To
Rosalie Nonnemacher Weaver

Acknowledgments

I wish to thank the following individuals and institutions for their help: Bemidji State University, for crucial writing time; Jonathon and Wendy Lazear, for believing in books; my sister, Judy Weaver Post, for her typing, proofreading, and general advice; the Minnesota State Arts Board and the McKnight Foundation, for their generous financial support; Stanford University's John L'Heureux and Nancy Packer, for showing me the short story; my editor, Patricia B. Soliman, and Susan Kamil, for their early and unflagging belief in *Red Earth, White Earth;* and thanks, finally, to my parents, who always had time.

Author's Note

Zhingwaak's stories are traditional Ojibwe legends. In some cases I have slightly altered their content and language. Special thanks go to Earl Nyholm, Indian man and maker of books, berry pies, and birchbark canoes, for his help with matters of Ojibwe culture and language.

Prologue

The letter came to his office. Its writing in pencil, wobbled diagonally across the envelope, fell over the edge, came back on a new track. No return address but the postmark was from Minnesota.

March 15, 1984

Guy—
Trouble here. Come home when you can.
                Sincerely,
                Your grandfather, Helmer Pehrsson

Guy Pehrsson, thirty, tall, fair-haired, with wide, bony shoulders, turned off his phone. He swung around in his chair to look out the high window of his office. His view was east. Across the blue end of San Francisco Bay were the inland foothills. It was March in California. The air was rain-scrubbed and clear. The hills rose up rounded and green. A thin blanket of gray clouds drifted just above their summits. Beyond the hills two thousand miles were Minnesota and the farm Guy had grown up on.

Guy looked again at the letter. He was surprised his grandfather could write. Twelve years ago Helmer's stroke had left him as stiff as a garden hose left outside in December. But some parts of him must have thawed.

Trouble.

Guy had left Minnesota because of trouble. Trouble with Martin, his father.

Trouble with the farm, with the bank, with Helmer.

No trouble with Madeline, his mother. But in the twelve years Guy had been gone she seldom wrote. The first year in California he waited for his mother's letters. When they did come he was always angry at their brevity. Her notes told of early killing frosts. Of Guy's classmates killed in farming or trucking accidents. Of the need for rain.

Guy wrote equally short notes in reply. After a year he stopped writing at all. Madeline's notes continued to come, usually around Christmas, his birthday, Easter, and other holidays, but Guy did not bother a reply. He had his own life now. A new life. He had nothing to say to his family.

He left his office early and drove home. His house sat in the foothills above Palo Alto. It was a square, steep-roofed house made of redwood with a glass front. As Guy pulled into his garage, inside the house Kennedy began to bark. Kennedy was his dachshund.

He fixed Kennedy a bowl of food and poured a glass of cold Chablis for himself. He stood with the wine, reading the letter again. Afterward, he looked out his picture window. The sun shone. Three houses down the hill, alongside the blue kidney bean of her swimming pool, the red-haired lady sunbathed topless while two Mexican men mowed her lawn. She always sunbathed when the gardeners were there.

Farther down, cars moved silently on Highway 280 toward Sunnyvale and San Jose. Down there beneath the flat lid of city haze was Guy's company, a white, supermarket-size building. Inside, a hundred men and women rolled carts of green and copper printed circuit boards from station to station. Outside, pink Toyota speedy-delivery trucks came and went like tropical ants as they shuttled Guy's circuit boards to the reciving doors of the big computer companies in the Bay Area. Doors and mouths. His company spit out circuit boards as fast as it could make

2

them. The large electronic factories of Silicon Valley swallowed them up in great, endless gulps.

Guy was glad he could not see his company from his house. He did not like to think about it when he was not there. He paid people to do that. Paid them well. Well enough that they took care of everything. Guy usually worked a half day, then drove up to the library at Stanford to read, or else up to the city, San Francisco, to the art galleries or to concerts. California had been good to him.

He unfolded his grandfather's letter again. The writing was as faint as sparrow tracks in sand. He ran his fingers across the words. Below on the page was a faint baby's foot of oil from the side of Helmer's hand. Guy held the smudged page up to his nose. When he closed his eyes he smelled straw, old wool, cows.

Come home.

He looked about his house. He was home. On one wall were his books, the rolling oak library ladder that reached the top shelves.

On another wall were his paintings. Centered was a wide oil entitled "A Thousand Cows." The cows were black and white holsteins, the cow lot was walnut-brown mud with a chartreuse June hillside behind, and every cow had turned its head to look out of the canvas into the room; when he first saw the painting in a gallery, Guy imagined that someone near the cows had fired a gun. Beside the big oil was a print of Friedensreich Hundertwasser's "Der Traum Des Toten Indianers"; its Indian lay dreaming at the bottom of a city.

On an opposite wall were stereo gear and shelves of records. Alongside the turntable were two albums, B. B. King and Strauss. He put on the Strauss. Some waltzes. Strauss was music to think by.

He sipped his wine, which outlasted the waltzes by a full hour. When he swallowed the last drop he stood up, called for Kennedy, and began to pack.

He would not stay long, two weeks at most. He took jeans, sweaters—there would still be snow in Minnesota—heavy socks. Leather gloves. Boots. A down jacket. More.

Music for the trip. He paged through his cassette tapes, picked out Strauss. Haydn. Gershwin. Brubeck. B. B. King.

3

Duane Allman. Boz Scaggs. Lynyrd Skynyrd. The Who. Bob Dylan. Leo Kottke. Emmylou Harris. Buffy Sainte-Marie.

He took his briefcase. Inside were miscellaneous company papers. From his coffee table he added a couple of books, plus the latest issue of *Rose Grower's Monthly*.

He called Karen, his secretary. He called Mrs. Cadillo, his housekeeper. He called Susan, a dark-eyed, black-haired Ph.D. candidate in literature whom he had met not long ago in the Stanford stacks. He told them he would be gone on business for two weeks.

He talked longest with Susan. They had dated enough times to sense that each saw large flaws in the other, but flaws not so large as to prevent them from sleeping together when either of them wanted to. Dating a grad student was like making hurried-up popcorn: lots of butter, high heat, instant noise. He thought briefly of seeing her before he left, but the faint puzzlement in her voice told him she was studying. She would finish her degree in the spring. There would be more time. They would see what developed then.

Last, he inspected his plants on his deck. The knobby jade plant he moved a bit more to shade. His tubs of roses he pushed farther into sunlight. The Simón Bolívar was past prime, and he cut away one of its orange-red blooms and two suckers. His Flaming Peace was only now opening, blood red inside with gold reverses. It would be in full bloom when he returned.

Fifty hours, a quarter gram of cocaine, and three speeding tickets later—one in Reno, a second near Idaho Falls, the third somewhere in dark North Dakota—Guy drove across the bridge in Fargo and entered Minnesota.

It was just after midnight. He held his gray Mercedes sedan carefully at ten miles over the speed limit. The oncoming headlights in Moorhead burned behind his eyes. Without slowing, he tipped back his head for more eyedrops, then blinked into the mirror. Oncoming headlights gathered in his white-blond hair, then slid down the long thin slightly bent line of his nose. Closer, the headlights revealed his eyes, small and blue in daylight, squinted and dark tonight. In their eclipse, the headlights illuminated his sharply Nordic features.

He blinked and rolled his eyes to see if they still worked.

4

For a moment in the dark glass of the mirror he saw his father's face. He looked away and concentrated on the road.

On the outskirts of Moorhead he drove beyond the last streetlight. He thought of the Robert Frost poem "Acquainted with the Night," of the line about outwalking "the furthest city light."

His mother had read him that poem once when he was young. Guy did not understand it, but the poem felt lonely. Madeline began to talk about the poem, but then Martin, his father, came in from the barn. She put the book away.

Beyond Moorhead the darker landscape and the eyedrops soothed his vision. But then the ache behind his eyes slid to his belly. He had not eaten since Salt Lake City. Yet there were only sixty miles left to drive. Then the farm. He could eat there.

The Strauss tape ended. He had forgotten it was playing. He replaced it with a Buffy Sainte-Marie tape. For a few miles he listened to her high, wailing songs, the Indian drums behind. It was good night music, full of bonfires and torches and dancing, music to stay awake by. But soon he turned that off too. There was always a point on a long trip when one drove beyond music or talk or even sleep. It was the point at which he drove from the present into the past.

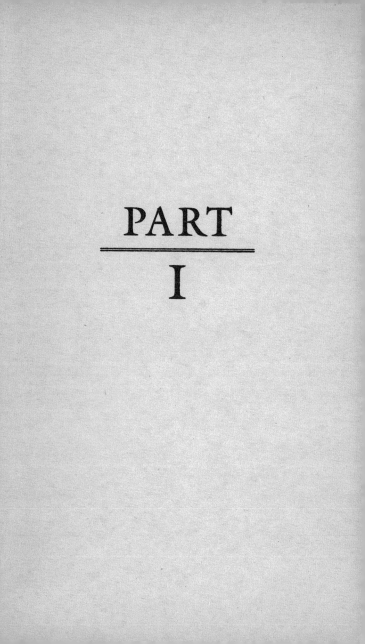

PART
I

PART

I

Chapter One

The summer he was five, Guy saw an Indian woman with four feet.

It was June. The ground was finally dry enough to play ball outside. Guy was in the yard pitching his leather softball against the side of the granary, for in that way he could play catch with himself. A car came from the south on the gravel road. Guy stopped to watch. He watched every car that passed the farm. The car, an old, rusted, blue, four-door Pontiac, slowed at the farm driveway and turned in. The car stopped far away from the house and turned around so that its nose faced the road.

For a moment nothing happened. In the flat yard, in the bright sunlight, far away a crow cawed. Then the rider's door of the Pontiac swung open with a squeak. An Indian woman got out. Guy picked up his ball and held it. When he looked again the Indian woman was crossing the yard. She was short but straight and walked on four feet. Guy's mouth fell open. Beneath the hem of her long skirt were certainly four feet. The feet moved her across the gravel and onto the grass like some weird insect on the ground beneath the yard lamp only on the hottest, most humid evenings of the summer.

9

An Indian Bug Woman.

The Bug Woman came toward Guy. Two of her feet wore shoes like the ones Guy's mother wore. The other pair was smaller, and wore moccasins. As the Bug Woman came closer, Guy watched the smaller feet. He thought of the little safety wheels on some of the farm machinery; if the big wheels went flat or gave way, the little wheels grabbed and kept things from tipping. Guy blinked against the bright sunlight.

"Eggs," the Indian woman said to Guy.

Eggs. Guy stared. He turned and pointed to the chicken coop beside the barn. There his mother's flock of leghorns bobbed within the square, chicken-wire yard.

"You have extra to sell?" the Indian woman asked.

Guy nodded and pointed to his mother's house. There were two houses on the farm. The big, white one was his grandparents', the smaller, brown one his parents'. The Indian woman nodded. Her eyes were as shiny brown as pocket-polished buckeyes and for a moment they gleamed wider and shinier. Then her bug feet propelled her forward.

Guy stared for a moment, then let his ball drop and followed the Bug Woman. He circled to one side of her. He saw something more. Not only did the woman have four feet, she had four eyes. Two smaller brown eyes peeped from around her skirt. The lower set of brown eyes could have been woven into the pattern of her skirt, but polka dots did not have black eyebrows. Polka dots did not peep out, then disappear, then peep out again. Guy thought of a chipmunk on a tree. No matter which way Guy or the Indian woman turned, the small brown eyes stayed on the far, safe side of her trunk.

Guy's mother brought the eggs out to the front steps. Without speaking, the Indian woman opened the cartons. She ran her short brown fingers across the white crowns of the eggs to inspect them for broken shells. Then she paid two dimes for two dozen, nodded to Madeline, and left. Her extra eyes and extra feet followed her across the yard to the Pontiac where an Indian man waited behind the wheel. Before the Bug Woman was half-way to the car, the Pontiac's engine started up. The door squeaked and slammed. Then the Pontiac's wheels crunched on gravel. Guy watched the car head south, then turn west. It continued across the flat plane of the fields and finally disappeared into the hazy green hills of the inner reservation.

In two weeks the Indian car came again. So did the Bug Woman's extra eyes and feet. This time Guy spotted on her a crow's wing of black hair connected to the smaller eyes. Then a brown ear. On each visit Guy saw more parts—a hand, an elbow—of the brown jigsaw puzzle he knew to be some sort of kid.

Once, toward midsummer, Guy was tossing his ball against the granary when the Indians' Pontiac came into the yard again. The Indian woman crossed the yard. As Guy leaned low to look for the kid beside her, he took his eye off the bounce of his ball. The ball rolled past him across the lawn toward the road. But the ball did not reach the ditch. The jigsaw puzzle of kid parts leaped away from the woman and formed itself into an Indian boy about Guy's age. The boy caught up with the ball. Like a red-tailed hawk slamming onto a stray chicken, he nailed it to the ground. Then he whirled and threw the ball to Guy so hard that Guy's hands stung.

Guy returned the favor. For a short while they threw the ball at each other as hard as they could fling it. But soon their throws began to arch into higher, softer lofts. The leather of the ball warmed their hands. Each throw, each catch, became a handshake.

The next day, and for the rest of the summer, Guy kept track of how many eggs his mother used. He marked down the eggs she fried for breakfast, the eggs she swirled into cake batter, the eggs she broke over flour to make cookie dough. When he was out for chores he made his mother list any eggs she used. For Guy guessed that the Indian family ate about the same number of eggs as did his own family. In this way he could calculate when the rusty blue Pontiac and the boy named Tom LittleWolf would come again.

Every other Saturday, Tom came. Those Saturday mornings Guy rushed through his chores. "What's the hurry?" his father said. "Indians don't get up before noon."

But as soon as he fed the calves and rinsed their pails, Guy raced up to the attic of the granary, to its small window that looked west. There he waited for the tiny cocoon of

11

dust to appear down the road, for the blue beetle to emerge from the center of the dust and grow into a real car. When he was sure it was the Pontiac, Guy raced down the ladder and hid himself in the yard. The Pontiac turned slowly into the driveway. Though there was good shade beneath the red oak tree near to the house, the Pontiac parked as always on the hot gravel by the machine shed. But its blue door squeaked open before its wheels stopped crackling on the gravel, and Tom LittleWolf's moccasins hit the ground running. Guy broke from his hiding place and their play was on.

Their games took them through the full measure of a farm's potential for fun. In the hayloft they hid and sought each other in the green city of bales. On ropes they swung back and forth across the wide loft like trapeze artists beneath the crown of a circus tent. Or they left the hayloft and crept back into the granary. There they crouched behind the grain fanning mill with slingshots loaded, their rubbers stretched and trembling the length of their arms as they waited for mice to peek from their holes in the corners of the bins. Sometimes they left the granary alone all morning and let it flock with sparrows. Later, with a baseball bat, they crept up the narrow stairs to the attic and burst in on the sparrows. In the long, narrow attic with its small windows at either end, the startled sparrows forgot their way down the open stairwell. They fluttered window to window, thudded against the glass. Guy and Tom took turns with the bat. The batter stood in the center alley of the attic. The pitcher used a stick to keep the sparrows flying down the batting lane into the strike zone. When the sparrows had all been belted for home-runs, fouled off, or hidden themselves in the cracks of the rafters, Tom and Guy turned to outside play.

Often they played in the scrap-iron pile beside the machine shed. There they tied worn harrow teeth to sticks and made spears. The rusted iron plates of a field disk were shields. A length of old sewer pipe bolted to a rusted wheelbarrow became a cannon. Discarded grease guns made natural ray guns. From old tractor seats, sheets of tin, and a broken, treadle-powered grind-stone, they constructed a space ship complete with a sparking alien death-ray beam.

But most often they played race and chase. They ran among the square buildings until their backs trickled wet with sweat and their skin glowed with heat. They tackled and tagged each other, then ran again. As the summer progressed Tom got to stay a little longer each time he came. That was because Madeline and Mary LittleWolf talked. At first the two mothers stood together for a few minutes on the front steps. Later they sat on the front steps in the shade. Once Guy saw that both of them held glasses of something cold to drink. Toward the end, the hottest part of the summer, the two women went inside the house. Tom's father sat motionless in the Pontiac.

When Tom's mother came out with the eggs, Tom immediately stopped their game and followed her in silence to the car. He never said good-bye. In the Pontiac he sat straight and did not wave as he left. Soon the car shimmered into the dust. Its blue shape wavered, shrank, then disappeared. And Guy was left alone again on the flat, dry lawn among the tall buildings.

Once after the Pontiac had gone Guy was in the house drinking his third glass of ice water. On the table were Madeline's and Mary's glasses, empty but for thin droopy ice cubes and wilty moons of lemon slices. There was a plate of gingersnaps, still warm. Guy took another. That day he was very hungry. He and Tom had played a long time. Then the porch door slammed as his father came in.

"So what have you boys been up to all afternoon?" Martin asked. His father was thin and tall and sandy-haired and stoop-shouldered from the dairy cows. Martin looked at the iced-tea glasses.

"Playing," Guy answered. He was still out of breath.

"Playing. There's work to be done on Saturdays, too, you know."

Guy was silent. He looked at Madeline. His mother was short and brown-haired, not from Minnesota. She began to clear the table.

"You better cut down on that running around," he said. His eyes were on Madeline. On the lemonade glasses. "Those Indians stay longer every time they come."

Madeline turned from the sink to look at Martin. "What do you mean, 'those Indians'?" she asked.

13

"The family with the black hair and brown eyes, they're Indians, I'd say," Martin said.

"LittleWolf is their name. You know that. Mary and Warren LittleWolf. And Tom."

"Warren," Martin said. "He's the one who never gets out of the car. Wonder why that is?" He laughed once.

"Likely for the same reason you stay in the barn when they're here."

Martin fell silent. A tiny muscle along his jaw began to move. "Mary, eh? Well, that's real friendly. But you better not start that. You shouldn't encourage them."

"Encourage them?"

Martin swung his arm at the plate of cookies, at the two empty glasses. "You do this, they stay longer. Just sell them the eggs. That's all they come for."

"There's nothing wrong with being neighborly," Madeline said.

"They're not neighbors," Martin said.

"I'd say they were," Madeline said immediately. "I enjoy talking to Mary."

"What can you have to talk about?"

Madeline spoke quickly; her words sliced through the air like tiny whips. "We're both women," she said.

Martin turned, slammed the screen door, and was gone.

In two Saturdays the LittleWolfs' car came again. But Guy and Tom had hardly begun their play when Guy noticed his father standing framed in the barn door. He was watching. Tom shouted but Guy missed the ball. It bounced across the driveway and rolled close to the Pontiac. Guy ran after it, then slowed to a walk as he neared the car. For the first time he saw, close-up, Tom's father. He had thick black hair that stood straight up in a long, sharp crew-cut. He had a wide face, small eyes, and his chin jutted forward like a fist. His chin looked large because he had no teeth, and his lips had shrunk back over his gums. From the car came the strong smell of peppermint.

Guy stared. But Warren LittleWolf did not see him. He was staring across the yard at Martin. Martin suddenly stepped through the barn door into daylight and stalked toward the house, where Madeline and Mary LittleWolf had gone inside. As Martin quickly crossed the yard, Tom's father tooted the Pontiac's horn once. Then again. But Martin had reached the front door by then. Guy and Tom turned to watch. From inside the house they heard loud voices. Then Tom's mother came quickly, almost stumbling, down the steps. She walked rapidly across the lawn. Tom ran to join her. This time when the Pontiac pulled away its wheels spun and snarled across the gravel.

Guy stood in the empty yard. A bumblebee droned by. In the windbreak a cicada buzzed. From inside the house he could hear his parents shouting. He heard something crash and break. He saw his father come out of the house backward, then cross the yard to the barn. Guy went to the shade of the red oak and waited. In a few minutes his mother came from the house. She carried a small suitcase, got in their car, and started the engine. She stopped the car by the driveway and the red oak. She got out and kissed him. He could smell iced tea and lemon on her breath. She had been crying too.

"Mommy will be gone for a few days," she whispered. "You can eat with Grandma, okay?"

Guy nodded.

On the sixth day Guy received a postcard from St. Anne's, Manitoba. That was where her family was. On the card was a picture of a river. On the ninth day Guy awoke in the morning to find his mother in the kitchen making scrambled eggs.

She did not speak of her absence. Guy did not ask. It was as if time, turning on the little sprockets of the clock, had jumped its chain, had slipped ahead several days, then caught again. Things went on as usual. Except for one thing.

The LittleWolfs' blue Pontiac did not come again. Every Saturday Guy watched for its blue speck to appear down the road. But only farm pickups, the milk truck, and occasional tractors pulling grain wagons came along. In the garden Guy hoed potatoes. He trimmed and hauled to the chickens the tomato vines and cabbage leaves and carrots that had run to seed. Soon he hardly looked up at the sound of a vehicle on the road. Around him there were only the endless rows of potatoes, peas, and beans.

But once when he was head-down, hacking along with his hoe, thinking of nothing at all, which was the best way to

15

hoe potatoes, he heard a scraping noise. The sound of gravel on tin. He looked up. There, out on the road, spinning in dusty circles on an old blue bicycle, was Tom. Tom! Guy flung aside his hoe and raced from the garden.

Tom would not come into the yard, so they took turns riding and then bucking each other down the road on the bicycle. Later they played in old man Schroeder's windbreak. Among the close, even rows of pine trees, on the red prickly blanket of dead needles, they played cowboys and Indians. They hid from, stalked, and shot pinecones at each other the rest of the afternoon. And never did they speak of their parents.

Chapter Two

On the Fourth of July, an hour before sundown, the rodeo ended in a pink haze. Guy and Tom sat atop the corral fence, faces into the sun. They were eight years old. Guy was nearly a head taller than Tom, his thin neck was sunburned red, and his hair was as white as the pigeons that dipped and fluttered above the grandstand. Tom had no neck; his black hair, shaved short, ended at his shoulders, wide shoulders that promised strong arms and a deep chest.

Guy and Tom sat on the edge of their plank perch like two birds near flight. They wanted to watch the cattle jockeys whip the Brahma bulls into the trailers, but they also wanted to be first at the edge of the river for the Big Blast. Already town kids were deserting the corral fence. Already behind them people were filing from the grandstand. Already in the parking lot pickups spun their tires on the gravel and threw plumes of dust into the red sunlight.

The biggest bull, a tatter of rope dragging between its legs, slammed forward into its trailer; Guy and Tom looked at each other. They leaped from their perch.

They had no bicycles, which proved they were not town kids, but they could run. They dodged through the crowd.

17

Their shadows weaved and darted among the walkers as they sped down the crowded, unpaved street. When they reached the asphalt streets of downtown the dust of the fairgrounds fell away. At Main Street the day's heat, trapped by the brick buildings, washed over them like an oven door opening in their faces. The tar was soft underfoot. A block beyond Main Street they smelled water.

At first the river's smell was only a faint coolness in their mouths. Then it flowed thicker over their cheeks and foreheads. In another block, the water scent divided itself into sharper layers of smells. Wet willow wood. Green algae. Somewhere a rotting duck. The faint vinegar and iron smell of the municipal sewage plant downstream.

But they were not first at the edge of the river. Already town kids lined the shore of the Bekaagami River. Tom jerked his head at a big willow tree whose roots snaked into the water. He squatted and made a hand cradle. Guy took a running step, hit Tom's hands with his right foot, and went up like a pole-vaulter. He caught the lowest limb and pulled himself up. Then he reached down for Tom. White hand on brown wrist, brown hand on white, they scrambled up the loose bark to the crown of the tree until the limbs began to bend under their weight. Above the crowd, they could see everything.

In front of their willow stretched the bay, a blue two-acre bulge of the Bekaagami River whose slow south side formed the Flatwater Municipal Swimming Beach. A long fly ball's distance from shore floated the dynamite raft, a rick of brown logs eight feet in length. The logs were made of papier-mâché. They concealed the stick—some said ten sticks—of dynamite. Fourth of July was Dynamite Daze in Flatwater.

Dynamite was the town's founding father. In the 1890s Flatwater had grown around the thick peninsula that slowed the current of the river. The great rafts of white pine and Norway logs floating south to the lumber mills in St. Paul always tangled and jammed at Flatwater. There lumber-jacks made a permanent encampment on the peninsula. Daily they dynamited the channel clear. Later Guy would come to see Flatwater as a town built on an impediment, see the constricted flow of the river and the town beside it as connected and metaphorical. But he did not understand

18

that now. Right now he turned with Tom to check the height of the sun.

"Nine minutes, tops," Guy said.

"Five," Tom said immediately.

"Bet," Guy said.

"Nickel," Tom replied.

"Shit, you don't have a nickel," Guy said.

"You don't have a watch," Tom said.

"Neither do you."

"Do too."

"Bet," Guy said quickly. He knew Tom had no watch. This was easy money.

Tom held out his arm and turned his palm and fingers sideways to the sun and to the horizon. Guy watched as Tom squinted over and then below his fingers. Tom peeled back two fingers, then a third. Sighted again.

"Free," Guy said suddenly, which meant the bet was off.

Tom grinned. The sun shone on his wide white teeth and through the gap between them wide enough to hold a pencil. "Lucky I let you off," he said. "See, here's how I do it." He squinted over his fingers again. "It's simple. Every finger's width is five minutes."

"Shit," Guy said.

Tom shrugged. "Try it with a clock sometime."

Guy was silent for a moment. "So where you'd learn that," he said.

"Zhingwaak showed me."

Zhingwaak was the old Indian who lived on the reservation. He sang and drummed at the powwows, and told stories to the children. Guy's father said that was because Zhingwaak was too lazy to do any real work.

"Was Zhingwaak a real medicine man once?" Guy asked.

Tom shrugged.

Guy turned back to watch the sun. He sighted over his fingers but the light hurt his eyes. Its orange glare shone on the white crown of the water tower, gleamed on the galvanized sides of the town grain elevator. Already Main Street was in shadow, and so were the white houses that ran in even rows like a picket fence down to the city beach.

On the brown grass near the diving platform stood a circle of tourists. Black camera straps cut across flowered shirts. Inside the circle four or five Indians shuffled to the thudding

19

of a drum. The drumming sounded weak and far away, like a partridge thudding his wings somewhere deep in the woods. The Indian powwows were organized by the Flatwater Jaycees. Guy's father said that the powwow was to keep the tourists' minds off the Bekaagami mosquitoes, keep the tourists' wallets in Flatwater as long as possible.

Tom followed Guy's eyes to the dancers. He watched briefly, then looked away.

Suddenly behind them at the shore an outboard motor coughed alive. Tom whooped. They whirled to face the river. It was time.

The sheriff's motorboat left the shore and plowed slowly toward the dynamite raft. In the late sunlight its waves spread like even windrows of wheat across a blue field. The boat slowed before the raft, bobbed sideways toward it. A green-headed mallard fluttered away from the water near the raft. Some people along the shore clapped. The sheriff leaned over the side of the boat and lit the fuse. When he jerked backward into the boat, his deputy gunned the engine. The propeller snarled once and the boat sped toward shore. More people clapped. The sheriff waved to the crowd. The green-headed mallard floated close to shore.

But suddenly the water around the mallard began to dimple and splash. The mallard fluttered once, then swam in a widening V toward deeper water. More splashes followed the duck.

"Look," Tom called, jerking his chin, pushing out his bottom lip to point downshore. Indians never pointed with their fingers.

Down the shore stood a cluster of town boys. With slingshots. One of their stones splashed a hand's length from the mallard, which scrambled into flight. It flew to the dynamite raft. There it perched on the highest papier-mâché log, ruffled its feathers, then settled down to stare at the crowd.

"Wait—no—" came one or two voices from the crowd.

"Holy shit," Guy murmured.

The mallard turned to peck once at a flea on its left wing, then sat motionless again.

The crowd fell silent. Suddenly the raft and the duck began to balloon in size. The duck swelled into a rooster. Then a Thanksgiving turkey. It rode the rising silo of foam

20

and shredded papier-mâché. At the height of the blast the duck reached sunlight. There it became a peacock in full spray. Then in a rainbow mist of meat and feathers it disappeared.

The Big Blast crashed through the willow. It whipped the thin branch ends across Guy and Tom's faces and they grabbed each other to keep from falling. Below them the crowd let out a long cheer. The fireworks began.

After the final red rose died away in the black sky, Guy and Tom stayed put. The crowd passed beneath their tree. Tom began to break off dead twigs and drop them onto the heads of the passersby. A man cursed and rubbed his head. When he looked up he saw Guy and threatened to bring back a chain saw, though his wife soon enough pulled him along.

"Thanks, fuck-face," Guy whispered.

Tom's teeth glinted white in the dark.

Within ten minutes the beach was empty but for Tom and Guy, and a few of the town boys who poked along the riverbank looking for unexploded fireworks. And the pow-wow Indians.

A steady drumming still came from among the dancers. The tourists had left, but the Indians still danced, six or seven of them now. The dancers moved clockwise in a jerky circle about the bright yellow eye of a gas lantern.

Guy and Tom slid down from their tree. "Come on," Tom said, jerking his head toward the shadowy town boys along the riverbanks.

"Naw," Guy said. He was tired. He had been in town all afternoon at the county fair. His mother had brought him. She was helping at one of the food shows. He was supposed to meet her near the powwow after the fireworks.

"Let's watch," Guy said, staring at the dancers.

Tom shrugged and followed him closer.

They sat close by on the grass in the shadows and watched. "They dance different when the tourists leave," Guy said. Now the dancers sang more. Couples crisscrossed hands and danced a dipping, weaving pattern. Sometimes women picked men from the crowd. Guy turned to Tom.

"'The Forty-Nine Song,'" Tom said.

"Why forty-nine? Forty-nine states?"

Tom laughed once and shook his head sideways. "Huh-

21

huh. Lots of Indian men went off to fight Germans in the war. Only forty-nine came back to the reservation."

They kept watching. Many of the men dancers had taken off their shirts. Their skin glistened in the lantern light. On the chests of two older men bounced necklaces, thin gray tubes of something strung on a leather cord.

"What are those?" Guy asked.

"Rabbit bones," Tom said. "Leg bones. You break off the longest leg bones, then poke out the guck inside and let them dry."

"We could make those," Guy said immediately. "This winter, in old man Schroeder's grove we'll trap some rabbits—big ones."

Tom was silent.

They watched some more. "What's that, a gingerbread man?" Guy asked. On the wrist of an old woman dancer whirled a tiny doll-like man.

"How should I know?" Tom said crossly.

After a while Tom said, "Not a gingerbread man. Flying Man."

"Why Flying Man?"

"Goddamnit, I don't know everything," Tom said immediately. "Come on, let's go look for bottle rockets."

"Can't." Guy looked through the darkness for his mother. She should have been there by now. He wondered where she was. His father was home unloading oats by tractor light. He was always working.

They watched another minute until Tom said, "Fuck, this is more boring than school."

Guy didn't answer. He was staring through the dancers to the far side of the circle. He was watching the drummer, old Zhingwaak. He suddenly realized that Zhingwaak was watching them.

"Tom . . ." Guy whispered. Tom looked. Without missing a drumbeat, Zhingwaak lifted his hand and motioned them forward.

"He wants something," Guy whispered. He looked around the powwow. There were only brown faces, and far beyond, the silent white houses.

"Us," Tom said. "We better go over there."

They approached the dancers and Zhingwaak. Guy walked behind Tom. In the flickering light and shadow of

22

the lantern, Zhingwaak's long face all ran into his mouth. The deep lines across his forehead and around his eyes, the deeper furrows on his cheeks, the gulleys and ravines along his nose all flowed downward over his thin lips and into the dark hole of his mouth. Zhingwaak spoke.

"Young boys should dance," he said. His voice was younger than his face. His words hummed.

Tom looked behind to Guy. Guy looked at the dancers.

"You, *Ningos,*" Zhingwaak said to Guy. "Your mother comes often to our school to help us. You live on the reservation and play always with Tom LittleWolf. Dance with us."

Guy swallowed. The passing dancers began to pluck at Tom and Guy as they passed.

"I . . . don't know how," Guy said.

"The dancing will come to you," Zhingwaak answered. "Because you come to us, the dancing will come to you."

Tom and Guy stood by Zhingwaak and watched. The drumming was like the steady beat of a hay baler, only faster. Riding on the hay wagons sometimes Guy and Tom did little jigs to match the pump-pumping sound of the machinery. Tom looked at Guy, jutted his lip toward the dancers. They grinned at each other and joined the moving circle.

Following the "Forty-Nine" dancers, Guy and Tom moved within a ring of Indians who only watched. The outside Indians were in shadow. Now and again the red eye of a cigarette glowed, then arched to the ground as one of them came forward. The new dancers smelled of whiskey and cigarette smoke and perfume. They were younger than Zhingwaak and the old woman; they were Guy's parents' age and some younger than that. As they entered the circle they laughed and shouted to each other. Sometimes they stumbled and fell. But the older dancers pulled them to their feet, kept them moving.

Zhingwaak's drumming quickened with an extra beat. Guy wove this new rhythm into his path of invisible, numbered footsteps on the hard-packed grass. As more dancers came forward, Guy and Tom were forced farther to the center. Guy could not see out, so he watched the new dancers. After they had danced for a while their faces began to shine. They stopped laughing and shouting to each other.

23

They stumbled less. Their shirts soaked through with sweat. The new dancers' smell of tobacco and whiskey and perfume changed into a sweet-sour odor like sileage. A dancer alongside Guy shrugged off his shirt and flung it over the heads of the dancers into the darkness. With it went his sileage smell.

Suddenly Zhingwaak wailed. It was a thin cry that started high in the air above the dancers and then fell. The cry slid down over the Indians' black hair and shining skin, down the rabbit bones and the old beadwork and dried feathers of the old women, all the way down to their feet on the dry grass. The lowest note of Zhingwaak's cry flattened into a humming. For Guy the humming became a floor upon which he danced. He leaped and soared. He was the Flying Man at the end of his leather thong. Only Flying Man was bound and Guy was free. Guy planed and leaped with Tom as Zhingwaak's wail came again.

Suddenly the darkness washed away. They were flooded with a bright light. Guy squinted away from the white beam. The dancers froze in place. Sweat glinted on and then dripped from their chins.

A voice came loud through a bullhorn. The police.

"The Flatwater Fourth of July festivities are over, as it is now the fifth of July. The Jaycees have paid the powwow dancers in full. Therefore, the powwow is over. Please disperse at this time."

For a long moment there was silence. Then Zhingwaak's drumstick thudded again. From the crowd something arced, shining, through the beam of the spotlight and shattered against the police car. A beer bottle. Then more bottles flying like falling stars. Crashing, tinkling. Then the harder thuds of stones.

Suddenly people were shouting and falling. Policemen pushed through the crowd, jabbing with long sticks. One of the officers grabbed away Zhingwaak's drumstick and broke it over his knee. He kicked aside the drum. "You—let's go!" He jerked Zhingwaak's arm behind him. Zhingwaak stumbled and fell. The policeman began to drag him across the gravel. Another Indian leaped on the policeman from behind. A policeman swung his stick. It hit the Indian's head with a watermelon sound, and the Indian slumped to the ground.

24

From nowhere Guy's mother was pulling him away. Beside her an Indian man retreated into the shadows. Guy did not see his face.

"Come," Madeline shouted. She ran. Guy twisted his head back to look for Tom, for Zhingwaak. But there was only the glare of lights and shouting and the glint of the polished wood as the policeman's sticks rose and fell.

"Why . . ." Guy cried, "why did the policeman come? Why did they take Zhingwaak?"

In the shadow of the stone beach house his mother held him. They looked back at the fighting. "Because . . . it's very late," she murmured.

"It wasn't late," Guy said. He started to cry, burning heaves in his throat and chest. "Not for the Indians it wasn't late."

His mother turned his face away from the fighting. Another police car, its red lights flashing, wailed past them.

"Yes, it's late," she murmured. "Especially for the Indians."

Chapter Three

One day at the end of July in the summer when they were nine, Guy and Tom were digging in against a panzer attack. All around the farm, dust clouds moved up and down the reservation. The Germans were clever. They had disguised their tanks and half-tracks as combines.

But Guy and Tom were not fooled. By two o'clock in the afternoon their foxhole was nearly ready. Tom was holding and Guy was nailing down the last boards when Guy realized his hammer was striking from sunlight to shadow. A shadow had crept across the yellow sand and up the plank wall so slowly that neither he nor Tom had thought about it. Guy stopped pounding. They whirled and shaded their eyes as they looked up. Above them was the dark, stubby outline of a kid. One corncob grenade could have finished them, so Guy and Tom scrambled out of the hole.

They stared at the kid. He had short, unevenly sheared blond hair that lay in flat, matted ringlets around his head. His face was melon-round and smudged with dirt. In its center were two blue eyes with black freckles of dirt in their four corners. He wore a gray T-shirt, which long ago had been white, and baggy bib overalls tied at the waist with twine and sheared off just below the knees. The frayed ends of the overalls hung down to brown feet that wore no shoes. Guy stared at the kid's feet. They looked like saddle leather.

"You a Nazi?" Tom asked.

The kid was silent. Tom and then Guy stepped closer. Then Guy could smell the kid. He smelled like the bottom of a calf pen where the piss settled and burned the yellow straw red and when you turned the straw over with a fork the ammonia smell made your eyes water. Guy jumped sideways, up-breeze.

"Jesus, you stink!" Tom said.

The kid struck forward low like a snake and took Tom down with an ankle tackle. Guy leaped forward and in a moment the three of them were wrestling on the dry grass. But it was like wrestling a skunk. In another moment Guy and Tom were struggling to get away from the smell. They leaped back into their foxhole and pointed their wooden submachine guns at the kid.

The kid stared down at them again. In the silence Guy looked at the kid's curly hair, his short pants, his T-shirt.

"If you're not a Nazi, then who are you?" he asked.

In the silence Tom whispered, "Spies can't speak English."

"You got no name?" Guy said.

"I gots a name," the kid said.

"So what is it."

"Maranhutmire," the kid said.

"Maranhutmire, what kind of name is that?" Tom said.

The kid picked up a stone.

"What I meant was," Tom said quickly, "is that your first name or last?"

"Could be both," Guy whispered. "Like Paladin."

The kid said his name again, slower this time. Maran. Hurtmire. Maryan.

"Mary Ann!" Guy said suddenly. He looked at Tom. They both stared and their mouths fell open. This was no kid. This was a girl.

Mary Ann Hartmeir was the only daughter, among four brothers, of Jewell Hartmeir. There was no Mrs. Hartmeir. She had died of leukemia when Mary Ann, the fourth child, was three years old. When she died, Jewell Hartmeir had moved his children from Georgia up to Minnesota because down south the niggers were taking over. If the weather was cold in Minnesota, at least he didn't have to work with niggers.

Later Guy would hear this and more as his father and Jewell Hartmeir talked. Right now he and Tom climbed back out of the foxhole.

"So where do you live?" he asked her. He knew most the kids on this part of the reservation.

The girl jerked her head north.

"On a farm?"

She nodded yes.

"Whose farm?"

"Ourn."

"Whose farm did it used to be?"

She shrugged. Guy thought of the farms north from his own. There was only one possibility, the old Abrahamson place with the burned-down buildings. The barn had burned, and Abrahamson, who was older than Guy's grandfather, had gone out west to live with his daughter. When the farm lay empty, the Indians had burned the other buildings.

"Are the buildings all wrecked and burned?"

She nodded.

"What are you going to do for a house?" Tom said.

"We gots a house," she said. "A wheel house."

"A wheel house," Guy said.

Tom began to choke with laughter. "A trailer house, she means. Shit. A wheel house, can you believe it?"

Mary Ann drew back her arm. She still held the stone. Tom jumped behind Guy.

"He didn't mean nothing," Guy said quickly. "He's my brother. My retarded brother."

Mary Ann's eyes widened. She leaned over to stare at Tom, who crossed his eyes and let spit roll down the side of his mouth. She snickered. Her teeth were yellowish-green along her gums. Tom hunched over and began to gimp about in a circle and make moaning noises and claw at the air.

She covered her mouth and began to laugh out loud. Guy,

28

too, began to laugh, and soon all three of them were lying on the ground trying to out-retard the other.

Suddenly another shadow fell over them, a larger one this time. Guy looked up to see Martin staring down at him.

"It's three o'clock. You got calves to feed, remember?"

Guy scrambled up. "Yessir." Tom stepped quickly away from Martin, went for his bike.

"See ya," Guy said quickly to Tom and Mary Ann. He followed his father toward the buildings. Halfway there, he realized Mary Ann Hartmeir and her silent bare feet were right behind him.

"Poor little ragamuffin," Guy's grandmother, Etta, murmured. "I've never seen a little girl that dirty."

"Shoulda caught her and give her a bath," Martin said.

It was after supper. They were all working in the garden. Martin swung the scythe and Guy threw the sweet-corn stalks onto the wagon; from the heat the sweet-corn ears had stopped coming but the cows could eat what green leaves were left. Madeline and Etta worked among the tomato plants, clipping back the runners that carried tomatoes too small and green to ripen. Down the garden west, outlined in a gown of orange dust, Helmer worked in the potatoes. His hoe swung him side to side, plant to plant. The even marks of its blade looked like machine tracks in the dry earth. Tank tracks.

"No, you don't meddle with other people's children," Etta said. "The Bible makes that clear." She named a chapter and verse. Guy's grandparents read the Bible every night and all day Sunday. His parents didn't.

Madeline looked up. "Somebody should," she said. "Somebody should pay that little girl's parents a visit and see what's going on."

"No, I wouldn't do that either," Etta said. "You don't want to barge in on someone. That's one thing you should never do, is interfere."

"If that little girl hasn't had a bath by the next time she comes, I'm going up there," Madeline said.

"You missed a runner, there," Etta said, pointing to the ground.

* * *

Mary Ann Hartmeir came the next day, unbathed. Guy was walking in from the barn for breakfast when her short shadow fell across his. He jumped.

"Damnit," he shouted, "you almost made me spill this milk."

Mary Ann stared at the jar of milk in his hands, at the yellowish layer of cream that had begun to form at the top.

"What's the matter, you never seen a jar of milk before?"

"Yes," she said. "I seen milk before."

"You talk funny," he said. She talked like she had a Jew's harp stuck in her throat.

"So do you," she said.

Guy kept walking. Mary Ann followed him. At the porch door he paused. She was still behind him. "Well, come on in then," he said.

During breakfast with Mary Ann, Guy's mother opened all the windows in the kitchen. Martin squinted and leaned away from the table as he ate. During Mary Ann's eighth pancake Madeline said, "Does your mother know you came for a visit?"

"No. Well, maybe." Mary Ann looked out the window and frowned briefly. "She's dead." She reached for another pancake.

Martin coughed. Madeline's eyes widened.

"Your father, he's . . ."

"They's building a barn. He and my brothers."

Madeline poured Mary Ann another glass of milk, which she drank empty in a series of gulps.

"Then . . . who cooks?"

"My brothers or me. I can make grits. I can make Jell-O. I can make milk."

"Make milk?" Martin asked.

"You only needs a can opener and a jar and a quart of water," she said. "Any damn fool can make milk."

Martin choked on a bite of pancake and had to take a long swallow of coffee.

"You live on the old Abrahamson place," Madeline said.

"It's ourn now," Mary Ann said immediately. Her eyes flickered across the table to the bacon.

Madeline passed her the plate.

"How long have you been here?" Martin said.

30

"Since Julia got attacked by the stranger and went into a coma, then she came to and got married to Dr. Les Granger. That long."

Guy looked to Martin and then Madeline.

"Julia?" Madeline asked.

"Julia. On TV. Today the stranger might come back again."

"One of the soap operas," Madeline murmured.

"My dad said the attacker was probably a nigger," Mary Ann said. "Niggers like white pussy."

Madeline caught her breath. Martin spit a mouthful of coffee onto his plate. His chest began to heave. "Get out," Madeline said quickly. "If you think this is funny, get out of the house."

Guy was puzzled but he began to laugh with his father. "You, too," Madeline hissed at him. "Out. Now!"

In the yard Martin wiped his eyes and laughed until he gasped for breath. "Niggers . . . white pussy. I never heard a kid talk like that in my life."

Guy grinned. White pussy. There were some calico pussies in the barn but no white ones. Anyway, he smiled at his father and listened to him laugh. It was a strange sound from his father, half magpie and half crow, a sound he seldom heard.

He helped his father grease the combine. They crawled underneath and lay on the prickly dry grass looking up at the sickle and reel. Guy held the grease nozzle in the places where a small hand worked better than a big one. Every once in a while his father laughed again and Guy joined him.

They were still on the ground, pumping grease into the last fitting, when they saw feet. Madeline's brown shoes and Mary Ann's brown ankles came toward them and stopped. Guy stared at Mary Ann's toes. The nails were clipped short and scraped clean. He could smell soap.

He scrambled from beneath the combine and stood up. Mary Ann was dressed in his mother's yellow blouse. A belt around her waist made the blouse look like a dress. Her blond hair lay flat and parted in the middle. Her cheeks were rubbed reddish and chapped. Her teeth were pink with blood, and she licked them and spit.

31

"I'm telling my dad," she said to Guy's mom. "You wait what he does to you."

"You go right ahead and tell him," Madeline said. Her dress was spotted with water. She carried a paper bag that held Mary Ann's clothes. Madeline's brown eyes shone in the morning sunlight and her jaw was set. "Guy, get a jar of milk for Mary Ann and her family. I'm going to pay a neighborly call on the Hartmeirs."

A half hour later Madeline returned in the dusty, family Cutlass. She came across the yard toward the combine carrying the yellow and orange blouse by its belt. Her face was red, her eyes angry. "Martin, you'd better get up to visit the Hartmeirs first chance you get," she said. "They'll be needing some help."

"Nope, don't need no help," Jewell Hartmeir said. He was a short, lean man whose bib overalls and red shirt hung on him like scarecrow clothes. His gray engineer's cap was pulled low across his eyes and had soaked itself full of oil from his forehead and black hair. He spit a long brown spurt of tobacco juice into the dust. His face was tanned leathery brown. Squinted half shut, his small blue eyes were double-lidded like the eyes of the black bull snake Guy and Tom had once killed by the chicken coop. Guy stayed on the far, safe side of his father.

Martin and Jewell Hartmeir stood leaning against the corral fence. In the Hartmeirs' yard there was a battered pink and purple trailer house. A flatbed truck. An old Massey-Ferguson tractor whose red paint had peeled mostly to gray metal. A large, bright yellow pile of lumber that shimmered away a pitchy smell in the sunlight. In the background were the burned wrecks of the old Abrahamson buildings. Jewell Hartmeir and Martin watched the four Hartmeir boys put up the rafters of the new barn. Mary Ann, too, was high up on the barn, walking barefooted along the rim. Below her was a pile of charred, pointed timbers left over from the Abrahamson barn.

Guy watched her walk. She did not hold on to anything.

"Throw down that square, you're not making a goddamn church," Jewell Hartmeir called to one of his sons. The biggest of the boys, the one with the thickest, reddest arms, slowly stood up. He threw the carpenter's square. It came turning and whistling across the corral toward the fence. Martin jerked Guy behind him. The flat metal square kicked up a cloud of dust a foot from Jewell Hartmeir's boots. Hartmeir had not moved.

"You want to hit me you got to aim better than that," Jewell Hartmeir called back. He spit again.

Martin glanced down at Guy, then back to the barn. He stared at the rafters. "What sort of pitch you got on that roof?"

"Just enough slope to run water," Hartmeir said. "That's all you need on a roof."

Martin was silent. Then he said, "Looks kind of flat for this country. We get a lot of snow up here in the winter."

Hartmeir glanced across to Martin. His blue eyes widened for a moment, then squinted narrow again. "Snow's light," he said. He looked back to his boys.

"Except sometimes two feet of snow comes all at once," Martin said.

"Light as a snowflake is what people say, don't they?" Hartmeir said. "Snow's like cotton, I'd guess. I worked in cotton, I kin work in snow. Bub—what you sittin' down for, you think it's suppertime or something!" he shouted.

"I'm empty on nails," Bub said. He spit a brown streamer over the edge.

"So go down and get yerself some for Christ's sakes," Hartmeir said.

"It's near two o'clock," Bub said.

"Two o'clock?" the other three brothers said at the same time. They stood up and let their hammers fall through the rafters to the ground.

"Two o'clock! Julia!" Mary Ann shrieked. She began to walk quickly—too quickly—along the narrow rim to the ladder. She slipped, pitched forward, but caught a rafter tail as she fell over the side. Martin sucked in his breath. Mary Ann slowly pulled herself up and walked on to the ladder as quickly as before.

"Tough little woman," Hartmeir said, grinning. "She's smarter than all them big boys put together."

Mary Ann raced across the yard toward the trailer. The boys followed her, walking faster and faster as they neared the door, four big geese pulled along by a fluttering mallard.

33

"Their goddamn TV show," Jewell said, checking his pocket watch. "If I wouldn't let 'em watch it, they wouldn't turn a lick of work around here."

Martin was silent for a moment. Mary Ann disappeared into the trailer. "Your girl," he said. "She's paid us a couple of visits."

"That won't happen again," Hartmeir said quickly. "We don't bother nobody and don't like to be bothered in return."

Martin nodded. He glanced back to the barn, to the rafters and the rim from which Mary Ann had slipped.

"That wasn't what I meant," Guy's father said. "I was thinking that she's almost big enough to work out. My wife says she'd take some work, like canning and garden and housework, from the girl in return for some beef and milk."

Guy stared at his father. His mother had never said anything like that.

Jewell Hartmeir stared across at the empty shell of the barn and spit again. "Doesn't sound bad. But I'd have to think about it," he said. He checked his watch and again looked toward the trailer.

The next morning Mary Ann Hartmeir knocked on the door at 5 A.M. She was wearing gloves and a scarf tied low over her head. "I'm here to work," she said.

"We don't start until eight o'clock," Madeline said, tying her bathrobe. "Until then you lie here on the couch." She pulled off Mary Ann's gloves and scarf, pressed her down, and covered her with an afghan blanket.

"And you get back to bed, too, Guy," she said.

When Guy woke up at six-thirty, Mary Ann was still sleeping. She was at the breakfast table when he came in from chores at eight. Later in the morning Tom rode into the yard on his bike. Mary Ann and Guy and Tom played together all that day and every day for the rest of the week.

On Friday afternoon Madeline and Tom and Guy drove Mary Ann home. Madeline delivered to Jewell Hartmeir a gallon of milk, some packages of frozen beef from the freezer, plus a sack of fresh tomatoes and string beans from the garden.

Jewell Hartmeir looked into the box and then at Mary Ann. He squinted. "She work that much?" he said.

34

"Could hardly have gotten along without her," Madeline said softly. "Like to have her again next week."

"We'll see," Hartmeir said, reaching for the box of food.

Next week Mary Ann came again, and every week for the rest of the summer. She and Guy and Tom played together. They showed her the hayloft, the attic of the granary, all their forts. By the end of August and the approach of school, it was like she had always been there.

Chapter Four

Chapter Four

That September the teachers in Flatwater put Mary Ann in first grade. Her first day she beat up three smaller boys who laughed at her size, then bit the wrist of the teacher, who dragged her off to the principal's office.

"Wasn't my goddamn fault they put me in the wrong class," she said. She and Guy and Tom sat together on the school bus. She spoke with her teeth clenched together and moved only her lips. "Dumb fuckers. I know how to do things they never heard of."

"What happens tomorrow?" Guy asked.

She shrugged.

Guy saw a folded note in her hand.

"What's that?" Tom said.

She looked down at the note. She wadded it in her palm. "From the principal. Supposed to give it to my daddy." She stood up and began to open the bus window.

"Wait," Guy cried. He grabbed her arm.

She struggled to throw the note out the window.

Tom grabbed it and leaned away to read it.

"It says . . . you can't read," he said. He and Guy turned to stare at Mary Ann, who looked down. "Shit, that's why they put you in first grade. You can't read."

36

Two older girls in the next seat, fifth-graders, glanced around at Mary Ann, then began to giggle. In an instant Mary Ann had one girl's ponytail pulled back and her arm around the girl's white throat. The girl's eyes bulged and she gasped for air; her friend flailed at Mary Ann with a notebook. The bus driver was slowing onto the shoulder of the highway before Guy and Tom separated the three girls. With the driver still glaring at them in the overhead mirror, the bus slowly picked up speed again.

"What the hell's the matter with you?" Tom hissed at Mary Ann. "You can't go around beating up on people every minute of your life."

"Why not? My daddy taught me how to fight back."

She glared at the two bigger girls in the next seat.

Guy stared at Tom and shook his head. "You don't always have to punch somebody," Guy said.

"Why not?" she said stubbornly. "My daddy says you turn the other cheek you just get your head knocked off."

"Because you're going to stay in first grade the rest of your life, that's why. You'll be the only full-grown person in first grade," Guy said.

"You'll get full-grown and your desk will stick on you," Tom added. "You'll have to walk around the rest of your life with this little desk that looks like it's sticking out your ass."

"Shit," she said. She grinned, but then stopped and turned to look out the window. Several telephone poles passed. Finally she said, "If I stop punching kids, I still can't read." When she turned back the late-afternoon sunlight gleamed in her eyes. Guy saw her blink back tears.

He and Tom stared at each other. "Shit, anybody can read," Tom said.

"We'll teach you," Guy said.

"Cinch," Tom said. "Two weeks, max."

The next Saturday Mary Ann came to school in the hayloft. Tiny shafts of sunlight fell from the barn's roof and made yellow eyes on the hay-bales-and-boards school desks. Guy and Tom had also made a plank-walk across a deep hole in the layers of bales.

"Any punching, spitting, shitting, pissing, or nose-picking during class, you walk the plank over the alligator pond, is

37

that clear, class?" Tom called out as Mary Ann climbed the bales toward the classroom.

"One problem, teach," Guy said. "We've got an alligator plank but nothing to read."

"Shit," Tom said. He scratched his head.

"I brought some magazines," Mary Ann said. She emptied a sack of them onto the desk.

"Jesus!" Tom said.

"Holy smokes," Guy said.

"They're Bub's," she explained. "They was the only magazines in the house."

Guy stared. The magazines gleamed in the sunlight. On the covers were women bent over being fucked or women with their eyes closed and men's cocks in their mouths.

"There's words later on," she said. "I know because Bub reads them to himself sometimes."

"Whoee!" Tom shouted.

"Shhh!" Guy hissed, stepping over to look down the ladder to the barn below. No one below but cows. He began to page through the magazines. He paused to stare at a black man who had a cock as big as a horse's and had it halfway inside a skinny, blond-haired woman who had her face all scrunched up. White pussy.

"Listen to this," Tom whispered. "Harry slid the tip of his throbbing, bulb-bulb . . ."

Guy looked where Tom's finger had stopped. "Bulbous. That means shaped like a light bulb."

"Bulbous banana into the hungry red mouth of her cherrypot as its waiting lips eng . . ."

"Engulfed," Guy said. "Must mean gulp. Like in don't gulp your food."

"Engulfed its spurting white . . ."

"J. Is. M.," Guy said slowly. The word was new to him.

"Hey—you said you could read!" Mary Ann said suddenly.

"We can," Tom said quickly.

"Sometimes you run across a word you never seen before," Guy said. "It just takes a second to figure it out. Jis. M. Jism. Jism," he said. "You see, that's how you read. You sound out the letters."

* * *

38

"I'm tired, I want to go home," Mary Ann said. The up-and-down shafts of sunlight now slanted across the loft.

"Three more sentences," Guy said.

"Five," Tom said. They sat bent over the magazine with Mary Ann pressed between them.

"Okay, four," Guy said.

Mary Ann sighed and began again. "The tick . . ."

"Th sound," Tom said impatiently.

"The thick, wit . . ."

"Silent *e,"* Guy said.

"White," she murmured.

"Good, keep going," Guy said.

"The thick, white rod of his coke . . ."

"I don't see no silent *e,"* Tom said.

". . . of his cock slid . . ."

"Great," Guy said. Mary Ann smiled and leaned closer to the words.

"Into her wet muffin."

"Not muffin," Guy and Tom both shouted. "There's no *f*'s in that word."

Mary Ann frowned. She stared down. "Pussy," she said.

"You're guessing," Guy said.

"I'll never get it," Mary said, pushing away the magazine.

"Hey—get this sentence right and we'll let you go home!" Guy said.

"Miss it, the alligator plank," Tom said.

Mary Ann glanced behind her at the bales. The hole was in shadow. She stared again at the sentence and scrunched up her forehead. "The thick white rod of his cock slid into her waiting . . . mouth!" she finished. "Mouth!"

"Yea, hooray," Guy and Tom shouted. "You were reading! That was reading!"

"Really?" Mary Ann said. Her eyes were more open and shining than Guy had ever seen them.

Chapter Five

Two days before Christmas came the first real snow. It snowed all day. All night. Until noon the next day. Thick, wet snow that, in three claps between mittens, made solid snowballs. When their arms hurt from throwing, Guy and Tom and Mary Ann rolled up bigger white balls for snowmen. The weight of the larger balls drew up grass and leaves from the lawn and left a map of brown trails across the white yard. On the farm buildings the snow dulled the ridges of the rooflines, lay drooped over their leaves like bread dough left rising too long in a bowl.

That afternoon Guy's father paid Jewell Hartmeir a visit. He brought with him the long-handled, aluminum snow rake.

"Maybe one of the boys can try that out tomorrow," Jewell Hartmeir said, leaning the snow rake against the barn.

Martin looked up at the Hartmeir barn roof. "I wouldn't wait," Martin said.

"I would," Jewell Hartmeir said. He glanced up briefly, then spit brown on the snow.

"Get in the damn truck," Martin said suddenly to Guy.

Guy obeyed. On the way home Martin swore again, then said, "At least nobody can blame me."

That afternoon, on his way to the barn for chores, Guy heard on the faint north wind cattle bawling. They didn't stop.

Martin and Helmer and three neighbor men worked with chain saws and a pistol. Cattle bawled and voices screamed from underneath the twisted tin and broken lumber of the Hartmeir barn. With the chain saws the men cut through metal and wood. Behind the men and saws, Guy and Tom threw aside the wreckage. Whenever a chain saw stopped, the pistol whumped as Martin shot another cow.

The men found Jewell Hartmeir pinned, cursing, in the gutter. He was okay but for a long scrape down his face. Martin cut him free and he stood up dripping manure and shouting for his boys.

Billy and Bob they found trapped alongside a big, dead holstein whose broken back supported a rafter. Martin cut a jagged door for them and they scrambled free. Chuck, the youngest, they pulled crying from beneath some timbers. The foot on his right leg was turned backward.

"Bub—Bub! Where's Bub? Bub and Mary Ann!" Jewell shouted.

There was silence.

"Bub, answer me, goddamn you!" his father shouted.

"That was him screamin' earlier," Chuck blubbered, his chest heaving. "Bub was further on but he ain't screamin' no more. Mary Ann neither."

Toward the middle, flattest part of the barn, the chain saw blades dulled from the tin and nails and did not cut as much as smoke. The men threw the saws aside into the snow, where they hissed and sank from sight. Then the men worked forward with axes and handsaws and hydraulic jacks.

"Need somebody small," Martin shouted back, out of sight beneath the tin and boards. "And a flashlight."

Jewell Hartmeir looked at his boys, then to Guy and Tom.

"I'll go," they both said at the same time.

"Git them a light," Jewell shouted.

41

Guy crawled forward to his father. Tom was right behind. "What are you doing in here?" Martin said.

"We're smallest," Guy said.

His father stared. Then he said, "Okay. Long as I can see you both, and you come out when I say."

Guy and Tom nodded. They crawled forward. In the darkness and dim beam of the light, cattle still bawled and groaned. The wood and metal around Guy thudded and quivered from their kicking.

"Mary Ann—Mary Ann!" first Guy and then Tom called. There was no answer.

Guy worked his way forward on his belly until his flashlight shone on boots. Two sideways soles of boots. A cow's head lay alongside the boots and its eyes reflected green. As the flashlight struck its eyes the cow flailed its head and struggled to get free. Every time the cow kicked, the boots jerked.

"Pistol, we need the pistol," Guy called.

"Pistol," Tom called back to Martin.

Then Guy felt the pistol butt tap on his boot. He took the heavy gun in his right hand, steadied it with his left, then aimed it down the beam of his light to a spot between the green eyes of the cow. He closed his eyes and squeezed the trigger. In the small space around him the pistol's noise crashed like a giant fist on all sides of his head. Afterward he felt the rapid death kick of the cow. In a minute the kicking slowed. When Guy's hearing returned, the cow's slow kicking sounded like cows' hooves running through mud. Blood bubbles popped from the cow's nose. When the cow finally lay still Guy crawled over its neck and shone the light forward. Bub lay pinned with his head against the cow's hooves. His face had been kicked until it looked like some small animal run over again and again by cars on the highway until you couldn't tell what it was. "Jesus," Tom whispered from beside him.

Guy turned off the light. He swallowed to keep from puking.

Then he heard a whimpering. He turned on the light again. From behind Bub's big body they saw yellow curls and round eyes. They scrambled forward.

Mary Ann was sandwiched between Bub and heavy timber, two of whose spikes had nailed her right hand to her brother's back. Guy and Tom braced against the wood and with their feet pushed Bub away. They jerked her hand free of the nails, then together carried her toward daylight.

Chapter Six

Winter Saturdays, Guy and Tom and Mary Ann sledded on the hills above No Medicine Lake. Mary Ann, who wore a double mitten on her right hand, was always with them. Jewell Hartmeir would wait until spring to rebuild the barn so there were only cooking chores for Mary Ann. Guy's parents often woke him late at night with their voices but they hardly spoke during the day. Tom came one Saturday with two black eyes and a puffed-up lip, none of which he would talk about. So the three of them played outside even in the coldest weather.

"Stumps there and there and there," Tom called, his nose dripping clear and shiny in the cold. He pointed to swells in the snow that ran down to the lake. Not far offshore was a fish house. The icehouse belonged to the old Indian, Zhingwaak. It was a small, white-painted shack no more than six feet square. Depending on the sunlight, Zhingwaak's fish house seemed some days close to shore and other days far away. With bright sunlight on snow, the little house was invisible but for a thin, gray string of smoke wavering from the ice.

They sledded and did not think about the fish house.

Sometimes a dark rectangle suddenly appeared on the lake and only then did they remember it. For once in a morning and once in an afternoon Zhingwaak would swing open the door and step behind the house. Then he went back inside. The black door on the ice closed to white and the fish house again disappeared.

"He ever get fish there?" Guy said. All the other icehouses were clustered on the sandbars two miles down the lake. There the water was clearer. The farther north you went on the lake, the cloudier the water became. That was because of the big underground spring which fed into the lake from somewhere under the hills that Guy and Tom and Mary slid on.

Tom shrugged.

"So why does he stay there?" Guy said.

"He thinks the big northern pike live closest to the spring."

"He ever see one? I mean a really big one?"

Tom nodded.

"How big?" Guy said. He turned from the fish house to Tom.

"Big as a shark," Tom said.

"Shit," Mary Ann said. "Ain't no sharks up here."

"Aren't any sharks here," Guy said automatically. "You want to stay in third grade the rest of your life?" He and Tom's reading lessons had pulled Mary Ann up to third grade, but they still held school for her when they could find a warm place without parents.

"*Ain't* is a word," Mary Ann said, pushing out her bottom lip.

"No it ain't," Tom said. He grinned.

"Then how come everybody uses it?" Mary Ann said.

"Everybody around Flatwater, you mean," Guy said, still thinking about Zhingwaak and the big pike. "You don't hear people on TV using *'ain't.'* Your heartthrob Dr. Granger, and Julia, you don't hear them using *ain't.* And that's how they got on television."

Mary Ann stared. "Really?"

"For sure," Tom said. "It's like the world is full of little microphones that listen for people to say *'ain't'* and *'ourn'* and *'hisself'* and stuff like you say. The microphones are

45

hooked up to a machine that keeps track of people. People who talk funny can never get on TV or become movies stars."

"Really?" Mary Ann said.

Guy nodded. "Dr. Granger and Julia, too, they probably never said *'ain't'* in their whole lives," Guy said, still staring across the ice, trying to spot the faint feather of smoke from Zhingwaak's house.

"Shit," Mary Ann said. She kicked at the toboggan. When Guy looked back her eyes had begun to shine with tears. "That means I already could never be like Julia."

Guy and Tom glanced at each other.

"Naw," said Tom. "It's like this. The people with the microphones and the machines take into account where you was born. Who your daddy and mom were. If your mom died, like yours did, they write that down too. If you got a slow start being a kid, like you did, they're not going to be so tough on you."

"Take Julia's or Dr. Granger's kids," Guy added, "they got a head start on the rest of us. But one *'ain't'* and they fall down a notch and we move up."

"Really?" Mary Ann said, beginning to smile.

"For sure," Tom said.

"Get on," Guy said, sliding the toboggan toward Mary Ann. He was still thinking about Zhingwaak and the big pike and the underground spring.

In January a warm front lumbered slowly from the south onto the reservation. The knee-deep, fluffy snow settled like white-bread whose yeast had failed. Cold weather came again and left a frozen crust on which their toboggan never slid better. Holding on to each other, Guy and Tom and Mary Ann swept down the hill toward No Medicine Lake. They soared shrieking over the ridge where the frozen water met the shore, slammed back onto the snow, then hissed forward across the ice. Sometimes their toboggan came within a snowball's throw of Zhingwaak's fish house.

Once Zhingwaak opened his door and left it open. He was watching them.

"Maybe we're bothering him," Guy said.

"Naw," Tom said, "nothing bothers him."

* * *

Another time when they were sliding, Zhingwaak came out of his fish house and walked down the lake. He carried a small saw. He walked to where he was finger-tall and a toothpick-sized tree lay blown over onto the ice. He bent over the tree. Guy watched his dark arm move back and forth like a wing. At first there was no sound, then came the faint rasp of the saw. When Zhingwaak stopped cutting and stood up the saw continued to rasp without him. Guy imagined the cut still deepening. Sawdust still falling.

As Tom and Mary Ann pulled the toboggan back uphill, Guy watched Zhingwaak. His dark figure against the white shoreline was connected to the black door of the fish house on the lake. Zhingwaak was a door.

He watched as Zhingwaak gathered a few sticks in his arms and began the walk back to his fish house. Guy looked at the long toboggan sliding toward him on the ice, then back to Zhingwaak.

The three of them approached Zhingwaak on the ice. The old Indian wore layers of plaid wool shirts and green wool pants that looked like army blankets. His pants were held up by suspenders made from braided strips of buckskin. On his head he wore a floppy cap of shiny black and white skunk fur. In the bright sunlight Zhingwaak's face looked like oak bark with knotholes for eyes. He smelled like woodsmoke and tobacco. He nodded to them and spoke some word Guy did not know.

"We have the toboggan, we'll haul your wood," Tom said.

Zhingwaak nodded, then placed his sticks on the sled.

They hauled and stacked a large pile of dead branches beside the fish house. Zhingwaak's little door remained closed. When they finished he swung open the door. He stared at the pile of wood. Then he said, "Come in, children."

Tom, Guy, and Mary Ann squeezed into the hot darkness of the little house. At first Guy could see nothing but the moonglow square of the spearing hole. While his eyes adjusted to the darkness, his nose took over. He smelled sweat dried in old wool. Tobacco. Pine pitch and creosote from the wood stove. And a sharper scent that was a cross between cedar shavings and something cooked for Thanksgiving but left too long in the oven, something burned.

47

Soon he could see better. Zhingwaak sat on a stool at the far end of the fish house. He leaned over the spear hole and his face drew light from the water. A zigzag scar cut like a crow's track across the furrows of his forehead. Guy thought of the policemen's sticks that summer night in Flatwater, the flash of lights, the swirl of falling bodies.

The big pike spear leaned against Zhingwaak's shoulder. The spear was a narrow rod of iron, taller than Guy. Its tines were a wide hand of ten barbed fingers that pricked in the wood floor. The spear's cord was draped across Zhingwaak's knee, then tied in a noose knot around his ankle. That way if Zhingwaak speared a big pike he could easily walk it outside and let it flop and stiffen on the ice.

Beside Zhingwaak was a wood stove, a five-gallon pail with a hole cut for a stove pipe on top and a door for wood cut in its side. On the wall beside Zhingwaak's head was a long gray feather, a feather bigger than Guy had ever seen. Beside the feather was a small leather pouch. Tied to the pouch was a tiny tin man. Below the tin man, hung on nails, were three bright-painted decoy fish carved of wood and with tin, curved tails.

A fourth decoy, a red and white one, hung in the water in the center of the hole a few feet beneath the ice. Guy stared down the bright door of the spear hole. The walls of the ice glowed white and smooth. The water welled slightly up and down, as if somewhere there were waves underneath the ice. Tiny, sand-sized bits of green moss hung in slanted drifts in the water like grain dust in sunlight. Faint white polka dots that could have been clam shells showed against the mossy-green lake bottom. Guy could not tell the depth of the water.

Zhingwaak began to work the decoy line. The decoy fish darted forward from a spray of green dust, then began to loop in slow circles about the hole. Zhingwaak's wrist clicked as he worked the line. In the dusty green water the decoy followed itself; its white sides left a ghost of phosphorescence that chased its real body in perfect circles below the ice. Guy watched Zhingwaak's wrist rise and fall. Click. Rise and fall. Click.

Then he realized Zhingwaak was watching him. The old Indian's dark eyes drew light from the water.

"You want to try?" Zhingwaak said, handing the line to Guy.

The decoy jerked and bobbed as Guy pulled on the line.

"Slower," Zhingwaak said.

Soon Guy had the red and white fish looping evenly about the hole.

"I'm next," Tom said quickly.

"Then me," Mary Ann said.

The three of them took turns with the decoy line. Zhingwaak watched the decoy swim.

"Not that way," Tom said to Mary Ann, "that's too jerky. Here. Like this."

Mary Ann stamped her feet on the floor and grabbed back the line from Tom.

"Children," Zhingwaak said, "we must be very quiet. The big pike Nimishoomis will hear us and he will not come to our hole."

They fell silent. They looked into the water, then back up to Zhingwaak.

"You saw him once?" Guy asked.

Zhingwaak nodded.

"How big is he?" Mary Ann asked quickly.

"As big as a man."

All of them stared back into the hole.

"Nimishoomis. He is the grandfather of all pike," Zhingwaak said.

They were quiet for a while. Zhingwaak handed the decoy line to Tom, then reached into his pocket. He pulled out a large potato. He held the potato over the hole and with his knife began to cut the potato into thin slices. The white slices splashed onto the water, then fell, wavering like leaves falling, to the bottom. Guy realized the water was only six or eight feet deep. Resting on the green moss, the potato slices drew light from the water and brightened the hole.

"Why are you doing that?" Mary Ann asked.

"Light for Nimishoomis," Zhingwaak said. "So he can find his way to our house."

Nimishoomis did not come that afternoon. He did not come the next day, nor the one after. But Guy and Tom and Mary Ann came often to Zhingwaak's fish house. When they tired of sliding or were cold, they crowded into Zhingwaak's house. Often he told them stories, stories like "The Little Boy and the Windigoo."

Long ago there was an Indian village. The men in the village were all hunters. One day some of the hunters went into the woods but never returned. Other hunters went to look for them. But those hunters never returned.

This kept on.

In the same village there was a little boy who lived with Ookomisan, his grandmother. He listened to people talk. He watched the hunters leave the village.

One day he said to his grandmother, "Ookomisan, may I go hunting in the woods?"

"Don't you know there's a Windigoo in the woods?" she answered him.

"A Windigoo is like a giant, only bigger," Zhingwaak explained, then continued.

"The Windigoo does not scare me," said the little boy. "So give me a little sack of buckskin to carry my lunch in and let me go into the woods."

"The Windigoo will catch you and eat you," Ookomisan said.

"Not me," the little boy said. "I will catch the Windigoo if only you will let me go into the woods."

The boy coaxed and coaxed Ookomisan. And finally she gave in. She knew the little boy was brave. She gave him a buckskin pouch and some dried venison for the trip.

The little boy walked from the village into the forest. He walked among the rivers and trees for four days. On the fourth day he stopped to lean against an oak tree. The tree moved. The tree was not a tree at all, but was the leg of the Windigoo.

The Windigoo thought, Here is a boy. But he is

too small to eat. So I will invite him to my house. When he eats he will grow big. Then I will eat him.

At the great hut of the Windigoo, the Windigoo brought out venison and duck and partridge and bread and blueberries and cranberries and more. "Eat," the Windigoo said to the little boy. "If you eat, I won't hurt you and you can stay here with me and grow big and I will be your friend."

But the little boy was as clever as he was brave. He knew the giant's plan. And the little boy had a plan of his own.

The Windigoo and the boy began to eat. They ate and ate. Once when the Windigoo's big eyes looked down to his bowl, the little boy felt for his own buckskin pouch. He moved the pouch so that it hung in front of him but under his shirt.

They kept eating. But the boy began to drop food into the buckskin pouch instead of into his mouth. The giant ordered more food. He began to stare at the little boy who could eat so much. But the little boy's fingers were faster than the Windigoo's eyes. He kept dropping his food into his pouch.

From the juice of the berries and the juice of the meat, the buckskin pouch began to stretch as all leather stretches when it is wet. In this way the little boy kept eating.

Soon the Windigoo thought, My! This little boy eats more than anyone I've ever seen, even more than other Windigoos.

Finally the Windigoo could eat not another leg of a partridge or even a berry.

"Have you had enough?" the Windigoo asked the little boy.

"Not yet," answered the little boy. He kept eating until his shirt puffed out in front as round as a goose before winter.

The Windigoo decided to kill the little boy. He could hang him from the rafters of his hut and then eat the boy tomorrow when he was hungry again.

But then the little boy said, "I can do something no Windigoo can. Watch this." With that he took out his skinning knife, pulled up his shirt, and slit open the buckskin pouch.

Now the Windigoo was angry and jealous. He took out his own knife and did the same thing to his own great belly. From the Windigoo's belly tumbled all the hunters of the village, who set upon the Windigoo and killed him.

When the Windigoo was dead, the hunters carried the little boy back to the village on their shoulders. They sang:

Windigoo *gii-nibo*, Windigoo *gii-nibo*.
The cannibal is dead, the cannibal is dead.
Mangademo, mangademo.
The trail is wide, the trail is wide.

Sometimes after a story Zhingwaak left them alone in the fish house while he walked up the lake to get more firewood or to look for animal tracks along the shore. Then Guy or Tom or Mary Ann got to sit in Zhingwaak's chair.

One February afternoon it was Tom's turn. As Zhingwaak's footsteps crunched away from the fish house, Tom tied the spear's cord around his ankle but leaned the spear against the wall. Since they had never yet seen a fish in Zhingwaak's hole, they played games with the decoy fish. Guy found another line and let a second decoy circle down into the water. He and Mary Ann played chase with the two decoys. The little wooden fish, one white and red, the other yellow, darted back and forth across the hole.

"Never catch me," Mary Ann called.

"Just wait," Guy said.

Soon their lines tangled. Still laughing, Guy and Mary Ann kept pulling on the lines. The little fish, like fighting kites, wound themselves closer and closer together.

As Guy opened his mouth to say "Tag . . ." there was a green swirl in the hole and both decoys disappeared. Guy pulled on his line but it was stuck on something.

"Holy shit," Tom breathed.

Then Guy saw the fish. It was Nimishoomis. His broad, dark back lay below them in the center of the hole like a great old log with yellow-black eyes. He filled the length of the hole and his tail was out of sight beneath the ice. His eyes looked all directions at the same time. His gills, as wide as Guy's grandfather's hands, swelled and sank, swelled and sank as he breathed the water. The two decoy lines disappeared inside his closed jaws.

"Spear—the spear!" Guy whispered.

Tom fumbled for the spear, then stood up. Slowly, as Zhingwaak had shown him, Tom lowered the spear until its barbs silently broke the surface of the water. The water trembled around the iron tines.

"Throw!" Guy said.

With both hands, Tom drove down the spear. In the same moment Nimishoomis heard the splash above him and swirled his tail. The spear did not strike behind his head and break his spine as Tom had aimed, but struck him far back, drove deep into the fleshy muscle of his tail. Harpooned, Nimishoomis fled. In the water of the hole the spear's cord hissed away. Hissed away from Tom's ankle. Tom had time only to open his mouth when he was jerked off balance and into the hole. Guy lunged for him but missed. Tom was in the water, then gone.

Mary Ann screamed.

Guy, too, was half in the burning cold water. He held on to the wood side of the fish house. "Zhingwaak—run for Zhingwaak!" he shouted. Mary Ann plunged through the door and was gone. Guy screamed Tom's name, then filled his lungs with air and pushed himself below the ice.

In the water, roiled by the pike's thrashing, Guy could see only a few feet in any direction. The cold cut through him. He swam a few feet straight ahead, then looked again. Nothing. He turned back to the hole but his head hit only ice. He tried to remember how many times he had kicked his legs. Four, five. He swam forward with his back against the gray ice. Suddenly he surfaced in the fish house. He gasped for breath, then pushed himself underwater again.

This time he swam south ten kicks. Nothing. Only green. He began to scream Tom's name but stopped himself from opening his mouth.

He found his way back to the air hole. This time he swam east. From the cold he could go only eight kicks. Far away above him on the ice he heard a faint thudding like a distant thunderstorm. He lost count of his kicks. Red stars popped in his eyes before he reached air again. He hung, gasping, on to the wooden legs of Zhingwaak's chair. Outside he could hear Mary Ann's voice screaming.

There was one direction left. North. Guy swallowed air and went under again. He swam six, then eight, then ten kicks north. He was just about to turn back when he saw something. He swam on. It was Tom. He was floating sideways against the ice, his legs and arms dangling, drifting. The spear's cord hung limply from his leg. The pike had torn free. The spear lay in the moss.

Guy pulled himself forward, half swimming, half clawing his way along the ice to Tom. He grabbed the cord and began to tow Tom back. But he had forgotten about the spear, whose barbs lay caught in the moss and weeds.

By now the last of Guy's air was leaking from his mouth and nose in a spray of bubbles. With a last lunge, he tore the cord from around Tom's ankle and pulled him forward.

But it was too late. He began to breathe water. He was a fish. He felt the cold rush of water in his lungs, saw red roses begin to bloom and burst in the sky above him. A tree fell from the red sky. He grabbed its trunk and held on as everything darkened. Night. Then the moon. A huge full moon to which he was sailing.

Hard hands pulled him upward. The tree was a ladder. The moon was a door. The door was air. Air was open. Open house, the fish house door. White earth, blue sky.

When Guy came to, he was alone in the fish house. A large, dead limb stuck up from the water. The tree. Mary Ann. She had put the dead limb in the hole.

Through the open door he saw Zhingwaak and Mary Ann standing on their heads on the ice outside. Tom was holding them upright. Guy blinked. Then he saw that Zhingwaak was holding up Tom by his ankles and Mary Ann was clapping on Tom's back. Tom was the one upside down. Tom puked once onto the ice, then again, a long gush of water. Then Zhingwaak called something and jerked his head toward Guy and the fish house.

54

"I'm okay," Guy said as Mary Ann gave him her coat. His teeth rattled. He began to shake all over.

Zhingwaak carried Tom into the house. Tom stared, white-faced.

"No . . ." he mumbled as he saw the spear hole.

"You're safe," Zhingwaak said. He closed the wooden lid to the spear hole and sat Tom next to the stove. He pulled Guy closer to the heat.

"More wood," he said to Mary Ann. Then he began to undress Tom. Mary Ann filled the stove with dead limbs. The wood crackled and threw yellow light onto the fish house floor.

"You too," Zhingwaak said. Guy struggled out of his shirt and pants, then sat naked with Tom. They shivered as the harsh heat washed over them. The sides of the stove turned gray, then dark red, then cherry.

As they warmed themselves, Zhingwaak looped the decoy line across the ceiling and hung up their clothes to dry. As he worked he began to hum a low song that rose and fell. Guy thought of the starbursts. Of the Fourth of July. In the heat Zhingwaak's face shone with sweat and he took off his fur cap. His long white hair fell down in a braid.

When the clothes were all hung, Zhingwaak took the big gray feather from the wall and ran its vane through his braid. He took the little tin man and tied it onto his wrist. Then he opened the leather pouch. He threw a pinch of something onto the flat top of the stove. The stove top hissed and smoked. A sharp, sweet, burning smell filled the fish house.

Zhingwaak sat again on his stool. He leaned over the now-shut doorway into the lake. With a thin, dead limb he began to tap on the wooden floor as he sang. He closed his eyes. He was like a singing blindman with a cane.

Guy and Tom watched. The stove's heat began to work its way through them and they stopped shivering. Zhingwaak sang on, stopping once to throw more sage onto the stove— that was it, sage—Guy thought. His mother used it at Thanksgiving. It smelled good then. It smelled sweet and strong and even better now.

Zhingwaak sang and drummed on the hollow wood floor until their clothes were nearly dry. Mary Ann had begun to giggle at their nakedness so they stood up and pulled them on. Zhingwaak set aside his sticks. He wiped his face and watched them dress.

Zhingwaak looked at Guy. "Ningos is a good swimmer."

"Tom taught me," Guy said.

"Lucky for him," Mary Ann said.

Tom did not speak.

Ningos opened the door of the fish house. Outside, the snow was blue.

"I've gotta go," Tom said. His voice sounded funny, like he was speaking through a pipe.

Zhingwaak nodded. Pulling the toboggan they began the walk home. Zhingwaak stood on the ice beside his house. He watched them until they stepped over the ice ridge onto land.

On the way home Mary Ann talked on about the accident. "Did you see anything under there?" she asked. "What was it like?"

Both Guy and Tom walked on in silence.

"You must have seen something," she said.

"Just shut up for once," Tom said. He just kept walking and staring across the purple fields.

Chapter Seven

In the spring when they were eleven, in late May when it was finally tennis-shoe weather, Guy and Tom were fixing Mary Ann's bike chain in the farm shop. Suddenly Tom dropped his wrench and stared at Mary Ann.

"Hey, you got tits!" Tom said.

Guy looked at Mary Ann's T-shirt.

"Jesus," Guy said. She did have tits. He had not noticed them because they were not the pointy kind. Sometimes in the summer Guy noticed girls in town who were eleven or twelve and had uneven little points under their T-shirts like horns growing on a calf. Sometimes the points were uneven, and once he saw a girl with only one. He began to watch for tits after his grandmother once clucked her tongue at one of the town girls and murmured that the girl was too old to run around dressed like that.

But Mary Ann's tits did not come out pointy. Rather, they were wide mounds growing like muscles across her chest.

"My daddy says they're going to be big ones too," she said. She held up her T-shirt.

Guy knocked over the oil can. He and Tom stared. Her

57

tits were swelled up like two big muffins with a glob of pink frosting in the center of each.

"Jesus," Tom murmured.

"Amazing," Guy said. He glanced through the open door of the machine shop into the yard. It was quiet and empty.

"That's not all I got," Mary Ann said.

Guy and Tom looked at each other.

They went to the hayloft, to their hayhouse, to see the rest of Mary Ann's secret. The hayhouse was a little lean-to building that Guy and Tom and Mary Ann had built in the corner of the loft out of old lumber; they went there, sometimes slept there, whenever their parents were drinking or fighting.

But now Martin and Helmer were dust clouds far out on the fields. Etta worked in the garden with her back to the barn. Madeline was gone to town. Sunlight came through the little windows and made a rectangular spotlight on the board floor.

Mary Ann stepped into the light, then backed out. "This will cost you," she said.

Guy and Tom stared at each other.

"A quarter apiece."

Guy and Tom fished into their pockets. Two nickels between them.

Mary Ann took the nickels. "A nickel apiece and do what I do."

Guy and Tom stared at each other, then nodded.

Mary Ann stepped back into the sunlight. She undid her pants, then pulled them down.

"Jesus," Guy said.

Mary Ann wore no underwear, and between her legs was a triangle of bright red hair.

"It's red!" Tom said.

"What the hell you expect, purple?" she said, pulling up her pants.

"Wait," Guy said, leaning closer for a better look at the hair, the tiny pink tongue at the top of her slit.

"Yeah, give us our nickel's worth," Tom said. They dropped to their knees so they could get a straight-on look.

58

"Time's up," she said soon. She pulled up her pants, then stepped away from the sunlight. "Your turn."

Guy and Tom stared at each other.

"Who goes first?" Tom said.

"Why not do it together?" Mary Ann said.

Guy and Tom looked at each other, then stepped into the spotlight.

They unzipped their zippers.

"Hey, that's cheating. All the way down," Mary Ann said.

They stared at each other a moment, then undid their belt buckles. Their penises, one white, the other brown, stood straight up; around them neither Guy nor Tom had any hair.

Mary Ann laughed. Guy and Tom started to pull up their pants. "Hey," she said, "give me my money's worth."

"You never paid anything," Tom said.

"But you got to see my tits too," she said.

Guy and Tom stared at each other, then let her look some more.

"Do you guys?" she asked, and made an up-and-down motion with her fist.

Guy looked to Tom. Neither of them said anything because they didn't know what she was talking about.

"Really?" she said. "My brothers do it all the time. Want me to show you?"

Tom turned to Guy.

She stepped between them, spit in first one palm and then the other, then took their penises into her hands. She began to stroke them. She started out slow, soon spit on them again, then moved her hands faster and faster. Guy began to feel a burning sensation. The burning started low in his crotch and moved higher and higher until he spurted a thin spray of white onto the hay. Tom groaned and did the same thing.

"There," Mary Ann said.

Guy felt wobbly on his legs. He pulled up his pants, as did Tom. They both got down on their knees to look at the white stuff. It was shiny, with white swirls in it like the glass of pearly marbles. It settled into the hay and drew bits of dust on its surface like lint on Jell-O.

Jism. His first jism. And Tom's too.

They looked up at Mary Ann.

"Where'd you learn that?" They said at the same time.

"From my brothers," she said. "They make me do it for them every day. They say it's part of my chores."

Guy looked at Tom. "Does your dad know?"

"Sure. Sometimes when my brothers are asleep he gets me up and I have to do him too."

Chapter Eight

"Niggers," Jewell Hartmeir said from underneath the tractor, "they've taken over everything from Des Moines, Iowa, south. That's why we came up here. Cheap land and no niggers."

Martin grunted and pulled harder on the chain hoist. Guy and Tom and Mary Ann sat on Martin's tractor. Guy operated the hydraulic loader that supported the Hartmeir Massey-Ferguson. They were in Hartmeir's field. Guy's father was helping to fix the front axle of the Hartmeir tractor. Billy, or maybe it was Bob, had been harrowing at road-gear speed. The front tractor tires hit a large stone, the axle snapped, the tractor flipped onto its side and threw either Billy or Bob fifteen feet out into the soft dirt of the field. Since neither would admit to being the driver, Jewell had whipped them both with a cattle cane. Now the two boys stood stiffly on either side of the tractor. From a long arm's reach they handed their father wrenches and sockets and pry bars.

"Should have bought a new axle," Martin said again. "That weld might not hold."

"Some people ain't got a hundred bucks," Hartmeir

61

replied. "Besides, my own daddy showed me how to weld."
He fit the socket onto another nut.

Martin was silent.

"But the niggers," Hartmeir continued, "I could tolerate
working with niggers when I had to. But not *for* niggers.
Take that last place we farmed. No crop two years in a row.
But that didn't matter to the landowner. If we were a day
late with the payment, we'd get a letter the next day. Never
saw who it was we gave our money to. Didn't think it
mattered at the time. But then we got behind, couldn't make
the payments. Got letter after letter. Finally the owner
comes out to the farm. Drives a big Lincoln. A hundred
degrees outside and the windows are rolled up. Air-
conditioning. He gets out of the car. A big nigger, he was.
Purple as an eggplant. Wearing an expensive suit. At first I
thought he was some kind of salesman. Then he serves us
the papers. Turns out he's an attorney from Atlanta who
owns a lot of land he rents out to poor whites and other
niggers. I looked at him. I said, 'Mister, for two years this
farm hasn't grown any more cotton than fuzz on a baby's
cunt and now I know the reason why.'"

Guy and Tom snickered.

"Shut up," Mary Ann said, and jabbed at them with her
elbow.

Martin did not hear them because he had leaned over to
stare at Hartmeir's work.

"Tighten that third hub bolt more," he said.

"I did."

"Give it another turn," Martin said.

Hartmeir spit but gave the nut another yank with the
wrench.

"Course up here you got Indians," Hartmeir said.

Beside him Guy felt Tom stiffen.

"Niggers, Indians," Hartmeir said. "Throw 'em all in a
toilet, flush it, and you can't tell one turd from the other,
they say."

"I never met any coloreds," Martin said, easing up on the
chain hoist. "But I met lots of Indians and I know this.
None of them want to work. They want everything handed
to them while the rest of us work."

Guy drew in his breath.

"Shall I let down the loader?" Guy called to his father.

"No," his father said immediately and turned. He stared. He had forgotten they were there. He glanced beside Guy to Tom, who met his gaze. Martin looked back to the axle. "Not until everybody's out from underneath—you know that."

Guy knew that. He was thirteen now.

"That's what I figured," Hartmeir said. "Bunch of parasites on the rest of us. Indians probably steal like niggers too."

"Don't have much trouble with that," Martin mumbled.

"I catch any of 'em around my place, I'll let the air out of 'em in a hurry," Hartmeir said. "No law against protecting yourself, least not down where I came from."

Jewell Hartmeir climbed out from underneath the tractor and slapped a cloud of dust from his shirt. Then he and Martin knelt to work on the chain-hoist bolts.

"I gotta go," Tom said suddenly to Guy. He leaped down from the tractor and started across the field.

"Wait," Guy said. He climbed off the tractor and ran after Tom.

"Let's go to my house," Guy said, grabbing his arm.

"Don't want to," Tom said, jerking away. He walked forward without looking back.

"Guy—give the chain some slack," Martin called.

Guy stopped. Tom kept walking.

"Guy, goddamnit!" Martin called.

Two days later Guy was harrowing the north forty with Helmer's little orange Allis-Chalmers. He was not yet old enough to run the big tractor. But soon.

Tom rode with him perched on the fender. As soon as Guy was finished harrowing they were going to look for agates in the washout. Across Hank Schroeder's field they could see the red Hartmeir Massey-Ferguson moving in and out of a cloud of dust. Occasionally its tall aluminum-colored rear wheels glinted dully through the dusty haze. The Hartmeir tractor made a round and a half to their one.

"Billy?" Guy called to Tom over the tractor's noise.

"Bob," Tom said.

"Bet?"

"Quarter."

Guy nodded and began to circle the Allis-Chalmers

farther north toward the fence, where they could see better. He was watching the harrow behind when Tom shouted and pointed across the field.

Dust drifted and thinned in the Hartmeir field. The red nose of the Massey-Ferguson lay on the ground below the big rear wheels. The tractor had overturned.

"Jesus!" Guy shouted. "Unhook the drag!"

Tom leaped to the ground. As Guy backed up, Tom unbuckled the clevis, then leaped aboard as Guy gunned the tractor down the fence line toward the road.

It took them five minutes at full throttle to reach the accident. And neither Guy nor Tom won the bet. It was not Billy nor Bob who lay pinned beneath his tractor.

"You sonsabitches help me!" Jewell Hartmeir shouted. Then he screamed. The tractor lay on its side, its engine across his legs. The hot engine block and exhaust manifold had charred his pants legs and Guy could smell burned meat. In the dirt, like the pattern of a brown snow angel, Hartmeir had tried with his hands to fan himself away from the tractor.

Jewell Hartmeir saw Tom. "You Indian bastard, what the hell are you standing there for—run—get Bub."

"Bub's dead," Tom said softly.

Hartmeir's eyes widened. Then he screamed long and loud.

"The chain—quick," Guy shouted to Tom. Guy hooked the thin harrow chain onto the side of the Massey-Ferguson and began to pull with the Allis-Chalmers. The chain tightened. The Massey creaked an inch upward. Then the chain parted—a link hummed past Guy's head like a spent rifle bullet—and Hartmeir screamed louder as the Massey rocked back onto his legs.

"You're trying to kill me," he shouted at Tom. "You niggers you Indians you're trying to kill me I know that! All of you—you're trying to do me in well it won't work, I'll get even with you sonsabitches!"

Guy shouted at Tom to step aside. Then he wheeled the little tractor forward toward the Massey. When its nose pushed against the Massey's big rear wheel, he gunned the throttle. With the Allis he pushed the big tractor two inches upward. Then the wheels of the little Allis began to slip and spin and dig themselves down. He killed the engine and set the brake. Though the Massey was too heavy to push farther, he had taken some of the weight off Jewell Hartmeir. There was a full water bottle on the Allis. He threw it to Tom, then leaped down. "Give him water—I'll run for help," Guy shouted.

"Water," Hartmeir groaned, and reached up for the bottle in Tom's hands.

Guy ran.

By the time Martin and Helmer arrived with the big John Deere, the sheriff's car was wailing toward the field. The Massey creaked upward. Jewell Hartmeir's legs looked like burned steak. Martin and the deputy slid him, mumbling curses, onto the stretcher. Hartmeir groaned something.

"Shock," the deputy said. He leaned closer to try and make out the words.

"Water," Jewell Hartmeir groaned.

"Water?" the deputy said. "He wants water. Anybody got any water?"

Guy turned to Tom. "Is there water left?"

Tom nodded. He handed Guy the jug. From its weight Guy knew there was a lot of water left. He spun off the lid. The jar was still full.

Chapter Nine

Guy and Tom and Mary Ann turned thirteen, then fourteen, then fifteen. Guy grew tall and thin, a sandhill crane with long bony wings and straight, skinny rods for legs. Tom grew wide rather than tall. His shoulders broadened, his chest deepened, his arms and legs thickened with muscle that, when he walked, gave him a springy, cat-like gait. Mary Ann grew not tall nor wide. She grew deep.

Tits. That's what Mary Ann grew. By thirteen they were the size of softballs. By fourteen they were large Texas grapefruit. By fifteen they were big cantaloupes verging on watermelons. At fifteen and a half she stopped showing them to Guy and Tom. She wouldn't even go skinny-dipping with them at No Medicine Lake unless it was pitch dark with no moon.

"Hey, you shouldn't feel that way about your tits," Guy said.

"Yeah, I thought most girls wanted tits," Tom said to her. "Now that you got 'em, you don't want 'em."

"I didn't need 'em this goddamn big," she said.

Two junior high boys turned around and giggled.

"You two look around again and the Indian is gonna tear

your scalps off. With his fingernails," Guy said. Tom made claws of his hands. The two boys' eyes turned golf-ball size; they turned around and sat straight in their seat without even looking out the window.

Guy and Tom and Mary Ann sat in their usual seat, midway back, on Bus #33, the Indian Bus. White farm and resort kids sat up front. Indian kids took the rear. Every morning #33 wound its way across the reservation on a circuitous, hour-long trip to Flatwater High.

The high school was a two-story brick building just off Main Street, a building with a slumped back and acne. To save money on construction in the 1920s, the Flatwater school board voted to use local pine rather than western lumber, and bricks made from local yellow clay rather than the hotter-fired red brick from southern Minnesota. Now, in 1969, the school roof drooped, and chips of yellow brick formed a deep, crunchy ring underfoot around the school's perimeter. A new school was planned, but a local bond issue failed four years in a row. Maybe when the Vietnam War was over, people said. Then they would build. Right now there were Communists to fight overseas. First things first.

When Bus #33 arrived at Flatwater High the town kids were already there. They leaned against the flagpole, lounged on the front steps and lockers with spitballs, paper clips, and rubber bands. They formed a gauntlet as the Indian Bus unloaded.

Guy and Tom and Mary Ann always walked inside together. Because their group of three was not white, not Indian, not boy or girl, the Flatwater toughs did not know what to make of them. Guy and Tom and Mary Ann usually walked unimpeded. Unstung.

Inside there were fights—a sudden flail of fists, the thuds of bodies against lockers. Usually the fighters were brown and white. But the fights ended quickly when Tom Little-Wolf appeared. Like a boxing referee, Tom butted, pushed, sometimes threw the fighters overhead into the crowd. Usually he ended up in the principal's office for his effort.

"You fuckin' apple!" a nosebleeding young Indian kid once screamed at Tom.

"Apple. Why did he call Tom an apple?" Mary Ann asked.

"Think about it," Guy said.

Later Mary Ann said she still didn't get it.

"Red on the outside, white on the inside," Guy said.

In their classes Guy was good at English and social studies but lousy at math and chemistry. Tom got A's in art but D's in civics and history. Mary Ann got C's in math but D's and F's in everything else.

"My mind goes blank," she said. She was sixteen now. Her tits had stopped growing, but then she had grown rounder all over. Her yellow hair was longer now, which made her look shorter and thicker. She wore excessive lipstick and rouge, plus strong perfume she bought in the dime store, and often she smelled sharply sweet and sweaty. To Guy, Mary Ann began to look like the women he saw at the feed mill. The women with squalling children. The women with sunburned faces and strong arms in sleeveless blouses. The woman with big, chapped hands. The women who came driving their husband's pickups that pulled wagons of ear corn and oats and then sat uptown in the cafes while the cow feed was ground. Often Mary Ann skipped her history class and went uptown to watch the soaps in the same cafes.

"The teacher asks me something and everything in my mind just freezes," she continued. "It's like there's a fuel line in my brain that gets a slug of dirt in it. The engine shuts down. I just sit there. People laugh."

"Tell me who laughs," Tom growled. They were sitting in the school's basement cafeteria. The tables were crowded. Indian kids sat at the far, corner table where the light was dimmest from a boarded-over window. Guy and Tom and Mary Ann sat at table number three, which was part Indian, part white. White kids took up most of the cafeteria, including the honor society and student council creeps who sat at the table closest to the faculty dining room and its picture window on to the rest of the cafeteria. The tables were crowded but, as usual, there was an empty seat beside Tom. "Just point the fuckers out," Tom said.

Mary Ann looked up from her plate of Spanish rice. "You can't go around roughing up people for me the rest of my life," she said. She looked away, up through the glass-block basement windows. "Shit, I should quit school and get a

68

job." She looked back to them. "I could. I'm sixteen. There's nothin' anyone could do about it. Get a job, buy a car, say to hell with all this."

"What kind of job?" Guy said, glancing at Tom.

Mary Ann shrugged. "Uptown. Waitressing maybe. Or somethin'."

"Or somethin'," Guy said.

"Get married maybe too."

Tom spit out some milk.

"Married!" Guy said.

"You can get married at sixteen," Mary Ann said, pushing out her red-painted lips.

"But who to?" Tom said. "First somebody's got to want to marry you."

"I could find someone. Easy," Mary Ann said.

Across two tables sat Kurt Fenske, the beefy brown-eyed basketball center. Alternately Fenske stared opened-mouthed at Mary Ann's chest and glowered at Guy and Tom.

The three of them continued to ride #33 the rest of their sophomore year, though Mary Ann often got rides home with Kurt Fenske.

"She's fucking him. For sure," Guy whispered to Tom. He and Tom, in the back row of biology class, had developed the Little Wolf-Pehrsson Ophthalmological Virgin Indicator Theory. It held that a close-up, extended look into a girl's eyes revealed whether or not she was fucking.

"What, have I got something in my eye or something?" Mary Ann said, leaning away from them.

"Thought I saw something," Guy said.

Tom leaned forward for a closer look.

"Yeah, I think you're right," he said.

"Fuck you two," she said.

Rather than get a job, Mary Ann decided to become a cheerleader. Her boyfriend, Kurt, mainly by reason of bulk, was the long-standing team center. If Mary Ann were a cheerleader, she could cheer especially for him. Plus there would be the long, dark bus rides home from games in other towns.

But Guy said, "Nah, you don't want to be a cheerleader."

69

He knew she wouldn't make it. The cheerleaders were all town girls, perky blondes with short hair and little tits and great cartwheels.

"I can jump as good as any of 'em," Mary Ann said.

She demonstrated. "Rah!" Her great tits bounced.

Tom grimaced. Guy looked away.

"Cheerleading is really dumb if you think about," Tom said. "You run around clapping and screaming. And the crowd just wants to see the game, not the cheerleaders."

"So why do the TV cameras zoom in on the Dallas Cowgirls all the time, huh?" Mary Ann said immediately.

Guy and Tom were silent.

"Tryouts are next week," she said. "I been practicing for a month. You just watch me."

Cheerleading tryouts were held before a school assembly. In the auditorium the bleachers faced the basketball floor. Across the floor, on the high cement-block wall, painted in red and black, was the school insignia, and Indian headdress crossed with a tomahawk. "Go, Fight, Win! Flatwater Indians!" was painted in tall letters below.

Miss Simpson, a gray-haired, long-skirted history teacher who was also the cheerleading adviser, stood before a microphone. Beside her was a table manned by three other teachers and a record player. The teachers started the same record for each girl, then noted on paper the duration and intensity of the applause.

The girls waited in a row of chairs to the left side. For uniformity's sake, each girl had to wear a short black skirt and a red school-letter sweater. Since there were not enough red sweaters, the first girls changed clothes in the locker room and gave their sweaters to the last girls.

Mary Ann waited near the end of the row as several girls wheeled and bounced their way over the floor. Her turn approached. Guy saw Jennifer Price, a blond senior and already a cheerleader for three years, confer with two other seniors. Jennifer giggled into her hand, then came forward and handed a sweater to Mary Ann. Mary Ann went to change. Guy didn't see her again until Miss Simpson called her name and the record began.

As Mary Ann ran onto the floor the boys began to whistle

and thud their feet on the bleachers. Mary Ann's sweater had been taken from the smallest girl, probably Jennifer Price herself; it hung on Mary Ann like a short, orange curtain on a big window. Every time she leaped, the sweater rode up and exposed the white bottom of her bra.

Intent on her routine, Mary Ann bounced this way and that across the floor. "Jesus, she did practice," Guy murmured. Her cartwheels were straight and high. She popped up from splits like a sturdy grasshopper. Her sweater rode up each time. Sometimes she remembered to tug it down and other times she didn't. From the corner of his eye Guy saw Miss Simpson waving her hand at the teachers who worked the record player. But the other teachers stared at Mary Ann with slack jaws.

Mary Ann's final series was a cartwheel, then a backflip in a split, something no other girl had tried. She wheeled, flipped. And on the last, scratchy note of the song, she landed in a perfect split—arms out, legs out—except that her sweater came to rest in a narrow band just under her armpits. Unaware, she beamed at the roaring crowd. The bleachers thundered. The boys screamed.

Miss Simpson scuttled across the floor and yanked down Mary Ann's sweater. Mary Ann looked down, shrugged, then smiled and waved to the cheering crowd.

On Wednesday, Guy and Tom waited with Mary Ann for Miss Simpson to post the list. "What about that backflip, huh?" Mary Ann said. "Did you see any other backflips?"

"No," Tom said.

"Listen," Guy began. Mary Ann had already paid six dollars down on a red and black letter sweater.

"Did you hear applause like that for any other girl?" she said, grinning.

"No," Tom said. He looked at Guy.

"Listen," Guy said again. "Miss Simpson . . . she controls the whole thing. She can pick anyone she wants to."

"The most applause wins," Mary Ann said immediately. "That's the rules. It's just like *Queen for a Day*. And I got the most applause."

At precisely twelve noon Miss Simpson came through the door of the faculty lounge, posted the list with one jab of a thumbtack, then disappeared back into the lounge. Girls crowded around the list. Alternately they shrieked or walked away in silence.

Mary Ann did not walk away. She stood staring at the list without her name until she was alone before it. She waited there. She waited as if the paper were a magnet that would gradually draw her onto its surface, or as if it were a window through which she could pass. Guy and Tom stood to the side and waited for her. Finally the bell rang.

"Come on," Guy said. He tugged her arm but she jerked away.

"Next year," Guy said. "You'll make it next year."

Without turning, she shook her head. "Ain't gonna be any next year," she whispered.

Chapter Ten

Mary Ann no longer rode #33 to Flatwater High. But then neither did Guy and Tom. As soon as Guy got his driver's license, which was the fall of his junior year, he bought a car, a black two-door 1957 Chevy with red interior. He bought it from a gray-haired widow woman who had begun to confuse the accelerator with the brake pedal. The Chevy was dented. The woman's middle-aged son made her sell.

Guy's mother helped him buy the Chevy. "I've got some egg money saved," she said without his asking. "You should buy it. Then you could get away from the chores more. Stay after school. You've always wanted to play basketball. You and Tom could go out for the team. You could get away more from the farm, from the reservation. You two could take a summer trip, go to Minneapolis, to Winnipeg, to California. Anywhere."

By the second game of the basketball season, Guy, who was now six feet four, displaced Kurt Fenske as starting center. Fenske quit the team and began at noon hour to smoke in the parking lot across from school.

Tom played guard, benching Arnold Granland, who spoke

to no one, not even to his girlfriend, Jennifer Price, for the remainder of the school year.

And the team began to win.

Guy and Tom, from their years of hayloft basketball, played to each other. Off each other. Guy cleared the rim of rebounds and passed up-court before his tennis shoes touched wood. Tom spurted ahead for twisting, hanging lay-ups. Guy followed up to tip in the few balls of Tom's that did not fall. They were Pehrsson-LittleWolf, LittleWolf-Pehrsson, depending on the bounce of the ball; any stranger tuning in to the local radio broadcasts of the games would mistake them for one person.

The team regularly won by twenty points. By thirty. More. There was talk in Flatwater, in the barbershops, in the cafes, of a trip to the state tournament in Minneapolis.

Opposing teams knew that to win they had to break up the Pehrsson-LittleWolf combination. They usually tried first by roughing up Guy underneath the boards.

"Maxi-Burger time?" Tom asked.

Guy shook his head.

"Come on, they're killing you!"

"Not yet," Guy said.

But when the elbows got too sharp and too low Guy finally nodded for the Maxi-Burger. On the next trip down-court the chief offender from the opposing team suddenly got an open chance to block a Pehrsson lay-up. But if Guy came from the right side, Tom sliced in from the left. Somewhere underneath the basket the three players sandwiched together with a crunch. Tom hit low, Guy high, and the opponent hit the floor on his back and head with a sound like a melon dropped from the top bleacher. The game stopped as the opponents dragged their player from the floor. The team managers wiped up sweat and sometimes blood from the floor with towels. Tom took the foul. Then the game resumed in a more civilized fashion.

Sometimes the abuse took a different form.

"Hey, Redman!" players hissed at Tom.

"Hey, Tonto—where's the Lone Ranger?"

Guy's passes usually kept Tom up-court or in the air, away from the mean shit at floor level. If it got too bad, Tom benched himself before he swung at someone. Then Coach

Anderson immediately put in Jimi Henderson, a skinny, frizzy-haired guard with thick glasses who played electric guitar not unlike his idol Jimi Hendrix, and who had fingernails to match. *Punji* nails, it was rumored. Jimi kept his nails a quarter inch long, filed sharp, and, some players said, he dipped them in shit before each game. One swipe across a neck or chest or down a forehead left behind rake-teeth lines of blood.

Jimi would take the foul. The offender would retire to the locker room, gauze, and disinfectant. For his efforts Jimi was afforded a couple of thirty-foot jumpers, none of which ever came close to the rim. And Tom soon came back into the game.

That year, except for the first two games, the Flatwater Indians won all the rest. In snowy March the team found itself headed to the state basketball tournament in Minneapolis.

The caravan of orange buses followed the Mississippi River south through Little Falls, Saint Cloud, Anoka. There began the north suburbs of the Twin Cities, unwinding rows of pastel tract homes each with a jungle-gym swing set in the backyard and a covered fishing boat on a trailer in the front yard. Both were submerged in snow. In the bus, to see better, the boys blew clear, blue ovals on the white frost of the windowpanes. Most of them had never been to the city. They fell silent as the houses turned to shopping centers, the shopping centers to sagging white two-story houses of north Minneapolis, and then to old brick warehouses and flour mill silos along the Mississippi. Once Guy saw a brilliant coppery ringneck pheasant poised at the edge of a parking lot; behind the pheasant, trees ran down to the river. Guy twisted in his seat, pointing for Tom to see, but the bus had already passed. The pheasant was a photograph flashed once on a screen, then gone.

The bus wove its way alongside the gray glass skyscrapers of downtown Minneapolis. The players scraped larger windows in the frost and pressed their cheeks against the glass to look up. The heat of their skin melted the ice and ran water. When from the cold they pulled away their faces, the water wavered and froze again. Then through the thin glaze of ice the tall buildings curved and bent, and stoplights and police lights throbbed like kaleidoscopic mirrors and lights in a fun house.

"Hey, look at that big nigger in the Caddy!" someone from the back of the bus shouted. The bus swayed as the right-side riders rushed to look out left.

Guy looked down. A big black man in sunglasses and driving a '62 Cadillac with a chromed continental wheel waited at a stoplight just below them. A red-haired woman leaned close against him in the seat. The black man slowly looked up at the bus and seemed to meet Guy's gaze. He held up his middle finger, then looked back to the traffic.

"You fucker—you bastard," the rear-seat riders jeered.

"Pipe down, you guys," the bus driver called.

"Fucking rubes," Guy murmured. But Tom didn't answer. He was scraping ice and blowing on the glass to keep it clear.

Leaned against each other, they watched the city pass. Once they saw two policemen with guns drawn push a black man spread-legged against the white police car. Another time they saw an old Indian weaving down the sidewalk holding a sheaf of newspapers under his arm. Tom twisted in his seat to watch the Indian until he disappeared into the crowd.

The Flatwater Indians played at the University of Minnesota in William's Arena. They lost their first game by thirty points to a Minneapolis suburban school that had more students than Flatwater had people. The Indians lost their second game, by sixteen this time, to an all-black team from north Minneapolis. Those players did things with the basketball Guy had seen only on TV. Finally, against a farm town from southern Minnesota whose scoring, like the Flatwater Indians', came mainly from two players, the Indians won their last game by one point. Early and not unhappily out of the tournament, the boys from Flatwater had a free day to explore the city.

"I'm supposed to take this to my mom's cousin," Tom said, removing a small, tightly wrapped package from the bottom of his duffel bag. "Wild rice," he said.

Guy looked at the address. Franklin Avenue. It meant nothing to him. "So let's go," he said.

With two wrong city bus rides, Guy and Tom ended up on Hennepin Avenue, dead center, downtown Minneapolis. The streets were salted and slushy, the traffic fast and loud. Rather than try another bus ride, they walked twenty blocks south to Franklin.

"Must be the right street," Tom said. They began to see only Indians. The city Indians wore their hair in long, greasy braids. Tom said hello, but the silent city Indians passed with only a sidelong glance at Guy. In twenty-degree weather they wore layers of old clothes or green army coats. The city walkers hunched over as if they were clutching something to their bellies. Often the gold cap of a wine bottle protruded from a pocket. None of the city Indians wore caps or gloves.

On Franklin Avenue most of the stores and gas stations were boarded up and closed. Sheets of plywood became street blackboards.

"BIA Steals."

"Red Power!"

"Custer Died for White Sins."

"Red Brother/Yellow Brothers Unite—Save Vietnam from Nixon."

"Control Rent—Kill Your Landlord."

One word they saw again and again was "AIM."

"AIM for All Indians."

"AIM for Street Safety."

"AIM for Neighborhood Watch Patrol."

"White Police Harassment? Call AIM." Always there was a phone number.

"What's AIM?" Guy asked.

"Beats me." Tom shrugged. He held up the address to the doorway number of a three-story brick apartment building. The steps were cracked, their edges crumbly and rounded. "This is it," he murmured.

They went inside. The foyer smelled of piss. A metal grid of buttons and buzzers hung forward by a snarl of thin wires. On the floor the old carpet was worn to its nap all over. Beneath an iron radiator rusty water dripped with the sound of a ticking clock into the overflowing water of a flat pan.

77

They found the stairs to the third floor. The stairwell smelled even stronger of piss. An old Indian man lay sleeping in a nest of rags and torn newspaper underneath the stairs.

"Jesus . . ." Tom said softly.

In the dim hallway they heard TV game shows and crying kids. Behind one door someone coughed deep and rattly. They found number 387. Behind the door people were shouting, women's voices. Tom glanced at Guy, then knocked. The arguing stopped. Someone stomped across the room toward the door. The footsteps slowed before the door, which opened only the length of its safety chain. One round brown eye peered out at Tom.

"I'm Tom LittleWolf. I'm looking for Mrs. Rosalie All-day."

The brown eye leaned closer. Guy smelled perfume or incense.

"So? What, you collecting for something?"

"No. I'm from White Earth. Mrs. Allday is my mom's cousin."

The door opened. Holding it was an Indian girl about fifteen who held her baby sister on one hip. She wore a scarlet headband, red lipstick, a peace symbol and an AIM button on her sweater. Her face was round, her skin pale brown and smooth, her teeth perfectly white and straight.

Tom's mouth opened as he stared at her.

"Somebody from White Earth," she called through the hallway toward her mother. "No suitcase."

Mrs. Allday came through the door from the kitchen. She was very dark and very stooped. She looked fifty but probably was about forty. She squinted. "We don't have much room," she began.

"We didn't come to stay," Tom said quickly. "Just to give you this." He handed over the rice.

Mrs. Allday squinted at the package. "Mary," she said suddenly. "Mary sent this?"

Tom nodded.

"Then you're Mary's boy?"

Mrs. Allday laughed. Her teeth were yellowed. Some were gone. "Come in, come in," she said, tugging Tom forward.

Tom looked back at Guy. The Indian women stopped also to stare.

"Who's this behind you, Jesus?" the Indian girl said.

"Terry—damn you, you shouldn't say things like that!" her mother said, raising her hand as if to slap her daughter. But Terry did not flinch or even look at her mother.

"He lives on White Earth. He's my friend," Tom said. "We came down here together."

Terry nodded. "Well, get in before somebody sees you," Terry said to Guy. "We don't want to give this building a bad name."

"You think you could do better, just try," Mrs. Allday said immediately to her daughter. "You go out there and try to find a place. You'd be back here in a day. Go ahead, just try it."

"Shut up," Terry said to her mother, and began to rock the baby in her arms. "Just shut up."

Mrs. Allday carefully untied the string of the little package, eased open the brown paper as if to save it. "Rice—oh, oh . . ." she murmured. She leaned down and buried her nose in the long shiny black kernels.

"Christ, you'd think it was Acapulco Gold or something," Terry muttered.

Mrs. Allday found a little kettle and began to boil water. While she waited she sifted the rice back and forth, back and forth, one hand to the other. She began to hum a low song that was half humming and half singing.

"Oh God, not that," Terry said. She turned on the radio. Grace Slick and the Jefferson Airplane came on loudly: "White Bird, sits on the windowsill . . ." The baby stirred, then began to cry.

Terry jiggled the baby gently, then harder in her arms. But the baby kept crying. "Oh shit, all you do is eat," she said. She sat down on the couch and jerked up her sweater and pushed the baby's face against her round, brown-nippled breast. When the baby began to make sucking noises Terry looked back to Guy and Tom. To Tom she said, "You brought my mother something, so what'd you bring me?"

Tom could only stare. "That's your baby?" he finally blurted.

"It's sure not yours," she said.

"How . . . how old are you?" he asked.

"Old enough, right?"

Tom blushed; his brown cheeks turned darker.

79

"I didn't mean that . . ." he said. His voice trailed off.

"I'm fourteen and a half," she said. "Nearly fifteen."

Tom was silent. He looked at Guy. Then he said to her, "What about . . . school? Do you go to school?"

"Fuck school," she said.

"So what are you gonna do?"

"Live. Just like you," she said, staring straight at Tom with angry eyes.

Later that night Tom and Guy sat in the blue haze of the Body Shop, a nude bar just off Hennepin Avenue. They sat along the strippers' runway and stared up at the women dancers. Or rather, Guy stared. Sometimes Tom watched the women and other times he didn't. Sometimes he just stared into his glass.

"Ready?" the barmaid said.

"Pardon?" Guy said.

"Another beer?"

"No . . . not yet."

The woman made a face and turned to the next table.

On the stage the strippers, in high heels and sheer black shorty gowns, danced one by one in the slow-turning red and blue and yellow lights. Sometimes old men laid dollar bills on the stage in front of them, then leaned forward. The dancer worked her way toward the money, danced down over it, legs spread, nipples an inch from the old men's mouths. Then with a quick spin she was gone to the next dollar bill.

Each girl danced three songs, then was replaced by another dancer. The third woman made Guy breathe through his cock. She was about nineteen, tall, blond, with upturned pink nipples that rode high, round breasts. Her tits hardly moved when she reached down for the old men's money.

"Jesus," Guy murmured.

Tom didn't speak. Guy turned to look at him. The blond dancer passed before Tom and he didn't even turn his head. He stared right through her. Stared somewhere far away. He hadn't spoken all night.

The dancers began a new rotation. It was late but Guy wanted to see again the blonde with the long legs and hard tits. Finally she came back onstage. She was tired this time.

She stumbled. But men still laid their money on the canvas. Once she bent down for money and her right breast sprayed a tiny stream that misted pink in the light. She wiped her nipple with the back of her hand and danced on.

"Christ, she's got a baby too," Guy said.

Tom looked up suddenly. "Let's get the hell out of here," he said.

Out on the street they walked in silence. It was late, after midnight. Fine, sharp snow slanted in the streetlights and fuzzed the stoplights and bar signs redder. Tom walked staring ahead.

"What's the matter, Turd?" Guy said. He draped his arm around Tom's shoulders.

Tom shook his head and kept walking. He did not shrug off Guy's arm.

After a block he said rapidly, "Tex—I think I got to do something. But I don't know what it is." He turned to Guy as if Guy had an answer.

Guy stared. The Indian stuff. He knew Tom thought about it, but there wasn't any answer that he knew of so he only nodded to show he understood.

"Tex—we got to get the hell out of here," Tom said. "That's the first thing."

"Hey, relax," Guy said, "tomorrow we're gone." He held Tom in a fake neck lock and pulled him along. The streetlights were fewer now, the hotel only a few blocks on. A block ahead, black against the white sidewalks, a drunk wove his way toward them.

"Am I supposed to do something about my cousin? About her baby? About the others?" Tom murmured. "How am I supposed to know? What the hell am I supposed to do?" Tom said, louder with each word.

"Listen," Guy began. But at that moment the drunk blocked their path. "Shay my friends, can you spare an old fellow a dollar, huh?" the bum said. Tom squinted through the falling snow. The bum was an old Indian. He wore an army blanket cape and no hat. Snow shimmered and melted in his wet hair, ran down his face. His mouth was covered with yellow-running sores. "What shay, buddies, huh?"

Then the old man looked again at Tom. "Ah!" he said, as if Tom had hit him hard with his fist. He said something in

81

Chippewa and lurched forward and threw his arms around Tom. Tom struggled to get free.

"Help—Guy—help!" Tom shouted.

Guy pulled at the old man's fingers, which he had locked behind Tom's back. He was hanging on like death.

"Help me!" Tom screamed.

The next morning in the hotel room, Guy woke up alone. Tom's bed was made, his duffel bag gone. Everything was gone. It was as if he had never been in the room.

The players' bus waited a full hour, until ten-thirty, but Tom LittleWolf didn't show. When the coach asked, Guy told him about the visit to Franklin Avenue.

"So there you go." The bus driver shrugged. The coach looked at his watch. At eleven the bus left without Tom.

On the way back to Flatwater, Guy had a bus seat all to himself. But he did not sleep. While the other players dozed he only scraped frost and watched out the window. There was nothing much to see, only groves of red oaks here and there in the white fields.

Chapter Eleven

That spring Guy drove to Flatwater High alone. Occasionally he saw Mary Ann riding with Kurt Fenske in his muddy pickup that carried a red gas tank and a rack of chain saws in the rear. Mary Ann did not wave. Once while Guy was driving through town he saw her walking on Main Street. She waddled. Her belly was as round as a tub. A week before the baby came, Mary Ann and Fenske were married. Guy did not attend.

Tom LittleWolf he did not see. But he heard. He heard that Tom was in Taos. He was in New Orleans. He was in Rosebud. He was in Berkeley. He was in Brownsville. He was in Anchorage.

Tom was working on a roofing crew. He was selling dope. He was in college. He was in jail. He was working on the oil rigs. He was married. He was not married. He was in the hospital after an accident. He was never injured.

He was coming back to White Earth.

He was never coming back.

All this Guy heard at the school and at Doc's Tavern on No Medicine Lake and in the pool hall on Main Street where the Indians hung out. After two months of rumors, Guy drove over to the LittleWolf house.

It was mid-May. Tom's parents' house was small and square and white. In front was a brown lawn greening beside the south foundation. Behind was a backdrop of dull green jack pines. To the right of the steps was a small, south-facing bathtub grotto. The grotto was fronted by a single cluster of red petunias. The petunias had been newly planted, and early at that. There was a good chance of frost through the end of May. But maybe the grotto would make the difference.

Mary LittleWolf answered the door. "Guy," she said, with a quick smile, "come in." Then she lowered her voice. "No, better we talk outside."

Behind her, sitting at the kitchen table, was Tom's father. His square head and jutting chin were outlined against the white sheers of a kitchen window. A half-empty bottle of whiskey and a single glass sat before him on the table. Where he was staring there were only cupboards and wall. He did not look around.

Outside, Guy asked about Tom.

Mary LittleWolf looked down, then back up. "He wrote. He said that there were a lot of things he had to figure out. He said not to worry."

Guy waited. Mary LittleWolf let her eyes drift beyond Guy to the open space behind. She stared as if she had forgotten his presence. Her black hair was snowed with white. A cut on the brown point of her right cheekbone was healing pink. She blinked and looked again at Guy. "He did ask about you and Mary Ann," she said, summoning a faint smile.

"Tell him . . . we're okay. We're doing fine," Guy said.

"His address was Minneapolis," she said.

"I'll write," Guy said, "let me get the street and number."

"Just Minneapolis. That was all."

Guy was silent.

"I'm sorry, Guy," she said.

Guy thanked her. He turned away.

"Don't worry," she called to him. "That's what he said."

Guy paused. He nodded, then he got into the Chevy. As he turned onto the road, in his mirror he saw Mary LittleWolf standing dark and motionless, framed by the white front of the house.

* * *

School ended. Planting began. Guy worked days and some nights planting oats and corn. Martin tended the cows—the milking, the breeding, the barn cleaning—while Guy plowed and disked and harrowed and planted. Helmer decided those things. It was, after all, his farm.

Once in the barn Guy overheard his father bring up, again, the subject of an electric gutter cleaner. Every morning and night Helmer drove the little Allis-Chalmers and a manure spreader into the barn, then down the cow's alley. Guy or Martin, sometimes both, pitched the wagon full of manure. Helmer then drove the dripping spreader directly to a field and let the beaters flail the manure directly onto the earth. In that way nothing was lost.

"We should be thinking about a barn cleaner," Martin said. "Guy won't be around forever. You can't pitch manure now. A barn cleaner is what we need."

From his tractor seat above Martin, Helmer said, "We'd have to go to the bank."

"That's what banks are for," Martin muttered, pitching another forkful into the spreader.

"Banks," Helmer said. "I'll tell you about banks."

"I know, I know, for Christ's sakes," Martin whispered under his breath.

Helmer had lost six hundred dollars and nearly the farm in the 1930s, but he did not tell that story again. Rather he said, "Bankers are parasites. They feed off people who work. Then they try to take what you've worked for. They give out money because they want the land. Once you take money from them, then they have you. We don't want that here. Maybe on other farms. But not on this one."

Martin drove his fork hard at the gutter and its tines sparked on the concrete.

"Besides," Helmer added. "Manure work is good work for its own sake."

"You should get away," Madeline said to Guy. "Now that planting's done there's time. I wrote up to Winnipeg. They haven't seen you for years. You've got the Chevy—go."

Guy went. Hank Schroeder took his chores. And Guy left for a two-week trip into Canada.

He visited Madeline's family, the LeCouerbrises, near Winnipeg. He visited two aunts, three uncles, several cousins. Then he drove farther north. After the million questions from the LeCouerbrises he enjoyed the silence of the open fields. He drove and listened to Bob Dylan and Johnny Cash on the *Nashville Skyline* album; on one cut they screwed up the lyrics and sang different words. But it didn't matter because it was music he could listen to over and over.

Maybe that's when music became art. If so, he knew of a few songs that went beyond music. The Beatles' "Hey, Jude," particularly the chorus. Roy Orbison's "Pretty Woman." Led Zeppelin's "Stairway to Heaven." The Bobby Whitlock piano solo on Clapton's "Layla." Some of Carlos Santana's *Abraxas* album. It happened, too, in classical music like Strauss waltzes. Handel's "Water Music," especially the part with the French horns. Much of the Brandenburg Concertos.

Music that transcended itself and became art was like a merry-go-round. A merry-go-round that you didn't get to ride—musicians were the riders—but rather that turned around you. It pulled you into the center of it. Once you were inside you forgot where it began and where it ended but you didn't care and you never got bored. You never got bored because the chorus or the theme kept coming back again and again like a merry-go-round whose horses were freshly painted every time they passed.

If he had two lives, he would give one over to music. But he didn't. So he drove and listened to his music and watched the land.

Once at sundown he came upon a great field of grain in brilliant, blue bloom. The field was so long its far end flowed into the sky. The blue grain matched the color of the air. He could not tell where the grain ended and where the sky began.

He stopped the Chevy and got out. He walked into the edge of the field, held a spear of the flowering grain in his hand.

A passing farmer stopped.

"Flax," he answered, glancing at the plates on Guy's Chevy.

Guy sat on the hood of his car and listened to the "Water Music" and watched the long blue field until the sun set. Before he drove on he dug up a sheaf of the grain in its

Canadian soil. He put it in the trunk. The next day he turned back south toward Minnesota.

When he returned from his trip his mother rushed into the yard to meet him. "Guess what," she said even before she asked about her family.

Guy had an interview the next day at the Flatwater John Deere dealership. For a real summer job, his mother said. Business at the dealership was best ever. The mechanics were overworked and needed another helper, farm boys only need apply.

"How did you hear about that?" Guy asked. He spoke softly because Martin approached from the right, from the barn.

"I've been looking around," she said. She smiled briefly. Guy paused.

"Maybe I shouldn't have . . ." she began.

"No—I don't mind," Guy said. He had thought about working away from the farm. But if town kids worked at the grocery stores and gas stations of Flatwater, farm kids worked summers at home. There was the hay, the grain, the corn, the cattle. Guy thought about Martin and Helmer.

"Let them hire someone," she said in a rapid, near-whisper. "They're going to have to learn to get along without you soon enough. When you're gone to college—"

But then Martin was there. It was ten o'clock in the morning and Guy could smell liquor on him. "So how were the Canucks?" he said. Madeline turned away.

The Flatwater John Deere dealership had shiny new tractors in the front showroom and greasy half-tractors in the rear shop. There Guy punched in at 7:00 each morning along with a half dozen other mechanics' helpers. All were farm boys. All knew machinery. All wanted to farm. Some, like Guy, were seventeen. Others were twenty-five or more. Some already rented fields and farmed them at night by tractor lights. Others worked for their father or an uncle, and waited for land of their own.

At lunch break the night-farmer boys slept. They slept sprawled across the wooden benches, slept curled in the closed cabs of tractors under repair, or, weather permitting, slept arms-out on the dry lawn behind the shop with clean grease rags over their faces to keep away flies.

At lunch break the boys who waited to farm sat and talked.

"So how old's your old man again?"

"Fifty-one."

"Shit," one of them said. They shook their heads.

"Yours?"

"Fifty-five."

"So what are you shittin' me for?"

"How 'bout you?"

"Sixty-eight."

"Lucky fucker!"

They turned to Guy. The new man.

"Forty-eight," Guy said.

"Jesus—I thought I had it bad!" one of them said, and spit.

"He's got a grandfather too," another said.

"Shit and double shit." All the boys shook their heads sadly at Guy.

Guy shrugged.

"Any health trouble?" one of the older boys asked Guy. "Arthritis? High blood pressure?"

Guy shook his head no.

"Old war wounds, machinery accidents?"

"Nope," Guy said.

They thought in silence.

"Boozer?" someone suddenly asked.

Guy stared at him in silence. All the others turned to Guy.

"Hey, that's something, anyway," another of the boys said brightly. The rest of the farm boys who waited nodded at Guy with new respect.

During the noon hour Guy read. He sat in the sunlit front seat of the Chevy listening to Bob Dylan, the Byrds, the Beatles, Strauss, and Handel on the tape deck, and read the Minneapolis *Tribune, Time* magazine, *Sports Illustrated, Argosy,* or *Field & Stream* from the dealership waiting room. Often he drove downtown to the old brick Carnegie Library and ate his lunch on the lawn and read there. He took out novels by Jack London, Hemingway, Faulkner, Steinbeck. One sunny July afternoon *The Grapes of Wrath* cost him a twelve-dollar speeding ticket on his way back to work and eight dollars in docked pay when he arrived there at 2:30, two hours late.

Sometimes on his lunch hour he drove down to the swimming beach and sat in the cool shade of the stone changing house and watched the girls. He chewed on clover and thought about them. He missed Mary Ann's handjobs. But then he didn't suppose Kurt Fenske would appreciate him dropping by for a quick one.

He thought about marriage. He didn't see where his parents had ever had much fun being married. So why get married?

About school. There was one year left and it was too late to find another friend like Tom so he would not try. Maybe a girlfriend. He would hold out for someone like Ursula Andress.

About college. Everyone said go to college. So he wouldn't, at least for a while.

About the Vietnam War. It was crazy. He would never go. Helmer had been a conscientious objector during World War I, had put on the uniform but would not carry a gun, and so had spent the war sorting potatoes in a dim army warehouse in Chicago. Helmer was Big Olaf in e.e. cumming's poem. Guy was always proud of that. But Helmer's first mistake was in putting on the uniform.

About rock 'n' roll. If Elvis was King, Roy Orbison and Eric Clapton and Jim Morrison were Crown Princes; Janis Joplin and Aretha Franklin, Princesses.

About books and writers. Hemingway left background stuff out of his writing. Faulkner put everything in, and more. If Hemingway sometimes left too much out of his sentences, Faulkner put too much in. So nobody was perfect. He liked them equally. Hemingway made you think. Faulkner made you read.

About his grandmother, Etta. She was dying of nothing in particular. Time. That was her illness.

About his grandfather. Helmer would never die. He was bigger than death.

About death. He imagined it as a falling feeling, like swinging on the big rope across the hayloft and then letting go.

89

About flax. Whenever he put new books in the trunk of his Chevy he saw the dried sheaf of flax, its brown Canadian soil. He thought of the long blue field. He wondered if the flowered grain would grow in Becker County. His father and grandfather never grew anything but corn, oats, and alfalfa. Oats sold for $1.60 a bushel, corn for $2.50, alfalfa for ninety cents a bale. Flax, however, sold for $12.00 a bushel. Guy stopped by the Ag. Extension Office in the courthouse. He asked the agent if anyone had grown flax in Becker County. The man said no. He said flax took a certain type of soil which this area did not have, plus cows wouldn't eat flax anyway. Guy thanked him, and the next day sent a cup of the Canadian dirt and an equal portion of his grandfather's loam to the University of Minnesota Soil Testing Service. The results came back in a week. The soils were nearly identical. The rest of the summer Guy thought often about the long blue field that ran like a river into the lake of sky.

About himself. Sometimes, daydreaming over the noon hour, he saw himself from outside his own body. Saw himself from high above looking down on the flat gray square of dealership and the rows of toy green and yellow tractors out front. He saw the tinny and shiny black roof, the chrome fins of his '57 Chevy. Saw inside the car a long, skinny, blond-haired kid with his hands behind his head staring off into the pale blue crown of the sky. One time, not daydreaming but reading, he turned the page and his eyes fixed not on the words but on the fingers that held the paper. They were scrape-knuckled, oil-stained, the nails chipped from wrenches slipping from greasy nuts. For a moment he thought the fingers belonged to a character in the story. They could not be his own real fingers because this was not his real life.

About his family. When he was small he never thought much about his parents. They were just there. He had no others for comparison. Being born was somewhat like being thrust into a room already furnished. In that room one's parents were the floor and ceiling. Occasionally, like Jewell Hartmeir, parents were walls—walls without doors or windows. Friends were the windows; through friends you saw the world. But parents most often were floors and ceiling, vaguely above and beneath one's life. No one paid them much attention unless they became cracked, or leaked, or were of particular beauty.

Whenever Guy's mother came to town for groceries she stopped to see him at work. Sometimes she surprised him, and he saw her for a moment as a person—a woman—and not as his mother. Madeline was short, an inch or so over five feet, and a few pounds overweight, mainly in her legs. She had thick, walnut-brown hair, cut short, and eyebrows the same full, shiny color. Her brown eyes were bright and quick. Always they were on the move, tiny flickering glances cast to the side or beyond. Talking with her, Guy often got the sensation that just moments before she had misplaced something. She wore plain, pastel clothes from Sears and Ward's, sensible shoes. On Main Street and in the stores she looked like the other women. Close-up, however, the constant movement of her eyes said she was not from this town or any farm nearby. Her full name was Madeline Anne LeCouerbrise and she was born in 1925 in the river town of St. Anne's, Manitoba.

Twice a week, usually on Tuesdays and Fridays, Madeline came at the noon hour and brought Guy lunch. Then they drove out to the A & W Drive Inn for cold root beer to drink with the chicken sandwiches, dill pickles, and pie. They ate and talked. They always talked more when they were away from the farm, from Martin and Helmer. Sometimes they ate quickly, then went to the greenhouse across the highway from the root-beer stand. There, inside the luminous plastic quonset, they walked in the close, humid air along the rows of plants and flowers. They pointed out this one and that. Guy's favorites were rose bushes; Madeline's, dahlias. They laughed at odd plants, praised others for their grace or beauty. Often Guy walked with his hand loosely on his mother's shoulder. When he had to return to the shop she always asked what time he would be home, though she knew.

Once they went to the city park and had a picnic on the grass. She was particularly quiet that day. Guy waited and finally she began to talk, for the first time, about Martin. About how they met. How they had come to be married.

91

The whole story. As she spoke, Guy imagined things his father must have said or done or thought back then.

In June of 1942, Martin Pehrsson was twenty. He was an inch under six feet tall, blue-eyed, thin, sandy-haired, with whisker stubble only on his chin. He had one thousand dollars, in tens, buttoned in the chest pocket of his bib overalls and he was driving fast toward Canada. The money and the black Ford pickup belonged to Helmer. Martin was on his way to Winnipeg to buy a combine.

Not that Minnesota had no combines. The sky was full of them, fluffy round cumulus clouds moving in a slow sweep across the blue field of the sky. However, the steel for real combines had all gone into tanks and planes and battleships for World War II. But war or no war, Helmer believed the best combines were Canadian. For three winters Helmer had studied a pile of combine manuals. He went over each one, marking small penciled notes here and there. He stared through a magnifying glass at the exploded drawings of augers, sieves, pickup reels, and gearboxes. He drew up lists and columns. He wrote down the number of grease fittings, the thickness of axles and shafts, the dimensions of the bolts that held down the power takeoff box, the gauge of steel, and, finally, the color of the combine's metal skin.

In the end Helmer threw away all the manuals except for the red and yellow combine made in Winnipeg.

For the first twenty miles of his trip Martin drove the Ford carefully. Helmer's eyes followed in the dust behind. But once Martin reached the blacktop of the main highway north he brought the Ford up to forty, which Helmer said was about the right speed. Then to forty-five. Then fifty. Checking the button of his money pocket, Martin rolled down the truck windows, threw off his cap, and let the June air splash through the cab.

No chores. No damn chores for three days. Hank Schroeder was to milk and clean the gutter. Helmer would feed the cows. Martin was free. His first trip out of Minnesota. A business trip. Yes, that's what it was. He was to buy the red and yellow combine and a trailer to haul it back. Once he returned with the combine, he would pull that old gray dinosaur of a threshing machine down the road to the big hill above No Medicine Lake and let that bastard roll. No

92

more shocking oats. No more pitching bundles. No more crawling inside to cut away wet straw. That was over. And with the new combine they could farm more land. Martin would be the combine operator. For that he would need sunglasses. Yes. The drivers of the big combines out West all wore sunglasses and white dust scarves around their necks. Martin would be combining so much of the day he would have no time for the cows. They could hire someone for that. Anybody could pitch manure and pull tits. But not everybody could operate a combine.

Of course with the new combine and the additional land, they would soon need another combine. Martin would again make the trip to Winnipeg. They would remember him there. Martin Pehrsson. That young guy from down in Minnesota with all the land. Thousands of acres, they'd say, and he runs the whole show.

Beside Martin on the seat of the pickup was the wooden egg crate his mother had packed with lunch. Four layers of lunch for the four days. Each layer contained six double sandwiches: two fried-egg sandwiches for breakfast; two chicken sandwiches for dinner; two roast-beef sandwiches for supper, plus an apple and a piece of mincemeat pie. At the bottom of the crate was a block of ice wrapped in an old wool quilt.

Though it was only nine o'clock in the morning, Martin ate a roast-beef sandwich and a piece of mincemeat pie. Still hungry, he dug into the second day's layer and ate its pie. He was thirsty after that. Though Helmer had sent along a vinegar jug of well water, Martin pulled into a truckstop and cafe.

The waitress had short, blond pin-curled hair. Martin lingered over his cola and watched her. He watched her stretch up for the plates the cook shoved through the little window. Watched her write out orders with the pink tip of her tongue clenched between her teeth. After an hour he finally paid for his cola. He had the dime in his pocket, but he slowly unbuttoned the flap over the combine money, peeled off a ten, and then left the waitress a whole dollar tip.

On the highway not a mile from the cafe, Martin's foot suddenly jerked on the accelerator and his heart began to pound. If the blond waitress had seen the roll of combine money, so had the men sitting near the till. He did not remember their faces, but at least one of them was dark-haired and another had a beard. He checked the rearview mirror. The highway behind was empty, but he felt under the seat for the tire iron. His heart continued to pound. Rather than wait to be caught—he could outrun nobody in Helmer's old Ford—he pulled off the road and parked behind a grove of spruce trees. He waited there out of sight. He lay on his belly and watched from beneath the spruce boughs for a half hour. No one passed but farm wives and occasional logging trucks. Finally he drove on. The men at the truckstop must not have wanted to tangle with him, Martin Pehrsson, no matter how much money he had. He brought the truck up to fifty-five to make up for lost time.

That night Martin slept in the truck out of sight from the highway just beyond Thief River Falls. The combine money was stashed in the left front hubcap of the pickup. Martin lay curled on the front seat under the blanket Etta had sent along.

He dreamed of the blond waitress. He was straight-combining a long field of wheat and the waitress was somewhere ahead of him in the field. Naked in the field. Her skin and hair were the same color of the wheat, so he could never see her. Neither could he slow the combine, because at field-side stood Helmer, waving him on. Keep going, had to finish by sundown, rain tomorrow, Helmer said. The sickle sang back and forth. He kept looking for the girl who was somewhere out there in front of his knives.

In the morning Martin ate the rest of the roast-beef sandwiches and all the pie. The remaining egg and chicken sandwiches he threw in the swampy ditch along the road. He watched the white bread crumble and melt away in the green water.

Late that afternoon Martin reached St. Anne's, Manitoba. St. Anne's lay strung along a tree-lined river, the Seine. He slowed at the city limits to stare at a brightly bannered jumble of tall green tents and white wooden halls. It looked like a county fair, if the Canucks called them that.

He parked. He checked the button on the money pocket. Then he walked toward the crowd. It was nearly sundown. Orange light glowed in the tent tops whose long ropes stretched from sunlight above to shadow below. The ground was littered with crushed tobacco tins and the grass was tramped into a green mud. To the right some cattlemen were loading a bull into a trailer. Ahead was a long, low wooden hall with yellow-lit windows. Martin could hear fiddle music and clapping from inside. He touched the combine money once again, paid his quarter at the door, and walked inside.

In the yellow haze of the hall, on a wooden stage at the center, was a fiddler and his band. The fiddler was a stout bear of a fellow with thick black eyebrows that grew together above his nose. His fiddling arm whirled the bow across the strings as fast as a pitman arm turned a mower's sickle. Dancers whirled in a large, galloping circle around the stage. To the right side stood a line of men with empty beer mugs. Their line stretched forward to a long wooden table that supported several barrels of beer. Martin grinned.

The beer was black and strong. Martin squinted his eyes at first sip, but after that it didn't taste bad, kind of like the juice at the bottom of a jar of canned mincemeat. Only stronger. Martin tapped his foot and watched the dancers. Those Canucks sure knew how to have a good time.

He let his eyes travel past the dancers toward the stage. There his gaze halted. On a girl. She had long black hair that waved forward from a comb above each ear. She had dark eyebrows, brown eyes, skin and teeth as white as piano keys. She stood looking up at the fiddler, who had her same dark eyebrows and small nose. Her eyes moved back and forth from the fiddler, who was certainly her father, to the musicians behind him.

The song ended to great clapping and shouts of "More!" The fiddler bowed deeply, grinned. He reached back for a new bow, then a puff of white smoke leaped from the fiddle strings as he began a new, even faster song. The dancers began to whoop and throw their partners. The fiddler, too, began to dance as he played, a jig of some sort. But Martin was not watching the fiddler. He moved through the crowd so he could see the girl better. Soon the fiddler's feet were eye level in the side of Martin's vision. The fiddler's feet were like the black hooves of a trotting horse that never seemed to touch the ground.

The girl began to wave frantically at the musicians and point to the fiddler. But the banjo player and the drummer did not see her. They were grinning and trying to keep up with the fiddler. The girl started to climb onstage. Just then the fiddle music wailed to a stop, like the electricity had failed. Martin looked up. The fiddler tottered, then fell. Martin leaped forward to catch him. They both crashed to the floor. In a moment the girl was alongside Martin, leaning over him to hold a small bottle of something—a whiff of ammonia brought instant tears to Martin's eyes—under her father's nose.

The fiddler coughed. His eyes rolled white, then turned up brown pupils. "What . . . what happened?" he said weakly.

"What do you think happened?" the daughter said. Her voice carried the scolding edge of a mother's. "Look where you are at this moment."

The fiddler sat up and blinked. He looked down at the board floor, then at Martin, who still lay pinned beneath him.

"He caught you," the girl said, nodding to Martin. For the first time, their eyes met. The fiddler rolled free of Martin. Still sitting, he extended a large, sweaty hand. "Bernard LeCouerbrise, rightly named, I'm afraid, 'The Fiddling Fool of St. Anne's.'"

"Martin Pehrsson."

"He always does this," the girl murmured, still staring at Martin. "Usually he falls backwards and the banjo player catches him." Her voice softened at the end, as if she had planned to say more but didn't.

"This is, of course, my daughter, Madeline, same last name though a more worrisome temperament. May I buy you a beer, Mr. Pehrsson, for your trouble?" Bernard LeCouerbrise said.

"You bet," Martin said softly, still looking into the brown eyes of this girl named Madeline.

For the next two weeks, without writing home, Martin remained in St. Anne's. He stayed as a guest of the LeCouerbrise family. He told them he usually stayed at a good hotel on business trips, but, if they insisted, he would stay with them. Twice he drove into Winnipeg to look at combines. On neither occasion did he sign any papers or spend any of the money. That is, what was left of it.

In the evenings he entertained the LeCouerbrises. He

took them to the best restaurants in Winnipeg. They ate seafood and steak and drank champagne, all compliments of Martin's expense account, as he called it. He met more and more LeCouerbrises. Aunts. Uncles. Cousins. Second cousins. All were black-haired, brown-eyed, and all of them Martin treated to dining and dancing.

During these nights out Martin did not explain much about himself because the LeCouerbrise family, excepting Madeline, were the talkers. They spoke in English that flowed into French and then back to English as easily as the water splashed this way and that along the rocks of the little Seine River, where he often walked alone with Madeline. With her, as with her relatives, Martin discovered the value of silence. His closed mouth, or at best his vague comments about land holdings and cattle and wheat, only made the LeCouerbrise relatives talk faster and nod and grin more often at him and Madeline. And his silence with Madeline on their long walks beside the river only drew her closer to his side. He figured that she had grown up around talkers. He guessed that she was ready for a man who held his peace.

And he was right. At the end of two weeks Martin began the trip back to Minnesota. He took with him forty dollars, no combine, and a wife.

On the drive south to Minnesota, Madeline sat close to Martin and talked excitedly. But as they drove farther into Minnesota, as they neared Helmer's farm, she grew silent. Finally she said, "It's so flat here. I thought it would be different than Manitoba. But it's the same. You never told me."

"You never asked," Martin said.

Chapter Twelve

The rest of that summer Guy worked at the implement dealership and saved his money, for what he was not sure. College maybe. He promised his mother he would visit some colleges during his senior year. But sometimes he thought he was saving the money for her.

One hot July night Guy came home and found Madeline in the dark yard sitting motionless on his old swing. Behind her, in the house, Martin's shadow passed back and forth through the yellow squares of the windows. Occasionally his voice penetrated the window screens. Or rather, voices. Martin spoke in dialogue, a high voice for himself, a low voice for Helmer. Sometimes, in a third voice, Martin swore at the other two. The third voice sounded like a director of a play cursing his actors. Martin kept walking, living room to kitchen to living room. Guy thought of a small brown bear he had once seen at a roadside zoo. How it lived on Pepsi. How it barked. How its feet had worn a circular path in the square concrete floor of its pen.

"Don't go in for a while," Madeline said. "He needs some time. I hid his bottle, made him some coffee. He was arguing with Helmer," she explained. "He'll be okay in a half hour or so."

Guy nodded. It was very late. He had been to Detroit Lakes, to the dance pavilion there. "Maybe I'll go up to the hayloft," he said.

"You shouldn't have to do that," Madeline said. Her voice caught.

"I don't mind," Guy said. He put his arm around her. Her shoulders began to jerk in slow rhythm.

"Hey now," Guy said. As she cried he began to push the swing, at first only a foot or so just to get her moving.

"Don't," she said, still snuffling.

"Sorry, the Pehrsson House of Thrills never closes," he said, making his voice loudspeaker-tinny, pushing her again.

She laughed once and grabbed the ropes tighter.

He swung her in longer loops upward.

"Guy—stop," she called.

"Ramone—the swing—it's jammed—we can't slow it down!" Guy called. He pushed her higher.

Madeline shrieked with fear and laughter.

"Ramone—where are you—you're the only one who knows the swing—it's gone mad!" Guy called.

"Guy, please—"

"Ramone, you must mean."

"Ramone, please, stop! I'm scared," she cried.

Guy made scraping, braking noises with his mouth, then gradually slowed his mother's flight. Laughing, he caught her in his arms as she jumped to the ground. As he held her, behind them he saw the scarecrow outline of Martin framed in the yellow light of the screen door.

"What the hell's the matter out there?" Martin called.

"Nothing," Guy called.

"Nothing," Madeline said.

Martin stared. "Get in the house then," he called.

Madeline pulled away from Guy. "I'll be okay," she said.

Guy was silent for a moment. He looked past her to his father. "He ever hits you, you tell me."

Madeline stared for a moment. "Okay, Ramone," she said. Then she turned and walked toward the house.

Summer ended and the school year began, Guy's last. Alone, he drove his Chevy to school. Once it needed a new coil wire and refused to budge from the farmyard until he got one. For one day, then, Guy rode the school bus.

Number 33 still carried its load of farm kids and Indians. The Indian kids in the rear, however, had not aged. It was as if the light or air or seats or graffiti in the back of the bus combined to form a growth retardant. Like a corn herbicide that killed weeds but left the corn, something in Bus #33 stunted Indians but passed over whites. The bus carried no Indian seniors. One or two juniors. Only a few sophomores. Mostly the Indian kids were ninth-, eighth-, or seventh-graders. Guy realized Tom LittleWolf would have been the only Indian senior in his class.

Arriving at school on the Indian bus without Tom and Mary Ann, Guy again walked the sidewalk gauntlet. Felt the old fear. But the absence of Tom LittleWolf was still a form of his presence, and the Flatwater thugs left him alone. He made sure, however, to buy the coil wire on his noon hour.

He played basketball again that year, but without Tom, and with Arnold Granland back at guard, the ball did not come much to him. The team lost more games than it won. To make the best of a bad season, Guy concentrated on personal moves, percentages; in that way, like a runner or a swimmer, he played mainly against himself.

He took more English classes. In one literature class the teacher was a younger man, Mr. Anderson, a newcomer to Flatwater who rode a bicycle and smoked a curved pipe at the same time. After an essay exam Mr. Anderson summoned Guy to the front, then walked him into the hall. "I want you out of this class," he said.

Guy stared wide-eyed down at the man.

"You should be in Advanced Lit.," Mr. Anderson said. "I'll see to it."

Advanced American Literature contained all Honor Society and Student Council kids. They stared skeptically at Guy as he joined them mid-class. He took a seat in the rear.

The advanced class was much smaller than any he'd had. The teacher, Mr. Richeland, chatted with the students, told off-color stories about writers' lives, explored allusions to literature that most everyone in the class except Guy seemed to have read. He sat silently as students spoke up without raising their hands. Mr. Richeland nodded thoughtfully at their comments and often said, "You're onto something there. Say more."

For the first few weeks Guy felt like he was in a school within a school. This English class compared to other classes was like the teachers' eating room inside the larger cafeteria. There Guy always suspected the food was better and now he knew for sure.

Guy's first essay was entitled "Faulkner's 'The Bear' and Keats's 'Ode on a Grecian Urn': Why the Boy Doesn't Shoot." In it he showed how Faulkner linked the end of his story to Keats's poem. Guy's main point was that if the boy shot the bear, there would be nothing left to hunt, just like if the man on Keats's Grecian urn caught the girl he was chasing, the fun would be over. Sort of.

Mr. Richeland read the paper aloud and laughed heartily at "sort of." The class laughed politely. Several girls turned down the corners of their mouths and doodled dark flowers through the rest of the paper.

"Brilliant—absolutely brilliant," Mr. Richeland finished. "Mr. Pehrsson, my compliments!"

Guy blushed scarlet and looked down. From then on no one in the class spoke much to Guy again. Which was fine by him.

Later in the term Mr. Richeland sent that and another of his essays, "Pointy Heads and Loincloths: Indians in *Little House on the Prairie*," to a former professor at the University of Minnesota. The professor wrote back inviting Guy for a visit.

"I'll think about it," Guy murmured to Mr. Richeland.

What he often thought of his senior year was flax. He carried the seeds in a little bottle in the glove box of the Chevy. They rattled like dried peas in a glass. Once in an art history class he came across Monet's painting "The Water Lilies." The field of flax he had seen in Canada was the same color as the water in the painting. The water in the painting was really the color of the sky—in the painting—which couldn't be seen. That's because Monet wanted the viewer to see the sky by looking down at the water lilies on their little round pond. Guy liked the painting but he liked the field of flax better. It pulled your eyes up and out in a straight line forever.

Saturdays Guy worked at the implement dealership, with its soot-blackened ceiling and frost-rounded corners. It was 1972. The Russians were buying wheat. Never had there been more tractors on order for spring. He tuned tractors and saved his money. With part of it he bought a rebuilt engine for his mother's 1965 Cutlass. She had not been driving much. When Guy happened to borrow the Cutlass and heard the engine, he knew why. The motor sounded like a polishing drum with a dozen new agates turning inside. On a quiet Sunday afternoon he warmed up the farm shop with the barrel stove and switched the engines.

"You should have told me sooner," he said as he finished.

"I didn't want Martin to know," Madeline said. She sat perched on a chair next to the barrel stove reading a paperback called *The Feminine Mystique.*

"Don't worry about him," Guy said. "Tell me first."

"Okay, Ramone," she said.

"I'm serious," Guy said, standing up and wiping his hands on the cleanest oil rag.

"I just didn't want to be a burden to him. Or to you."

"Hey," Guy said, "did you or did you not carry me around nine months inside and two years outside?"

His mother smiled.

In March the University of Minnesota wrote a letter inviting Guy down for an April tour of the campus. His first thought was of Madeline. By March in Minnesota, houses, like barns and schools, had shrunken. Their late-winter size depended on how well the inhabitants got along. In the waist-deep snow, his parents' house was hardly bigger than a dollhouse. The Minneapolis trip, any trip, would be good for her.

Guy drove his Chevy. The highway south cut narrow and gray through the winter fields. Now April, still with a thin coat of snow, the white of the fields and the sky was broken only by occasional groves of green pines and red oaks. Once Guy saw far out in a field the red dot of a sleeping fox. In some fields south of Little Falls, the snow had melted on the higher crowns of the fields and left great black eyes on the landscape.

They drove and talked and listened to music and the news

on the radio. Nixon had sent troops and planes into Cambodia. "It can't go on much longer," Madeline said.

Madeline had packed lunch but they stopped in St. Cloud and had ice cream and strawberry pie. They played the little jukebox in their booth. Guy chose songs by Santana, Madeline picked Kenny Rogers and Judy Collins. An hour later they were in Minneapolis.

Guy remembered the way to the university. But several blocks from the campus a line of helmeted policemen blocked the street. They wore their visors down. The nearest policeman pointed for Guy to turn left. Guy rolled down his window. "I'm trying to get to"—he glanced down at the little map the university had sent—"Morrill Hall."

"Just turn. Now," the policeman said. He pointed with his black stick. Guy could not see the man's face through his gray visor. Beside him the line of policemen looked like a welders' class turned into a chorus line.

"Okay, okay," Guy said. He turned left. On the next street they began to see people heading toward the center of the campus. Many of them carried placards:

"Out of Cambodia."
"Nixon—Killer!"
"Peace Now."
"Mothers for Peace."
"Strike for Peace!"

"So," Guy said to Madeline with a grin, "here we are."

His mother's brown eyes were round and alive. "What great luck," she said, "a demonstration!"

They parked on a side street and joined the crowd heading along University Avenue. Rock 'n' roll blared from the windows of the fraternity houses, whose members sat in their windowsills, legs dangling. Most held a stein of beer in one hand and an American flag in the other. Some waved the steins instead of the flags. Some just stared. Others shouted:

"Eat shit, you fucking peaceniks!"

"When the Commies hit San Francisco, then what . . .?"

One short-haired boy sat perched atop a stone lion in the yard and screamed repeatedly, "My brother died for you fucking bastards, my brother died for you fucking bastards!"

Someone from the crowd called out, "So some people are smarter than others!"

The short-haired boy leaped from his perch and ran, swinging, at the crowd. People fell. The frat-house boys leaped from their windows and, shouting, dragged their member back into the yard where they held him.

Guy pulled his mother away from the crowd. Following the map, they wound their way alongside the backs of several large buildings toward Morrill Hall. By accident they entered the rear of the building. Soon they found their way to the admissions tour office on the second floor. There a thin, erect woman with blue-gray hair, a rose-colored spring coat with a cantaloupe-size maroon and gold "Gopher Booster!" button on the right lapel, was introducing herself to a group of students and their parents. The students wore letter jackets. The fathers wore tight sport coats and out-of-style narrow ties. The mothers wore their hair short and newly curled.

". . . proud to be a Minnesota alumna," the blue-haired woman was saying. "My name is Mrs. Knutson and I'm honored to guide you this afternoon through our beautiful campus. After today, you, too, will feel like a Minnesota Gopher." She beamed. "Our first stop, the university mall and the famous Walter Library, where no doubt you'll be spending a lot of your time—and therefore very little of your parents' money." Mrs. Knutson paused for effect.

The parents laughed nervously.

Then they all followed Mrs. Knutson through the front door. "The mall," she said, with a sweep of her umbrella.

"Jesus Christ," Guy murmured. The mall looked like a Super Bowl playing field immediately postgame. The great, colonnaded buildings along the sides were like bleachers emptied of fans, all of whom had surged onto the field. To the right, on the wide steps of Northrup Hall, a ponytailed man screamed through a bullhorn and the crowd chanted with him.

"One, two, three, four—we don't want your fucking war!"

"Notice the words etched in stone," Mrs. Knutson called to them. Her eyes skipped the protesters entirely as she pointed above them to the top of Northrup Hall. "Dedicated . . . honor, pride . . ." Guy couldn't hear.

"Five, six, seven, eight—fucking Nixon we all hate!"

"And justice," she shouted. "Without those truths no university can survive. Follow me." She forged through the crowd. With her umbrella point, she cleared a narrow path and looked neither left nor right.

A muscular woman with a red kerchief tied low over her forehead handed Guy's mother something mimeographed. "Off our backs, on our feet—fight male dominance," the woman droned. Madeline took the brochure and murmured, "Thank you."

Guy could smell smoke. Looking over the crowd, down the mall he saw a house-high barricade of wood and cardboard blocking the next street. Smoke wicked up from the rubbish. The smoldering barrier divided black-suited, helmeted policemen on one side and protesters on the other. Occasionally a protestor hurled something burning over the top toward the policemen.

"Walter Library was built in 1897 and named after somebody Walter," Mrs. Knutson began. From the shouting around them Mrs. Knutson's voice came on and off like a record player with faulty wiring. The students and parents stared beyond her. "If I may have your attention . . ." Mrs. Knutson called.

Guy looked back to the plaza at Northrup Hall. To the left side of the crowd he saw a red Vietcong flag. Beside it was another flag that carried a black thunderbird on red. A sign below read, "Native Americans—Amerika's Vietcong." Below was a tight cluster of Indians in tribal dress, sunglasses, and long hair. One of the Indians was shorter, stockier than the rest. Guy's heart began to pound. The shorter Indian's hair was not long enough to braid and so fell in a black hood over his shoulders. He wore sunglasses and a red and black Flatwater Indians jacket from which all letters had been torn.

"Tom!" Guy shouted. Tom's head jerked around. He searched the crowd. Guy grabbed his mother and pulled her away from the tour. He pushed closer through the crowd. People cursed him.

"Tom!" he shouted again. For an instant, still separated by the breadth of twenty bodies, their eyes met. Tom's mouth came open. At that moment, however, people began to scream and run. Up and out of the red flag beside Tom,

105

like a wasp rising from a rose, a helicopter chut-chut-chutted toward them. Low. Guy thought the helicopter was a crop duster that had lost its way. But the tumbling gray spray from its long pipe was not herbicide.

The fog rolled onto them. The crowd broke and ran. Holding onto Madeline, sometimes stepping on people underneath, Guy lost sight of Tom. Then he forgot about him entirely as he and Madeline choked and cried and stumbled away from the tear gas. They ran north, which took them to University Avenue. There they clutched a tree as they coughed and wiped their eyes.

As Guy's vision cleared he saw more lines of the black-suited, visored policemen. The policemen marched straight down University Avenue, thrusting their long batons with each step like clumsy fencers. The protesters retreated, walking backward, spitting at the policemen. Suddenly a short policeman rushed forward to swing at a student. The police line broke, the protesters screamed and ran. Some fell. The policemen hacked at them with their sticks, then leaped over the writhing bodies to chase the runners.

"Stop it!" Madeline screamed. She ran into the street. A policeman turned toward her with club upraised. Guy sprinted forward and grabbed his mother on the run and slung her over his shoulder. He smashed through the crowd of spectators who watched from the sidewalk. He looked behind once. The policeman, having lost Guy and Madeline, swung at someone else. Guy saw an arm swing up in defense of a face, saw the club strike the upraised forearm. The arm flopped at its new joint. People screamed. Still carrying Madeline, Guy ran until there were no more people on the streets. Afterward they found the Chevy and then he drove north until there were no buildings or people but only fields.

106

Chapter Thirteen

"Two-thirds, one-third. And no Sunday farming."

"Deal," Guy replied to his grandfather. At the same moment they reached out to shake hands. His grandfather's hand was wide and thick and cool, as if the earth they stood upon was reaching up through the old man to touch Guy. They stood beside the barbed-wire fence of the hundred-acre pasture, which had lain in sod for ten years or more. But now it was late April of 1972. Guy was eighteen. In less than a month he would graduate from Flatwater High. But before then Guy would plow up the old sod and plant a crop, his first. His own.

Guy had a sudden urge to throw his arms around his grandfather, but their handshake locked them an arm's length apart. Anyway, Pehrsson men were not huggers. Not huggers, but holders. Guy continued to grin and to grip Helmer's great palm as long as his grandfather held on.

The rest of Helmer was as big as the hand that closed around Guy's. Helmer's broad face was perfectly square, his chin as wide as his forehead. His pale blue eyes were not deep-set and so were hardly creased at their corners. Still straight-backed at age seventy-eight, Helmer was taller even than Guy. As square as a shirt pinned on a clothesline,

Helmer's shoulders were the straight, broad beam of a plow to which everything else hung bolted. Helmer's arms, in shirt sleeves buttoned at the cuffs, ended with the big cups of his hands, then the flat, thick fingers. His legs were posts. He wore long underwear, wool in winter, cotton in summer, every day of the year. His big feet wore soft leather high-top boots tightly laced and double-knotted around his ankles.

Helmer's only weakness was his heart, for which he took little white pills. "Keeps the oil thin," he said. Though he did not work as much as he used to, Helmer was still usually there—in the barn, in the machine shed, at field-side—to watch Martin and Guy work.

Helmer left the farm only for a daily visit with Etta, who had been in the hospital in Flatwater most of the winter. During his absence Martin often came in the house and napped. If he did not sleep, he sat and drank coffee royales and looked through brightly colored sales brochures of electric barn cleaners and vacuum-sealed, bottom-unloading silos.

It was also his grandmother's illness that had made Guy speak to Helmer about renting the hundred-acre pasture.

"He's got other things than the farm to think about," Madeline said after Guy told her about his idea for flax. Her eyes sparkled when he talked about Manitoba. "He's got to let loose of this place someday, and why not now? Ask him. Try the flax—what can you lose?" she said.

The rental arrangement between Guy and his grandfather, except for the no-Sunday-farming part, was common. Guy would bear all the expenses, provide all the labor. For that he would receive two thirds of the crop. His grandfather, as landowner, would get the remaining third, payable at harvesttime.

Guy expected the quiet-Sunday clause. Helmer never farmed on Sundays. He believed Sunday was a day of rest for both the farmer and his land. But Guy could get by without Sunday farming. He would log more tractor hours the other six days. Sunday would not be a problem.

"So what are you going to plant?" Helmer asked, looking across the field.

"Not sure," Guy lied.

"Raise a good crop of corn. Oats for sure."

"Have to get it plowed first," Guy said, "see how it looks."

His grandfather nodded at that.

And Guy was thinking of flax. He did not speak about it now, however. He did not want to worry Helmer. He did not want to argue endlessly with Martin about the dangers of a new crop. Right now, Guy needed all his time for school and work and sleep.

That winter, with Helmer alone in the big house, Guy slept upstairs in his grandfather's house. There his alarm rang at 5:00 A.M., when he went to the barn to help his father milk. By 7:00 he was showered and was driving his Chevy to school. At 3:00 P.M. he left school and went to the implement dealership, where he worked three hours. At 6:00 P.M. he punched out, drove home in time to help his father and Helmer finish milking. Supper was in Madeline's kitchen at 7:30. Afterward he walked with Helmer back to the big house.

Evenings in Helmer's house, Guy spread his homework across on the bare oaken kitchen table. He sat bent over the table reading lit and history texts. His grandfather sat in a straight-backed chair reading his black Bible. In the house without television or radio, the only sound was the whispering slide of their pages and faint kissing noise of his grandfather's moving lips as he read. Guy liked the silence. School he had always found noisy. The clang of lockers, the radios in the narrow hallways. Work was louder still. The thudding air compressor, the eardrum bite of hammers hitting steel. In Helmer's house no one pounded, no one argued. Things there were straight and square and silent, like a library.

At nine o'clock he usually got them both a bowl of ice cream. They ate together. Then bed.

Upstairs, under the slope of the roof, Guy read more and listened on his little transistor radio, turned low, to WLS out of Chicago. He listened to Journey, Santana, Led Zeppelin, Aretha Franklin, Janis Joplin thump in his pillow. Sometime later in the night he would awaken and turn off the radio.

Guy did not plan to stay at home forever. Or even for another year. He would go to college at some point, but first

109

there was the field of flax. The flax would be money. Money would be possibility. If at first the flax forced him to stay on the farm, later it would allow him to leave. In style. But that was thinking too far ahead. First there was the summer to get through.

By helping his father with the Holsteins Guy worked out the use of his father's tractor and plow. This arrangement Martin had figured closely. "Money between relatives is like sand between the sheets," he had said. By keeping close accounts, everyone slept fine. Without room and board to pay, Guy was able to save his mechanic's money, $89.96 per week.

On a small calendar tacked to the sloped ceiling above his bed Guy had figured his summer's farming expenses. With his summer savings and his weekly checks, he would have the flax seed paid for by the end of April. May was marked for plow parts. June and July were checked off for diesel oil and fuel. August was labeled for harvest expenses—custom combining and trucking. September, however, was unmarked. There would be no September for Guy at the implement dealership. With his flax crop sold, he could jam his grease rag into the mouth of the time clock and walk away. He would have money to start his own life.

By April 19 the snow, except for slouched, weeping banks on the north sides of the farm buildings, had vanished. A week of sunshine and fifty-degree weather followed. By April 22 Guy could drive a shovel eight inches into the pasture sod. Along the road to Flatwater, tractors and plows began to emerge from their sheds and sit centered in the yards. On April 25, a Wednesday, as if by common signal, tractors entered the reservation fields and began to turn strips of the gray land black.

Guy cursed because he was not among them, plowing. But he had promised his mother he would not skip school.

Saturday finally came. At sunup, with only a cup of coffee for breakfast, Guy turned the tractor into the field. He let the plow settle onto the ground, then brought up the RPMs and headed downfield. The coulter disks cut six slices into the pasture sod. The moldboards lifted and turned the soil, left six gleaming waves behind. Stopping only for diesel fuel

110

and a sandwich at midday, Guy plowed until sundown, and then, later, by the tractor's yellow running lights.

At 11:30 that night the field was an airport. The black strips of plowing were runways. The tractor, with its blue and green dash lights and its yellow headlamps outside, was a jumbo jet. With each taxi around the field Guy came closer and closer to lifting off the ground, to rumbling over the fence up into the black night.

Abruptly he stopped the tractor mid-field. He opened the door of the cab. The cold air slapped him awake. He got down to piss. He surveyed the field. There were only ten or so acres left to plow. He could finish that tomorrow. But then he cursed. Tomorrow was Sunday.

He looked across the field to Helmer's house. Tiny yellow boxes shone from the living room. Helmer was waiting up.

What the hell. He would keep going, finish tonight. But then he cursed again, involuntarily including Helmer this time. There were at least two hours of plowing left. In less than one hour, it would be Sunday. And a deal was a deal.

Guy slept most of Sunday. He finished the plowing Monday evening after school. In the dark he hooked onto the field disk and rumbled by headlights in slow circles about the field until 3:00 A.M. Tuesday, he stumbled through chores, school, work, and chores. He disked again Tuesday night and into Wednesday morning. The week became a slow-turning kaleidoscope of tractor lights, welder's sparks, white lines on blackboards, and falling stars.

On Friday, Martin called him at school.

"There's some guy here from Manitoba with four hundred bushels of flax seed," Martin said. "I told him he was in the wrong county if not the wrong country. But he showed me your name on an order sheet. And it looks like your handwriting."

"It's my writing," Guy said. His heart thumped. He imagined the face of the truck driver, the brown burlap bags of seed.

"Flax? For here? For the old pasture?"

"That's right," Guy said. "Flax."

"Jesus, you must be out of your goddamn mind—nobody ever—"

111

Guy carefully hung up the receiver. "Fuck you," he murmured.

"I beg your pardon?" one of the school secretaries said.

Saturday he planted. The slippery brown flax seed flowed easily through the hopper of the grain drill. He was finished and in Martin's house for the ten o'clock news and weather.

May 6. Fifty-five degrees and sunny. Flax seed fat. Some with sprouts. None through.

May 13. Warm front stopped over North Dakota and central Minnesota. Seventy-four degrees, sunny. All seeds sprouted and heading to daylight. Need a rain, though.

May 16. Raining and fifty-four degrees.

May 18. Flax up! Green needles, a billion of them.

May 24. Two inches of rain last night. Sunny today and warming fast. Flax finger-high. Black field shading green.

May 28. High School Graduation. Hot robes, boring speaker. Standard grab-for-all-gusto, education-sets-you-free speech. Drove home fast to look at flax.

May 30. Seventy-seven degrees and sunny. Flax long-hand-high. One hundred bright green acres. Martin says oats would have been knee-high by now. Fuck him.

June 13. The third day of ninety degrees, southwest wind at more than twenty mph. Flax stems rolling, whitening at the edge. Need rain. Now.

June 14. Wind switching to northwest. Cold front moving down. Keep coming!

June 15. Raining like hell and fifty-eight degrees. Raining in Becker County and little elsewhere. Beginner's luck.

And so Guy's notes on his calendar and his luck continued. When his flax needed rain the skies gradually bunched with clouds and water fell. When his flax needed heat the weather moved on and the sun shone.

By the end of June the field of flax, as if there were a great magnet buried under its green surface, began to slow the pickups of passing farmers and pull many to a halt. The farmers got out of their trucks. They walked along the hedge end of the field. They knelt and sighted across the grain. They pulled up stems of the flax and rolled them through their fingers. They chose one green shoot for their mouths and then slowly chewed it as they watched the flax move in long rippling sheets in the summer breeze.

Every evening Helmer gave Guy the flax report: how many farmers stopped. The aphid count per square foot. Rust. For Helmer spent much of every day walking along or within the field. Guy began to believe that Helmer's presence had something to do with his good luck. That his grandfather was some sort of guardian angel of the field.

Or maybe his good luck came from Madeline. She, too, took daily walks around the field. Often she walked into the grain to pull up a bull thistle or a stalk of black nightshade. Guy could tell it was her; she left a fainter path in the grain than did Helmer.

Sometimes in the evenings, after chores, Guy walked with her. When they had completed the two-mile circuit they often sat together on the rock pile by the gate. They watched the sun set on the field. Madeline talked of Canada, of home. They watched the green flax turn orange, then blue.

On July 20, however, Guy's luck began to run out. The temperature and humidity were matched at ninety-five. A cold front had bulged down from Canada and would meet the warm air somewhere close to Becker County. Guy alternated between watching the TV's weather radar and the west sky over the flax.

By 7:00 that evening the TV weatherwoman was predicting high winds ". . . and damaging hail," Martin finished for her. He said to Guy, "You see, that's the trouble with flax. Hail catch it coming close to bloom and it's dead. But I don't imagine you thought about that. Now take corn or oats, they almost always . . ."

Guy left the house. Outside, he stood among the flax and watched the oncoming weather. Now waist-high and blooming blue on the higher swells of the field, the flax's uncertain colors matched the sky. Southwest were the high, shining cumulus towers. "Holy-card clouds," Mary LittleWolf called such clouds. White heat lightning flashed underneath them.

From the northwest came the lower, darker, faster-moving clouds of the cold front. Guy for a half hour watched the two fronts collide. Their clouds in slow motion churned and tumbled and rolled upward dark and bulbous. Supported now by yellow spider legs of lightning, the two

113

fronts were no longer clouds but great spiders struggling for control of the reservation sky.

Cold air suddenly washed over Guy's face. Rain shimmered across the flax toward him. Behind the rain, whitish and racing, came the hail. Guy cursed and ran for the machine shed. The rain overtook him and he was instantly wet through. Under the eaves of the shed he turned to witness the destruction of his field.

But even as he watched, the hail veered sharply south. It churned through Jim Hanson's oats, then raced from sight. It was then Guy saw his grandfather. Helmer stood on the front steps of his house. His arms hung straight down, his palms faced out, his brown face and white hair streamed with water. His eyes were closed. His mouth was open. His lips moved as if he were speaking or drinking in the cold rain.

After the storm and two days of sunlight, the flax eased into bloom. First a broad, milky blue, the field drew color from the sky. In full bloom, the flax's color surpassed the sky, gave back a deeper blue to the high summer air. Past full bloom, the field shaded daily to yellow, then brown. The flower petals dropped away. Seed pods formed.

July 18. Etta Bornholdt Pehrsson: April 1897–July 18, 1972. Gramps all alone now. Except us. And his flax.

By July 20 the flax seeds, each clutched in their tiny five-leaved cups, were the size of garden peas. That same week a frost burned most of Manitoba's flax fields black. Within two days flax futures began to trade up their daily limit. Cash price for a bushel of flax climbed to an all-time high of $25 a bushel. The Flatwater *Quill* ran an article about Guy and his flax entitled "Gambling and Farming May Pay Off." The article estimated Guy's flax yield at sixty bushels to the acre.

"That's $150,000, Gramps," Guy blurted as Helmer's eyes moved slowly across the page.

But Helmer did not reply or look up until he was finished reading. Then he carefully folded shut the paper and turned it face-down on the table. He stared through the west living-room window.

"Best not to think too far ahead," he murmured. "It's not in the bin yet."

Guy nodded. He wished the newspaper had not started figuring bushels and dollars. Now the money was all he could think of. The money ran through his mind like a continuous movie that showed all the things he could buy. For his grandfather he would buy a new furnace and a tank of fuel oil as big as a silo. He would buy his mother a new car and a microwave oven. He would buy Martin a barn cleaner, a sileage unloader, and a full-time hired man. Then he, Guy, would never touch a cow again.

"No," Madeline said. It was sundown and she and Guy were sitting on the rock pile beside the field. The rocks held the day's heat. Guy was talking about the money. "No—nothing for me!" she said angrily. "Save the money—save it all. Then take it somewhere. College, a business. But don't buy land, that's all I ask."

Guy was silent.

Her voice flattened as she looked across the field. "The land hooks people, especially farm boys like yourself—not that you're like all the rest. You take a tractor and plow to it, turn a green field black and then make it green again, you start to feel powerful. I can see it in the way men talk. They talk like they control it, like it's their slave." She paused. "But that's not true at all. The land controls you. It controls everything. Farmers get hooked. They think the land is all there is. That the land is enough. Well, it's not."

Guy did not understand all of what she said. The land was a lot, that he knew. Rather than talk more, he put his arm around her. At first, still angry, Madeline sat stiffly. But slowly her shoulders loosened and she leaned against him. They sat that way for a long time and watched the flax pull down the sun.

"Well, well—what a cozy couple," Martin's voice said behind them. Martin. He had walked up on them. They hadn't been watching, thinking of him at all. He had caught them off guard.

Guy jerked away his arm. His father stood squinting down at them, his feet planted a telltale two inches wider apart than normal. "Arm in arm. I thought that was my job." His voice slurred.

Madeline jumped to her feet. The sunlight burned orange in her face. "You bastard," she said to Martin.

That was the first time Guy ever heard his mother swear.

By August 8 the flax was nearly ripe. The seeds were hard enough to hold a fingernail dent. Guy made final harvesting arrangements with Jim Hanson, whose big John Deere would combine the grain. "No problem," Hanson said, staring straight at Guy. "After that hail, I don't have much of my own grain to worry about now, do I?"

To cut and windrow the flax, Guy bought on credit a new John Deere swather from the dealership where he worked. The swather cost $18,000 and all Guy had to do was sign two papers—one for the dealership, the other for the banker, Lyle Price.

"Hearing good things about you," Price said with a quick smile as he watched Guy sign.

The sales manager at the dealership smiled and said, "With a crop like that coming in, I'd sell you a swather for every day of the week."

The weather held hot and dry. On August 12, a Friday, with a clear, blue sky and the next weather far off in the Rockies, Guy cut.

The flax folded golden over the sickle of the swather. With Helmer watching from the rock pile, Guy swathed until sundown. Then the flax began to draw moisture from the cooling air, and the sickle began to pound in complaint. Guy pulled away from the grain with only ten acres left to cut.

"Hail can't hurt me now," he called to Helmer as he drove the swather through the gate. From the roar of the engine he did not hear his grandfather's reply.

On Saturday he finished cutting. The field lay ribboned with waist-high, yellow windrows. Sunday dawned cool but clear. Monday came sunny and eighty degrees, which cured the top several inches of the windrows. Guy could chafe the flax hulls between his palms and watch the shiny brown seeds drop into his lap. Now at $26.50 a bushel, he wondered what each seed was worth.

Tuesday, Wednesday, and Thursday were days that grainmen dreamed of. The sky was cloudless, unendingly blue.

116

The temperature was ninety degrees with a steady, dry wind from the southwest. In the yellow oven of the field the windrows baked and shimmered away their moisture. At the touch the flax stems crackled and broke. At field-side, Guy lined up a parade of grain wagons.

Friday morning at 11:00, an hour later than agreed, Jim Hanson's green combine came rumbling down the road. Guy ran to meet him at the driveway. Hanson swung down from the cab. He wore several days of beard stubble along with a pair of oil-spotted coveralls. He farmed several hundred acres, and Guy often saw him at the parts counter at the John Deere dealership.

Hanson strode up to the first windrow, ran his hand underneath. He pulled free some stalks, smelled them, bit into them. He looked at the sky. "Won't go until two o'clock," he said.

Helmer, who had already checked the flax windrows in the same fashion, nodded. Hanson climbed back into the green-tinted cab of his combine and slumped backward in immediate sleep.

Helmer walked closer to the combine. He stared intently at the tires, the grease fittings, the pickup reel. He reached out to one of the spring teeth; the tooth rattled loosely at his touch. With the small pliers he always carried, Helmer knelt and tightened the nut. Hanson did not wake up.

While Hanson slept and Helmer walked along the flax windrows, Guy went to the house to listen to the weather report on the radio. Rain in Omaha, Idaho Falls, Bozeman, Kalispell.

At 2:30 P.M. Hanson suddenly sat up in the cab of the combine. He turned the key and the combine's engine coughed alive. He brought up the RPMs until the combine's green sides shuddered, then wheeled its mouth toward the first windrow. The pickup reel began to turn, the thin forks pulled the grain forward. And like a great green beetle, the combine headed downfield swallowing the flax as it went and spitting a spray of straw behind. Guy ran alongside. In the roar of the engine, the shuddering clatter of the sieves, with grit in his mouth and eyes, Guy watched the little Plexiglas window of the grain hopper. Flax seed inched up its sides like an hourglass filling with sand. Or gold.

But suddenly there was a massive thud. Then a clanking

sound, as if the earth beneath the combine had given way. The combine heaved to a stop. Hanson leaped down from the cab, threw his cap onto the ground, and began to stomp on it.

Guy drove Hanson home. Hanson stared straight ahead with his jaw clenched. "Fucking flax, I shoulda known better," he muttered.

Repairs would take at least three days. Guy knew what a new gearbox cost and so did not speak of it.

"Windrows that big, you need the big custom equipment."

"Like who?" Guy said quietly. There was no combine he knew of in Becker County bigger than Hanson's John Deere.

Hanson scratched the beard on his throat. "There's a small crew I know that ought to be near Fargo about now. Probably headed for South Dakota. Flaherty, a red-haired Irishman, runs some big Allis gleaners. Maybe he'd detour around this way and clean up your flax."

"I can pay," Guy said quickly. He would go to Lyle Price again. There would be plenty of money when the flax was in the bin.

At six o'clock that evening, with two hundred dusty new miles on the Chevy, Guy located Flaherty's crew. Sixty miles west of Fargo, his four combines were running a staggered front against the last half of a long wheat field. Guy's heart pumped with excitement. Flaherty's Allis-Chalmers gleaners looked as large and as sturdy as Sherman tanks.

He drove the Chevy up to the motor home and the trailers. At the edge of the field stood a man, hatless, with coppery hair, with binoculars to his eyes. He watched his combines.

Guy walked up to Flaherty. His heart thudded before he spoke.

"Flax, huh?" Flaherty said, again lifting the binoculars to his eyes. "Don't see much flax around here. But I dunno. A hundred acres isn't much for a day's detour. I'm supposed to be down in Sioux Falls by Monday."

"I can make it worth your while," Guy said.

Flaherty lowered his glasses. A slow grin grew in the sunburned creases around his mouth. "Oh you can, can you?"

"Yessir," Guy said. He realized Flaherty was probably about the same age as his own father.

"This must be quite a field, then."

"Sixty bushels," Guy said.

Flaherty laughed and raised the binoculars again. "Son, I been shakin' grain for twenty years and I've never seen flax run even fifty."

Guy suddenly remembered the newspaper article, which, not wanting to look at, he had stashed under the seat of his car. He retrieved the paper and handed it to Flaherty. Flaherty fished reading glasses from his pocket, blew away their dust, and began to read.

"Hell," he said finally. "I've never yet met a reporter who could figure bushels. But the picture looks good, yes it does." He brought the newspaper closer to his face. Then he looked sideways at Guy. "And you're this gambler fellow they're writing about?"

"Yessir," Guy said.

"And you want to gamble on Flaherty?"

"Yessir." Guy grinned.

By three o'clock Saturday afternoon, Guy thought he had gambled wrong. Flaherty's combines had not come. He wondered if Flaherty had had trouble. Had gotten lost. Had lied to him.

Helmer sat at his kitchen table so he could see out the window and down the road west. "He'll come," Helmer said. "If the man said he would come, he'll come."

But the combines did not come Saturday afternoon, nor Sunday by the time Helmer had driven in his pickup off to church. Guy paced the silent living room of Helmer's house. He listened to the transistor radio upstairs; he had to hold it close to the open window, where there was less static.

Rain in Sioux Falls. Rain in Billings. Rain in Bismarck and Valley City. He cursed the radio. In the same moment he heard trucks. From the southwest, like a caravan of circus elephants appearing out of the dust, came Flaherty's combines.

Guy thundered down the stairs and ran into the yard. He

waved and the trucks turned into Helmer's yard. Flaherty stepped down from his motor home. His eyes were as red as his beard stubble. His hands were stained dark with oil. He shook his head. "On that last forty acres, whatever could go wrong, went."

He looked at the flax even as he spoke. Without waiting for Guy, he strode into the field. He ran one arm underneath the grain and hefted it.

"Be damned," he said, a tired grin spreading outward from his eyes. "I'm in the wrong business. Ought to be growing this stuff instead of shakin' it." He turned to his men. "Unload those ornery critters," he called. "We got a real field here."

Guy started to speak, but Flaherty turned away to direct his men. Guy looked back to Helmer's house. Its two porch windows were eyes, its door a mouth. He walked up to Flaherty again, but this time a combine's engine roared alive, then another and another. Guy's voice was lost in the noise.

Flaherty's men unleashed the combines' tether chains, then lowered the ramps of their trailers. The drivers began to ease the combines down the ramps to the ground, where they then formed a convoy pointed at the field of flax.

As the last combine touched ground Guy saw from the corner of his eye Helmer's small pickup turn into the yard. It came slowly toward the field. Helmer got out. In his dark Sunday suit Helmer walked up to Guy. He looked at the combines, then back to Guy. For long moments, as the combines began to move toward the field, Guy met his grandfather's gaze. Then he broke away. He ran in front of the lead combine, driven by Flaherty himself, and blocked its path.

Flaherty leaned out of the cab. "What the hell's the matter?" he called. He swung down from the combine.

Guy was silent. He looked briefly at Helmer, then back to Flaherty. "We . . . can't combine today."

Flaherty stared. "What the hell you talkin' about?" he said. "The grain is ready. I should know."

"No—it's not that," Guy began.

"Well, what then?" Flaherty climbed down.

"It's . . . Sunday," Guy said slowly. "This is my grandfa-

120

ther. This is his land. He doesn't farm on Sunday. We made a deal."

The other drivers swung down and stood behind Flaherty. Flaherty turned his red-rimmed eyes to Helmer. "Sunday? Sunday? Old man, are you crazy or something?" The other drivers laughed. "Your grandson's got the field of a lifetime, there's rain no more than a day away, and you're worried about Sunday?"

Helmer met Flaherty's gaze in silence. Finally Flaherty looked down and ran his hand through his hair. "Goddamn," he muttered, "but I've never run into this one before."

Flaherty turned to Guy, pulled him aside. "Listen," he said. "Sunday don't matter to me. It don't matter to the flax. And it probably don't matter to you. So why don't you take your granddad back to the house. Fix him a cup of coffee. Take him for a drive. Something. You take care of him, we'll take care of your flax. Half a day and we'll be on our way. In a few days he'll forget all about it."

But Guy could only shake his head. "I gave my word," he said.

Flaherty's eyes narrowed. "Well, goddamnit, look—you hired me. If you want me to wait a day, I'll wait. But every hour we sit here will cost you same as if we were combining."

"I can pay," Guy said.

"Bunch of fruitcakes," one of the other drivers muttered.

"Get some shut-eye, anyway," another said as they turned away to shut off the combines.

Flaherty spun on the heel of his boot, stalked into the motor home, and slammed the door behind. Then there was silence in the field.

That night Guy lay in his bed under the slope of the roof. It was dark. His eyes were open. He did not listen to the radio. Sometime much later he heard the sound he knew would come. At first the sound was so faint that he mistook it for the slide of his own blood in his ear against the pillow. Then the sound grew. A whispering on the shingles. A steady patter. Finally a drumming. Rain.

He rose from the bed and went to the window. In the yard

121

below, in the yellow glow of the yard lamp, Flaherty's combines shone like great, wet blocks of ice.

The rain continued Monday and Tuesday.

"We can't wait any longer," Flaherty said Wednesday morning. He was clean-shaven now, his face puffy with sleep. "You're not on our regular route. We're supposed to be down in Sioux Falls. Maybe somebody else . . ."

Guy nodded. He felt older. Harder. Like some part of him had turned to wood or stone. "How much do I owe you then?" was all he asked.

"Just for Sunday," Flaherty replied.

Guy wrote out the check and handed it over. Flaherty looked down at the check in his hand, then across to the flax, and, finally, to Helmer's house.

"Goddamnit," he said suddenly. In one motion he crumpled the check, flung it down, and ground it into the mud with his boot. Then he turned away and waved his combines down the road.

Thursday the skies cleared, but only for the afternoon. Friday and Saturday the rain came again.

The windrows of flax rusted brown. From their new weight the windrows began to crush their supporting stubble and sink. By the following Monday the windrows lay flat and shrunken on the cold wet earth.

Rain and mist continued for the next two weeks.

"It's going to clear up," Helmer said every day. "It always does. There's still time."

But Guy had few words for him, for Madeline, for anybody. He continued to sit with Helmer awhile in the evenings. He was glad his grandfather spoke no more nor no less than usual.

In the mornings Guy once again drove to his job at the implement dealership. Often he saw his grandfather walking at sunup among the dark windrows of flax. He carried a fork. He poked at the wet grain, tested its weight. Once when Guy returned at sundown he saw Helmer in the field just as the sky cleared. Orange light slanted harshly across the windrows, whose seeds had begun to sprout. Guy braked the Chevy to a stop. His grandfather stood motionless far out in the field among green rivers of fire.

September came, and with it a truck from the dealership to take back the grain swather. Now it was a used implement; Guy lost two thousand dollars on it. One thousand he owed to the dealership; that money he could work out against wages. The second thousand he owed to Lyle Price of the Flatwater State Bank. The bank began to call, then send letters. At first the letters came in thin white envelopes, then thicker ones, then with pink receipt-acknowledged cards stapled on their sides. All he threw away unopened.

Late September brought Indian summer. The skies cleared. The sun shone hotly for a week. The flax windrows dried on top. If the windrows could be lifted and turned to dry their undersides—a hayrake might work—there was still a chance for a partial harvest by a cautious combine. There was a chance at least to pay off the bank.

Guy stopped working at the dealership. He readied the hayrake. On a Wednesday, along with four neighbors who showed up uninvited with their own tractors and rakes, Guy tried to turn the flax. Helmer watched by the gate.

Still sodden underneath, still heavier than any hay, the flax wound and webbed itself around the reels of the rakes. Every few yards Guy and the other drivers had to stop, dismount, and cut away the flax with butcher knives. If they drove without stopping, the rake's reel belt began to slip, then smoke with the smell of burning rubber or twine.

One by one the neighbors turned away from the flax and drove toward the gate. Guy kept going. He drove fifty yards, leaped down to slash at the flax, then drove again. The rake's drive chains began to chatter and slip. The tips of the gear teeth began to wear away. Guy kept going. On the tractor's steering wheel his left hand felt wet, then numb. When he looked down the tan palm of his glove held a rose of blood, blooming even as he watched. The butcher knife. He closed the rose in a fist of leather and kept driving.

Suddenly the main chain on the rake parted and flopped. The rake was now a plow. Guy turned the steering wheel away from the windrow.

As he drove toward the gate Helmer waved him off. "Go

123

back—keep going—go back!" he called. He waved his fork at the other drivers. "All of you—go back, go back!" But they looked away. They took off their caps and ran their hands through their hair.

Guy got down from the tractor and walked toward Helmer. "It won't turn," he called. "It won't work!"

Helmer shook his head. "It's got to work. The flax has to be turned. When it's turned we can get that red-haired man and his combines to come back. Then we can—"

"No!" Guy shouted close to his grandfather's face. He grabbed him by the shoulders and shook him. "It's finished! It's over—over—over—over—can't you see that?"

But Helmer could not look at Guy. His blue eyes were frozen to the field.

Guy awoke sometime after dark. He was uncertain of the time. He had gone to bed without supper, had retreated deep into a sleep that contained no people, no tractors, no fields, no dreams of any kind.

He stumbled toward the window. He had a brief vision of Flaherty's combines, wet under the yard light. But the yard was empty. The black sky was clear and moonlit. There was nothing at all to see except, far out in the field of flax, the movement of some night animal.

Suddenly Guy called out. He raced barefoot downstairs, across the yard, pounded on his parents' bedroom window, then ran toward the field.

Far out in the field, Helmer had fallen to his hands and knees.

"Gramps!" Guy called. As he neared him, Helmer turned his face to look. A black course of blood ran from his nose across his cheek. Beside him lay his fork.

"Few more hours, maybe," Helmer whispered, panting. "Few more hours, have it all turned. Then we'll get that red-haired man . . ."

Guy saw that Helmer, by hand, had turned a half mile of one windrow. Helmer reached again for his fork.

"No!" Guy said, kicking away the fork.

"Yes, have to turn . . ." Helmer breathed. Helmer found the fork and pushed himself to his feet. Guy caught the fork's handle; he could feel his grandfather through the wood.

"Please, Guy-boy, let me finish . . . tonight," Helmer whispered. He pulled on the fork. Suddenly Guy was holding him, feeling his grandfather's woolen shirt wet with sweat. Feeling his old heart shuddering in his chest.

"You're a good boy," Helmer whispered, and kissed him. Kissed him like he used to when Guy was small. Guy tasted his grandfather's blood.

But then Helmer pushed him away.

"Stop him!" Martin shouted. Guy looked back. Martin and Madeline were running toward them.

"No," Guy said. Something in his voice drew his parents to a stop and did not let them pass. They all watched. Helmer, one arm clutched across his chest as if to hold in his heart, drove his fork again and again into the grain. Staggeringin the moonlight, he slowly worked his way downfield into the dark.

Chapter Fourteen

October 10. Helmer in hospital. Just stares. The doctor said a stroke is when the brain gives up on the rest of the body.

October 12. Tried for a full-time job at the dealership, but they said no. You've quit twice already, need someone dependable, they said.

Guy kept up brief notes on the little flax calendar above his bed. But the notes did not mention his flax. Now the flax was only a field of dark green quack grass with black pinstriping, a field that needed plowing.

But Guy did not plow. Much of the day he lay on his bed upstairs in Helmer's empty house. He did not read. He did nothing but listen to the radio. Any station. When he thought about anything at all he tried to imagine a stroke. After a stroke you just lay there and stared at some spot on the ceiling. He tried to imagine something different from lying on the bed listening to the radio but couldn't. He began to understand that there were many kinds of strokes. Some strokes froze the body. Some froze the heart. Some froze ideas. Others froze dreams and love. Everybody had some frozen part to them. But the worst stroke of all was the one that froze time, the stroke that locked in place the present. Forever.

Once he was startled from half-sleep by a pounding on the door. At Helmer's door stood a gray-suited young man trying to look old. He was from the Flatwater State Bank.

"Mr. Price has instructed me to visit with you and make arrangements for a transfer of chattel to the bank sufficient to cover the amount of"—he looked down at his clipboard—"one thousand dollars even."

"Mr. Price can fuck himself," Guy said quietly.

The young banker looked up and blinked. "I'll . . . relay your message to Mr. Price," he said. "In the meantime"— he looked back to his clipboard—"there's the matter of the chattel."

"You can fuck yourself too," Guy said.

The banker did not look up from the paper. "You've listed as chattel several items, the most valuable of which appears to be a 1957 two-door Chevrolet, license number RMN-349. That must be it there," the man said, turning to look across the yard to Guy's Chevy.

Guy grabbed the man's lapels and shook him. "Hit the road, mister. You come here again I'm going to pound you into the ground like a fence post." His voice shook.

The man's eyes widened and he swallowed. Guy released his grip and the man walked quickly toward his sedan. Inside, he rolled the window halfway down and called out, "I'm instructing the sheriff to visit you to retrieve the Chevrolet. You have seven days before that time. The next move is up to you."

Guy paced the living room for a while, then went back to bed. He lay there.

Four days later Guy stood deep in a sandy excavation hammering long spikes into lumber. West of the small grove, out of sight from the farmyard, he had taken the tractor and hydraulic loader and dug a hole in the field. The hole was the size of a house basement. In the middle of the hole he had nearly finished building a heavy-timbered, flat-roofed structure. His materials were treated fence posts and old railroad ties. And long spikes.

On the fifth day he finished the nailing. He walked out of the hole, then stooped to sight across the surface of the field. The roof of the building was two feet below grade. That afternoon he cleaned out his Chevy and drove it into the field. He laid two tracks of planking down the ramp of the excavation. Then he carefully backed the Chevy down the slope and into the underground garage.

He parked the Chevy, jacked up first one end, then the other. He placed blocks under the axles so the tires turned freely. After that he turned to the engine. With the motor running, he removed one sparkplug at a time and squirted heavy tractor oil into each cylinder. By the eighth plug the Chevy was laboring, chugging like a John Deere, puffing black smoke from its tailpipe. Guy finally shut off the engine and scrambled, coughing, from the hole. When the smoke cleared he returned. From a five-gallon can he poured diesel fuel, itself thin oil, over the Chevy. He poured the fuel into the carburetor. Over the engine block. Over the radiator. Over the hood and fenders. Over the roof and windshield. Last, he laid the keys on the dashboard and closed the door.

Then he draped the garage with black plastic. He wound the dark sheet around and over and around again. He felt like the artist who covered buildings and ships and islands.

Finally, with the tractor and loader, he backfilled the hole. Soon he was dumping dirt atop the roof. The excess earth he hauled away and dumped in a field washout. When the field was once again smooth he broke open several bales of hay and shook them over the fresh digging. When he walked away the hay was the same color as the field. The Chevy was gone. On ice. In suspended animation. A woolly mammoth dreaming underground.

Like Helmer.

Like himself.

On the sixth morning his parents did not wake up as he stood by their bed. Madeline lay close to her edge of the mattress and breathed softly with her mouth closed. He touched her hair, then turned away. He left the farm, walking, in the purple light before dawn.

He carried a pack and sleeping bag on his back. Around him the fields were dark and silent except for the twitter of nighthawks.

He walked south toward the highway. Slowly the sky pinked up like color coming into skin. Meadowlarks began to call from atop fence posts. Their breasts drew light from the air and stood out atop the fence posts like pale, heart-shaped flowers blooming from the wood.

Ahead was a car in the ditch, a battered Oldsmobile without window glass. He stopped to look inside. An old Indian man and younger Indian girl lay sleeping in the back seat. Two empty Ripple bottles lay between them. The old man's pants were half down and there were goose bumps on his gray skin.

Guy walked on.

He reached the highway, #10 West. Just as the sun came up a farm pickup pulled over. His first ride. A woman about his mother's age drove. She wore her hair up in a kerchief, a man's jacket, jeans, and boots. Her hands on the steering wheel were chapped and calloused. On the seat beside her was a flat, round pan that rattled with fragments from some kind of bearing.

"Told him to watch that seal," the woman said. Guy stared at the shrapnel in the pan. "'The seal goes, the bearing goes,' I told him. He knows that. But he's always in such a goddamn hurry," she said.

Guy nodded. They talked briefly. Then they drove for a long while in silence. Later she turned to look at him again. She glanced at his pack in the rear of the pickup. "Detroit Lakes, you said. Looks like you're going farther than Detroit Lakes."

"Want to pick up the freeway there," Guy answered. He looked out the window. He didn't feel much like talking. He didn't know what he felt.

"West?"

Guy nodded.

The woman smiled and squinted as she lit a cigarette. She offered one to Guy.

Guy shook his head no.

She exhaled. "Out West is where I'm from. Idaho Falls. Every year I tell the old man we ought to sell the place and move back. The winters aren't so bad there. 'Next year,' he says. I say to him, 'Sometime there ain't gonna be a next year. Sometime your tractor will come driving through the yard without you and it'll be me who has to go and find you out in the field and it'll just be your boots sticking up from the ground.' But he don't listen."

She fell silent for a long time. Guy watched the trees. Detroit Lakes approached.

"There at the stoplight will do," Guy said.

She nodded and slowed.

"Thanks," Guy said.

The woman waved briefly and drove on.

Guy was walking toward the freeway ramp when he heard her brake and begin to back up.

She rolled down the truck window. "They'll be finishing the fruit harvest out there about now," she called. "Peaches. You get through Idaho Falls, eat a peach for me, okay?"

Guy held up his thumb to her. He watched her drive off. As she went out of sight around a gas station, he thought of crying. But cars began to pass. He turned his thumb west.

Chapter Fifteen

North Dakota was western Minnesota with fewer trees. Only when the Badlands began, pinkish mountains hidden in great holes, did Guy feel distance between himself and the farm. At a freeway rest stop he slept an hour stretched out atop a picnic table. He awoke in sunlight. A shiny black grackle was perched on his table, eyeing his pack.

He ate a chunk of bread, an apple, gave the crust and the core to the bird. Then walked again toward the freeway. He had thirty dollars in his right pocket. He wore jeans, boots, a red and white plaid flannel shirt. A feed cap. The sun was warm on his neck and shoulders.

His rides came intermittently. A step van whose racks of fresh bread he smelled even before they came to a full stop.

A farmer headed to Valley City for plow parts.

An old woman in an immaculate '69 Bonneville that drifted lane to lane as she talked.

Two Indians in a rusty '58 Buick who first asked him for gas money. When he shook his head and stepped back from their car, they drove on, but then stopped a few blocks ahead and waved him forward.

Mandan.

Wibaux.

131

A four-hour wait just outside Hebron. He crossed the North Dakota-Montana border in an air-conditioned Oldsmobile driven by a businessman who smoked Tiparillos and read the *The Wall Street Journal* as he drove. "Help yourself," the man said of the little cigars.

"Thanks," Guy said. He lit one.

That evening he had a hamburger and a beer in the American Legion Club on the main street of Glendive, then walked west. At the edge of town was a small park with good bushes and thick grass for his sleeping bag. But there was still an hour of sunlight. He put out his thumb again. A dark blue Saab with New York plates passed. A woman drove. From her sunglasses and the Saab's tinted glass, he could tell only that she had dark hair and very white skin. She turned her head at him briefly but her car did not slow. In a few minutes the blue Saab returned. This time it slowed. The woman swiveled her head to stare. For a moment the Saab's brake lights flashed on. Guy began to reach for his pack but then the brake lights went off. The Saab continued west, picked up speed, and disappeared into the twilight.

He kicked a stone into the ditch, shouldered his pack, and walked on.

"You can't sleep here," someone was saying loudly while shaking Guy's arm. A fat man in an apron. The manager of a cafe. A cafe in—where was he?—Bozeman. He had eaten three hamburgers and a malt, then leaned back and closed his eyes just for a moment. In the park in Glendive the mosquitoes had eaten on him all night.

"Don' want no vagrants in here. Keep moving." the man said.

Guy shook his head and looked around. A family, three small blond-haired kids and their parents, stared at him from the next booth. He nodded to them. The children leaned behind their parents.

South into Idaho.
Dillon.
Lewisville.
Blackfoot.
Between towns. Five hours in the sun with no water.

132

Finally a ride from a balding carpet salesman who asked him if he ever dreamed about naked men.

Fort Hall.

In a half-sleep in a swaying truck seat he opened his eyes and saw a sign for Idaho Falls.

"Idaho Falls," he said quickly, sitting up. "Have to get out at Idaho Falls."

"Suit yourself," the driver said.

It was the afternoon of Guy's third day on the road. He had eighteen dollars left. The sky was clear and blue, the temperature somewhere near sixty. He could smell a river. He walked toward the town. A quarter mile ahead, on the outskirts of Idaho Falls, he saw a fruit stand along the highway. He was hungry and he walked faster.

He neared the small, white, wooden building with colored fruit shapes painted on the side. Red apples. Orange oranges. Green and red watermelons. And yellow peaches. The stand was ringed with crates of peaches tipped up for inspection. He jogged forward, his pack bouncing heavily on his back. In the sunlight the peaches glowed as if they were eggs on a lighting tray. He knelt before them. He ran his hand over their pink curves, held one's downy belly up to the sun. But it was bruised underneath.

After several minutes he found it. The peach was heavy in his palm, nearly the size of a cantaloupe. Sunrise pinkish yellow. Cloudless, unbruised. One green leaf still clung to its stem. He paid for it, then carried it with him for several blocks until he came to a park bench next to a small fountain.

He smelled of the peach, then hefted its weight again. Finally he took a deep, slow bite. Its juice ran down his chin and onto his wrist and all the way down his arm until it dripped off his elbow. He ate it down until he could taste the rough bitters of its pit. When all the pink meat was gone he thought of walking back and buying another. But didn't.

Pocatello.

Salt Lake City.

Two blond, young Mormon men heading to Nevada repeatedly offered him a Bible from a box of the same. When he declined, repeatedly, the Mormons let him out in the middle of the Salt Flats. He threw a rock after their car as it shrank away west into the colorless, shimmering haze.

Winnemucca.

Sparks.

That night he slept on a gravel streambed with stray dogs creeping toward him. He would awaken, shout, throw a stone. The dogs would scare. But every time he awoke they were close to him again.

Emigrant Gap.

Gold Run.

Seven dollars left.

Up and up the Sierras.

He reached Donner Pass late at night in the front seat of a Winnebago running hot. The driver pulled over, popped the hood, went inside to sleep, and locked the door. Guy shouldered his pack and walked on. A sign said Continental Divide. The night air was cold and crisp, like Minnesota in November. A truck passed and left behind a sweet-smelling contrail of onions. He was hungry.

He walked forward on the flat dome of Donner Pass. There was thick, black forest on both sides of the highway but the cut of the roadway shone with faint light, like a doorway to a big room beyond. He walked toward it. As he passed around a black grove of trees, he sucked in his breath and halted. Below, in a flat grid of lights, lay California's Central Valley. Sacramento lay glowing like the settled center of a midnight campfire. Smaller towns stretched away, embers escaped from the center, larger coals closest, smaller sparks flung farther away, but all of them fallen on dry tinder, where they burned on. Beyond the valley west was the faint, broad glow of San Francisco and the Bay cities.

Guy stared at the lights. He was an astronaut. An astronaut newly landed on a mountain of a strange planet. The lights pulled him forward. He was no longer hungry and tired. He forgot to put out his thumb to the cars that passed. From the downward grade his steps lengthened of their own accord. Soon he was jogging, then bounding. His pack was weightless. On great strides he floated downhill. Eyes on the lights, he followed the long, descending glide path. He was coming in to land.

PART
II

Chapter Sixteen

Eastbound, April 5, 1984, Guy held his gray Mercedes sedan at ten over the speed limit. It was 3 A.M. He was in Minnesota now, close to home. Close to trouble. He thought of Helmer's letter. He let the Mercedes' needle creep to eighty.

Twenty minutes east of Moorhead the dark plane of the freeway began slow undulations. The Mercedes whispered down the long grades into river valleys where clumps of basswood and elm rose up in the periphery of his headlights like great black mushrooms. As the car slung itself upgrade the trees shrank, thinned, disappeared. To the sides lay farmland. The moonlit fields were a crazy quilt of black and white, of plowed earth and snow. Only a couple of weeks until planting time. Not that it mattered to Guy.

In the back seat Kennedy's stomach rumbled and he twitched in his sleep.

"Hang on, Jack. When we get to the farm Madeline will fry you a burger all your own." Kennedy awoke and yipped once.

Soon Detroit Lakes appeared on the horizon like a thin cluster of grounded stars. Detroit Lakes marked the end of the western plains. Beyond the town the land changed from

137

open farmland to rolling hills of maple and white pine. Helmer's farm lay twenty miles northeast, where the plains made one last attempt to reassert themselves. Failing, the land around Flatwater and beyond gave way to the rocky hill and lake country of northern Minnesota.

Guy slowed for the city limits of the town. He thought back to the summer nights at the dance pavilion on the lake. Bobby Vinton, Roy Orbison, the Uglies, the Trogs, the Buckinghams; the air inside the wooden hall syrup-thick with cigarette smoke, perfume, and, later, patchouli oil; outside in the humid darkness the thump of rock 'n' roll through the walls, the shriek of skinnydippers along the shore; in the dark park across the street the clink of beer bottles; the soft giggles deeper in the trees. He went to the pavilion often after Tom left. He went alone. Returned alone. Sometimes in between he found a girl to dance with or kiss with in his car, but mostly he just watched.

The last streetlight fell away. Only twenty miles left. Guy reached back and touched Kennedy's smooth coat. In ten minutes he turned off the main highway onto the narrow tar road that zigzagged north to the farm. A large green sign with white lettering leaped luminous in his headlights:

Entering White Earth Reservation, Home of the Anishinabe.
Hunting, Fishing, Berrying Permits Required for Non-Tribal
Members. Violators Arrested. $500 Fine for Theft of
or Damage to This Sign.

This was new. When Guy left the prairie twelve years ago it was not important where the reservation began and ended. Someone with a can of white spray paint had changed the sign's letters to read, "Humping and Pissing Permits Required." On the lower right corner crawled a dull spider of a shotgun blast.

Guy smiled at the shotgun's pattern. The reservation road signs, from bullet holes, had always made better spaghetti strainers than signs. There were lots of guns up in Minnesota, maybe more on the reservation than anywhere. He could feel them in the dark. Winchester .94s and Remington .30-06 deer rifles in gun cabinets and bedroom closets. Dusty single-shot twelve-gauges standing in the corner of the garage nearest the chicken coop. Twenty-two-caliber pistols lost under the seats of pickups. Guy had always carried a shotgun in the trunk of his Chevy. If he saw a partridge on the road around No Medicine Lake, he stopped. If Canadian honkers lit in a field of winter wheat he parked a mile down the road and crawled back toward them in the ditch. Once at night he hit a deer with the Chevy and broke its back. He was glad to have the gun to stop the doe's buckling lunge down the center stripe of the tar.

But there was no gun in the Mercedes. He did not hunt in California. People in California had strange ideas about guns. Once at his house, at a party, Guy talked with a man from Red Lodge, Montana. The man hunted, loaded shells, and had in his car a Winchester Model Twelve twenty-gauge with a low serial number. He brought the gun inside to show Guy. When the man walked back into the room with the gun and some handloads, talk died. It died as if the voices in the room were on tape and someone had pulled the plug. Near Guy's picture window a man with frizzy black hair and wire-rimmed glasses jumped to his feet, pitched Guy's coffee table through the glass, pushed a woman through the hole, then jumped after her. The pair leaped from Guy's deck ten feet to the ground. Limping, stumbling, they clambered into a Volvo and sped away.

Charles Manson he was not, but at the sight of his broken window and shattered coffee table, Guy grabbed the Winchester, ran to his deck, and fired two rounds of quail shot in the general direction of the window-leapers' taillights.

Which did nothing for his party. With effusive thanks for a wonderful evening, his guests—Susan and a couple of her Stanford friends among them—were gone within five minutes. The man and his girlfriend from Red Lodge stayed, and the three of them shot beer bottle skeet from the deck until a police car came nosing up the hill from Palo Alto.

Guns and this road, he knew. Heading north, he pinned the Mercedes accelerator to the carpet. As he knew it would, the square, unbanked curve came up fast—too fast. The rear tires broke loose from the cold asphalt. Kennedy barked. Front wheels pulling west, rather than brake, Guy accelerated through the apex of the curve up onto the flat road west.

Indian Killer Curves. On a map this road looked like stairs. One mile north. One mile west. One mile north, another mile west. So on for ten miles. The road had been built by Scandinavian farmers. Helmer had operated a horse and tin gravel boat for most of one summer. The road scrupulously followed the section lines; in that way it left square fields, straight fences, even rows. One mile of the road had been built at great labor, and two men drowned in a swamp when a curve of no more than a hundred yards would have carried it onto higher, safer ground. The square-cornered road killed a half-dozen Indians and one or two drunken whites every year.

As Guy navigated the corners his stomach rumbled again. He saw the white and rounded enamel belly of Madeline's refrigerator, then inside it. He saw cold chicken pieces poking up from a brown glaze of gravy. He saw a fat loaf of homemade white bread with thick, egg-brushed crust. He saw a tall jar of homemade garlic dills. He saw a wide bowl of strawberry Jell-o lily-padded with banana slices.

He saw Martin.

"Wake up, Jack." He hoisted Jack onto the front seat and stroked his back.

Light from a passing farm pulled his eyes from the highway. The Woods farm. There had been four boys, all older than Guy. The sign by the mailbox still read Herb Woods and Sons, but the last "s" on Sons had been crossed out.

And the light was different too. Dark before, now the Woods farm was lit up like a shopping mall in San Jose. Mercury vapor security lights hung from the silo, from the machine shed, from a pole beside a barbed-wire compound that enclosed the gas barrels, from the gable end of the Woods house. Guy wondered how they slept. He squinted away. When he had passed into dark fields again he saw across the prairie one mile, two miles, other farms similarly illuminated. The lights were like giant fireflies on the land.

Suddenly Guy swerved the Mercedes. Along the road people were running, dark shadows moving in the ditch. In his periphery he saw a pickup, still upright, sideways in the ditch.

Accident. He braked hard. He began to back up. But suddenly the truck, a newer Ford with a tall wooden rack in back, roared alive. It lurched onto the highway and sped lightless down the road.

Guy stopped and stared. About to drive on, in the red wash of his brake lights he saw the glint and curl of fresh-cut barbed wire. Something in the ditch. He swung the Mercedes' lights around, then walked forward between its beams.

A Hereford cow, brown with a white mask, lay on the frozen grass and snow. A tall arrow rose from its chest. Blood bubbled from the Hereford's nose and ran into an open eye, which did not blink.

Guy touched the arrow. He put his foot on the Hereford's chest and pulled it free. A long aluminum shaft. A four-point broadhead half the size of Guy's hand. He guessed it was shot by some kind of mechanical crossbow.

He stood up and looked around. Rustlers. So who was rustling? Whoever it was knew cattle. The Hereford looked to be a younger steer not far from market weight. He looked down the highway after the truck. He would recognize that truck when he saw it again.

He drove back to Woods's farm and pounded on the door. In a minute a light came on upstairs and in another minute Herbert Woods appeared at the front door dressed in his long underwear and holding a pistol straight down. Guy explained. Woods listened without expression. Then he nodded and put the pistol on the sill above the door. He closed the door and soon reappeared dressed in coveralls, boots, and cap. He carried a long, thin skinning knife. In the yard Woods swung the knife at the darkness beyond the farm. The blade glinted in the glare of the vapor lamps. Between clenched jaws he said, "Fucking Indians."

Guy helped Woods roll the Hereford into the front-end bucket of the tractor's loader.

"Get him back to the yard, me and the boy can skin him. We'll eat this one instead of the goddamn Indians." He flopped the Hereford's head over the side and cut its throat. Guy stepped back from the fall of blood. Woods wiped the knife blade on his pants leg, then squinted up at Guy. He glanced at the Mercedes, then back to Guy. "That white hair. I should know you."

"Guy Pehrsson."

141

"Sure. Helmer's boy."

"Helmer's my grandfather. Martin is my father."

"Oh."

Woods fell silent for a moment. Nobody ever knew what to say about Martin Pehrsson.

"So how is Helmer these days? Haven't seen him in years."

"I'm not sure. I haven't seen him for some time. Just on my way up there now."

Woods stared at Guy. Behind him the other Herefords in the pasture sniffed at the cut wires. They shied at the smell of blood and blew steam in the air.

"You don't live around here then?" Woods asked.

Guy shook his head.

"Probably better. Things here have gone to hell for a lot of people."

Guy was silent. Behind Woods the largest Hereford stepped cautiously in the gap of the severed wires.

"Well, I got fence to fix," Woods said without turning. "Best get at it."

Guy nodded and walked to the Mercedes.

"Be around here long?" Woods called.

Guy paused. "Not sure. Have to see." As he spoke he suddenly felt the great weight of the land all around him. Heard his voice the way it had sounded twelve years ago in the cab of the pickup of the farm woman from Idaho Falls. He suddenly understood that farmers spoke in short sentences or none at all because the land weighed down their voices. The land took away speech because it was always bigger than words to describe it. The land had no need for words.

Woods lunged, with a shout, at his cattle. The Herefords bolted back into the field. Their irregular white patches tumbled across the dark field like pillowcases blown from a clothesline at night, but then the cattle slowed and turned to stare again at the door in the fence.

Two miles farther and Guy turned the Mercedes onto gravel. One mile later, he was home.

Helmer's farm, too, was more brightly lighted. Before, one yellow bulb shone above the garage. Now two security lamps lit the yard. One of the lights hung high up on the side

142

of a new, blue, vacuum-sealed silo. Top-of-the-line silo. Guy wondered what it cost. Below the silo, beside the barn, was a new John Deere tractor, a four-wheel-drive. But the tractor tilted sideways from two flat tires, and did not appear to have been driven for a long time.

Other than the new silo and tractor, all else was the same. In the far corner of the square farmstead stood the white dairy barn. Next to the barn were the two galvanized grain bins, two-thousand-bushel canisters. Beside the metal grain bins was the small wooden granary and its tiny wooden doors that had been built around Helmer's scoop shovel. Farther left, moving toward the road, was the long machine shed and shop. Then, closest to the road, were the houses.

Helmer's house was gray and weathered. It seemed smaller, but that was because the spruce trees beside had reached out to nearly touch its foundation. Eighty steps southeast was Guy's parents' house. In the summer, when the sun set far to the northwest, the pointed shadow of Helmer's roof crept at sundown across the lawn toward Guy's house. Its dull point walked its way up the front steps. And for two or three days each summer, when the door of Guy's house was open, as it had to be from the heat, the shadow cut squarely through the living room. Guy did not remember if his mother stayed home those days or not.

Tonight both houses were dark. Guy let the Mercedes coast up to the oak tree. He killed the engine and got out. A tatter of his old swing rope hung down and disappeared from sight in the black branches above. Guy tugged on the rope. It broke and coiled down over his arm. He felt the rope, then let it drop.

The front door of his house was unlocked. He eased inside the porch, then into the kitchen. His father's snore growled from the bedroom. Guy walked to the bedroom door. He could not see his parents, only lumpy shadows. He quietly shut their door, then turned to the refrigerator.

The refrigerator bulb threw light on two oranges, bearded green with mold. A half can of Spam, its lid torn open by a knife or a pliers. A half bag of store bread, it, too, dusty with mold. And three twelve packs of Hamm's.

No chicken in cold gravy. No dill pickles. No pickled beets. No foil-wrapped turkey slices. No jar of milk, no smaller pint of cream.

In the metal vegetable drawer he found four apples shrunken to the size of plums. He leaned farther into the refrigerator—but then behind him came the metallic hiccup of a rifle shell sliding into its chamber. He slowly backed away from the refrigerator and turned.

Martin, naked, gaunt, his pubic hair steel-gray and chest hair now entirely white, lowered the .30-.30. "Lucky you got blond hair, boy," he said. He turned back to the bedroom.

Guy flipped on the light. The lime-green linoleum. The bits of straw on the rug by the door. Martin's boots. The white enamel range. The varnished pine table—it was all the same.

But no plants. No geraniums wintering in the corner away from the light. No ivy hanging in front of the east window. No furry-leaved violets carpeting a card table by the west livingroom window.

And no small, oak, claw-footed writing desk, the one Madeline had brought from Canada when she married Martin. No bookcase. No books. No best of Robert Browning or Whitman or Frost. Not even a Sears catalog.

Guy stepped to the bedroom door. Martin sat on the bed buttoning his shirt.

"Where's mother?" Guy said, keeping his voice steady.

Martin buttoned his cuffs, ran his hand through his hair.

"She don't live here no more," he finally said.

Guy waited.

"Oh, sometimes she shows up here. Washes some clothes. Cooks a meal for me. Then she goes again."

"Where?"

"Where?" Martin repeated. He turned. Green half-moons held up his eyes. His nose, long like Guy's, was shot through with tiny red veins. His teeth were stained brown from tobacco. "With the Indians, that's where."

Martin walked past Guy to the kitchen. Thinner and more stooped, he had shrunken. His eyes barely came up to Guy's chin. From the cupboard he pulled a jar of Sanka, poured some into a cup, and filled it with warm tap water. He reached into the cupboard again and topped off the Sanka with a long gurgle of Jack Daniel's.

"How long has she been gone?"

Martin took a long drink. "On and off now for two years."

144

"Her letters. She never said."

"And I doubt that you asked, now, either, did you?" Martin said quickly, glaring over his cup at Guy. "I don't remember you giving us the time of day after you walked away from this place."

"I was eighteen. There was no room for me here, you know that."

"You could have waited."

"How long? As long as you?"

Martin stared at Guy, then looked down. He pursed his lips and stared at the table.

Guy put away the Jack Daniel's. "It's too goddamn early for this. You better eat something."

"Not hungry."

Guy cut mold from the bread and made toast. He found a half jar of peanut butter and made sandwiches. "Eat," he said to his father.

Martin chewed slowly, still staring at a pine knot in the wood of the table. Finally he said, "Maybe running off is the thing to do. I shoulda done it twenty years ago. Say to hell with everything. The old man. His cows. Lyle Price and his goddamn bank." He looked up. "Just walk down the road. Shit," he said, turning to Guy, "I'm the only one in the house who hasn't tried it."

After the sandwiches, Martin went out for chores. It was blue, 5 A.M. Guy brought Kennedy into the house and fed him from a sack of California dog food. Then he lay on the couch and covered himself with a wool blanket. The blanket smelled of cows.

He lay looking about the near-empty living room. On the wall was the faint star pattern of a missing clock. The small china lamp with its rose-petal shade was gone too. He remembered Martin once holding the lamp high in the air, threatening to smash it. But the lamp was gone now . . . safe.

He dreamed of broken things. Dishes. All the dishes broken against the side of the house. Tiny spears . . . shards of pottery. Broken cups with their finger rings intact on the grass . . . odd hailstones from an angry sky. That night no mention of the broken dishes. Madeline gone. Martin

145

serving potatoes and gravy in great splashes on the bare pine table. Bread dams. Bread dams keeping the gravy from leaking away. Bread dams holding it all together.

He dreamed of hiding. Martin after him . . . but never catching him, not with all his secret places, forts, and houses. Could live for days sneaking milk from the bulk tank, carrots from the garden . . . but voices calling, calling. Safe, here, in the attic of the granary, the tunnels of straw. Playhouses. He had lots of playhouses . . . but then a new voice calling. Tom. Tom's voice. Tom on their side? Never . . . never . . . climbing into daylight for Tom's voice. Then Mother running toward him, arms out, catching him, falling to the ground, not letting go, holding on . . . but then Martin's face staring down like a thundercloud in blue sky, staring, staring, then suddenly gone . . . screen door slamming . . . slamming.

"Daylight in the swamp," Martin called. Cold air and the smell of fresh manure washed over Guy where he lay on the couch. He jerked awake. There was pink sunlight in the east window. Martin was in from chores. "Hurry," Martin said, checking his watch. "It's nearly eight o'clock. It's time to check on the old man."

Guy followed his father on the shallow, frozen path to Helmer's house. The house was in decline. On the roof, shingles were missing. Tar paper showed here and there like teeth gone from a mouth. A broken chimney brick clung to the lip of the eave; the first hard rain would bring it down. Underfoot, the porch steps sagged as if melted by heat. Or time. By the steps sat a rusted black '62 Galaxie.

"Day help," Martin said of the car. "She comes in every day for three hours in the morning. Gets him up, washes him, cooks some. Then I take over later on."

Guy was silent.

"I mean, hell," Martin said, "I've got forty cows and myself to feed."

Guy stepped into the kitchen, which smelled of old linoleum and fresh milk. A squat woman with blond hair tied in a pink kerchief stood with her back to them washing dishes and watching a little black and white TV on the counter. Two of her kids sat perched close to the TV. On the screen Wile E. Coyote was shrinking in size on a long fall into a canyon.

The woman turned. It was Mary Ann.

"Guy!" Her face had rounded with flesh that closed in about her eyes like a dough doll's. Her upper arms in their sleeveless blouse were as big as legs. But her grin was the same. She held out her dripping hands and Guy gave her a hug.

"Boys," she said to her kids. "Boys—this is Guy Pehrsson. I've told you about him," she said. But neither of the two would look away from the TV. "Kids," she said, and shrugged. Then she frowned, looked down at her apron and water-spotted blouse. "If I'd a known you was comin' . . ."

"You look great. As is. As always," Guy said.

She blushed briefly.

"So . . ." they both said at once.

"So what brings you back?" she asked.

Beyond her, in the living room, Guy could hear a whirring, clicking noise. "Helmer?" he said. She nodded and pointed through the doorway.

He stepped into the dim living room. His grandfather sat in an electric wheelchair with his back to Guy. His white hair, thick still, curled onto the collar of his dark wool shirt. His great back and shoulders dwarfed the chair.

Helmer sat before a table. His Bible was propped open and upright at eye level. The Bible was clamped on a metal rack. A cord ran from the rack to an electrical outlet below. As Guy watched, the rack whirred, and a part of it moved. A pencil-sized metal arm snaked out. At the end of the arm a rubber roller wheeled across the page. Then a thinner metal finger dropped down, swung left, and turned the page.

"Mary Ann plugs him in mornings, I unplug him at night," Martin said. Then, louder, he called, "Dad, visitor."

Helmer's head twitched. Batteries beneath him whirred and his chair slowly swung around. His right eye widened and drew light from the dim windows.

"Guy-boy—you're home." Helmer's words came out drawled but clear. They came from the right side of his mouth even as the left side tried to hold them back. His right hand rose from his lap. Guy took it. Though softened from disuse, Helmer's fingers were still thick and strong— so strong Guy could not pull away.

"Guy—you've come home."

"For a while," Guy began. But as he spoke the page turner buzzed and clicked through his words. Helmer dropped Guy's hand and wheeled around to face the Bible again. After a long minute he swung back.

"Trouble here, Guy. With the farm. With your parents. Your father is weak."

Martin did not blink.

"Your mother . . ." Helmer fell silent. Behind him the page turner clicked again, but this time he did not turn around. "Your mother," he finally said, his voice slowing to a rumble, "she should be stoned."

Chapter Seventeen

Trouble.

Madeline had left Martin and now lived with an Indian man.

Martin, a week after Helmer's stroke, had appointed himself legal guardian of Helmer and, by extension, of the farm purse. Within two weeks he had bought an electric barn cleaner, a pipeline milker, a new tractor, a vacuum-sealed, self-loading silo. The farm was now a hundred thousand dollars in debt to Lyle Price's State Bank, a year behind in payments, and Price wanted title to the farm—within sixty days.

Helmer spent his days poring over crime and punishment in the Old Testament, preparing himself for the apocalypse.

And Mary Ann's Galaxie wouldn't start.

First things first. At noon Guy drove Mary Ann and her kids and her TV home. Home for Mary Ann was Jewell Hartmeir's battered pink and purple wheel house. She had left Kurt Fenske and taken the four children. Now she cared for them and for her father, Jewell, who had eventually lost both legs just above the knees from the tractor accident. He stood to lose more if he didn't keep his stumps clean, which was now Mary Ann's job. Her brothers were all gone. Bub dead, Billy killed near Khe Sanh, Chuck and Bob sharecropping in Georgia.

All this Mary Ann told Guy in one mile of gravel road as she ran her hands over the leather seats, the walnut console of the Mercedes.

"So what about you?" she asked, smiling.

"A long story," Guy said, smiling back.

"Hey, Ma—tell him to speed up, we're gonna miss *Masters of the Universe!*" one of the boys said.

"Dry up," Mary Ann said automatically. She waited for Guy's reply.

"I'll be around for a while. I'll tell you everything," Guy said as he pulled into the Hartmeir yard. Beside the pink and purple trailer was a shiny, white TV dish antenna.

"What's your wife like?" Mary Ann said suddenly as he stopped the car. "That's one thing I always wondered about. What Guy's wife would be like."

"I'm not married," Guy said.

"Really?" she said. She made no move to get out. Color came into her cheeks. Then she looked down for the door handle. "Well . . . thanks for the lift."

"I'll see you, we'll talk," Guy said, and smiled.

She got out, then walked beside his car as he backed up. "First time I ever rode in a foreign car," she said.

"Anytime," Guy said. He turned toward the road.

"Come up and watch TV some night," she called as he pulled away. "We get two hundred channels."

He stopped at the Hartmeir driveway and looked across the reservation. Low, gray clouds moved quickly across the flat land. The sun dumped light onto the frozen fields, then pulled it back. Guy turned right and slowly began to drive. He wondered where his mother was.

White Earth Reservation was broad and generally square, thirty miles or more to a side. Its boundaries held about a hundred square miles, or over 600,000 acres. Most of the reservation land was owned by whites like his family. It was the timber that had drawn whites onto the reservation. When the timber was cut down, the open land, not rich but flat and rockless, brought farmers. Most of the white families on White Earth were now second- and third-generation farmers. Their land formed a fenceless, geographical corral about the hilly pine and lake country at the center of White Earth. There the Indians lived on the land that could not be farmed. The main village was No Medicine Town.

As Guy drove, a battered red Pontiac came toward him. He gave it plenty of room. At the moment before their eclipse, the Pontiac swerved toward him. But Guy held his ground. He had grown up with this game. The Pontiac cut back into its own lane. In the car was a crush of young Indians who gave him various obscene high signs.

He kept driving. He thought of Madeline.

Two miles north of the Hartmeir place he let the Mercedes coast to a stop. Across the road, on the next quarter section, was an irrigation rig. That was new here. He stepped from the car and crossed the ditch filled with black topsoil blown from the field. The northwest winds. Helmer permitted no fall plowing on his land. His ditches remained empty, and in the spring ran water.

Guy walked underneath the irrigator pipe. Bright aluminum and leg-thick, the pipe stood higher overhead than he could reach. Supported by aluminum stilts on rubber wheels, the pipe stretched back to the center of the field to its pivot, the deep well.

As his eyes followed the irrigator's pipe, far across the field he saw a brown sedan moving slowly on the next mile's road. He watched its progress for a moment, then looked closer at the irrigator. Lodged in the rubber tread of a big tire were a dozen small potatoes.

Guy kicked one free. He held the frozen potato in his palm. They were new here. Here and there in the frozen furrows he could see potato vines. When he stood the brown sedan turned on the road that would bring it past the Mercedes, so he walked back to his car and drove on. At the next corner he looked down the field and saw another and another irrigator. They looked like giant praying mantises walking the fields.

Suddenly the brown sedan, with a red light flashing, was close behind.

Guy pulled over and looked in the rearview mirror. Backward letters read, "Deputy Sheriff, Becker County." The deputy, in mirrored sunglasses and a brown fur hat

151

with a gold star on it, walked forward. Guy turned to get out and found himself staring into the black eye of a pistol barrel.

"Out and spread," the deputy said.

Guy eased open his door and got out.

"I'll be damned," the deputy said, "It's Pehrsson. Guy Pehrsson."

Guy stared down at the man's brass nameplate. Wicks. Bradley Wicks. Wicks had been two or three years ahead of Guy in high school.

"Brad." Guy nodded. They did not shake hands. Wicks holstered the pistol and took off his sunglasses. He had the same small gray eyes, the dark beard shadow. But his jaw. His nose. His cheekbones. There was something different about his face.

Guy glanced down at the pistol butt. "Pretty big stick you're carrying there," he said. The pistol was either a .44 or a .357 Magnum.

"Indians got thick skin," Wicks said, rapping the pistol butt with his knuckles. He grinned. He had new, perfectly straight teeth. Suddenly Guy understood that Wicks must have suffered some great injury, that his face had been rebuilt. "Joke, right?" Wicks added.

"Right," Guy said.

"So what are you doing around these parts?" Wicks asked, his grin thinning.

"Visiting," Guy answered, turning his head south toward Helmer's farm.

"Got no problem with that," Wicks said. "I was just patrolling and saw someone out by that irrigator, so I pulled you over. Them irrigators ain't cheap. Seventy-five grand, minimum. The owners like to protect their investment."

"Owners?" Guy said. This land belonged to old Hank Schroeder.

"Losano brothers. They own most of these fields with the irrigators. Or if they don't now, they soon will. That is, unless the Indians get them."

"Losano brothers?"

"From out West. Idaho and California. They grew spuds out there, but that land is fucked now, they say. Too many potatoes, too much chemicals for too many years in a row. That adds up to scabby spuds. So the Losano boys moved into here. Flat land, good drainage, high water table, low taxes. They say potatoes grown here make Idaho spuds look like rabbit turds."

Guy looked across the field.

"Big money in potatoes," Wicks continued. "You take one potato, slice it up, and suddenly you got ten or twenty where you had one before. Like magic," Wicks said. "Get it? French fries."

Guy nodded. "Where's Hank Schroeder?" he said suddenly.

"Easy Street. Lives in Detroit Lakes. Got an apartment, there and a pocketful of money from the Losano boys. Sleeps late in the morning and eats out every night, they say. Best deal these old-timers could make."

Guy looked beyond Wicks to the faraway grove and buildings of his grandfather's farm.

The sun broke through and Wicks put on his glasses. He turned his gaze to Guy's Mercedes. "Fancy car. California plates." He looked back to Guy. "You wouldn't be carrying any drugs in that car, now, would you?"

"Drugs?" Guy said. "Why? You need some?"

Wicks stared.

"Joke," Guy said.

Suddenly Wicks grinned. "Joke, right," he said. He turned back to his car. As Guy opened the door to the Mercedes, Wicks called out, "Be around here long?"

"Hard to say. Awhile anyway."

Wicks nodded. "I ride herd on this side of White Earth. Some night I'll come by and you can ride posse with me. Cowboys and Indians. Gets wild some nights, so I don't mind the company."

"All right," Guy said. "But I'm no cowboy."

Wicks grinned his lopsided grin. "Up on the reservation these days you got to be one or the other. Ain't no riding the fence."

After Wick's patrol car receded in his mirror, Guy stopped and dug under the seat of the Mercedes for the thimble-sized brown bottle. His freeway No-Doz. There was one toot left, but he threw the little bottle, unopened, far into Hank Schroeder's field.

* * *

153

He drove on. The flat farmland began to rise and sink. Scrub oak and jack pine grew on the hills too steep to farm. In the draws and ravines were hazel brush and aspen. Soon he began to pass Indian houses. Often in the same yard were three types of Indian homes. They represented the three main periods of Indian housing.

Farthest from the road, deep in the yard, often overgrown by brush and jack pines, was the log house. Its thick gray logs and narrow white lines of mortar formed a weathered, flag-striped exterior. On the roof, black paper flapped in the breeze. Where the paper had torn away, the wide sheathing boards were exposed. Where the sheathing boards had rotted through, Guy could see sagged and buckling beams.

The second type of house, usually only a few steps kitty-corner from the first, was the tar-paper shack. Lower, with a flatter roofline, the tar-paper shack's exterior was black tar paper held in place with vertical slats of pine. Some of the tar-paper shacks were sided with tan, fake-brick asphalt siding. The windows of the smaller shacks were usually larger but often fewer than the windows of the log house.

Closest to the road was the third type, the government prefab. These houses had come to White Earth in the early sixties. They came ten houses to a semitrailer load. Carpenters from somewhere other than the reservation pounded them together, one house per day. The carpenters were supervised by crew-cut men driving beige government sedans. These men determined that the prefab houses should sit perched on four-foot concrete foundations.

"Expecting high water?" Martin had asked them. "Mississippi River's only sixty miles off."

Before leaving the reservation, the government carpenters painted the prefab houses bright pink, lemon yellow, sky blue. Kids, afterward called them rainbow houses.

Guy remembered the rainbow houses burning. The Indians took several years to move into the rainbow houses. By then many of the houses were stripped of copper pipe and sinks and toilets, then burned.

Now, in 1984, the pastel sides of the rainbow houses were battered and smudged by children's play. Broken windows were cardboarded over. Screen doors, their mesh ripped away, hung askew. Their low-pitched roofs sagged; locals said the prefab houses had been destined for Indonesia, but at the last minute were diverted to northern Minnesota. Guy believed it. Now if smoke rose from the rainbow-house chimneys, others showed no fire. In one yard, beside a particularly battered lemon-yellow house, smoke rose again from the tar-paper shack.

No matter what number or configuration of houses, Indian yards held more cars than buildings. Guy passed a yard with four and a half '72 Chevy Vegas. The cars were parked in order of repair. Closest to the house, parked in its own tracks, was a blue Vega with two yellow doors. Left of the blue Vega was a yellow Vega with two doors missing. Beside the yellow Vega sat a black one; its front end tilted up from a missing engine. The fourth Vega, white but mostly rust, lay overturned, stripped of its drive shaft and transmission. The half-Vega consisted of a vertical front fender and grill, as if the remainder of the car were below grade.

Guy thought of his '57 Chevy. If the Indian had a spare car, so did he.

Deeper into the reservation, the Indian yards contained fewer cars and better houses. The rainbow houses had been repainted, this time in browns and greens. In place of wrecked cars were outlines of garden plots. Farther back in one yard, the brush had been cut away from the old log house and its roofline was sharp and reshingled. In another yard, in a small clearing beside the log house, were two low grave houses. They, too, were reroofed and repainted white. Plastic, purple flowers bloomed beside them in the snow. Waist-high at their roofline, coffin-long, the small houses covered graves. The little spirit houses had been a common sight when Guy was growing up. But they were rotting even then. By the time Guy finished high school, trees and vandals had pushed most of the little houses onto the ground.

Guy kept driving. He let the Mercedes turn where it wished, any road. By memory or maybe by ruts in the frozen road, he found himself driving along No Medicine Lake Road toward Doc's Tavern.

Doc's lay at the south toe of No Medicine Lake. The

tavern stood on the lake side of the road, which separated the flat, gray ice of the lake from a long slope of birch trees on the inland side. Through the birches Doc's beer lights blinked pale yellow and blue. It was only late afternoon, but Doc's parking lot was already half full of farm pickups and dented Indian cars. It was, after all, only a few hours until Saturday night.

Guy had spent more than a few Saturday nights at Doc's, most of them after Tom left. Back then the three-piece bands played loud Creedence Clearwater, Johnny Cash, Waylon Jennings. People danced: Indians, whites. Often they danced together. Back then Doc's was like a great blender. Everybody danced, swirling together in a thudding haze of cigarette smoke and beer lights and bass guitar. At closing time, Indians and whites reconstituted themselves and went their separate ways. In the parking lot there was often a fight—a sudden lunging and flailing of fists. Sometimes the fighters were Indians against whites. But most often the fights were about men and women too drunk to care with whom they went home, fights over whiskey bottles and stolen car batteries. If the fight persisted, or drew in bystanders, Doc intervened—from the rear kitchen window came the sudden orange flash and roar of his twelve-gauge. By the time his lead shot whistled overhead, reached its apogee somewhere over No Medicine Lake, spattered down on the water, and wafted its way to the bottom muck, the fighters had scrambled into their cars and the parking lot emptied fast.

And Guy had come to Doc's years before that, when Helmer used to bring him. In the summertime, in July and August, his grandfather often brought Martin and him here. They came during oat harvest, in the evenings after the combines were shut down. They came on the hottest, driest days of the summer. The oat dust had reddened their eyes and ran black at their corners like cheap mascara on tears. That same dust had worked its way through their shirts, and the barbed oat hulls found their way around buttoned cuffs and collars, and boated on tiny rivers of sweat down onto their chests and bellies and into their crotches. They itched all over. But the worst itch was for something cold to drink.

On those days Helmer always bought six Orange Crush

156

soda pops. Two apiece. Guy always drank his so fast that pinwheels popped behind his eyes and his nose hurt. Martin drank his only a little slower. Helmer's pop always lasted the longest.

Once, on a day when the thermometer read 101 degrees, the coolest it had been for three days, Helmer bought four orange pops and a tall draft Hamm's beer. Martin and Guy stared. Helmer did not drink beer, never touched alcohol. People down the bar turned to stare. Doc glanced at Martin and Guy, then slid the frosted mug in front of Helmer. Helmer's big Adam's apple moved the dusty skin of his throat. He leaned forward toward the beer. The head of foam rose up and hung bubbling over the rim of the glass. Slowly Helmer brought his hands toward the mug until he gripped the cold glass. Guy forgot to drink his own pop.

Helmer tried to lift the mug; the long, brown muscles puffed up his arms. But the mug was frozen to the counter. Either frozen to the counter or glued. Either glued or else the beer mug was not glass at all but iron. The mug was made of iron and the pine-tree bar was not pine at all but rather a great magnet. Or, if the beer mug was not frozen or glued or magnetized, it was made of something like osmium or some asteroid material so heavy that no man, not even his grandfather, could lift it.

Then, instead of allowing itself to be lifted, the beer mug began to draw Helmer's mouth down to it. It was now the magnet, and his grandfather's lips, iron. Helmer's mouth opened. His lips quivered as they touched foam. Suddenly the mug flew from his hands and shattered against the wall behind the bar. Down the stools, someone clapped slowly. But Helmer didn't look around. He paid for the pop, for the beer and the mug, then drove home and drank a gallon of cold well water.

But now Guy was thirty and the old tavern door squeaked. In a haze of cigarette smoke, forty or more faces turned to look. Half brown faces. Half white. They were easy to count because the brown faces took the right side of the bar, the white faces the left. Between them was a five-stool empty space. Guy took a seat in no-man's-land.

At least the bar was the same, a long white-pine log split

exactly in half lengthwise, planed smooth, and then varnished dark brown. Above the smoky mirrors still hung the black-velvet painting of John Kennedy and Abraham Lincoln. Beside the velvet presidents, the tattered moose head still wore its propeller beanie. And in a moment, canted steeply to the left from a bad back, a bar towel over his shoulder and his gray eyes still twitching from the smoke, there was Doc.

"Pehrsson. Guy. Long time."

"Hello, Doc." They shook hands.

"What'll it be? On me."

Guy smiled. "Hamm's and a schnapps."

Doc talked as he poured. "Heard you're out in California. Struck it rich, they say."

Guy took a long drink of the musty-tasting Hamm's, then leaned forward and whispered, "Gold, Doc, nuggets the size of oranges. Just reach down and fill your pockets. But don't tell anybody. This place would fold."

Doc did not smile. "Let her fold. Then I could get out of here." He wiped an imaginary spill. "Sometimes I think I ought to drop a cigarette in the back room, lock up, and go home. Come back the next morning and collect the insurance money. I've got a sister out West, you know. Sacramento."

Guy knew. But he remembered Modesto.

"Or maybe it's San Francisco. Anyway, she works on the line at Lockheed. Makes twelve dollars an hour and has two orange trees in her backyard. She said once I could get on at Lockheed. Now would be the time to go. You don't know what the hell is going to happen around here. Another year and this place could be called the Chippewa Firewater Inn."

"What do you mean?" Guy said. Wicks. If the Indians don't get it back, he'd said.

"You serious?" Doc said. "You don't know?"

Guy sipped the schnapps and waited.

Doc looked down the bar to the Indians, then back. He lowered his voice. "This place. The resorts. The farms, and that includes your granddad's place—the Indians want them. The Indians say any land owned by whites within the boundaries of the reservation belongs to them. They say they got cheated out of the land. They say they want it back. They're digging back into the old treaties, the old deeds, to

158

prove it. The whole business stinks," Doc said, wiping the bar again.

Guy finished the schnapps. He laughed once.

"What's funny about that?" Doc said.

Guy shook his head. "Tell me some good news, Doc. Just one piece of good news."

Doc squinted across the bar toward the window. He rubbed his chin. "Ain't any," he finally said.

"Some information, then," Guy said. "My mother. And Tom LittleWolf. Where are they?"

Doc started to speak, then fell silent as he looked over Guy's shoulder. At that moment someone clapped Guy hard on the back and spilled his beer. "Well, if it ain't Guy Pehrsson, basketball star of yesteryear."

Guy turned. It was Kurt Fenske.

Beefy in high school, now Fenske was thicker still. He had put on a thick coating of meat from his eyes down. His black beard grew from just below his eyes all the way down his throat, where it disappeared into a sweat-stained red and black wool shirt.

"Hello, Kurt," Guy said.

"Hello, Kurt'? Is that all you can say to an old friend? A teammate, for Christ's sakes? We went to the same school, remember?"

"I remember," Guy said evenly. He remembered that Fenske was trouble back then, and he was trouble now.

"I mean, aren't you supposed to say something like, 'Kurt, old buddy, how's the wife?' After all, I mean, you and Mary Ann and Tom LittleWolf. It's not like you didn't know each other, if you know what I mean."

Guy drained the last swallow of Hamm's. "Kurt, old buddy, how's the wife?" he said slowly.

"That cunt? She walked. Hit the road. Just like your mother walked out on your old man."

Guy felt his breath leave him.

Fenske gestured at the barroom around them. "So I come here. Sometimes I run into her. That's logical, ain't it? A woman runs off, you go to the nearest place where there's other men. That's why you're here, right? You're looking for your mother?"

"Go easy, Kurt, you've had plenty—" Doc said.

"But if you're looking for your mother, you're sitting in

159

the wrong location," Fenske continued. He pointed down the bar toward the Indian section. "Brown-town, that's where she'd be."

So here it came. The oldest male demon of all, the fight.

"Down with the Indians or maybe out in the parking lot. Check the back seats, if you know what I mean."

Guy swung on his bar stool and kicked Fenske in the crotch. Fenske grunted and went down, but caught Guy a glancing blow on the mouth as he fell. Guy's lips went numb. On the floor, Fenske held his crotch and tried to get up. Guy kicked him once more, hard, in the face. Fenske's right cheek split beneath Guy's boot, and blood leaped in his eye. Fenske swore and flailed.

"Guy—that's enough!" Doc was shouting. "He's finished. You better go!"

Down the bar, the whites stared and the Indians grinned. Fenske crawled to his hands and knees.

"Doc," Guy said. His heart pounded in his ears. "What about my mother?"

Doc looked down at Fenske. "She got a little wild . . . drank for a while. Used to see her in here a lot. She was kind of crazy. I tried to hold her back, but what can you do? She's an adult, right? She's better now, I guess. Lives up in No Medicine."

"Where in No Medicine?"

"North of town."

Fenske staggered to his feet. Doc pushed Guy toward the door. "Get—and don't worry about finding your mother." He jerked his head toward the Indians. "After today she'll know you're here."

Outside, Guy spit red on the snow.

Chapter Eighteen

Guy slept that night on his father's couch that smelled of cows. Toward morning he began to dream. No pictures. No colors. Only a gray fog. But something in the fog. Something . . . the promise of weight or force. Something or someone.

He jerked awake and sat up. Silhouetted against the pink light of an east kitchen window, in a chair beside the couch, was someone. A woman. Madeline. Mother.

Guy reached for her. In his arms she was thin and hard and she smelled like fresh air and wool and leather and soap.

"How long have you . . ." he began.

"A half hour. Since your father went out for chores."

"I didn't hear you come in," Guy mumbled.

"Neither did he."

Guy let her go and leaned forward to look through the window into the yard. There was no car. "How did you get here?"

"Walked."

Guy shook the last gray webbing of sleep from his head. He rubbed his eyes and stared at his mother.

"Your lip, what happened?" she asked.

Guy felt it. His top lip felt like a dried bread crust.

"Minor accident at Doc's," he said. He stared at Madeline. Her eyes. Only her eyes were the same, as round and deep brown as walnuts. The rest of her was somebody else. Her hair was very long and was split into even braids. The roundness, the softness in her face was gone. Now her cheekbones were sharp and reddened, chapped by sun and wind. Around her neck hung a leather thong strung with three beads of turquoise. She wore a gray, coarse wool sweater under which her small breasts lay free. A buckskin jacket sat folded on the chair. Her faded blue jeans ended at battered Adidas.

No short-curled hair.

No Sears dress.

No leather shoes.

No wristwatch.

No pale lipstick.

No makeup at all.

"Walked," Guy said suddenly. "From where?"

"From No Medicine Town. I stay there," she said, looking down briefly.

Guy looked out the west window toward the far-off timber. His mother had walked fifteen miles and only now was the sun fully up.

"I started early," she said, as always, a half step along the path of his thoughts. "If you walk fast, it doesn't take long."

"Where's the Cutlass?"

"Your father sold it. About five years ago. Said he had a tractor payment to make."

Goddamn him.

"You should have a car," Guy muttered, standing and pulling on his jeans. "You shouldn't be out walking around in the middle of the night." He would buy her a car. They would go together this morning to Detroit Lakes and he would buy her a car.

"I don't want a car," she said. "I've gotten quite used to living without one. If I had a car, then I'd have to worry about insurance, mechanics, all the rest. Without a car, things are simple."

Guy stared down at her.

"I know," she said. "I'm a different person than when you left. But you probably heard that." She looked down again.

162

"Sort of," Guy said. He did not mention Helmer's letter or Doc's explanation.

"Sometimes I feel like I should apologize for changing—but I won't," she said before he could speak. She began to say more but suddenly Martin's boots stamped on the porch. For an instant his mother's eyes widened with fright. Then she said rapidly, "Guy, don't worry about me. And don't stay. There's nothing here for you anymore. You've got your own life, go back to it. Don't think about us. Forget all this . . ." She waved her hands at the living room, at the farm beyond.

Martin came into the kitchen doorway. He stopped to stare. "Well, well, a family reunion."

"Just visiting," Madeline said softly. She put on her jacket.

"Buckskin, now," Martin said, staring at her jacket. "You look more and more like an Indian every time I see you."

Guy was standing halfway between his parents. "I'll cook some eggs," he said. "Make some coffee."

"No eggs 'cause there's no chickens," Martin said. "Not hungry anyway." He shrugged off his jacket and threw it in the corner.

"I better go," Madeline murmured to Guy. As she passed she stopped to pick up Martin's jacket. She began to hang it on the hook, then looked at a rip on the elbow. She folded the jacket over her arm.

"Where the hell you taking my jacket?" Martin shouted. "Your Indian buck lose his?"

"The elbow's gone," she said softly. "I'll mend it. And wash it."

Martin stared. A tic worked his right cheek like a worm just beneath the surface of the skin trying to break through.

Guy walked his mother into the yard. Behind them in the house, something made of glass shattered.

"Just like the old days," Guy said, then wished he hadn't.

His mother swallowed but kept walking. "Your father and I were in love once," she said quietly. "For a couple of years, anyway. When you're in love, love doesn't let you think about anything except itself. So we were mostly happy, then. But slowly we fell out of love. Other things crept in, came between us. Your grandfather. The cows. Never having

163

anyone to wake up with because your father was always gone for chores at five-thirty every morning of the year. Canning with your grandmother. The garden. Other things. Small, dumb things. But they all were like grains of sand in a shoe. For a while, maybe a long while, you can keep walking. The sand doesn't matter. But at some point you start to limp. Then after a while you can't walk another step. You've got to stop and empty it out."

She stopped walking. "That's what I did, I suppose. I knew I had stopped moving. So when I stopped was a good time, I thought, to empty out of my life some things that weren't working. I started throwing away things. And kept throwing and throwing. Soon there wasn't much left. That's when I got moving again."

She looked back over the farmyard, then back to Guy. The harsh light of the early sun lit her face, showed the mesh of wrinkles around her eyes and mouth, showed the gray in her hair. Guy realized she was nearly sixty years old. He reached for her. In reaching he felt the old blood try to pull back his arms, try to stop his hands from reaching, from pulling her close.

The old blood. In one instant he understood it. The old blood was a river from the red lake of the heart that flowed into the past. The river started wide in the present; his father, grandfather, and himself, three generations of living men, formed a wide breach in time. Beyond Helmer, into the fourth generation and further back, the river narrowed. Beyond Helmer were shadowy photographs of big men and long-skirted women beside sagged cabins. Beyond photographs were only images, memory. A tall man with blue eyes and great hands . . . a woman with red hair. But all of them were men and women who worked the land. If right now he spaded up a hole and put in his hand, in the cool earth he could feel them shifting, turning; hear them whispering to him; feel the pull of their fingers on his.

But right now the old blood was not so strong. It was not strong because he was older and because he had been away from the land for a long time. He had broken its hold. Now he controlled the river of his own heart.

In the sunlight in the open yard, he held his mother for a long time.

"Come," he said finally, steering her toward his car. "I'll drive you back."

But Madeline shook her head. She stopped him, then pushed him, gently, away. "No—I have to walk."

He watched her go. Her thin figure passed down the driveway. On the road, she walked without looking back. As she receded, the two brown braids on the light buckskin of her jacket gradually grew together, fused. At the half-mile corner she angled across the field. He watched her move steadily toward the green timber of the reservation, a tiny figure taking rapid steps across the land.

Chapter Nineteen

Monday morning. Thirty-one degrees, partly cloudy. Guy and Kennedy hauled a load of cattle feed into Flatwater for grinding. Martin had let the grain bin run dry. The cows bellowed and followed Guy with their heads as he passed their stanchions; he went to the grain room and kicked the bin. Only dust fell.

He pulled an orange wagon full of ear corn and oats behind Martin's pickup, the '64 Ford. Where the farm driveway met the road, Guy went into the ditch. There were some brakes but not enough. Luckily the wagon did not tip, and he was able to drive back into the road. There he drove slowly and watched the Ford's gauges as he headed to town.

The truck's oil gauge showed less than forty pounds of pressure. The water temperature needle rose fast and stayed high. The steering linkage was loose. The tires shuddered. The brakes grabbed metal on metal whenever he slowed. Rather than take the main highway, Guy turned onto the gravel of Chippewa Highway, a narrow, potholed road that wound its way generally parallel to the main highway, to Flatwater. It was called Chippewa Highway because it was the main route from White Earth to the liquor store in

166

Flatwater. If Indian cars, with their broken headlights and expired license plates, stayed off the main highway, the county sheriff and his deputies stayed off Chippewa Highway.

As did the road graders. Guy drove ten miles an hour on a surface so washboardy it chattered his teeth. Ten miles from town, he came around a bend and let the truck coast to a full stop. Ahead on the road was a woman beating a car.

Against a backdrop of evergreens, a woman in a gray coat was kicking a dusty yellow Chevy Vega. The woman was white, young, with short dark hair. Steam rose from beneath the Vega's hood. And if her car smoked, so did the woman; her breath puffed frosty steam with each kick. So far she had caved in the driver's door and was working her way back. Intent on her work, she did not notice Guy. He rolled down the window. He listened, then grinned. "Kennedy, cover those ears, you're too young for that kind of language." Kennedy yipped. The woman turned to stare.

Guy walked forward. "Trouble?" he asked.

The woman surveyed him up and down. Her cheeks were scarlet on white from the cold air and exertion. She was tall, six feet at least. Her coat was gray wool, a thin cashmere. She wore leather dress shoes, wool slacks, a wine-colored turtleneck. Her shiny brown hair was short on the sides, long on top, and hung forward in a diagonal slant across her forehead. Her teeth were straight, white, and expensive. The whole woman was expensive. She was the kind of woman Guy saw in magazines like *Vogue* and *Cosmopolitan*.

"This fucking car," she said, jerking her head at the Vega. "If I never see this broken-down bastard again, it'd be fine with me."

"I see," Guy said. He swallowed a grin. You did not grin at angry women. That much about women he understood. Rather, because he had on a pair of Martin's spotted green coveralls and a dusty feed cap, he nodded and spit. "Mind if I take a look?"

She looked him up and down again. "Why not? Every goddamn would-be mechanic from here to Fargo has looked at it, so why stop now?"

"Right," Guy said. He popped the hood. The water pump hung loose. Antifreeze dripped green where it had boiled

167

over. The valve cover rattled, its gasket broken. Oil had leaked down the side of the engine block and smelled like butter left burning in a frying pan.

First he checked the oil. The dipstick came up dry but for a dot of oil on its tip. At least three quarts low.

Next he checked the radiator; its cap blew off at his touch. He jerked backward, striking the back of his head on the hood latch. White milkweed pods floated and popped behind his eyes. He steadied himself against the fender.

"You okay?" the woman asked, making no move toward him.

"Fine," Guy muttered. He stared at her for a moment. She had clutched her coat around its neck and hunched her shoulders against the breeze that came down the road from the northwest. "You could sit in the truck if you like," he said.

"I'm fine," the woman said crossly, stamping her feet to stay warm.

Guy leaned back over the Vega's engine. With a finger and then with a twig, he fished the radiator for antifreeze. He found none. "How long did you drive it this way?" he asked. When he received no answer he looked up. The woman was opening the door to the pickup. He leaned back over the engine, wet a finger, and touched the side of the engine block. His finger sizzled for a moment. He cursed, jerked it away, and sucked on it. He guessed the engine was fried. Still, if he tightened the water pump the Vega might make it to Flatwater.

He returned to the pickup for tools. "Doesn't look good," he said, digging through Martin's toolbox.

"No kidding," the woman said. She looked up from the dashboard and its crushed Hamm's cans, grease seals, and bolts to the empty road ahead.

"So how long have you had this car?" Guy said.

"Me? Have this piece of shit? I rented it yesterday in Fargo. The last rental car in town, the man said. The bastard."

"Right," Guy said, backing away with ratchet and half-inch socket.

Back in the engine compartment, he fit the socket, turned the ratchet. In the first quarter turn he broke off the stud

168

that went into the engine block. Fucking aluminum. But no matter—three of the four studs would hold the pump. The next stud broke immediately.

He cursed. Now the water pump was finished. He leaned back to think. As he rested his wrench on the wheel well, electricity jerked through his arm all the way to his teeth. He stumbled back—his wrench had touched a broken wire from the battery—and hit his head again on the hood latch. This time he sat down hard on the dirt road. When he could see clearly, his first image was of the woman staring at him through the windshield of the pickup like she was on TV. She didn't move. He shook his head and got to his feet. He kicked the Vega in the grille. It shattered. Plastic. The whole goddamn car was aluminum and plastic and vinyl. Kennedy's dog shit was better made than this car.

He stalked back to the pickup and threw the wrench into the toolbox. "Any luggage?" he said.

"Yes," the woman said, "in the back seat. Why?"

Guy didn't answer her. He retrieved one medium-sized, Italian leather suitcase, plus a locking briefcase nearly as heavy, and put them in the pickup. Then he dug behind the seat and found Martin's dusty twelve-gauge shotgun.

"Oh God!" the woman said, shrinking away, feeling for the door handle.

"Relax," he said. In the glove box he found shells. Then he walked back to the Vega, found the gas line to the carburetor, jerked it loose. Gas spurted and ran down the sides of the engine. Then he walked halfway back to the pickup, turned, and fired three rounds into the Vega, the last through the gas tank.

He waited. Black smoke began to creep from the engine compartment. On the Vega's upraised yellow hood, paint began to bubble and creep; a black sun appeared.

Guy returned to the pickup and cased the gun. "Couldn't save it," he said, "sorry."

The woman still held her hands over her ears and stared open-mouthed at the Vega.

Guy started the pickup's engine and pulled past the car. The woman's head turned as they passed. Black smoke boiled inside the car. They had driven half a mile before she yelled, "Where are you taking me?"

"Nearest town. Flatwater." He rubbed his head.

"But . . . my car. What about my car? What am I going to say about my car?"

"This is the reservation."

"What do you mean?"

"Your car broke down. You got a ride into Flatwater. Somebody came along. It happens all the time." He rubbed his head again. There was a daddy longlegs crawling on his neck.

"Jesus," she murmured, turning to stare out her window. Then she looked back. Her eyes fell to his neck. "Jesus," she said, "you're bleeding."

"Silver, Cassandra Silver. My friends call me Cassy," she said, extending her hand over the table. Guy dumped the cattle feed at the mill, then went to the clinic for three stitches in the back of his head. Now he sat with her in a booth at the Red Caboose Cafe just across from the mill. His head ached.

"Miss Silver," he said. She wore no wedding ring, did not strike him as married. "Guy Pehrsson."

"Mr. Pehrsson."

They shook hands, one pump.

They sipped their coffee in silence. At length she said, "You . . . shoot and burn cars often?"

"Not that much. Just when it seems right," Guy said. He grimaced. His stitches hurt when he talked.

"Kind of like *The Dukes of Hazzard?*" she said. "This must be Duke country."

"I don't watch the show, sorry," Guy said.

Cassandra Silver stared at him a long moment, then looked about the cafe. Guy followed her eyes. Men in insulated coveralls and seed-corn caps sat at the counter eating plates of eggs and hash browns and catsup, drinking coffee, and smoking. Through the steamy picture window, across the street, was the feed mill, a cement-block building with a brown drift of oat dust across its metal roof. In front of the mill, below the loading dock, a farmer in the rear of a blue pickup was handing feeder pigs up to another man standing by a crate and a scale; he swung the pigs up by a leg; the second man caught them. To the left of the feed mill,

170

on the sidewalk, a black-coated Indian walked trembly-legged, as if he were on thin ice. Her eyes returned to the table next to theirs. A man in tattered orange deer-hunting coveralls was slamming the butt of a catsup bottle with his palm. Catsup spurted onto his eggs.

"Jesus," she murmured to herself, and went to buy cigarettes. Guy sipped his coffee. As Cassandra returned the man in the orange coveralls said to another man, "It's the Jews, you know. They're behind everything. Take this cholesterol business. It's a big Jewish conspiracy. All you read now, all you hear on TV—it's cholesterol. People shouldn't eat red meat. People shouldn't eat eggs, drink cream. That's all you hear, right?"

The second man drank coffee from his cup and listened.

"And that's all you hear because the Jews control the newspapers and the TV, plus the American Medical Association. I mean most doctors are Jews, right?" the first man said.

The other man nodded.

Cassandra's jaw slowly slacked.

"So when people hear this stuff day in, day out, they get scared," the first man said. "They think—shit!—red meat and eggs is plugging up my arteries. I gotta lower my cholesterol intake. So they stop eating meat and eggs and ice cream. Millions of people, they all stop, right?"

The other man nodded.

"Suddenly there's no demand for red meat, eggs, milk. No demand, prices fall. I mean, you can see that happening right now."

"You got that right," the other man said.

"No demand, farmers go out of business. No farmers, the value of the land drops to nothing. Bingo—then it happens. Suddenly the Jews are buying up all the farmland. I mean, every goddamn acre. Then when they got all the farmland under their control—along with the newspapers and the banks and the Federal Reserve Board—then bingo. It happens again. Suddenly we'll start to hear reports and see articles that say 'Hey! Sorry. We were wrong. Cholesterol? No problem with cholesterol! In fact, the more cholesterol you eat, the longer you'll live.'"

The second man nodded, as did two other men nearby.

"I mean, it's happening right now but nobody can see it," the first man said. "Nobody except the Jews, that is."

All the men who had listened drew on their cigarettes and took long drinks of coffee as they thought about that.

Cassandra slowly closed her mouth. She stared far away for a moment. "Maybe if I think of this as embassy work . . ." she murmured to herself.

"I'm here on business," Cassandra explained, tearing the cellophane on a pack of Virginia Slims. "I work for Senator Howard Stanbrook. Most of the time I stay in Washington, but occasionally I come out in the field. To put out fires, as they say in the business."

"So what's burning in Flatwater, Minnesota?" Guy asked.

"Howard—Senator Stanbrook—has been getting a lot of calls and letters from some particularly angry-sounding constituents who live on White Earth. They're worried about their land. The Indian land claims," she explained. "So Howard sent me out to take care of it."

"It?" Guy said.

"The legal stuff," she said. "That's what I do. I research things, reassure people that the law is on their side, that nothing bad is going to happen to them, fix things if I can, then leave." She lit a long, thin cigarette.

An expensive-magazine-woman attorney. In Flatwater.

"Then back to Washington," Guy said.

She nodded.

The waitress poured them more coffee, staring all the while at Cassandra Silver's hair, her clothes.

"So this fire in Flatwater," Guy said. "How long do you think it will take to put out?"

She shrugged. "Right now in Washington the cherry blossoms are starting. I'd like to be back when they're still in bloom."

Guy smiled at her.

"So what about you?" she asked abruptly. "Who are you?"

"Guy Pehrsson," he said.

"I remember your name," she said immediately. "I mean, who are you really?"

172

Guy drank coffee.

"See it my way," she said. "This seedily dressed fellow comes along in an even seedier truck that's pulling something cows eat. The man tries to fix my car, can't, so shoots and burns it. But in his truck he's got this perfectly dear little dachshund wearing what looks to be a gold-plated collar. He has a briefcase, inside which are a lot of papers about some business in California. Also in the briefcase are two very literary, hardcover novels, along with a copy of *Rose Grower's Monthly*, to which it appears he has a subscription."

"You always go through other people's briefcases?" Guy said. The bitch.

"Only when it seems right," Cassandra Silver replied.

They talked. He told her he grew up in Flatwater, tried farming briefly, but left. He did not tell her the circumstances of his leaving or about his family. He told her he now owned an electronics company in Palo Alto, but did not explain how he came to own it. He was back for a short visit.

Cassandra told him she had grown up in Boston and went to law school at Yale. She told him she liked law because it was a system like a jigsaw puzzle, whose pieces, if you studied them long enough, all fell into place. She told him she owned a condominium not far from M Street in Georgetown. Twice she mentioned a friend named Clark who worked for the Justice Department. She said she thought the solution to this White Earth land trouble was probably fairly simple; the Feds would have to pay off the Indians, which is what the Indians invariably wanted anyway. Then everybody would be happy.

As they talked Guy stared increasingly at her mouth, her long straight teeth, the shiny cut of her hair, the whorls of her ears, her long fingers and perfect nails. She looked better the more he looked. In fact, she was that rare type of woman who looked better and better the closer you got. Once she stopped talking to stare at him in return.

Separated by the table, by their coffee cups, Guy thought of an advertisement he had seen recently in some magazine, a cigarette ad. In it were a man and a woman, dressed up, at a party, and leaning toward each other from opposite sides of a gaming table. The woman's hands covered some cards. The man's hand was circled around a stack of black chips that he was thinking of moving. But in the moment of the photograph the man and the woman just stood there, eyes locked into each other's. It was the ad of the eighties. They were both waiting. Your move.

Before he left Flatwater with the ground feed, Guy found Cassandra Silver a room at the Lumberjack Hotel on Main Street. He also found her a rusted but mechanically sound '68 Chevy Impala. The Chevy had been abandoned at the Shell station because of an engine overhaul bill; the mechanic was glad to be rid of it.

"Thanks," Cassandra said, glancing at the hotel behind, at the Chevy parked in front. "I think."

They shook hands again, two pumps this time. She had strong fingers.

"So I'll be here, I guess," she said. "I have to spend some time in the courthouse looking through deeds and abstracts, that sort of thing."

"Good luck," Guy said. He turned away.

"So . . ." she said.

Guy stopped and waited. He guessed this was hard for her. Guessed that she had a difficult time being nice to most men.

"So if you're in town, stop by," she said. "You can tell me more about Flatwater, Minnesota. I'll buy you lunch at the Red Caboose."

"Maybe I'm married," Guy said.

Her jaw sharpened and her cheeks reddened with anger. "Maybe I don't give a damn," she said.

Guy stopped for gas on the way out of town. At the station he looked over a rack of souvenirs of Flatwater under a scratched glass counter. Teacup-sized birchbark tom-toms. Beaded necklaces. Rubber tomahawks. Brightly dyed chicken-feather head-dresses for kids, all made in Taiwan.

In the end he chose a postcard to send to Susan at Stanford. The picture on the card was an aerial view of

Flatwater in summer. The town looked white and clean. The river beside it was a shiny blue sleeping garter snake that had swallowed an egg. The fields around were square and green. From the great height you could make out occasional tiny tractors and cars. But no people.

Chapter Twenty

The following day Guy stayed on the farm and fixed things. In the barn he fixed a sparking light switch and its broken wire. He fixed two broken steps on the hayloft ladder. He called a tire service in Detroit Lakes to come and fix the tractor's tires, which had lost both air and fluid from two bullet holes. "Indians," Martin said.

In the shop he worked on Martin's pickup. He removed the wheels and hubs to check the brake shoes. The Ford was barefoot. Its curved brake pads were worn to their rivets, and the rivets had scored long circular gouges across the face of the brake drum the way glaciers drew hard stone across soft.

He checked his watch: 3:00 P.M. There was still time. He levered off the other hubs and put them in a box. Their soot blackened his hands and wrists, and he could see a fuzzy dark smudge down the side of his nose. He threw a blanket over the front seat of the Mercedes and drove fast to Flatwater.

At Ken's Machine Shop the machinist checked his watch and scowled, but fit the Ford's hubs onto the turning lathe. As the hubs began their slow turning, a carbide dressing point settled on the drums like a phonograph needle onto a record. Guy watched the sparks for a minute. Then his stomach began to rumble. He'd forgotten to eat lunch. He looked down at his dirty hands, his coveralls. No one at the Red Caboose would care.

At the Caboose afternoon coffee drinkers stood packed in the entryway drinking coffee from cups and saucers as if they were attending a stand-up cocktail party. The Red Caboose was a real caboose, long and narrow and always short on room, but today the Caboose was particularly crowded. Guy saw why. Taking up three full tables in the center of the cafe, only half visible behind tall stacks of large books, was Cassandra Silver.

Guy wove his way forward among the cups and saucers. Cassandra sat bent forward over the table. Beside her was a nearly full ashtray of half-smoked cigarettes, a nearly empty cup of coffee. She was wearing reading glasses, a red flannel shirt, the top two buttons open. She held the pink tip of her tongue between her teeth as she wrote rapidly on a yellow legal pad. Feeling Guy's presence beside her, she said, "No more coffee." Then she looked up and blinked.

"Mr. Pehrsson!"

"Miss Silver."

Her gaze traveled from his smudged face down his coveralls to his boots, then back up. He glanced briefly down her open shirt. He liked what he saw.

"I had no idea there were coal mines in Flatwater," she said.

Behind Guy, several men laughed.

"Beneath these clothes I'm really very clean," Guy said. The men laughed again, slightly louder this time. Cassandra's lips opened in a half smile. She leaned back from her writing and removed her glasses. Guy sat down.

Her eyes were red-rimmed, her forehead faintly shiny with oil. She rubbed her eyes and looked across the table. Guy followed her eyes across the big books, their tiny gold lettering on flaky leather bindings. "Deeds, Becker County," they all read. They started in 1869 and came to 1984. The covers of the later books were embossed plastic, like large credit cards.

Cassandra shook out another cigarette and lit it. She drew deeply, then looked around before she spoke. She lowered her voice. "Mr. Pehrsson, your family's farm wouldn't by any chance lie within the boundaries of the White Earth Reservation?"

Guy nodded yes.

"Too bad," she said.

That afternoon she explained as she drove. "There are, to put it mildly, some very odd transfers of land from Indians to whites. Most of these transactions took place between fifty and eighty years ago. But that doesn't make the holes in them any smaller. Then there are treaties." She drove her Chevy with one hand, smoked with the other while she looked across the reservation fields.

"So the Indians are onto something," Guy said.

"That's forgone by now," she said. "My job is to strike a compromise, make both sides, Indians and whites, feel like they came out ahead."

Guy looked out his window. The April fields were dirty white from the thin crust of snow that remained. The flat land stretched away and ended at the low, green hills of the inner reservation.

He wondered who Helmer had bought the farm from. There had been no mention of Indians. Guy had never seen a deed or title. But then he didn't really care, either. Helmer's land would pass to Martin. Martin would piss it or spend it away, as he was doing right now. And Guy didn't care. He was through with the land. Of that he was very sure.

Cassandra talked more about the disputed land, the opposing claims, the title troubles. Clouded title, she called it. Guy listened but did not comment.

"This bores you?" she said suddenly, turning to look at him.

"I'm listening."

"You sure as hell don't seem very interested, considering your family's land is involved."

"I don't live here."

"But your family does. You grew up here and they're still here."

Guy nodded.

"What's your story, anyway?" she asked. "How can you not care about the place you grew up on?"

178

"Easy. You just walk away one day and don't come back."

"But you're back," she said, turning to look at him.

They drove into the hills. Jack pines lined the road, which curved up and down, around tiny lakes and sloughs. The glacier had come through here and it had been bored, Guy always imagined. After grading the farmland flat, the glacier had been bored to tears, bored enough to rear up and dance. The tiny lakes, the steep hills were the result. The largest and bluest of the glacier tears was No Medicine Lake.

Cassandra and Guy were headed to the east side of No Medicine and a land sale there. At auction were twenty acres of lakeshore lots. The lots were owned by Lyle Price, the banker, and Walter Whittaker, an old attorney. The two men owned most of Main Street in Flatwater, thousands of acres of farmland, and the entire shore around several lakes. The land and lakeshore they bought during depression years; together they kept track of tax-delinquent lands and were there at the courthouse, checkbooks in hand, the day the land went tax-forfeit.

Now, in 1984, Price and Whittaker, along with assorted real estate agents and lawyers, were subdividing and selling the lakeshore. Price-Whittaker Developments, Inc., advertised in large newspapers such as the Fargo *Forum* and the Minneapolis *Tribune*. Price-Whittaker did not bother to advertise in Flatwater. They knew nobody besides them had time or money enough to build a vacation home.

All this Cassandra explained to Guy, who listened, nodding. He waited for her to get some of the Flatwater history wrong but she didn't.

"I understand now why you work in the Red Caboose Cafe," he said.

Cassandra smiled. "In Washington you have to be at the right parties; in Flatwater, the right cafe."

And if Cassandra knew about Price-Whittaker and the land sale on No Medicine Lake, so did the Indians. On Monday a small, black-bordered notice had appeared in the Flatwater *Quill:*

> The White Earth Anishinabe Tribal Council opposes
> the sale of lakeshore so-named "Hiawatha Acres" on
> No Medicine Lake. What is not owned cannot be sold.

Cassandra steered the Chevy to follow yellow auction pennants tied to trees. She turned onto a frozen, rutted road leading toward the lake. The road builders, sometime last fall, had not bothered to cut down the pines but let the bulldozers push them over. The Chevy followed the rough-blazed road downward. Guy realized they were only a mile or so from his old sledding hill. His and Tom's and Mary Ann's.

At the end of the road was a line of parked cars. Big cars with electric windows. Cassandra stopped behind a burgundy Cadillac. The car carried the sticker of a Minneapolis auto dealer. Ahead of the Cadillac were Thunderbirds, Buicks, two more Cadillacs. Just beyond the cars was a yellow-bannered path that led out of sight, through big Norway pines, down toward the lake.

Guy and Cassandra followed the path downward. In the snow and dirt were the flat footprints of men's dress shoes, occasionally the sharp heel and toe points of women's high heels. Suddenly Cassandra grabbed Guy's arm and sucked in her breath.

Guy looked up. An Indian blocked their path; he had stepped from behind a tree. He wore a fox-skull headdress whose jaws were eating his head. The Indian had long black braids, wore tribal leathers, moccasins, and carried a long-handled, thin-bladed hatchet on his belt.

"Good afternoon," he said without smiling. "Welcome to White Earth, home of the Chippewa-Anishinabe people."

"Good afternoon," Cassandra murmured from behind Guy's shoulder. Guy nodded.

"Please look through one of these," the Indian said, handing them a flier. His braids swung as he spoke. "And have a nice day."

Guy glanced again at the hatchet.

Cassandra took a flier from the Indian, who stepped aside, back behind his tree. They walked on, looking over their shoulders. Another group of men in Burberry-type raincoats came behind them. Guy and Cassandra watched as the Indian stepped from behind his tree. The raincoated men stumbled to a halt like sheep in a chute.

Guy led the rest of the way down to the lake. Cassandra followed, reading the flier, muttering as she walked. Guy glanced over her shoulder. A thunderbird and bear logo rode the letterhead: "White Earth Anishinabe Legal Services, Inc." The text below was a long legal description—dimensions, lot numbers, township, section, and range—of the lakeshore development. Guy let his eyes skip farther down to "Preliminary Title Opinion." Below that he read, ". . . sufficient ambiguities of title and transfer as to encumber the land heretofore described in favor of legal heirs or assignees of the White Earth Chippewa/Anishinabe People." It was signed, "Ma'iingaans, President, Tribal Council."

"I'll be damned," Cassandra murmured, still reading the legalese. But Guy was more interested in the scene below.

In a clearing, outlined against the gray ice of No Medicine Lake, was a raised wooden stage covered with bright green Astroturf. The artificial grass said funeral, but a polka band was setting up to play. At the front of the stage was a battery-powered loudspeaker; at the rear, a red portable generator. To the right, on the snow beside the stage, was a portable bar around which Lyle Price, Walt Whittaker, the real estate agents, and their buyers had clustered. Rather than face the bar, the lake, or each other, the small, well-dressed crowd stood in a tight half circle facing out, as if they were buffalo and the short brown bar was their baby. For in the woods were Indians.

There were Indians in the trees. Eight or ten Indians, dressed in tribal leather and fur, some in hawk's-head capes, sat unmoving high up in the bare crowns of oak trees like prehistoric birds.

There were Indians in the bushes. A dozen or more Indians, dressed in coyote- and fox-skull headdresses, sat hunkered on their heels here and there up the side hill. Some were visible only by the toothy grin of their animal-skull headgear.

In all there were less than twenty Indians. More than forty whites. But the Indians had the high ground. Had the auction site surrounded.

Guy laughed. Cassandra looked up from her flier. She gasped and grabbed Guy's arm as she saw the pterodactyls in the trees. Then her eyes widened farther as she began to spot the fox- and wolf-skull Indians crouched in the brush.

Guy steered her along toward the bar.

"What'll it be, ma'am?" a short-jacketed, shivering waiter asked. "Ma'am?" he repeated.

"Ah . . . scotch," she murmured, still staring behind at the Indians. "A double. Up."

Guy, too, sipped Black Label from a plastic glass as the polka band thumped. The band was not half bad.

"Dance?" he said to Cassandra.

"In many ways you're a strange man," she said, still staring up the hill.

Beside Guy was a middle-aged woman in a gold blazer and pink-tinted glasses. He leaned over to her. "Dance?"

The woman's eyes widened as she stared up at Guy. "Excuse me," she said, and turned away.

Guy shrugged.

"Which one is Whittaker?" Cassandra whispered.

Guy tilted his head. "The one in the gray porkpie." Beside Whittaker was Lyle Price in a black overcoat and wool scarf around his throat. Guy still owed Price a thousand dollars, plus twelve years worth of interest. But Guy had on sunglasses and Price was too busy watching the Indians to recognize him. Guy followed Cassandra toward Whittaker.

". . . all the way from Washington," Whittaker was saying to Cassandra, while watching the Indians, "no idea my advertising carried that far, and I assure you, you'll never be sorry for investing in beautiful Hiawatha Acres."

At that moment Lyle Price, whose face was frozen in a continuous half smile, poked Whittaker in the ribs and spoke rapidly into his ear. Then Whittaker excused himself from Cassandra and spoke into the bartender's ear. He was a sallow-faced man who blinked continuously in the sunlight. Whittaker pointed to the Indians on the hill.

"Me?" the bartender said loudly, leaning away from Whittaker. Whittaker glared at him.

The bartender shrugged, took an order pad and pen, and walked up the hill toward the Indians. He looked back several times. Whittaker waved him on. Among the Indians, the bartender went tree to tree, bush to bush with his pen and pad as he wrote down their orders from the bar.

He returned and began to fill up a tray with cans of 7-Up and Pepsi. Lyle Price's eyes bulged. He grabbed away the bar list, stared at it for a moment, crumpled it, then began to set bottles of scotch and vodka on the tray along with the soft drinks.

The bartender shrugged again. Then he struggled, slipping often on the wet, softening earth, back up the hill with his tray. He held up the fifths of liquor to the tree Indians, but they shook their furry heads and beaks in declination. The bartender looked back to Whittaker and Price for directions. Receiving none, he tossed up to the Indians their Pepsis and 7-Ups, then left a bottle of liquor at the base of each tree and bush that contained an Indian.

The Indians drank their pop. The whites drank scotch and champagne. And the polka band played on. During the fourth polka a tree Indian dressed in a coppery hawk's-head cape climbed halfway down his tree toward a red and gold fifth of Johnny Walker. The other Indians began to yip and chirp and hoot at him until he returned, empty-handed, to his perch.

Finally the polka band stopped playing. Walter Whittaker took the microphone. "What a great day, want to thank you all for coming. We're now about to sell at auction the beautiful development of Hiawatha Acres on sparkling No Medicine Lake."

An auctioneer in a black cowboy hat and green sunglasses trotted onto the stage. "Ladies and gents—what a great crowd out here today. You remind me of the type of people . . . ." And he told a joke about a man with two wives. When he finished no one laughed.

"Well, let's get right down to it then," the auctioneer said. "I can see that's what you want, yessir. You're not here for jokes. You're here for the deal of your lives. I call your attention to your plat maps and lot number one. Five hundred feet of sugar-sand beach with virgin white pine on the shore."

Suddenly, from somewhere in the trees, came the hollow thudding of a drum. Guy's head jerked around. An Indian drum. Buckskin stretched on wood. He knew that drum, that was Zhingwaak's drum. But he must be long dead. Still . . .

The auctioneer fell silent. The crowd looked around uncertainly. The auctioneer looked down to Lyle Price for directions. Price jabbed his finger at the microphone.

"Okay, folks, never mind the music, let's begin with lot number one. Somebody give me twenty thousand to start. Twenty thousand for lot number one."

There was silence but for the slow drumming.

"Fifteen thousand then. Fifteen," the auctioneer said.

The drum thudded.

The auctioneer's sunglasses tilted down to Whittaker, who beamed a frozen smile back and forth across the buyers.

"Well, we got to start somewhere, folks," the auctioneer said. "They say the first time's the hardest, if you know what I mean." The auctioneer chuckled. No one else laughed.

The drum thudded.

"Ten thousand then."

Somewhere deeper in the trees a woodpecker tripled the drum's beat, then was silent.

"Six thousand," the auctioneer pleaded. "Folks and friends, how can you pass up six thousand dollars for lakeshore like this? Buy a parcel, broker it off, you're talking about easy money here, my friends. If you don't get in now, you'll kick yourself all the way back to the city."

At the mention of the city, several people buttoned their coats and looked back up the path to their cars.

"Three thousand. Two thousand."

The drum thudded.

"Offers, friends—let's get going with an offer. Who'll make an offer on lot number one?"

No one said anything. The crowd began to drain their drinks and button their coats and look sideways at each other.

"Goddamnit then, this auction is over," the auctioneer called. He jammed the microphone into its holder and stalked off the stage. Walter Whittaker stumbled onto the green plastic grass and grabbed the microphone. "No," he called. "Nothing's over. Folks, don't get frightened off by the Indians. Don't worry about that brochure, that title-opinion baloney. Buy now, straighten out the title later, there's no problem here, I assure you!"

But the crowd began to move in a tight herd up the path

184

to their cars. Lyle Price joined Whittaker on the stage. He was not looking at the disappearing crowd. Rather, he began to jab a finger into Whittaker's chest. Price hissed into the still-open microphone, "If you can't sell something, then it's not worth anything, is it now, Walter?"

"Come back—come back!" Whittaker called to the crowd.

Guy took a bottle of Black Label from the bar before it closed.

Chapter Twenty-One

"Let's go to the Tribal Council office," Cassandra said. She tried to speak with Whittaker and Price after the sale, but they stood red face to red face, jabbing their fingers and hissing at each other. "I have to meet their lawyers, plus this tribal chief"—she pulled the flier from her pocket—"this Ma'iingaans."

Cassandra drove. The big cars all disappeared west toward Detroit Lakes and the freeway south. The Indians disappeared into the woods; soon after, Guy had heard several loud-mufflered cars departing at high speed. As Cassandra drove she looked again at the Indian flier. "I must say, this preliminary title is quite classily written."

"Your competition," Guy said.

Cassandra turned for a moment to stare. "I wouldn't say that. I'm not on anyone's side here. Whatever the laws read, whatever the judge says, that's my side."

Guy watched the road curve through the pines. "So what happens when you run into a law that's wrong? You still defend it?" He took a swig of the Whittaker-Price scotch.

"Put away the damn bottle," she said. "You want to get me arrested?"

* * *

They drove through thinning pines down into No Medicine Town, population two hundred. The whole town could be contained in the snapshot of the smallest camera. The photo would show two Labradors barking at each other from opposite sides of the highway, skinny black lions guarding the gates. One of the dogs belonged to the junkyard on the right. Cars lay overturned and askew, butchered for parts as if the yard had been a parking lot mistakenly bombed by one of the B-52s stationed in North Dakota. "Red Power!" was scrawled in purple across the doors of a wheelless, rusted Coupe de Ville; another dog, a German shepherd, was chained to the Cadillac's bumper.

On the left side of the highway sat an abandoned Shell station. Its yellow scallop sign was shattered by shotgun blasts, its grease room burned away to reveal, still upright, the rusted column of the hydraulic hoist.

In the center of town was a post office flying a large American flag. A hardware store. A combination grocery store and cafe. Two taverns. Some of the building fronts were newly painted white. The white paint covered pink scrawls underneath.

"BIA STEALS."

"BETTER RED THAN DEAD."

"PAINT UP AND TAKE IT BACK!"

Cassandra drove slowly down Main Street. A gray-haired Indian woman stared at them from behind a store window. Guy wondered where Madeline stayed.

Ahead was the Catholic church. A square building once white, its paint had been as unfaithful as its parishioners. Around its foundation was a thick dandruff of white paint chips on brown dirt. The Sunday schedule of masses on the nearby sign had been reduced from five masses, one each hour, to one mass at 10:00 A.M.

Beside the church was a new building, a low brick and glass structure Guy had never seen before. The building was five-sided, with five pointed eaves flaring away from a glass dome at the center. A pentagon, Indian style. By the front doors stood a tall totem pole of carved bear heads and bird beaks. Beside it was the name of the building: "Hubert H. Humphrey White Earth Anishinabe Community Center."

"I'll be damned," Guy murmured.

Cassandra parked. Two cars down, Guy saw a muddy

black Ford pickup with a tall wooden rack in back. The rustler's truck.

They went inside. In the foyer they stopped to read the guide to the building. A clinic. A five-bed nursing home. A day-care center. A library. A legal service and tribal government office.

To the left in the foyer was a plaque, a bronzed cameo of Hubert Humphrey. Guy vaguely remembered Humphrey's visit to White Earth many years ago. Beside the iron cameo was a photograph of Humphrey at the building's dedication; his plump cheeks were sunken by then, but he was still grinning from beneath a fox-skull headdress. A double grin, with the fox's teeth.

Beyond the foyer their path was blocked by a receptionist's desk. An Indian woman behind the desk stopped typing and looked up. Beside her was a large stack of fat white envelopes she was addressing. Her dark eyebrows rose in a skeptical stare. "Yes?"

"The Tribal Council office? I'd like to speak with Mr. Ma'iingaans."

"Mah-ing-gonz," the receptionist said. "Do you have an appointment?"

Cassandra handed her a business card.

"One moment." The receptionist spoke softly into her phone. Guy heard her say, "Senator Howard Stanbrook." After a moment she looked up. "Go ahead. Bear Wing, last office."

Guy and Cassandra passed into the center of the building. In the sunlit atrium was a circular mural of Indians before the coming of the white man, Indians working and playing through four seasons. Spring green. Summer yellow. Fall orange. Winter white. The Indians played games with balls and sticks, flayed wild rice over the sides of canoes, skinned deer. They smiled both in play and work. In one scene a long-haired Indian youth chased a laughing girl. "Bold lover . . . do not grieve. Forever wilt thou love and she be fair," Guy murmured.

"What?" Cassandra asked.

"Nothing," Guy said.

Below the bright mural, in a curving row of chairs, sat a line of young Indian women and their children. The women stopped talking to stare. To the right of the women was a half door behind which sat a white-capped nurse. A sign said, "Today's Anishinabe Children Are Tomorrow's Anishinabe." Beside the sign was a schedule of prenatal classes, postpartum infant care, daycare activities, and story hours in the library.

"I'll be damned," Guy murmured again.

"Why?" Cassandra asked.

"This place. It's . . . remarkable."

"What's so remarkable about a community center?" Cassandra said.

They followed Bear Wing to the last office. Through an open door came Led Zeppelin's "Stairway to Heaven," the clattering of electric typewriters and computer printers, the smell of cigarette smoke, sage, and, even stronger, the sharp scent of liquor.

They stepped inside. The small office was crowded with Indians, desks, file cabinets, typewriters, desktop computers. Centered in the office was a long table stacked with books like those Cassandra had studied at the Red Caboose Cafe. Several Indians, their wolf- and fox-skull headdresses and hawk capes draped over chairs, were pouring bottles of liquor down the drain of a sink. The Whittaker-Price liquor.

"All of it?" one of the Indians said, pausing with an unopened fifth of Cutty Sark. "Jesus, man, there must be two hundred bucks worth here. We could sell it, you know?"

"Every drop," someone commanded from across the room. That voice. Guy turned. Standing with his back to Guy and Cassandra, beside an IBM computer, was a stocky Indian in a gray wool sport coat with leather elbow patches. The back of his head was parted in a vertical white line by the shiny black flow of his braids.

"Excuse me," Cassandra said from the doorway, "I'm looking for Mr. Ma'iingaans."

The stocky Indian turned. His eyes moved from Cassandra to Guy. His brown face opened in a wide, gap-toothed grin.

"Hello, Tex," he said to Guy.

"Hello, Turd," Guy answered.

This was no Indian. This was Tom LittleWolf.

189

Chapter Twenty-Two

Their handshake ended in a bear hug. Tom's arms were as strong as ever, but he smelled like Zhingwaak. The nut-meat smell of scalp and hair oil. The musky scent of sage and leather and wool. Behind them the Indians in the office stared, but Tom and Guy held on for a long time. When they released each other Tom's shiny black eyes returned to Cassandra Silver, swept down her body, then returned to her face.

"Cassandra Silver," Guy said.

"Ah so," Tom said gravely, "emissary from Big Chief Stanbrook in Washington." He let his voice slip into a Chippewa lilt, a cantering rise and fall of words.

"Senator Howard Stanbrook, yes," Cassandra said, not smiling.

Tom turned to Guy. "White woman has no sense of humor."

Guy grinned.

"Too much college, mebbe," Tom said in singsong.

Cassandra's eyes passed over Tom's shoulder to the wall behind, then back. "Looks like you've had some college yourself."

Guy turned to look. On the wall hung a black-framed

diploma. "Thomas Steven LittleWolf (a.k.a. Ma'iingaans)." It was a law degree from the University of Minnesota.

"Jesus, Turd!" Guy said.

Tom grinned. "Find the right store, they print you anything—hey?"

But Guy knew at a glance the diploma was real. "I heard every rumor but that one," Guy said, staring at it. "The closest rumor was the craziest—you were studying medicine."

"Medicine was right," Tom said. He swung his arm toward the lawbooks, the deed and abstract tomes, the IBM computers. "This is medicine. Indian medicine."

Cassandra raised her eyebrows in puzzlement.

"The law," Tom said, his Chippewa voice disappearing. "Your law. It works for Indians like their old medicine—only stronger." He spoke in flat, white textbook sentences. "Before we never had enough medicine for our people. Now we have plenty. You finally gave us what we need."

"You're a medicine man, Cassandra is a medicine woman," Guy said.

"That so?" Tom said. "Big Chief Stanbrook get angry letters from white folks with Indian medicine spell cast on them?" Tom asked, falling back into his Chippewa lilt.

"A few, yes," Cassandra said through tightly clenched lips.

"Then Indian medicine working," Tom said, grinning.

"Look, Mr. Ma'iingaans—I didn't come here to—"

"Of course," Tom said. He shook out a cigarette and lit it in one motion, then looked about the office. The other Indians returned to work on the deed books, to the computers, to draining the Price-Whittaker liquor. Tom glanced at his wristwatch. In his shirt pocket, beneath strings of bone and turquoise beads, were reading glasses. "Let me show you around. We can talk at the same time."

They toured the rest of the building. Tom walked quickly, spoke rapidly without the Chippewa intonation. His gait was faster than Guy remembered it. He still walked like a leopard, but the contented amble was gone. Guy thought of the Marlin Perkins cycle-of-life nature shows on TV; Tom walked like a hunting cat angling toward prey, walked like at any moment he would burst into a run.

191

They toured the clinic. He pointed out the five-bed rest-home wing, but did not take them inside.

"Five beds," Cassandra said. "That seems small."

Without slowing, Tom said, "Only thirty-five percent of the Indian population lives past age sixty-five. That's half the rate of white longevity. You don't have any old people, you don't need a big rest home, right?"

Cassandra was silent.

They toured the library, the day-care center. Whenever Tom came around a corner or into a room, other Indians straightened. A janitor leaning on his broom began again to sweep. Young Indian women with their babies grinned, looked down, then whispered to each other after he passed.

As they walked Cassandra spoke of Howard Stanbrook. Committee assignments of international scope made it impossible for him to leave Washington—that's why she was here. Senator Stanbrook had asked her to bring to the Tribal Council the senator's ideas for a solution to the White Earth land-claims problem in the form of a federal land bill.

Tom said that if the Big Chief were not reelected next time, he would have plenty of time to spend in his own district. And any land bill that did not include full restitution of White Earth lands as established by Congress, March 19, 1867, would not be discussed.

Cassandra's cheeks reddened. She asked more questions. Tom gave her few answers. She asked to meet with him again. He told her maybe. He brought them full circle to the front door.

"So," Tom said to Guy, "come by later this evening. I'll be here. We can talk, alone." He glanced from Guy to Cassandra, then back to Guy. "Nice to see old friend Guy and his white woman."

"I'm not his woman," Cassandra said immediately. Her cheeks flushed car-beating scarlet. Guy guessed she had always felt betrayed by her face's easy capacity to color.

"But he would like you to be," Tom said with a grin.

"Oh? And how do you know that?" Cassandra said.

"Indian medicine man has X-ray eyes."

Cassandra stuck out her jaw. "All right, Mr. Ma'iingaans. If you have X-ray eyes, what do you see ahead for whites and Indians on the reservation?"

Tom squinted like a fortune-teller and turned his gaze through the windows of the Anishinabe Community Center. "Hmmm," he murmured, looking far away. Then he blinked and turned to Cassandra. His grin faded. "Me see only Indians where white folks used to be."

"Somebody ought to check that man's degree," Cassandra muttered. They had left No Medicine Town, Guy at the wheel. Cassandra stared straight ahead. Her hair was mussed over her forehead, but she had not thought to smooth it. Her cheeks still glowed pink. "I mean, who is that guy anyway, the Shecky Green of the Chippewas?"

"Chief Shecky," Guy corrected.

"And the two of you," Cassandra said, "what's your story?"

"We go back a ways."

Cassandra stared at him. She glanced in the mirror, ran her hand through her hair, then stared at him again.

Guy drove toward Helmer's farm, turned into the driveway. Cassandra would continue to Flatwater.

"Nice," Cassandra said, looking around. Guy followed her eyes. The new tractor sat upright on its repaired tires. The blue silo shone. The holsteins stood silent in the sunlight by the rear barn door. "Needs a little paint here and there, but nice," she said.

"Right," Guy said. He glanced over to Helmer's house. Boxed by the low kitchen window, like a frame around an old photo, Helmer sat in his wheelchair, watching. It was six o'clock; he was checking to see if Martin was on time for chores.

Cassandra glanced at her watch, then back up. "You could show me around. The closest I've ever been to cows is four seats from the screen and Paul Newman in *Hud.*"

"Some other time," Guy said. Martin was coming from the house to the barn.

"Hey, wait," Cassandra said as Guy got out. She held up the Whittaker-Price bottle of Black Label. "Take your scotch, anyway."

Martin, passing, saw the scotch. He slowed his walk.

"Keep it," Guy said.

Martin spit, walked on.

Cassandra stared. "Who was that, the hired man?"

193

Guy was silent for a moment. He looked after his father. "Sort of," he said.

Cassandra looked again at the scotch. "Black Label. I prefer Glenlivet, but Black Label is drinkable, though not alone."

Guy waited.

Her cheeks reddened slightly.

"We could share it, that is," she said.

"You mean like, I'll take one half and you the other?"

"Jesus Christ!" she exploded.

"Okay, okay," Guy said, not pressing his luck.

"Goddamnit, I'm inviting you for a drink. I mean, Jesus, I deserve one after today. Indians in trees. Polka bands on ice. Tribal comedians. Tonight I'm going to hole up in the Lumberjack and drink. Come visit if you like. It's either you and me or me and Johnny Carson."

Guy paused. "Thanks, but I'm going to see Tom tonight."

"Come by early. See him later," Cassandra said, starting the Chevy's engine. "But it's up to you."

"I'll think about it," Guy said. He watched her drive away.

Cassandra's room on the top, second floor of the Lumberjack Hotel was square and tall. Its walls were papered with faded pink and purple paisley petunias that swirled into each other. The ceiling was old rococo tin painted white, complete with a large, brown-bordered oval water stain. The furniture consisted of a wooden dresser painted pink. An armchair with a pink slipcover. A sturdy armoire, probably oak, painted pink. A small white writing desk top-heavy with an old black and white TV. A large, bow-backed double bed with an iron rail, scallop-shaped headboard. And a pink bedspread.

"Cozy," Guy said, looking about the room.

"Pink," Cassandra answered, with her long teeth tearing open the plastic on a bag of ice cubes. She was wearing a red flannel shirt, new blue jeans—Guy wondered if she had any old clothes—and sandals. Her toenails shone with a clear lacquer. The tips of her hair were wet. She smelled clean.

Guy had worn Helmer's long overcoat, whose elbows were gone.

"Nice coat," Cassandra said.

194

"Thanks. It has a special feature." From inside its folds he produced Kennedy.

"Oh!" Cassandra's eyes lit with surprise.

"I needed the coat to get him past Mrs. Smythe at the main desk. She was the high school librarian," Guy said.

Cassandra took Kennedy and held him, but Kennedy wanted to get down and sniff. "I never had a pet," she said, staring at Kennedy for a long moment. Then she poured two glasses of scotch.

They drank and talked. The TV played. Cassandra sat curled up on the bed with Kennedy in her lap. Guy sat in the pink armchair with his feet across the end of the bed. She asked a lot of questions about Tom LittleWolf. He gave her general answers. Told her some of their stories. Told her a little about Tom's family. About Zhingwaak. Tom's father. Mary LittleWolf. Powwows on the Fourth of July. No Medicine Lake. Flatwater High. Franklin Avenue in Minneapolis.

She asked more questions and poured more scotch. In the middle of Guy's third scotch and a scratchy *Bonanza* rerun—Dan Blocker was hoisting a knife-wielding Indian high over a cattle-watering tank—Cassandra leaned against the iron-rail headboard. She looked like Venus on the half shell. Guy checked his watch. He had better get going if he wanted to see Tom.

"Is that strange, do you think?" she said suddenly. "A kid never having a pet?" She stroked Kennedy's back with her fingertips.

"Yes," Guy said. He leaned forward to stand up.

"Thanks," she said. She ran a slim fingertip down Kennedy's nose, around his eyes, over the little washboard bumps of his spine. Guy watched her fingertip move. He did not stand.

"My mother said pets were unhealthy," she continued. "Pets woke you up at night, my father said. So I read. Books were good pets. No messy food dishes, no smelly litter boxes." She paused. "My friend Clark doesn't like pets, either."

"Why?"

"Mostly the same reasons. Also because a psychologist once told him pets were substitutes for things missing in people's lives. Missing friends. Jobs. Children. Lovers."

195

"You believe the shrinks?" Guy asked.

"Sure, why not?" she answered. She ran her hand in slower strokes along Kennedy's back; he was asleep by now.

"So I have a pet and you don't. That means I'm lonely and you're not?" Guy said.

Cassandra looked up and met his gaze. "Kennedy's in my lap, not yours."

Guy drained his scotch. He got up, lifted Kennedy from Cassandra's lap, and set him in the armchair. Then he reached for Cassandra. He pulled her up from the bed and kissed her. She was very tall in his arms. He kissed her for a long time. At first her folded forearms held him apart from her. Gradually they loosened and her hands slid to his shoulders. He slowly unbuttoned her shirt. Her breasts were round and upturned and firm. They hardened more as he stroked them. Slowly he leaned her backward until they fell onto the bed.

Which broke in the middle with a great crash. Kennedy leaped to the floor and began to bark. In moments Mrs. Smythe pounded on the door.

"What's going on in there?"

"Everything's fine," Cassandra called, struggling to stand up. But Guy would not let her go.

"I heard a dog barking in there!" Mrs. Smythe said.

"The TV," Guy whispered.

"The TV," Cassandra called.

"*Lassie,*" Guy whispered.

"*Lassie*—on TV—that's what you heard."

Mrs. Smythe was silent for a moment. "*Lassie* isn't on any channel that I'm getting."

Cassandra's eyes widened.

"A commercial," Guy whispered, continuing to kiss her neck. She continued to try to get away, but Guy had her trapped in the pink V of the broken bed.

"Ah . . . a dog-food commercial on TV—the dog looked like Lassie, that's what I meant. Everything's fine here. I . . . dropped my suitcase."

Mrs. Smythe muttered something, then her footsteps receded down the stairs.

"Damn you," Cassandra began. But Guy closed her mouth with his own.

* * *

Afterward it was the three of them, Guy, Cassandra, and Kennedy, in the crashed pink bed. Kennedy sniffed the air and tried to burrow up between Cassandra's legs. Guy gave him a good whack. Then he curled up, pouting, between their legs.

Guy and Cassandra's lovemaking had been quick and complete. From the long naked smoothness of her body, from some perfume whose aroma he did not smell until his tongue licked her skin, Guy came quickly. He stayed hard, however, as she kept moving against him. She had more than a few instructions for his hands and fingers and tongue. She moved faster and faster until she buried her face in his neck and moaned once.

Fifteen minutes later, Guy and Kennedy were on the cold, empty streets of Flatwater.

Cassandra had quickly become businesslike, efficient. Work tomorrow. Get up early. Or maybe it was miles to go before I sleep, Guy didn't remember which.

Outside the hotel the cold air cleared his head, and Guy suddenly remembered he was supposed to see Tom. Down Main Street the clock over Lyle Price's State Bank blinked, "Corn—2.29/Oats—1.63/Time—11.08."

Guy glanced back up at Cassandra's hotel window just as her light went out. "Come on, goddamnit," he said to Kennedy. "We're late."

The Hubert Humphrey Anishinabe Center was dark but for a faint glow at the rear. Guy tried the front door. Locked. He intermittently pounded and waited, but no one came forward. Then he circled the building toward the light. As he neared the one yellow window that threw its bent square of light onto the ground outside, Guy could hear a faint thudding. Drums. He looked inside. It was Bear Wing, the Tribal Council office. Its only occupant was Tom Little-Wolf. He sat with his back to the window, his head cradled on his arms, asleep. On either side of him stood a stack of leather-bound books; an ashtray full of butts hung half over the table edge beside his elbow. Just beyond Tom's folded arms a cursor blinked blue at the bottom of a computer screen. The screen was full of text. On a shelf beyond, a stereo played. Tiny red lights fanned out and back, out and back as the record played. A Lynyrd Skynyrd album jacket leaned against the stereo receiver. The thudding bass sounded like "Free Bird."

Guy pounded on the window. Tom did not stir. Guy knew "Free Bird" was the last cut on the album, so he waited until the red lights blinked off and the record arm lifted. He pounded again. Tom stirred, changed positions, but left his head on his arms. The record arm hesitated above its fork, then swung back and dropped onto the album. Automatic replay. Guy pounded harder on the glass, but Tom did not awaken.

Chapter Twenty-Three

The next morning at eight-thirty, as Guy walked from Martin's house toward his car, the postman's pickup pulled into the driveway and honked. Guy was on his way to see Tom, but walked over to the truck.

"You a Pehrsson? You look like one."

Guy nodded.

"Need a John Henry then," the postman said, who wore a green visor though the skies were overcast. He held out a fat white envelope. It was addressed to Helmer. Its return address was the White Earth Tribal Office, Humphrey Center. On the seat beside the postman was a large box of identical white letters.

As Guy signed the postman fanned his rubber-tipped thumb across the tops of the other letters, then looked down the road north. "Take me all goddamn day, five o'clock for sure," he muttered to himself. Then he tore off the pink signature form; he briefly hefted the letter before he handed it back to Guy. "Funny," he said. "You haul mail long enough you get so you can feel things through the paper. Give me ten letters, nine good news and one bad, I'll pick out the bad one for you."

"Have a nice day," Guy said.

The postman muttered something and threw his truck into reverse.

Guy started toward Helmer's house with the letter. He hefted it again. Then he switched directions, took it to Martin's house, and dropped it on the kitchen table.

Outside, Guy got in the Mercedes. He, too, had mail: on the seat lay a large packet of thin white envelopes. They were criss-crossed, tightly bound with thin brown strips of leather. The letters all carried his name. His twelve years of California addresses. They were letters from Madeline, letters she had written but never mailed.

October 18, 1972

Dear Guy,

Your car was gone from the yard this morning. Martin thought maybe you had gone to town for something. I knew better.

It kept raining until about two o'clock in the afternoon. The sky cleared some, then. I walked outside, down by the barn. I just stood in the wet yard and looked around. It was so empty.

Then I did something I've never done before. I climbed the silo on the outside ladder. I shouldn't have done it because the metal rungs were wet and slippery and my feet slipped twice. Martin saw me when I was halfway up. He started to shout for me to come down but I kept climbing. He thought I was going to jump or something. But I just wanted to get to the top. To that little iron crow's nest where you and Tom used to sit and fly your balsa airplanes from.

Well, I made it up there, too. Once I was inside the cage my heart was pounding and it took me a minute before I dared open my eyes and turn around to look. I always had the idea you could see nearly forever from up there. But when I did look I was kind of disappointed. I could see only across to the hills of White Earth and the white top of the water tower in Flatwater.

The wind up there was very cold. Martin kept calling for me to come down, but I stood up there for a while. When I closed my eyes it felt a little bit like I was flying. Like I was moving and the land was still.

I wonder if I'll ever see you again.

Love, your mother

October 20, 1972

Dear Guy,

No word from you yet. Martin says he always figured you'd run off unexpectedly and leave him with all the chores.

Helmer is doing all right in the hospital. Don't think about what happened. It happened and that was all.

Love, your mother

October 24, 1972

Dear Guy,

First snow today. Twenty-eight degrees and wind from the northwest. It snowed just enough to make everything white. Now the fields are the same color as the sky.

I've got to get the bird-feeder up. The grosbeaks will be here soon. Strange how they come down from Canada to winter here. This country to them is like Arizona to us. I wonder if people in Arizona have an Arizona that they think of going to.

You're far away now. I know it.

Went up the silo again to the crow's nest. When I was there it was snowing lightly. The snow was slanting into the wind. Everything seemed tilted. Everything but me. It was like I was the one standing straight and the farm and land were tilted.

I'm thinking about my first letter. I didn't mean to sound crazy. I only set out to tell you how sad I was you had left. But that didn't come out in the letter. Maybe that's because I'm not sure I am sad. I won't write any more about that until I'm sure of what I feel.

That might be the way to write these letters—not write anything I'm not sure of. That will make the letters short.

Love, your mother

November 2, 1972

Dear Guy,

The snow has melted, but the weather turned cold again. Twenty-one degrees today. The leaves on the box elders have fallen. I'm glad the big red oak in the yard keeps its leaves all winter. Which is not far away. The November grays are here. Field gray, sky gray, aspen gray, nuthatch gray, chickadee gray.

But I had a dream last night, and in it there were lots of colors—reds and pinks and yellows and greens. I think it was a different country and you were there.

Yesterday I went to town alone for groceries. I stayed all afternoon and through suppertime. I looked in all the stores. I hardly remember time passing, but when I looked up once, the street-lights were coming on. I stayed in town and had supper by myself at the diner. It felt funny eating alone. When I got home Martin was very angry, as you would expect. He kept asking me why I did it, why I ate supper by myself in town. I told him I didn't know.

But I do know. It was because you were gone. I'm sure of it.

Love, your mother

November 10, 1972

Dear Guy,

I always write these letters between 5:30 and

6:30 in the morning. Martin is gone then for chores and I'm free. I take a bath and then when I'm warm I either write or read a little. The house is completely quiet. The birds start to come to the feeder with the first daylight. Saw the first rose-breasted grosbeak yesterday, which means winter is here. Still no snow but only nineteen degrees at 6:00 this morning.

I was thinking of my last letter. It must have sounded silly, me writing about staying in Flat-water and eating supper at a restaurant—it's not as if I haven't taken trips or eaten alone before!

But doing it in Flatwater was the different part. People in Flatwater come in pairs, like mittens or boots. In the restaurant people stared at me because they knew who I was and they wondered where Martin was. I said it felt funny. Exciting is a better word. I felt like I had a secret. And you know what the secret was? It was that I didn't feel lonely being alone. I didn't feel like I was missing something or someone. This sounds crazy, but I felt more like someone who had long ago lost an arm or a foot, had lost one so long ago I had gotten completely used to buying one left mitten or one right boot.

I don't feel like I've lost you, though. I don't think children can be lost ever—even when they're dead. I'm sure of it.

Love, your mother

November 18, 1972

Dear Guy,

Today I looked out the kitchen window to see what was taking the milk truck so long. Martin and the driver were fighting, hitting each other and rolling on the ground. Through the window it was like I was watching men fighting on TV, with the sound off.

I ran outside and stopped it. Martin had a gash across his eyebrow but the driver wasn't hurt.

203

Apparently the driver had scratched the milk-house door when he backed up.

Helmer watched the whole thing from his window.

Love, your mother

November 20, 1972

Dear Guy!

Got your card today!! California! I was right, my dream, I mean. It must be very green there with lots of flowers. The postmark said San Jose. I looked that up on the map. It looks to be about fifty miles south of San Francisco and the same distance from the ocean. I've never been to an ocean, though Lake Winnipeg always seemed like one to me.

Please send a street address next time. But don't if you don't want to. Don't worry, I won't give it to anyone. I left your card on the kitchen table where Martin would see it. He made a big deal of not looking at, but later when he thought I wasn't looking, I saw him holding the card.

Helmer is doing better. We're arranging for him to come awhile for Christmas.

Unseasonably cold these days—minus eighteen and strong northwest winds.

Love, your mother

November 22, 1972

Dear Guy,

Nine years ago today, President Kennedy was shot. I remember how you liked him so. I remember your scrapbook. You shouldn't have burned it. The day the President was killed I was standing at the sink peeling potatoes. I heard it on the radio. You and Tom were outside in the yard fooling with that bike-powered sled you made. I turned the radio off. I felt like no one should tell

you the bad news. I felt that if you never found
out you would remain nine years old and happy
forever.

Love, your mother

November 23, 1972

Dear Guy,
   You were happiest with Tom, I always knew.
Sometimes with me, when we were alone. Once in
a while you were even happy with Martin, but
that was always when you and he were working on
something where you had tools in your hands or
some machine between you.
   I remember thinking that for the first time
when you were twelve or so. It was June and
Martin was driving the tractor and baler. You
were behind on the wagon, bucking bales.
   I had come to the field with lunch. Martin and
the tractor came down the field with you behind.
Martin was in front, the baler was in between,
and you and he were connected only by the iron
pin that joined the wagon to the baler. I remember thinking that that was just the right distance
between the two of you. I remember crying.
   I always thought I would cry when you left
home. But I haven't. So far.

Love, your mother

November 27, 1972

Dear Guy,
   I hate Thanksgiving. How's that for a confes-
sion? Thanksgiving, most holidays for that matter, are always so much work. That, and everyone
is supposed to feel happy and thankful.
   Holidays should come naturally, I think. People would celebrate Thanksgiving and Christmas
in June or October or whenever it seems right for
them.

205

But that would mean not many holidays around here.

Sorry. I'm kind of down today. Will stop.

Love, your mother

December 10, 1972

Dear Guy,

A foot of snow, twenty degrees. From my egg money I bought a pair of cross-country skis. I've made a trail around the windbreak, I suppose it's about a mile around the trees altogether. The first time I made the circle I thought my heart was going to pop. But it gets easier. In the trees I saw a pileated woodpecker, plus a partridge sunning himself. Hope an owl doesn't get the partridge.

After I've skied around the windbreak the farm always looks smaller. It must be because of the deep snow.

Here's some more news. I signed up for an evening class in Detroit Lakes, an English and creative writing class. A professor from Moorhead State will teach it. When I told Martin he said, "But you already know how to write." I told him to expect me gone on Tuesday nights, 6-10. The driving will be difficult when the weather gets bad. But it's the class, not the driving, that scares me. I know I'll be the oldest one there.

I'll save the rest of this letter to tell you how it went.

Love, your mother

Terrible, that's how it went. I got to Detroit Lakes two hours early. The professor was an hour late. And when he walked in he was not at all what I had expected. He was short and burly, mostly bald with a curly red rim of hair. He looked Irish. I was expecting for some reason to see someone who looked like Walter Cronkite. Anyway, this red-haired man walked into the room smoking a pipe and glaring at us. Without saying anything he handed out photocopies of some poems by Rod McKuen. "Read these," he said. "When you're finished we'll talk about them." Then he repacked his pipe and started working on another stack of papers he had brought along.

After about twenty minutes he seemed to remember we were there. Everyone had finished reading by then, but no one dared make a sound. He looked up.

"Well now," he said. He smiled for the first time. I began to think maybe he was nice after all. "Did you like the poetry?" he asked. "How many of you liked the poems? Raise your hands, please."

I thought the poems were pretty good, certainly better than I could ever write. I waited, then raised my hand with everybody else. He counted our hands, then turned to the blackboard and scrawled, "McKuen 19, Poetry 0."

"What the hell is the matter with you people?" he shouted. "This is not poetry—this is dog shit!" Really, he said that.

We have to write something for the next class. I don't know if I'll go back.

Love, your mother

Guy smiled and leaned away from the stack of envelopes. He counted them. Close to one hundred letters. He took out his pocket knife and slit open all the envelopes, then dug in the glove box for a paper clip. If bound, the accumulated letters were as thick as a book.

January 19, 1973

Dear Guy,

I finally turned in my first poem to Dr. Corley. I got it back with a big red "Lousy!" marked across it. The poem was about sunset. He also wrote that if he had to read one more poem about "the sun's

207

dying gleams" he would kill either himself or possibly the writer or both. He told me to forget rhyme and meter. He told me to write about something I knew a lot about, something unpleasant.

So I did (and it wasn't about Martin). I wrote a poem called "Seventeen Ways a Cow Can Die." You know, as a calf from scours or pneumonia or from getting trampled. Or later from too much green grass. Or as a full-grown cow from eating barbed wire or from calving paralysis or milk fever . . . The poem was just sort of a list. But Dr. Corley gave me an "A++++++++++!" on it. He wanted me to stay after class and talk about it. We even had coffee together in the student cafeteria before he drove back to Moorhead and me home. He's really a nice man underneath.

Love, your mother

Guy read ahead, skipping, skim-reading through the next several letters. Dr. Corley's long comments on Madeline's poems. Robert Corley's extra books for her to read. Ginsberg, Ferlinghetti, Plath, Sexton, Rich, Le Sueur. Bob Corley and Madeline talking books and family after class at the Hi-Ten Truckstop on the edge of Detroit Lakes. Bob. Bob's wife, who didn't understand poetry any more than she understood him.

Guy skipped farther ahead and found the letter he knew was coming: ". . . told Martin I had car trouble and that I stayed with a woman from my class. Bob told his wife the same thing. Afterwards I felt both terrible and excited. I didn't want to go home ever again. But I went."

March 2, 1973

Dear Guy,

The class has been over three weeks now. Bob said he would send me some more books, plus a poem he wrote especially for me. But he hasn't. What an idiot I am.

Love, your dumb mother

May 4, 1973

Dear Guy,

I think I'm getting over being angry. I've done a lot of walking. That seems to be good for me. I usually walk ten to fifteen miles a day. I like the way I feel after I walk—empty, flushed out. Right now I just got back from a very long hike and I'm writing a letter which, for once, has nothing to do with me.

I'm glad I will not have to send this letter. It's about Tom's parents.

God, I hate to write this.

They were killed last night. Their house burned, the oil burner exploded, I guess. Something like that. The coroner said Warren's blood alcohol was .28. Apparently Mary tried and tried to drag him out but she couldn't. The fireman got her out but she died early this morning in the hospital in Flatwater. The funeral for both of them is the day after tomorrow.

I want to send you this but I can't. Because if I do, you'll come home. I'm so, so sorry.

Love, Madeline

Guy let out his breath. He looked up from the letters, looked through the windshield of the Mercedes toward the west pine hills of the reservation. He turned the key in the ignition. As the engine idled he read the next letter.

May 6, 1973

Dear Guy,

The funeral for Tom's parents was held in the Catholic church in No Medicine Town. It was so cold in that building, like it was still winter inside. Tom was there. He has longer hair now, nearly to his shoulders, and he was wearing a beaded turquoise necklace. He just sat there in the front row, staring straight ahead. I watched him. He never cried. His face was like wood or stone.

After the service in the church there was the burial outside. It felt good to be in the sunlight. There was dancing and drumming. Zhingwaak drummed. He's very old now, stays in the rest home in Flatwater in the winter but comes back to the reservation in the summer. He can still drum like always. The dancers were mainly older people, women in their jingle dresses and the old men in vests and rabbit bones and white feathers.

Tom just stood and watched the dancers. Just stared. I was going to walk up to him, tell him how sorry I was. But then he suddenly walked forward to Zhingwaak. Zhingwaak didn't miss a beat as Tom came closer. Then Zhingwaak handed another drumstick to Tom. The two of them began to drum together. They fell into this double rhythm that brought goose bumps onto my arms and down my back. It was strange. There were only the two of them drumming, but when I closed my eyes it sounded like there were three or four or more drummers.

I listened with my eyes closed for a long time. The old women began to wail. I started to cry. When I could see again Tom was crying too. His face was all shiny and his tears were falling on the deerskin of the drum. They left dark spots there. He and Zhingwaak just kept drumming harder and harder.

I never did get a chance to speak with Tom. When I went out to lock up the chickens, the wind was in the west and I could still hear the drumming.

Love, Madeline

Guy sat back in the Mercedes. He let the letter drop. Then he got out. He took a long walk around the grove and out to the old washout where he and Tom used to play. When he

210

returned to the yard he got in the car and drove to No Medicine Town.

He walked without slowing past the surprised secretary. Ahead, through the open doorway of Tom's office, came loud voices. Guy stepped through the door. Inside, Tom and an Indian in tribal dress were arguing; it was the same Indian, Sonny Bowstring, who had handed out fliers at the Price-Whittaker lakeshore sale.

". . . Tom, your folks—I didn't know . . ." Guy said from the doorway.

Tom turned. The other Indian stared. Tom let drop the papers he was holding. "I'll be gone for an hour," he said quietly to an Indian woman typing on a computer.

"You can't walk out of here," the other Indian said. "We need this stuff taken care of—now!"

"I'll be gone for an hour."

Bowstring pounded his fist on the papers Tom had let fall. "We wait and we wait and we wait . . ." he began, his voice rising. "For a hundred years we wait and now we wait some more just because you and some white dude—"

Like a snake striking, Tom jerked forward and slammed Bowstring up against the wall. He held him there; the Indian's moccasins dangled.

"Here's what I want you to do," Tom said in a flat voice. "I want you to go chew some pemmican or do some beadwork for about an hour. It'll help your nerves. Then when I come back we'll start where we left off, okay?"

Sonny Bowstring's eyes glittered blackly at Tom, then turned to Guy.

"Your parents—I just found out," Guy said, outside the building. "An old letter from Madeline. If I'd known . . ."

"If they'd known," Tom murmured. He took a deep breath, then let it slowly whistle away through his front teeth. He looked down to the ground. The sun was out, the dirt was wet from the melting snow.

"My father. My father had been drinking hard," Tom began. "It was cold for May, that year. He was pouring fuel oil from a can into the oil burner. Something happened. The can exploded, then the house. My mother tried . . . She didn't make it. A very short story," Tom finished, turning to

211

Guy. "One column in the Flatwater *Quill*. 'Drunken Indian burns down house, two killed.' Something like that."

Tom was silent. He drew his finger along the gray paint of the Mercedes. "Sometimes I think the newspaper people have that story already written. They just change the names. Change car wreck to burning house. Leave the drunken Indian part. That always stays the same."

They were both silent.

"Get in," Guy said. "Let's take a drive."

Tom blinked. He looked briefly at the Humphrey Tribal Center, then back to Guy.

Guy turned east. He put in a cassette tape of *The Byrds' Greatest Hits* and began to drive. He drove and they talked, at first hesitantly, then openly, about where they had been, what they had done. Tom talked first.

Chapter Twenty-Four

When he left the hotel and the basketball team that cold Sunday morning in March in Minneapolis, Tom walked for two days and nights. Any street, any place. Just walked. Eventually he arrived back on Franklin Avenue at the office of the American Indian Movement. AIM found him a room, mostly heated, and that spring a job with an all-Indian roofing crew. That summer he worked on the rooftops of Minneapolis among air conditioners and pigeon shit, carrying buckets of tar, wearing tennis shoes that weighed ten pounds apiece from hot asphalt hardened on them.

Then the fall. A broken scaffold rope, a drop three stories into a crab tree alongside an apartment building. Two months in St. Mary's in traction. Plenty of time there to think.

Long talks at night with an old black hospital orderly named Clements. Clements worked the graveyard shift emptying bedpans, dusting. Clements began to bring him books, not the pulp paperbacks that most people read while they were in the hospital, but Eldridge Cleaver's *Soul on Ice*, Ralph Ellison's *Invisible Man*, books by James Baldwin.

The books belonged to his son, Clements said. Clements said he himself didn't enjoy reading all that much; when he handed the books to Tom, Clements squinted and tilted the books as if to focus their titles.

One day Clements brought not books but a visitor. The visitor was a man who was Clements himself, only a lot younger. Younger and taller and straighter and dressed not in a white smock but in a yellow, camel's-hair overcoat and underneath a gray flannel suit with a striped tie over a light blue shirt. The man was Clements's son. His name was Frederick Douglass Clements and he was an attorney for the Urban League in Washington, D.C.

When Tom was released from the hospital he went home to convalesce with Clements. Once a week, on Sunday night, Fred called his father from Washington, and once a month Fred came home. Not long before Tom was ready to go back to roofing, Fred invited Tom to come with him to Washington.

"The first time I walked around in the Capitol Building I felt like I was in church," Tom said. "You know, wanting to whisper. Looking at the detail work of the ceiling, the walls, the floor. I couldn't stop looking at the details. But then I began to watch the people there, the men with their briefcases and suits and ties. They never looked at the ceilings or the paintings on the walls. They just walked down the halls in little clusters of briefcases. They argued. They went to meetings all the time and to the bars afterwards.

"I couldn't figure out what it was they did all day," Tom continued. "So I started to follow them around. Aides, lobbyists, congressmen, senators, I didn't know who was who except when I recognized some of them from newspaper photos. It didn't matter to me. I followed anybody that looked like he might know what was going on." He laughed. "Once I was following this senator and suddenly two guys in gray suits and wires in their ears grabbed me and hustled me off to a basement room where there were lots of phones and television monitors. I had to call Fred. He came and got me. I told him what I had been doing. He didn't get mad. Rather, the same day he took me to a shopping mall, made me get a haircut, bought me a gray suit and striped tie, a cheap gold watch, and a leather briefcase. The next morning he stuffed my briefcase with two Washington *Posts* and sent me back to the Capitol.

"After that, after my make-over, nobody looked at me twice. I went most anywhere I wanted. I even started to attend meetings." Tom grinned. "Whenever there was a group of men arguing and heading toward the same door, I tagged along. I'd just merge in and glance down at my gold watch as I slid through the door with the rest of them. Once I got into a meeting with Humphrey, who was Senator then, and a bunch of congressmen. Went to a lot of Senate hearings. You name it. It was a game—see how many meetings I could get into.

"Only one problem, it was easy to get in but then I'd be stuck there. So I started to listen. I started to hear what went on. I listened to how a law got on the books. I listened as laws got kicked around and beaten so full of holes they wouldn't hold roofer's tar in January," Tom said, his eyes narrowing. He paused. "That's when I started to get pissed. Every night when I came back to Fred's apartment I told about what'd I seen that day, about the shit I saw go down in those meetings. I told him I thought most of those white fuckers should be roofing instead of walking around with briefcases in their hands and real gold watches on their wrists."

Guy watched Tom's face as he talked. His jaw was clenched. His eyes, focused somewhere far off through the windshield, blazed obsidian black.

"'So what do you want me to do about it?' Fred would say. Over and over he'd say that—'So what you want me to do about it?' The more shit I told him about, the more he'd say that, sitting there grinning and saying, 'So what do you want me to do about it?'

"I remember once shouting, 'Something—do something!' He leaped clear across the room," Tom said. He smiled briefly. "Fred played basketball for some attorneys' team. Anyway, he had me up against the wall in a second. 'I am doing something,' he said, 'but what about you, boy, huh boy? Huh, boy?'

"I went back to Minneapolis the next day. Six months later I finished the high school stuff with a general equivalency diploma. I stayed on with Clements and took bus #16A every day to the University of Minnesota and finished the undergrad degree in three years. Right after that I went on to law school there. I had lousy grades but the law school was desperate for a little color in its classrooms." Tom paused to stare off across the reservation. "Some days I can't believe I did it. But then again, Fred Clements said he'd send a bunch of big niggers from Washington to work me over if I didn't finish." Tom grinned. "I think he was serious too. Whenever I saw a black guy on campus I had this flash that he was some spy sent by Fred Clements. Anyway, when I finished, I came back to White Earth."

Chapter Twenty-Five

Listening to Tom, driving by memory down the reservation roads, Guy had without thinking brought the Mercedes to Tom's house. Or rather the yard where Tom's house used to be. Tom looked up. His mouth came open.

"Turd—Jesus, I didn't mean . . ." Guy said. He began to speed up.

"Wait, it's all right," Tom said. "I never drive down this road. I should but I never do. Stop."

Guy braked the Mercedes. He backed up and pulled into the driveway and shut off the engine. Tom stared for a moment, then slowly got out.

Trees formed a three-sided backdrop for the yard. Still winter green above, dusty brown below, the jack pines were silent, unmoving. Centered in the open space was Tom's house. All that remained were the low, square walls of the concrete footings. Inside their perimeter was the rusted hump of the oil burner. A mattress burned clear of its stuffing, now a Medusa's head of wire coils. Charred timbers from the fallen roof.

Tom walked slowly forward. At the opening of the doorway he nudged the sill with his boot. The wood crumbled away. He stepped inside. Guy followed. The floor of the house was now a foot of muddy, wet ashes that smelled like lye. Like the soap Guy's grandmother had always made, charcoal and tallow and lye.

The neck of a whiskey bottle protruded from the black debris; Tom stooped to pull it free. He stared at the bottle, then flung it against the concrete, where it shattered. A woodpecker flapped from a nearby tree to one deeper in the pines.

A white enamel kitchen range, drooped from the great heat, lay on its side. Tom heaved it upright. Then he stared down at the clean square where the range had lain. Slowly he bent down and brought up in his hand a tiny, rusty aluminum man. The little man was made from a snuff tin.

"Jesus," Tom whispered. "My Flying Man." He held up the little doll to Guy. "My mother made this," he said. "This is mine. She made this." Tom's voice broke. His eyes glazed with tears. In the sunlight he looked blind. "Jesus Christ, she made this." He dropped to his knees in the ashes and began to sift through them with his bare hands.

"Tom—no," Guy said. He stepped toward Tom, but then stopped. He watched him crawl and dig and cry. When he stopped digging and only cried, Guy pulled him from the soot and held him. Tom buried his face in Guy's neck. His big chest heaved. Guy held him and rocked back and forth, back and forth.

After a while, Guy got Tom into the car. Tom stared down at the Flying Man doll in his hands. He rubbed at its rust.

"You all right?" Guy asked again.

Tom nodded.

Guy sneezed from the ash in his nose. They were both covered with soot and ash, like coal miners just come up to daylight. He started the engine. "Let's drive to my mother's place," Guy said. "We can clean up there."

Tom looked up slowly, as if he had not heard.

"My mother's place. Do you know where she lives?" Guy repeated.

Tom nodded.

"Where, then?"

"With another man," Tom said. He turned for Guy's reaction.

218

Guy shrugged. "Most people live with someone."

They came to a crossroad. "Right or left?"

"Left," Tom said. They drove on.

"An Indian man," Tom said after another mile.

Guy was silent.

"Right again," Tom said. Guy turned down a narrow road.

"So what's this guy like?" Guy said.

Tom paused. "Decent most of the time, I guess. Not around much, sometimes. There," Tom said, pointing ahead to a small, newly painted white house just off the road into the trees. Guy turned into the driveway. The mailbox carried no name.

They got out. Tom stood brushing off his clothes as Guy went to the door.

"What on earth happened to you?" Madeline said. She stared at Guy's clothes. Then she saw Tom behind. "Oh no," she said softly.

"Tom's okay," Guy said. "We stopped at his folks' house, looked around, got dirty. Tom said he knew where you lived, so we thought we'd stop."

"Knew where I lived . . ." Madeline said. She looked up to Guy. "You didn't know? You didn't get my letters?" she said quickly.

"Got your letters. But I haven't read them all. When I got to the one about Tom's parents I stopped reading and went to find him."

"And now you're here."

Guy smiled.

"Well . . . come in."

They both turned to Tom, who stood bent over brushing his pants.

"Tom . . ." Guy called.

"No, go on in," Tom said. "I'm too dirty."

"You better come in, too, Tom," Madeline said.

Inside, Guy could smell bread. Plants hung by the windows. Furry-leaved violets covered a card table. Through a short hallway Guy could see the varnished pine floor of the living room and Madeline's small claw-footed writing desk. Atop the desk sat her china lamp with its glass, rose-petaled shade. For an instant the house was Guy's when he was small.

219

But on a rug by the kitchen door sat a pair of moccasins, men's, large. Above the moccasins hung a man's winter parka.

"You both better clean up first," Madeline said. Guy took the kitchen sink. Tom walked down the hallway to the bathroom. Madeline measured spoons of coffee into the basket of the percolator.

Guy returned to the kitchen. They started to speak.

Guy waited. "So how's your father?" Madeline said again.

"Drinking hard," Guy said.

She nodded. She turned on the burner, and adjusted the blue flame. She remained with her back to Guy. She looked out the window to the bird feeder, the one she'd had on the farm. "I'm expecting robins any day," she said. "The redpolls are gone. Robins never come until they go."

Guy waited. He looked about the kitchen again. "Cozy house," he said.

"Right after the robins come the brown thrushes. I always like the brown thrushes—they're so—"

Guy walked up behind his mother and put his hands on her shoulders. "Tom told me," he said. "You're living with someone. I can handle that. Your boy is thirty years old, you know."

His mother turned. But she wouldn't look him in the face or smile. "I hope you can handle it," she murmured.

Tom came back into the kitchen. His brown face was scrubbed clean. He was wearing a different shirt. Guy stared. Tom crossed the kitchen toward the moccasins on the rug. Suddenly Guy's vision contracted until he saw only Tom's feet. In slow motion Tom's black-stockinged feet passed over the white linoleum squares like dominos falling. His feet lifted, first left, then right, and slid themselves into the moccasins.

That afternoon Madeline explained. Guy and Tom listened.

"You read some of my letters," Madeline said to Guy. "The early ones make sense. The later ones . . . I was getting a little crazy by then."

She told of her trips from the farm to Winnipeg, to Fargo, to Duluth, eventually to anywhere but the farm. Sometimes

220

she was gone for days. Since Martin would give her no money, she slept in the seat of the Cutlass at night. Days she walked. She walked through the stores and shopping malls and museums. Usually she was hungry. Once she stole a bag of peaches rather than drive back to the farm, where there was a refrigerator full with half of a holstein steer.

"But it was fun," she said, her brown eyes shining. "For the first time in my life I answered to no one for days at a time. I only had myself to think about and look after."

"I started to go into bars," she said, "at first only during the middle of the day, mainly for the free popcorn and peanuts. But the daytime bar people were friendly, kind, especially the old men who played cards and dice. They'd buy me a beer just so I'd sit and talk with them. Or listen, rather. They talked and I listened, sometimes for hours.

"So I got to like the bars. The music, the pool tables, the colored lights, the dimness, but especially the sound of people talking. In bars people talked; suddenly that was important to me. People didn't mind telling you things about themselves, about their lives. They'd tell you the biggest mistakes they'd made, what they'd do different. The old men especially. They'd tell you their whole life story. Sometimes they would cry and I'd cry too. And they'd keep buying me beer as if they were afraid I was going to leave before they'd finished.

"But it got out of hand," Madeline said abruptly. She rose and poured more coffee. "The bars seemed so homey that I'd end up sitting there drinking beer all afternoon. Sometimes whiskey along with the beer. Just drinking and listening. Then one day I remember suddenly seeing myself —hearing myself—as if I were outside of my body. I was talking. I was the old-timer, the barfly. I was telling some younger guy who sold linen supplies to high schools all about my life.

"I remember suddenly leaping off my barstool. I frightened the linen salesman nearly to death. I stood there halfway between the bar and the front door. At that moment my life had only two parts to it—walking out the door or staying in the bar a little longer. I thought about each. I thought how out on the street if you saw someone who looked terribly sad or terribly angry and you walked up to him and asked him what was the matter—or if you yourself

221

were depressed or angry and wanted to talk about it—people would think you were crazy. But if the same thing happened in a bar, people wouldn't think you were crazy, only drunk. So I chose drunk."

Guy smiled but Madeline didn't.

"That's when I began to see Tom in the bars," she continued. "I got so I didn't feel the need to drive a hundred miles to get drunk. It was just as easy in and around Flatwater. But Tom had started this program through the Tribal Center. He called it Firewater Rescue. Weekend nights he drove this van around to all the bars near the reservation. He loaded up drunken Indians and delivered them back to the reservation so they didn't kill themselves fighting or on the highway. He called the van the Firewater Express. He still drives it on Saturday nights and most nights during ricing season.

"Anyway, I, as they say, had 'developed a taste.' So whenever Tom found me drunk he would load me up in the Firewater Express and deliver me back home. This worked fine. But then there was Martin," she said. She paused and looked out the window to the trees. "I mean, what was he to think? Here comes a vanload of drunken Indians and me with them. Once he went after Tom with a butcher knife. Tom managed to slam the door on Martin's arm and drive off fast. Then Martin started keeping his .30-.30 by the door. After that, whenever Tom found me I'd fight him so he wouldn't take me home and get himself shot. So he started to take me to his house to sleep it off.

"Finally Tom made me stay here at his house. He put me through the reservation detox program, got me a part-time job at the Tribal Center in the kids' reading program—said I was part Canadian-Indian." Madeline smiled. "That was a year ago. Now I live here, cook, keep house for Tom. Things are okay now, better than they've been for years."

Guy swallowed. He turned to Tom. The Turd. The Turd had saved his mother. There was never any friend like the Turd. The Turd and Madeline living together now all made sense. Security for Madeline. Decent meals for Tom. It was perfect. For long moments when he had seen Tom put on those moccasins he had thought . . . But that was completely crazy. No. Everything made sense.

* * *

222

Then Guy told his story. He talked about California. His first job—how he'd waited in a hot lobby full of Mexicans and bikers for a job that said only "General Labor." How a man had come out of the front office with a sheaf of applications in hand and called out, "Who's the one from Minnesota?"

How the job had been scrubbing the insides of empty acid tanks and running plastic pipe and making wooden pallets for water to run through beneath the tanks.

How he worked a hundred hours a week setting up the tanks and stamping machines and drills for the owners, who spoke only German when they were alone.

How soon the sheets of copper came to the loading door and were cut in rough squares. How ponytailed silk-screeners transferred photos of circuitry onto the copper with their ink; then how the acid baths etched away all the bare copper except that covered by ink. And how then the ink was washed off the tiny trails and the circuitry remained.

How the company made and sold the printed circuit boards as fast as it could produce them. How the Germans worked Guy for a month at each station, then made him general manager.

How the wrong papers once came to his office and he saw the company's profit figures. He made one thousand dollars a month, the Germans ten thousand each.

How he began to buy the Germans' leftover equipment, old acid baths and etching machines.

How once a bearded, skinny man approached him outside the company and said he had a pinball game that needed circuit boards but he had no money and no credit.

How Guy went to the man's garage and spent a whole afternoon batting a little gray ball on a TV screen. How the man called the game Pong.

How the Pong circuit boards were nothing special to make, so Guy began to make them at night in the basement of his apartment building.

How within six months Guy had quit the Germans, rented a garage, and hired two Mexicans to help him make the Pong circuit boards. How within a year the skinny Pong man was driving a 280 SL and Guy had a company as big as the Germans'.

How there were lots of Minnesotans in California. How bars were known by their states. How at the Minnesota Bar sandy-haired people drank until last call and talked of home. How most of them eventually returned to the Midwest and then talked about California the rest of their lives.

It was late when Guy finished. Madeline had a meeting at the Humphrey Center. Guy and Tom drove down to Doc's for some food.

"Back door," Tom said as Guy turned into the parking lot. "I'm not exactly Mr. Popularity here."

They took a dim booth and ate a hamburger that was mostly onions, and french fries that were mostly cold. Guy drank a Hamm's, Tom a 7-Up. They sat with their knees touching and talked more. About California. About Cassandra Silver, about Howard Stanbrook. Midway through their burgers, Guy saw some men in seed-corn caps looking their way. On the bar were some white envelopes and open pages of their contents. Guy remembered the postman and his box full of bad-news letters. "Eat up," Guy said, nodding toward the bar.

"Shit," Tom muttered when he saw the men. They finished their burgers, drained their glasses, and headed toward the back door.

"Not so fast," one of the men said, angling to block their way. He was thin-faced, unshaven for several days; his lower teeth were dotted black at the gums with chewing tobacco. He held out the pages of a letter to Tom. "How's about you explaining this?"

Tom glanced at the letter but did not take it. "The letter suggests that there likely is a problem with the title to your farm," Tom said quietly.

"Title. Like in land title," the man said.

"That's right."

Three more of the men got off their barstools and gathered around Guy and Tom.

"You're saying here, then, that I don't own my own farm. That none of us own our own land." The man nodded to the men behind him.

"In a sense," Tom began.

"Don't play word games with me, Geronimo," the man said. "I didn't ride into this country on a load of pumpkins.

224

What you're trying to do is get us whites the hell off our own land—that's clear enough. And I'll tell you about mistakes. The only mistake you made"—he swung from below and caught Tom with a sucker punch to the belly—"was coming in here today!"

Guy hit the man hard across his cheek and nose, felt his nose crunch. But then he took several punches to his neck and gut. He struggled to keep his breath and kicked and flailed. Tom scrambled into a center's crouch, then took out three of the men with a lunge forward. Guy took another hit to his face, felt pinwheels rise, and saw them flare in the sky. But he also kicked someone hard in the crotch and felt his fist strike teeth on another. "Guy—let's go," Tom was calling. Guy ducked and ran. Tom held the door.

Outside, they scrambled into the Mercedes. Guy fumbled with the key, then the tires were spinning and they were sliding onto the highway. Behind them Doc's shotgun crashed.

"Just like the old days!" Guy shouted.

Tom was looking back. "Not quite," he shouted. "Get down!" At that moment the gun crashed again and the Mercedes' rearview mirror on the driver's side blew away in a shower of glass and chrome.

"Jesus!" Guy called. He glanced behind. One of the men in a seed-corn cap was pumping another round into his shotgun. Guy ducked low and concentrated on driving. He swerved the Mercedes violently until they were safely around the bend of No Medicine Lake and into the timber.

At Tom's house Madeline's eyes widened as she saw their faces and clothes, the blood.

"Oh God, I knew it," she said.

Guy's right eye was closing fast. Tom's nosebleed had dried in a Hitler mustache above his lip.

"Tom—you sit over here—Guy you sit here!" she commanded, sliding two chairs to opposite sides of the kitchen. Guy and Tom stared at her, then at each other. They began to laugh, long deep hoots of laughter that hurt their lips and their bellies and everywhere else they had been punched. They couldn't stop laughing, and soon Madeline joined them.

* * *

225

Guy stayed with Tom and Madeline that night. First Guy, then Tom, took a hot bath. Madeline dressed their cuts with iodine and cotton. Later it was time for bed. There were two bedrooms. Madeline took one, Tom the other, and Guy slept on the couch.

He fell asleep immediately. Later he awoke, half in a dream, and heard wooden floorboards squeak and quiet voices talking. He slept again. Much later he started awake unsure of where he was.

He remembered.

His bladder hurt from the kick of somebody's boot, so he eased off the couch and felt his way down the dark hallway to the bathroom door. He quietly turned the knob and opened the door. But the room was not the bathroom. Faint moonlight came through the curtains, threw shades of gray across the room. In the bed were Tom and Madeline, under the covers, curled against each other, asleep.

Chapter Twenty-Six

Zhingwaak's story "The Boy Who Turned into a Magpie."

A long time ago in an Indian village by a lake, there was an Indian woman who had a baby boy. The woman's husband was often away hunting, as hunters are. When the husband was gone the woman often left the wigwam too. She left the little boy alone tied in his hammock.

The little boy always cried whenever his mother left. "Stay home, stay home, stay home," he cried. But the mother never listened.

One day as the mother prepared to leave, the little boy said, "I wish I could be something else. Something that is not a little boy."

Quickly his mother said, "Never say that!" But still she prepared to go.

"Stay home, stay home, stay home," the little boy cried. But the mother went from the wigwam anyway.

When she returned the little boy's hammock was empty. She cried out. She rushed about the

227

wigwam looking for him. She looked in the blankets. She looked in the baskets. But the little boy was nowhere to be found. The mother began to wail and pull her hair. Then she heard a rustling noise above her. She looked up. Above her in the crossbeams of the wigwam she saw a half-bird and half-boy. Her son had changed into a magpie, half-black and half-white.

The magpie began to croak:

> Abin, abin, abin,
> Stay home, stay home, stay home;
> Animise, animise, animise
> He flies away, away, away.

With that the magpie fluttered up through the smoke hole of the wigwam and was gone.

From the Mercedes Guy watched a magpie flap black and white across the field. It was dawn. He was stopped on the road to his father's house. Guy could not sleep anymore at Tom and Madeline's place. He had left before either awoke.

He watched the magpie fly along the barbed-wire fence. Magpies seldom came farther east than North Dakota. The bird alit on a fence post, then flapped on to another, then another and another, as if none was quite right. Red sunlight burned orange on the white part of its feathers. Then the magpie crossed the wires and flew toward the shadow of the timber. It flashed white once or twice in the trees, then disappeared.

Guy did not drive on. He watched the sun rise. Watched its back broaden with red. He put in a tape, the Strauss waltzes. His face and neck and belly hurt from the fighting last night. After a while he ejected the Strauss music, tried Haydn, then Gershwin. He did not have the right tape. But he did have the rest of Madeline's letters.

More than her words, Madeline's handwriting told her story. Her early letters were written in her careful Palmer style; you could see nuns in the circles and gowns of the letters. Each "T" and "L" were miniature carpenter's squares. Each "O" was a full moon. Each "I" wore its dot like a skullcap. Each "S" curved exactly back on itself. Short sentences.

By 1975 her words began to lean. They tipped, slightly, toward the right margin, as if the paper were a garden and her words were flowers before a westerly breeze. "A's" angled. "L's" slanted. "O's" elongated. The words had sharper points, had begun to grow teeth.

By 1978 her words leaned forward like bicycle racers crouched over their handlebars, silhouettes bent forward for speed.

By 1980 her writing would have been illegible to anyone who had not followed its decline. The words rushed across the page like racing children in a crazy game of touch tag. Sometimes a long letter was without punctuation, stopping only when the words ran off the end of the paper.

She wrote about giving birth. About menstruation. About watching her father make love to her mother; once at a family picnic she had discovered them in the pantry, her mother on her hands and knees with her skirt up over her head like a veil. But when the skirt was lowered it was not her mother but her Aunt Annabelle. She wrote about the ten different sounds the wind made in the leaves of ten different trees. White pine needles made the wind lonely, aspen leaves made the wind nervous . . .

About Martin. About the worst of his drinking. About shooting to death a cow that stepped on his hand. About her beginning to carry a knife when he was drinking hard.

About herself again, about waking up in the Cutlass in towns with buildings she did not recognize.

March 6, 1982

Dear Guy,

I stayed at Tom's house again last night—he said he wouldn't take me home anymore. He made me drink coffee and take a bath. Then he put me to bed. He slept on the couch. Late that night I woke up and didn't know where I was. I walked around, found Tom sleeping on the couch. He was dreaming, I heard him crying, "Mama,

Mama, Mama." So I lay down beside him and put my arms around him. He didn't wake up, and I fell asleep too. In the morning when I woke up he was shouting at me—he was so angry I had slept there with him. I told him he was having a bad dream. He said he always has that dream.

After he left for work I cleaned up and baked him some bread. When I look out the window I can't see any land, only trees. I feel safe here.

Love, Madeline

March 20, 1982

Dear Guy,

Someday you'll read this, and I hope it doesn't sound insane. I've been staying at Tom's house and going through the Tribal Counseling and Detox Program. Your mom, the drunk. Anyway, Tom let me stay here. Last night, like every night, I heard him moaning in his sleep. He's told me about his dream. There's a wall of light, and people on the other side keep calling to him but there's no door. Their voices get louder and louder but there's never any way for him to break through. Anyway, he was shouting in his sleep worse than I'd ever heard. So I went to his room and lay down with him and put my arms around him. It was cold, so I slid under the blankets with him. He didn't wake up. Later he started to moan again, and I put my arms around him really tight. He woke up, but just lay there. He'd been crying in his sleep. I just held him. Toward morning sometime, it happened. It was like neither of us did anything; neither of us moved. It just happened. We made love is what I am saying. We made love, Tom and I. It's been a long time for me, maybe for Tom too.

Afterwards Tom cried and said how sorry he was. I said I wasn't sorry at all. I said if he wanted me to leave, I'd leave, but I wasn't going to feel

230

guilty about what we did. It felt good for me last night. And if I didn't think about anything or anybody else, it still felt good for me this morning. And that was enough.

This is not crazy. Maybe I am, but this letter is not.

Love, Madeline

Guy put down the letter, her last. The sun was now fully round above the fields. He thought about the last line of her last letter. She was right. Things—paper, ink—were not, could never be, crazy. Only people could be crazy.

He looked across the fields. The thing that was the least crazy in the world was the sun coming up on the land. Everything worked out right in nature. Nature was dependable, logical. But nature was dangerous if you came to depend on it too much, because nature didn't care about anything except itself. That he knew also.

Yet people were always crazier and more dangerous than the land. Without Helmer, Martin would not have gone crazy. Without Martin, Madeline would not have gone crazy.

Guy never had any trouble with craziness. But that was because he stayed apart from people so their craziness would not touch him. His heart slowly began to beat louder in his chest. His hayhouse. The woods and fields. Tractors and farming always far from the buildings or the road. Always he had used these things to distance himself from people. Most farmers did that. Farmers and their sons. That's why they farmed. They chose land over people.

He watched the light crawl yellow across the fields. Farmers chose land but the land wore you down. It wore you down just like it wore down and broke the strongest parts of the tractors and implements. Bolt on four new, steel plow lays, each of them thumb-thick and arm-long, pull them underground for one hundred acres, and when you levered up the plow again, the lays were as thin and shrunken as polio legs. To know about land you had only to dig through the scrap-iron pile beside Helmer's machine shed for the twisted harrow teeth, the bent axles and shafts. They were twisted and bent the same as the men he saw at the feed mill and in the hardware stores of Flatwater. The farmers with limps. With corn-picker hands hooked and hard like driftwood.

Later he'd moved closer to machines. His '57 Chevy. Cars in general. Cars, and perhaps trains, had always been the next logical step up from the land. Once he began to take cars apart, he'd understood something he'd always known —that some cars were more than just themselves. The best cars touched art. His Mercedes, for example. The finely oiled dance line of pistons and their choreographer the camshaft, the silhouette of the Mercedes in relation to the flat earth it sat upon—all lifted the car toward art. People collected old Mercedeses, Porsches, Corvettes and put them in galleries. But the worst cars, like Chevy Vegas and Ford Pintos, were less than themselves. If the best of technology touched art, the worst of it touched the land. Vegas and Pintos turned earthward. They rusted. They settled. They sank. When he was sixteen he could not afford a car that was art, so he settled on the next best combination, his black '57 with a red interior. And it was on the tape deck of his Chevy that he first listened seriously to music.

Good music, like land and machines, had no people in sight. He liked it for that reason. Music also did not wear people down or wear itself out. Music was not dangerous and it was not crazy. It was the best of people without people themselves.

He understood, now, that there were only four things in the world. There was the land. There were machines. There was art. And there were people.

Helmer was land. Land coming into winter.

Martin was a machine, a Chevy Vega badly rusted, running on empty.

Cassandra Silver was technology who thought she was art—but she was probably just good-looking technology. Probably.

Madeline had moved up from land, passed through technology, was entering art.

Tom was art, always had been.

Guy thought again of Tom and Madeline in their bed. Against the gray blankets they had looked like a black and white painting. He thought of the boy and the girl on Keats's Grecian urn; they were safe because they were art.

232

But Tom and Madeline and Martin and Helmer were real people. Maybe a little crazy, but real. In California when people got crazy you did not see them anymore. He could disappear too. Right now he could drive away. Things would be much simpler. Sunup was always a good time for leaving.

He rolled down the window. The fields were quiet and empty but for a single meadowlark calling far down the fence posts. He listened to the bird for a long time. He came to understand that if he left now, he would be no better than the silent fields around him.

Chapter Twenty-Seven

Guy drove past the singing meadowlark on his way home. He would take some aspirin, eat, sleep, then see what he could do for Martin.

He drove into the yard. A newer tin-gray Chevrolet sat by the barn. As he got out, stiffly, Guy heard Martin's voice through the barn walls. He walked across the yard, swung open the barn door to investigate.

"Help!" someone called immediately to Guy. A short man with thinning, sandy-colored hair and wearing a gray suit was standing in the gutter. He held a manure fork. Alongside him was the old manure spreader hitched to Helmer's little orange Allis-Chalmers. Martin sat atop the tractor's seat with a shotgun in his arms.

"Help me—he'll kill me!" the man pleaded. His pants were brown-cuffed to the knees with manure and cow piss. His shoes squished. The big holsteins stood chewing with their heads turned behind to stare at the man in the suit. Suddenly Guy recognized him. It was the man from the State Bank who, twelve years ago, had come to take his Chevy. The young man who had wanted to look old. Now he looked scared enough and old enough to be his own

234

father. And in the dim barn light, on the tractor seat, Martin was Helmer.

"Morning," Guy said evenly to the banker and to Martin. The sunlight through the barn door was at his back. As Guy stepped inside and closed the door the banker started to speak—then his mouth dropped open. He squinted at the bruises, the scrapes on Guy's face, then closer still into his eyes.

"Hello again," Guy said to the banker.

"Aaaaagh!" the banker shouted hoarsely. Then he threw up into the gutter. Guy looked up to Martin. Martin stared briefly at Guy, then back to the banker. Guy could see the brass rim of a shell on the bottom side of Martin's twelve-gauge pump. Martin's hands curled tight around the stock and slide; white moons rode the red fields of his fingernails. His eyelids were red-rimmed, his nose blazed with Jack Daniel's.

"Barn cleaner break down?" Guy said to Martin. He spoke slowly, did not make any sudden moves.

"Barn cleaner works fine," Martin said.

"New hired man, then?"

Martin's lips parted in the beginning of a grin. Then his face re-formed in a snarl. "Keep shoveling, you bastard," he shouted to the banker, who was wiping his mouth with his tie. The banker quickly bent forward with the fork. "You're gonna stay here till you finish this goddamn gutter—then you'll know what it's like," Martin said.

Guy leaned on the wheel of the manure spreader to watch the banker and think.

The banker struggled with a great, dripping forkful.

"Faster, you sonofabitch," Martin said. "You want this farm, then by God you'd better know how it works."

The banker was more than half finished with the gutter. Guy couldn't see any reason to stop him now. Martin wouldn't have any more counts against him with an empty gutter than with one half full. Guy picked up a clean stalk of alfalfa and chewed on it. The only sounds in the barn were the cows' sea-rhythm chewing, the banker's panting, and the scraping of fork tines on concrete.

When the banker finished they all walked toward the house. Martin brought up the rear with the shotgun. Helmer watched from his window. In the middle of the yard the banker suddenly started to jump up and down and wave frantically at Helmer and point to Martin's gun and to make telephoning gestures. Helmer watched the banker dance. "He's paralyzed," Martin said, pushing the banker along. "No telephone, anyway."

The banker made squeaking noises.

In Martin's house, Martin sat the banker in a chair and laid the gun across the table. "Now," Martin began, "you came barging into the barn and said something about transferring title of our farm to the State Bank?"

The banker's jaws dry-pumped several times, then produced words. "You're aware, certainly, of your loan balance with us—though you're by no means the only farmer in difficulty," he added quickly. "I personally don't care anything about loans or money of any kind. I mean . . . when I'm not working. Weekends, that is. Weekends I'm just like any other poor slob trying to make ends—I mean—not that your family are slobs by any stretch of the imagination," he said quickly. He tried a grin but it only made his face look like an undertaker's overenthusiastic stitchwork.

Guy began to make coffee. The banker continued his paralytic smile.

"So how much money would make you happy today?" Guy said, plugging in the percolator.

"Heh—heh," the banker said. "Why, just about anything, any type of movement on your account—"

"How about a goddamn dollar?" Martin said. He fished in his wallet and slammed a green dollar bill on the table.

"Well . . ." the banker said, his eyes on the money. He did not reach for it.

"How about ten thousand?" Guy said, pouring in the dry brown coffee.

Both Martin and the banker looked up at Guy.

"Ten thousand dollars, right now, to give us some time to work through a few problems here," Guy said, setting two cups on the table.

"Ten thousand dollars would make my day," the banker said. "And Mr. Price's day also. We'd be very happy to start with ten thousand."

236

Martin squinted at Guy. Guy picked up the phone and dialed California. His accountant answered. Guy spoke briefly with him, then hung up. "Wait here," he said. He went to the Mercedes for his briefcase and checkbook. Back inside, he wrote out the check.

"What the fuck is this, some kind of joke?" Martin said. The banker's grin faded.

"No joke," Guy said. "Your full name," he said to the banker as he prepared to write out a second check.

The banker told him.

Guy handed over the first check. "This one is made out for ten thousand dollars to your bank," Guy said. He held up the second one. "This one is made out to you. It should be plenty to buy you a new suit, new shoes, new breakfast."

The banker reached for the second check. His eyes widened as he read its numbers.

"And if there's any future unpleasantness for my father as a result of your visit here this morning—your ass won't be worth canner and cutter price on any market anybody's ever heard of," Guy said.

The banker nodded, wide-eyed.

"Right now you're stinking up our kitchen. You've got three minutes to be out of sight down the road."

The banker scrambled through the door.

Martin stared up at Guy.

The percolator chugged. In the yard the banker's car door slammed, his engine raced, gravel spun inside wheel wells.

"Just who the fuck do you think you are?" Martin began.

Ten minutes later Guy and his father staggered around the house in a boxer's clinch. Martin had accused Guy of wanting to take over the farm and, once and for all, get rid of him.

Guy tried to tell his father he didn't want the farm, tried to tell him about his life in California, about his company.

"Dirty money, that's what it must be," Martin shouted.

Guy told him how he worked hard, had been in the right place at the right time.

Dirty money.

About the Silicon Valley.

Dirty money.

About printed circuit boards.

237

Dirty money, dirty money.

Guy looked once about the house, saw the TV, took it outside and smashed it on the steps, then ripped out the circuit board and threw it across the table to his father. Fiberglass, .052 inches thick. Copper, .009. Solder-plated circuitry after the silk-screen image. A green solder mask. Then capacitors, resistors. He shouted the whole litany at his father.

Martin stared at the board. Then he looked up to Guy's face for a long moment—seemed, briefly, to see him fully for the first time. Then Martin's eyes traveled to Guy's swollen lip, the scraped eyebrow from last night's fighting.

"So you got money, but you still get beat up just like the rest of us."

Guy was silent.

"Maybe you finally found out where your mother lives."

"You knew," Guy said.

"Sure."

"Why the hell didn't you tell me?"

"Some things are best found out alone."

Guy walked away, into the bathroom. There he shook out four aspirin, ran a glass of water. Martin followed, stood behind him.

"So you got nothing to say?"

"She seems happy enough."

"What's that supposed to mean?"

Guy shrugged.

"Talk to me, you sonofabitch." He jerked Guy by the arm; the muscles in Guy's ribs screamed with pain.

"You don't think it's a little strange?" Martin said. His breath was hot and rank. "Your mother living with Tom LittleWolf? I mean, it's not as if she ran off with a traveling salesman, is it? First—she ran off with a goddamn Indian. Second—the Indian is twenty-five years younger than she is. And third, Tom LittleWolf used to be your best friend—you don't think that's strange?"

Guy stared at this early-morning drunk of a man. A man who was killing himself by degrees. The man who was his father.

"Nothing to say? Nothing at all? Then what the hell kind of man are you? What the hell did I raise?" Martin shouted.

238

Guy turned. "This kind," he said, suddenly reaching, palms out, for his father. But Martin mistook the gesture for a blow, and swung. Guy took a glancing punch to the face that brought sun sparkles, but then he got inside the fists. He grabbed Martin around his chest and hung on. He took blows on his back, but they didn't hurt. The two of them reeled into the living room.

"You want everybody to give up on you—then you can kill yourself—well, it's not going to work!" Guy grunted, hanging on.

"Shut up, you sonofabitch."

They crashed into the kitchen. The coffee percolator jerked off the table and shattered on the floor.

"I give up on you—then you kill yourself with whiskey— how am I supposed to feel?" Guy said. From his barn work his father was as hard and strong and lean as a coyote.

"You don't feel a thing for me—you never have!"

"You never let me. You never let anyone," Guy panted.

"Go back to California—you didn't have to come back here!"

"Go to hell—I'm here and I'm not giving up on you—"

"Let go of me—"

"No—that's what you want—forget it—"

A chair broke beneath them. They crashed to the floor. Guy was vaguely aware of someone shouting at them, pounding on the screen door.

"Go the hell back to California and your goddamn rich life!"

"I'll go back when you stop killing yourself."

"I can do what I want—you can't tell me what to do!"

"I'm half you—that gives me the right." Guy panted, trying for an armlock. "You're my goddamn father, for chrissakes!"

Martin stopped struggling. He pulled back from Guy, blinked, stared. His nose was bleeding on Guy. Both their shirts were bloodied.

"Stop it," someone was screaming at them, "you're killing each other!"

For one long moment, still in their wrestler's embrace, Guy and Martin did nothing but hold each other.

But the voice at the door continued to shout at them.

They looked up. It was Cassandra Silver, staring down at them, rattling the screen door. "That's enough—look at yourselves!" she called.

They stared at her.

"Go away," Guy said slowly. "Leave us alone."

Martin looked from the woman to Guy to the woman again. "Yeah, hit the road, lady, you heard the man," Martin added, still in Guy's arms.

Chapter Twenty-Eight

Guy drove Martin to Flatwater for breakfast.

"The Krauts know how to make cars, that's for sure," Martin said after several miles. He felt the seat, craned his neck to look under the dash. "You can't hear anything outside, you don't feel the road—it's like you're in a goddamn submarine."

Guy grinned. His face hurt. His whole body hurt. He briefly cataloged his stay thus far. Twice he had looked into the black hole of a gun barrel—Martin's rifle and Brad Wicks's pistol. Three times he'd been in fights—twice at Doc's, once in his own living room. He'd averaged three hours of sleep a night and a day and a half between beatings. His face looked like Muhammad Ali's after the Thrilla in Manila. His body felt the same way. His Mercedes had taken a blast from somebody's shotgun. Plus, he'd just placed ten thousand dollars on a very long shot. Betting on Martin was like betting on an aging horse that lived on sourmash whiskey.

"What'll she do?" Martin said, nodding at the speedometer.

Guy waited until they reached a straight stretch of highway, then brought the Mercedes up to 115.

"Goddamn!" Martin shouted. "Pour it to her, son!"

On the outskirts of Flatwater the highway patrolman clocked them at 117 in a 55 zone. The speeding ticket was $124 with another $100 "reckless disregard" tacked on, $20 court costs, an $8 law-library acquisitions fee, and a possible week in jail.

From the courthouse Guy sent Martin to find Cassandra Silver. She came immediately. To Guy's surprise she argued with the traffic judge that Guy was racing to take his father to the clinic—that there'd been a farm accident. She pointed to Martin's bloody shirt.

The judge looked from Martin to Guy's face, then back to Martin, who at that moment leaned aside to the deputy and said in a hoarse whisper that carried across the room, "Hell—we was just trying to see when that Kraut car would bottom out!"

"Two hundred forty-eight dollars," the judge said, and rapped the table with his gavel. He looked at Guy's face again. He thought for a moment. "Incarceration suspended for medical reasons." He turned to Cassandra. "You'd probably accuse us of beating the prisoner."

At the Red Caboose, Guy and Martin dug into their hash browns and sunny-side eggs. Cassandra watched from her side of the booth. She only drank coffee and smoked. She kept looking at her watch.

"Sure you don't want some eggs?" Guy said again.

"Not hungry," she said.

"Losing a case ruins the appetite?" Guy said. He grinned. She didn't.

"My witnesses usually hold up better. But I kept you out of jail, for chrissakes," she said. She narrowed her eyes at Martin, who was jolting the catsup bottle with the butt of his palm.

Martin said to three men at the next table, "Shit, I know she'd have hit a hundred and twenty-five, I could feel her letting loose."

"Listen," Cassandra said to Guy, "I've got to see you."

"I'm right here."

"Alone."

"I'm having brunch with my father at the moment," Guy

242

said. "We're waiting for the fruit plate and the champagne. After that maybe."

"Hey—who found time to rush up to the courthouse and make a fool of herself?"

"Okay, okay," Guy said. He finished his eggs, then drained his coffee cup. He handed the Mercedes keys to Martin. "You take the Kraut car, I'll get a lift home later."

Martin stared at the shiny keys, then grinned at Guy and Cassandra. Outside the Caboose, Guy adjusted the seat for Martin's shorter legs, showed him the ignition lock. He watched as Martin backed with a jerk from the parking place. He waved briefly to Guy, then departed in a shriek of the tires and two little blue thunderheads of smoke.

In Cassandra's pink room at the Lumberjack, Guy lay on her bed. She had given him a Valium for his aches, and occasionally the paisley wallpaper swirled like a school of pink minnows. He shivered. She stared briefly, brought him a blanket.

"Thanks, Florence."

"I'm not your goddamn nurse," she said. "I'm trying to make sure your father doesn't kill you or you him, that's all. I'm trying to keep you alive, that's all."

She snapped open her briefcase and drew out some papers. Guy watched. Her hair was combed back on the sides, hung forward at the front. She wore a white silk blouse, blue wool slacks. Sunlight came through the east window and gleamed on the white back of her neck.

"Oh, nurse," he said.

Cassandra looked up from her papers.

"I've lost my pill," Guy said, looking down to the folds of the blankets.

She came over to the bed. Guy grabbed her.

"Damn you, stop it," she said.

"You said we had some things to talk about. I'm ready." Guy held her down atop him and buried his face in her neck.

She struggled free and stood up, angry, by the bed. She straightened her blouse. "This is work, all right? It's one o'clock in the afternoon, there's a lot of things—big things

243

—happening between Indians and whites. And they're going to get a lot worse before they get better."

"So I'm listening," Guy said.

"I need your help . . ." she began. She stood with her back to the sun in the window. The light bloomed in her silk blouse. She wore one of those thin bras that showed not lines but curves.

"Take off your clothes," Guy said quietly.

Her eyes widened.

He repeated it.

"Are you . . ."

"Serious. Take them off and don't move an inch from where you're standing."

"Why the hell should I?" she said, recovering from surprise. "Because you're some sort of Marlboro Man who tells women what he wants and then expects them to do it?"

"Not that," Guy said.

"Or maybe you think you're Clint Eastwood—you expect to get laid after every fight—well, fuck you, buddy!"

"No Marlboro Man, no Clint Eastwood," Guy said. "If you undressed now, in the sunlight, I would remember it the rest of my life. That's all."

She stared down at him. Somewhere outside of the hotel an airplane droned overhead.

She was killing him. His ribs hurt, his hands hurt, his face hurt, his knees and shins hurt. His head ached. But he wouldn't stop and she wouldn't either. Before he came he pulled away and rolled them over. He slid her forward over him until his face was centered between her thighs. He held her there, his mouth full on her. He did not let her go until his tongue ached as badly as the rest of his body. By then his face and neck were slick with her wetness, some of which was blood. "I should have told you," she murmured, slumping over him like a long stick of butter in a warm dish. "Now you look worse than you did this morning."

"But I feel better," Guy lied. They rolled over again and kept moving.

* * *

244

While she was in the bathroom Guy fell asleep. He dreamed. He dreamed Zhingwaak's story "The Blood Boy."

Once upon a time there lived a hunter and his wife. They lived in a wigwam by a lake. While babies cried in other wigwams, their wigwam was silent.

At night the woman sang into the smoke of the cooking fire. She sang, "I have no son, I have no son, I have no son."

Every night the hunter sat by the fire and smoked his long pipe while the wife sang. The hunter's smoke joined the song of his wife. His smoke traveled with the smoke of the cooking fire like willow shoots woven into a basket. Every night the smoke of their fire rose up through the hole in the wigwam's roof and went into the night sky.

Spring came early that year. The hunter killed a deer with one arrow. With his knife he cut open the belly of the deer. As he worked a spot of blood fell on his hand. He kept working in the smoke that rose from the belly of the deer.

He kept cutting away the deer's guts, reaching up for the lungs and heart. His hand began to itch, but he did not stop to rub it. The hunter's name was Waits All Day. But soon he could no longer hold the knife. Something was growing in his hand.

The hunter stood up to look. Something was growing from the spot of blood that had fallen on his hand. At first it looked like a mouse, pink and with no hair. A mouse in his hand. But then it grew more and the hunter could see that it was a boy.

The boy grew long legs. Then arms. Then a head. Soon the boy was as big as, then bigger than, his father.

His father could no longer hold the boy in his

hand, so with his knife he cut the boy free. Then he lifted him. He carried him in his arms down to the river and washed away the blood. After that he took the boy home to show his wife.

As they neared the wigwam the hunter could hear his wife singing. She sang, "Now I have a son, now I have a son, now I have a son."

The son became a hunter like his father.

Soon he became a better hunter than his father. The father began to stay home in the wigwam and to let the son bring home the deer and the ducks and the partridge. The son was happy to do this for his father. He was the best hunter in the village.

But one day the son left his bow and arrows in the wigwam. He did not go hunting. He had decided he must leave the village. "Father," he said, "I must go away to look for some people."

"Who?" the father asked. "What people?"

"I will know them when I see them," the boy answered.

The father was both sad and happy. He was sad because now he would have no son. He was happy to be the hunter again.

The son prepared his canoe. Like the son himself, the canoe was the best and most beautiful canoe that anyone had ever seen. Its birchbark was whiter than sunlight on snow. Polished clam shells decorated its sides. The shells shone like rainbows.

The father walked his son to the shore and watched as he paddled into the distance. Then he turned back to his wigwam.

Inside the wigwam he heard his wife singing. She sang, "Now I have no son, now I have no son. Who will bring the meat? Who will bring the meat?"

The hunter was very angry. He took up his bow and arrow and ran to the shore of the lake. He

246

drew back his bow and shot an arrow as far as he could. The arrow flew from sight.

The next day some other hunters found the rainbow canoe. It had overturned in fast water. In the canoe they found an Indian girl dressed in her best fawn-skin robe. The father's arrow had pierced her heart. The son was not found. In the canoe where he had sat was only a spot of blood on the birchbark.

Guy was awakened by rustling paper. Cassandra was speaking to him. He opened his eyes. She had pulled a chair close beside the bed. She was fully dressed in tan slacks and a red pullover sweater and new, pale pink lipstick. "Okay, here's what's happening," she began, spreading some papers over his belly.

They sat in the Caboose Cafe. Guy had refused to listen or talk to her until he, too, had dressed and had drunk at least one cup of Caboose coffee.

"I've never seen a woman like you," Guy muttered into his mug. "You've got an off-on switch like a circuit breaker."

Her cheeks colored. "Don't be coarse. And don't press your luck."

"Luck? That a half hour ago was luck?" Guy said, setting down his mug so hard that coffee spilled onto the table-top.

"Shhh," she hissed, looking about the cafe. Two men in seed-corn caps looked over at them.

"My luck or yours? Answer me that?" Guy demanded.

"Our luck. My luck. What does it matter?"

"It matters," Guy muttered.

Guy read the pages of the letter, return heading, the White Earth Anishinabe Legal Services Tribal Council.

"Dear Landowner."

It was the same letter that had come for Helmer, he guessed. First came the long legal description of some reservation farmland. Then came the punch line, the same phrase he had seen on the flier at Whittaker's sale: ". . . sufficient ambiguities of land title as to encumber the land heretofore described in favor of the legal heirs of the White Earth Chippewa/Anishinabe People."

"You've seen this?" Cassandra asked.

"Sort of."

"You realize what this letter is doing?"

Guy waited.

"Yesterday two large real estate deals fell through on the reservation. One was a dairy farm, the other a resort. Both the buyers were from out-of-state. One of them lost several thousand dollars of earnest money but felt lucky. You want to know why he felt lucky?"

"Tell me."

"Because he escaped buying land with a bad title."

"So who cares."

"Your family—you—should, like every other white on the reservation." Cassandra paused for a moment. "Remember at Whittaker's lakeshore sale when Lyle Price said, 'If you can't sell something, then it's not worth anything?' "

Guy nodded.

"Well, the same thing goes for farmland as for lakeshore."

"So?" Guy said. "If you're not trying to sell the farm, why worry about it?"

"Unfortunately it's not that simple," she answered. "Think of it this way. Farmers take out loans against the value of their land, right?"

"Right."

"We're talking here about regular old mortgages. My land is worth X amount per acre, therefore I want to borrow X amount of money against it."

Guy nodded.

"Their loan collateral is their land."

"For Christ's sakes, yes." Guy's head still ached. He thought of Cassandra's clothes falling in the sunlight.

"So what does farmland around here sell for these days?" she asked.

Guy thought a moment. "It depends," he said.

"You bet it does," Cassandra answered. Her fingernails drummed a sharp staccato on the Formica tabletop. "It depends where the land is located. Good farmland off the reservation sells right now for about five hundred dollars per acre. Good farmland on the reservation sells right now for nothing. Don't you see what Tom LittleWolf has done with this letter? Before the letter, people thought this Indian land-claims thing would go away. Some bad blood, but business fairly much as usual. Before, he'd just scared the farmers and resorters. Now he's frightened the bankers and lawyers. They don't want anything to do with White Earth."

Guy began to speak but Cassandra interrupted him. "Who cares, you might say, right?"

Guy was silent.

"Lyle Price cares," she answered. "He cares a lot."

Guy grinned.

"Not funny," she said. "Put yourself behind Price's desk. He's holding all these farm loans. One day he's fat and happy. The next day—when Mr. Ma'iingaan's letters hit the mail—his loan portfolio nose-dives to nothing."

Guy laughed until his ribs hurt and he had to wipe his eyes to see.

"What the hell is so funny?" Cassandra demanded.

"Crime and punishment. God, after all, may be just."

"It's not God who's punishing Lyle Price and all of the white landowners on the reservation—it's your buddy, Tom."

"So why are you so worried about poor old Lyle Price?"

"I'm worried about him, but only peripherally," she said. "I'm more worried about Senator Howard Stanbrook. And Cassandra Silver." She paused. "Guy—you've got to slow down Tom LittleWolf," she said. "You're the only one who can."

Chapter Twenty-Nine

Martin was in jail in Detroit Lakes. He had tried to outrun a highway patrol, was clocked at 130. The Mercedes had gone into the ditch at somewhere just under 100, planed over the ramp of a driveway, traveled 272 feet in the air, splashed down in a bed of cattails. The car appeared undamaged but for several hundred pounds of mud wedged in the undercarriage.

"Jesus, those Krauts are something," Martin said as Guy posted bail. "I was pulling away—that highway patrol looked like a pinball machine at a half mile. Then this goddamn old fart in a pickup comes drifting out of his driveway—I had to go for the cattails."

Guy nodded. This hadn't really happened. It was a bad dream. In California right now he could be driving down Palm Drive along the half mile of roses to pick up Cassandra at Stanford; they would eat a seafood salad and drink a bottle of cold Riesling, then head up to the city for the evening. In the Mercedes. Susan, he meant. Not Cassandra, Susan.

He walked with Martin outside to the courthouse parking lot. The Mercedes hung from the rear of a tow truck like a dirty gray horse in a veterinarian's sling. Cattail fuzz bearded to the muddy flanks of the car and gave it a receding, melting look.

Guy groaned.

"What else could I do?" Martin said.

Guy counted to 130 by tens. "You did the right thing," he said.

"I did?" Martin said, turning to Guy. He looked back to the car, then grinned. "I did, didn't I?" He nodded. "Those Krauts, Jesus. When I left the ground I thought I was a goddamn jetliner and the wheels were gonna tuck up underneath and I was gonna fly away right up over the trees and clear out of sight. But then the nose started to drop."

Guy winced. "Come on," he said, steering Martin toward Cassandra's Chevy. "Let's go home."

Carless the next day while mechanics cleaned the Mercedes, Guy stayed home. He called Mary Ann Hartmeir, told her to take the day off; she said she could use the time because Jewell's stumps needed trimming. Extra loudly over the telephone, Mary Ann said she once read where a man had everything amputated below his belly button—needed a plastic bag to hold in his guts—all because he didn't keep himself clean. From the background Jewell Hartmeir shouted something at her.

First, Guy gave his grandfather a haircut. He combed out the lank, long hair, then used scissors. White leaves of hair fell over Helmer's shoulders and down the trunk of his body. His grandfather's scalp smelled like oiled saddle leather. He clipped and told Helmer about California.

How rose bushes grew into trees of flowers.

How the redwoods along the coast took their moisture not from the ground but from the fog.

About the fields of artichokes along the coast by Half Moon Bay, how artichokes were really big thistles but people ate them anyway; Helmer nodded at that and the left side of his face grinned.

As Guy clipped hair he soaked Helmer's feet in two pans of warm water. One foot in each pan, the hooks of his toenails were like yellow roots of coral stretching toward deeper water.

He told his grandfather about the red fields of tomatoes.

251

About the harvest race to the canning companies when the trucks, pyramided with the red fruit, drove no slower than eighty, and how the last tomatoes loaded jiggled and floated and finally blew off, then exploded on the highway and on the windshields of cars that followed them too closely.

About the great rice paddies northeast of Sacramento, the great, balloon-tired combines.

About the orange checkerboards of apricots drying on wooden racks along the freeways south of San Jose.

How farmers grew strawberries using acre-size sheets of black plastic and how Mexican workers lay on their stomachs on special wagons that allowed them, like ducks feeding along shore, to pluck up the berries as the tractor pulled them along.

He turned to Helmer's feet. He sat them on his lap on a towel and dried them. Fine blue veins ran like tiny rivers on two white maps. His toes were river deltas spread from the main, their alluvial deposits soft at the edges, hard at the center. Toenail shards spun away. A nail clipper broke. He needed his rose-bush shears but worked instead with his grandmother's sewing scissors and a rat-tail file. He told more about California.

About the ivy that covered the freeway medians.

About the sweet hum of the exhaust fans of the canning companies—Libby, Dole, others—that for weeks at a time scented whole neighborhoods with the sweet smell of peach syrup.

He did not tell his grandfather other things about California.

He did not tell him how the gray air in summer burned your eyes and throat like tractor exhaust trapped in a machine shed.

How in June, July, and August the green hills turned yellow, then brown, and the grass crackled and broke underfoot like glass; how the freeways buckled from the heat; how then mad Blacks and Chicanos and poor whites from their sweltering belljar trailers and shack homes in San Jose and the east side of Highway 101 drove up into the hills and set fire to the brush to burn out the big homes of the rich.

How earthquakes sometimes thudded in the night like

giant, Hephaestian hammers swung up from below to strike square on the floor of the house or whatever building you happened to be in; how in the days of aftershocks people slept uneasily if at all; how liquor stores and night-watchmen companies and emergency wards in the hospitals put on extra staff and were busy.

How once on his way with Susan on a winding, wooded road toward the beach they were stopped by a roadblock and red lights; how the policemen struggled up the hill onto the road carrying a blanketed stretcher; how when the policemen stumbled, a gray arm, cleanly severed at mid-forearm, dropped from the stretcher onto the road, was retrieved by a policeman and replaced beneath its plastic blanket; how the roadblock was cleared, the cars waved on.

How at night everywhere when it cooled, slugs came out from beneath the ivy and fruit-tree leaves like packs of tiny legless dogs from the forest; how they left foamy, webbed trails across the warm concrete as they hunted fresh greens.

When he was finished with the haircut and pedicure, he turned to Helmer's hands. He talked more. When he finally finished it was sundown, and Helmer rumbled, "You have much land there?"

"No. Only a house, a yard."

"You could buy land there?"

"I suppose so."

Helmer was silent for a while. "A man should have land," he said.

"Some men don't," Guy began. But he stopped.

"What would a man do without land?"

Guy was silent.

With great effort, Helmer turned to look at Guy. With his haircut he looked younger. The late sunlight lay orange across his lap. "You have no land in California, but you know so much about it," he said.

Guy was silent.

"You go to it," Helmer said. "You watch the farmers."

Guy nodded yes.

The next morning, at ten minutes past ten, spring came to northern Minnesota. Guy was walking from the house to

253

the mailbox when he noticed for the first time real heat in the sun. He stopped. In the yard and fields the snow was all gone, had slipped away. The ground had thawed similarly, absorbing the melting snow and ice without gurgle or splash. In the cow lot the holsteins stood sideways to the sunlight. Guy, too, turned his face up to the sun, felt its heat on his throat. For a long moment he imagined every person and animal on the reservation standing outside faceup to the sun, breathing in the heat, warming. When he opened his eyes he saw his grandfather through the kitchen window. Watching. In shadow. Guy stared for a moment, then turned his eyes to the steep front steps, the open yard below. He walked on.

In the mailbox, along with a Flatwater *Quill,* were two letters, both addressed to Martin Helmer Pehrsson. No "and/or." No hyphen. The first letter was from the State Bank of Flatwater.

Dear Mr. Pehrsson,

   As you are no doubt aware from a recent letter issued by the White Earth Tribal Council, a certain Indian attorney and his staff have called into question ownership of land by whites on the reservation.

   This investigation has dramatically reduced the value of land on the reservation, if not called into question the entire future of farming and resorting in this region.

   Because you have loans outstanding with our bank, loans based on land equity figures that are no longer valid, I would like to discuss with you at your earliest convenience your loan balance with our lending institution.

   With every good wish,

   Lyle Price, President, Flatwater State Bank

"What's that slippery sonofabitch trying to pull now?" Martin said as he handed the letter back to Guy.

"The rug," Guy said.

* * *

The second letter was from the White Earth Tribal Council.

Dear Mr. Pehrsson,

Since your farm lies within the original boundaries of the White Earth Anishinabe Nation, and since you are actively engaged in use of the land through farming, and since the lands of White Earth must be protected from pollution and degradation—for example, the seepage of herbicides, pesticides, and chemical fertilizers into our groundwater endangers the sacred gift mahnomen (wild rice) from the Great Spirit—for the well-being of future generations of Anishinabe, the Tribal Council has passed a Natural Resources Preservation Ordinance.

Main points of the Ordinance include: (1) restriction of the use of agricultural chemicals such as commercial fertilizers, herbicides, and pesticides; (2) restriction of agricultural irrigation; (3) restriction of fall plowing to prevent wind erosion, and (4) restriction of further clearing of timber land for agricultural use.

White Earth tribal members will make periodic inspections of tribal lands to ensure compliance.

Meegwetch!
Ma'iingaans, Tribal Chairman

"And what the hell's this all about?" Martin said, pouring whiskey into his coffee. "Great Spirit, wild rice, herbicides, fertilizers, pesticides." His eyes scanned the letter.

Guy waited.

"Shit," Martin said suddenly, tipping over his coffee. "This is a goddamn list of rules and regulations on how we farm!" Martin's eyes skipped to the bottom! "'. . . tribal members will make periodic inspections of tribal lands to ensure compliance.'" As he read aloud two farm pickups drove fast past the farm, heading south to Flatwater.

"This says the goddamn Indians will be coming to tell us how to farm!" Martin said, looking up at Guy.

255

Guy took the letter from Martin. He read it again. He could feel Tom in the writing. The long, rambling sentences. Their rough stitching of commas and dashes and parentheses and exclamation points. It was Tom riding a feathered pony at night around and around the fenceless corral of the white page. He was herding the words together like they were camp ponies, jostling them back to the center just when they seemed likely to break out and stampede through the night trampling everything in their path. So far he was holding them in. But for every sentence he reined back, another tried to break free.

Outside, a third pickup jolted fast toward town.

"Goddamn, what's the old man gonna say to this shit?" Martin muttered, pouring whiskey without coffee.

Guy took the letters and let them drop into the garbage sack. "Nothing," he said.

That afternoon Guy worked with two stout, black-haired brothers as they built a wooden ramp over the steep and crumbling front steps of Helmer's house. The brothers logged in winter when the frozen ground supported their skidders, carpentered May through October. "Round trees in winter, square ones in summer," the brothers' newspaper ad read. Helmer watched them work from his window.

By late afternoon the ramp was finished. Then, using strips of plywood and two-by-four stakes, the brothers formed a wide sidewalk from the house to the barn door. The Redi-Mix truck, its beehive mixer grumbling, came up the road from the south, turned into the driveway, lowered its chute, and backed up.

"Indians are on the warpath, I guess," the driver said, rolling a toothpick in his mouth as he watched Guy and the brothers push the heavy wheelbarrows of concrete.

"Fuck 'em," one brother said for both.

"Wetten it up a little," the other brother said of the concrete. "It's too stiff."

"That's what my wife says," the first brother added.

"Once a year she says that?" the second brother grunted, dumping a load.

"Once an hour. All night," the first brother said.

"My ass," the second brother said.

256

Guy grinned and kept trotting back and forth with his wheelbarrow.

By sundown the sidewalk concrete was trowled, brushed sandpaper rough with a stiff-bristled barn broom, and the black-haired carpenters were driving fast toward Doe's.

Martin finished chores and came across the yard. "Who the hell is paying for all this?" he said, surveying the construction.

"California," Guy replied, turning on the water hose.

"By the way, that Silver woman called," Martin said.

Guy nodded and sprayed water on the wheelbarrow.

Martin watched him for a minute. "'Spose that means you'll be heading in to the Lumberjack for the night."

"Maybe I ought to send you," Guy said.

Martin thought for a moment. "Nah—she might not ever call you again."

Guy turned the cold spray on Martin, who whooped and cursed. Then he chased his father, laughing, as far as the hose would reach.

At ten o'clock the next morning Guy dressed Helmer in a plaid wool jacket and cap, put the earflaps down, though the temperature was fifty-five degrees, and wheeled him through the front door onto the ramp. In the sunlight, Helmer squinted. He stared for a long time down at the wood, its lag bolts and beams, then beyond at the ribbon of concrete that stretched to the barn.

"What do you think, Gramps?" Guy said happily.

"Who pays for all this?" Helmer rumbled.

"Me," Guy said. "Hang on." He rolled Helmer down the ramp onto the ground. Suddenly Helmer canted his neck to look up at the sky. He tipped back his face. The sunlight fell full into the deep sockets of his eyes, the crevices around his mouth. He sat that way for long minutes, as if he had fallen asleep. Then he looked back to the sidewalk.

"Try it out," Guy said, nodding to the concrete path ahead.

Helmer squinted back to his house, then ahead. Slowly his right hand moved the lever that powered the batteries. The wheelchair whirred; its wheels turned slowly toward the barn. Guy walked behind. Soon he was trotting, then jogging to keep up.

"Hey," he called, laughing. But Helmer kept his lever to the metal.

Helmer spent the rest of the day parked in the center alley of the barn. He refused to go in for lunch. Guy brought some sandwiches and coffee, two bales of straw for a table, and ate with Helmer in the empty barn. At three o'clock Martin came to put down grain. When each stall was fronted by a small dusty pyramid of ground oats and corn, Guy and Martin prepared to let in the holsteins, who, having heard the scrape of the grain shovel on concrete, milled and thumped and hooted just outside the door. Guy wheeled Helmer backward and parked him out of the cows' path, by the front door. Then Martin swung open the rear door, cursed at, whacked at the cows with his auctioneer's cane as they thundered past him toward their grain. Guy started to lock the stanchions when Martin cursed louder. The cows' rush had stalled, backed up. Martin was sandwiched against the wall. "Get going, you sonsabitches—what the hell's the matter with you!" he shouted.

Guy saw the trouble. Helmer had wheeled his chair back into the center of the alley, mid-barn. The tide of cows balked at the sight of his wheelchair. Then, from the weight of cows still pressing in from behind, the dam broke. The cows surged past Helmer on both sides. Helmer was a boulder. The cows were floodwater in a stream. Helmer held out his right hand. His fingers traced the sides of the cows' necks, sketched their big shoulder bones, vibrated along the washboard plains of their ribs as they flowed past.

Guy held his breath. For a long minute he lost sight of Helmer among the surging cows. The flood diminished. The last of the cows, in clumsy, king-salmon leaps, cleared the gutter, slammed forward into their stanchions, and buried their noses in the grain.

Helmer sat alone in his wheelchair.

"Jesus Christ, Dad!" Martin began. Martin's face was bone white.

But Helmer didn't look up. He lifted his right hand to his face. He closed around his nose the fingers that had touched the cows.

* * *

Outside, Guy walked behind the wheelchair as Helmer rolled home. The sun was full in their faces. Midway from the barn to the house the chair slowed, then veered to the right. Guy grabbed the handles to keep it from tipping. He leaned forward to check on Helmer. His grandfather's face was streaming with tears.

Chapter Thirty

Guy returned Cassandra's car that evening. He found her in her pink room at the Lumberjack. She was on the phone. She motioned him through the doorway and shifted the phone to her other shoulder as she kept writing on a yellow pad. On the pink bedspread lay her brown leather briefcase and assorted papers. Cassandra murmured, "Yes, yes . . . yes," into the receiver. Guy sat and looked across the bed.

One of the papers caught his eye, a grainy, narrow-script, finger-thick, stapled photocopy: *"Report in the Matter of the Investigation of the White Earth Reservation,* 62nd Congress, with Transcript and Testimony Taken and Exhibits Offered from July 25, 1911, to March 28, 1912."

"Yes, Senator," Cassandra said. "Everything is set."

Guy looked up.

"That's tomorrow. I'll meet you at the airport, then we'll drive into Flatwater. The meeting is at one P.M." she continued.

She was silent for a moment.

"Yes, Senator, the local and state media."

Stanbrook's voice said something.

"The Minneapolis *Tribune,* Fargo *Forum,* WCCO, KSTP," Cassandra began. She continued with a list of newspapers, radio and television stations.

"Good-bye to you too," Cassandra said, holding the receiver at arm's length a moment and making a face.

"The Big Chief," Guy said.

"Yes," she said.

"So what's cooking?" Guy said. He leaned forward to pick up the photocopy of the old congressional report.

Cassandra intercepted his reach, swept the papers into her briefcase, and snapped it shut.

"You didn't hear?" she said.

Guy waited.

"Your friend Ma'iingaans has created what we in the business of politics call a media event. One o'clock tomorrow, your old gym," Cassandra said, "a town meeting."

"At which the senator appears. On live TV."

"Something like that," Cassandra said.

"What about the Indians?"

"They'll be there. Tom LittleWolf said he'd come, though later some woman called and said he'd come only on the condition that I guarantee security, crowd control."

"Who was the woman?" Guy said quickly.

"She wouldn't say. She did say that there's some sort of men's club called the Township Defense League, headquartered at"—Cassandra glanced at her notepad—"a place called Doc's on No Medicine Lake. She said this defense league would be there and should be watched."

"She's right," Guy said.

"You know this group?" Cassandra said.

"I met some of them once at Doc's," Guy said. He thought of the Mercedes' mirror exploding in glass and sunlight. "Security. What have you done about that?"

"I called the sheriff, who said his chief deputy, a fellow named Bradley Wicks, would take care of crowd control. I talked to Wicks. 'No problem,' Wicks said."

Guy fell silent.

"And you?" Cassandra said.

"I'll be there," Guy murmured.

"Good," she said. She thought a moment. "So my work is done, today anyway." She turned to face Guy. She stared down at him for long moments. With a faint smile, she said, "Anything you'd like to do between now and tomorrow?"

Guy stared up at her. She had on tight new blue jeans, a

261

pale red fishnet sweater. He could see the shadows of her nipples through its weave.

"I gotta go," he said suddenly.

He drove fast to White Earth. It was dusty-blue dark, nine o'clock. Far out from the rutted roads of the reservation, big tractors plowed by their yellow and blue running lights. The tractors looked like neon tetras drifting in the dark tank of the fields. Along the black coral reefs of the potato irrigators, often three or four tractors moved side by side.

At No Medicine Town, the Humphrey Center was dark. Guy circled to the rear, where light came from Tom's office. Tom sat at a desk, typing, with his broad back to the window. His record player was unlit. Guy pounded on the glass.

"Guy," Tom said, squinting at him as he unlocked the front door. "What's going on?"

"First, you need some goddamn window shades," Guy said.

Guy began with the town meeting. "There's gonna be a thousand pissed-off white folks waiting for you tomorrow in that gym," he said.

"So?" Tom said. He stood with his arms folded and drew deeply on a Camel; his long braids lay over a rabbit-bone necklace and were bound with beads of turquoise. There were greenish circles under his eyes. "It's time they heard the truth," Tom said.

"You think they're gonna enjoy hearing you tell them to get the fuck off the reservation?"

"I hadn't planned on using that phrasing," Tom said, his lips spreading in a white-toothed grin. "But something like that."

"Jesus, Turd, sometimes I think you spent too long under the ice that day down at No Medicine," Guy said. "I mean, I know what you're doing—the land and all the rest—but you got to watch out for yourself. You're no good to anyone beaten into a McNugget. Or worse."

"Or worse?"

"Goddamnit!" Guy said, kicking a wastebasket across the room. "You don't remember getting beaten up at Doc's? You don't remember getting shot at in the Mercedes? Jesus!

262

You remind me of something I read once about being drunk. Some guy figured out the ten stages of drunkenness. I forget the first several levels, but stage nine was bulletproof and stage ten was invisible."

Tom grinned. "Lots of invisible redskins up on White Earth."

"That's for sure," Guy said. "People get real invisible when they're dead."

They were both silent for a moment. Tom stubbed out his cigarette. "I don't worry about that," he said.

"You dumb redskin! You may not worry, but other people do. Like me. Like my mother!"

Tom turned to stare at Guy.

"Don't go tomorrow," Guy said. "Let it be The Howard Stanbrook Traveling Show. You're doing fine without him."

"No," Tom said abruptly.

Guy fell silent.

"Don't you see, Tex?" Tom said. "Tomorrow there will be Indians as well as whites at that meeting. Most of the Indians support me. There may be a few that don't," he said, pausing to look out the black glass of the window. He turned back to Guy. "But what I need, Tex, is consensus. I need a mandate, as Stanbrook would call it. I need the support of every damn red man and woman on the reservation." Tom's voice rose, his eyes glittered blackly. "Then the Anishinabe will be on their way—there'll be no stopping us. We'll take back the lands. We'll close the reservation. With our own land, we'll have our own laws. We'll tear down the irrigators. We'll pour concrete down their well pipes. We'll plant the fields back to pine—thousands of acres of pine. The lakes will return to *mahnomen*, and the rice will be our main industry, and . . ."

Guy's mouth slowly fell open as Tom talked. In the glare of the overhead fluorescent lights Tom's eyes were obsidian black and pupil-less. They were filmy. Dreamy. Tear out the TV dish antennas and their white pornography. Burn down the taverns . . . no liquor allowed on the reservation . . . nobody killing each other . . . no guns . . . someday not even any cars.

"Wicks!" Guy said suddenly, loudly.

Tom shut up. He blinked and looked around.

"Bradley Wicks. He'll be responsible for crowd control—

263

for your safety—tomorrow," Guy said. "Wicks and this Township Defense League make James Earl Ray look like a Flatwater Jaycee."

"Wicks," Tom said.

Guy nodded.

"Shit," Tom murmured, turning to look over his shoulder out the dark window.

Tom agreed to be careful, to bring his own security. Then they talked another hour.

They talked about Madeline.

About Cassandra Silver.

About Mary Ann.

About Black Elk and Russell Means and Chief Hole-in-the-Day and wild rice and flax and Hubert Humphrey and Helmer Pehrsson. When Guy talked of Helmer, Tom listened, then stubbed out his cigarette. "Come," he said.

They walked down the dim hallway to the five-bed rest home. A night nurse sat watching a *Bonanza* rerun. Beyond her the rooms were dark and empty but for one. Tom stopped at the doorway; he was framed in a soft, red, slowly pulsating light. Inside was a bed cranked half upright, its back to the door. Steelgray hair flowed down both sides of the sheets, touched the floor. Beyond the bed, the red light came from a Plexiglas box, backlit by a light bulb, of oil and colored water. The box tilted first one way and then another. Its moving colors lapped like slow sundown surf across the walls of the room.

"He doesn't sleep without it," Tom whispered. They stepped to the side of the bed.

"Zhingwaak!" Guy said.

Zhingwaak, staring at the light box, turned toward the voice. His eyes, whitish and slick with fluid, searched for Guy. "He can't see you," Tom whispered. Zhingwaak spoke in Ojibwe, a long flow of words that whispered and hummed like wind in the pines. Tom leaned down and spoke Ojibwe into his ear.

Zhingwaak's hand came up from the bed like a dry leaf floating up from the ground. "Ningos," he said.

Guy took his hand. The skin was thin, nearly translucent, cool. Zhingwaak spoke more Ojibwe.

"'You're the swimmer. I thank you,'" Tom said. Then

264

Zhingwaak's hand slackened, and he turned his face again to the light.

Guy watched Zhingwaak's eyes. As they followed the red light, his pupils moved across the night sky of his face like two moons rising.

They stepped from the room. "How old is he now?" Guy said softly.

"At least a hundred and five. Maybe more. He speaks only Ojibwe now. Some of his words even the oldest men don't know."

Guy looked back into the red glow of the room. "Does he still have his drum?"

"No," Tom said. "He gave it to me. It's mine now."

Guy arrived an hour early at Flatwater High School, but still parked three blocks away. Muddy pickups and cars lined the streets, filled the dirt softball field in a gridlock of Chevrolets and Fords that flowed toward the wide doors of the gymnasium. Guy wound his way around the cars and trucks. On their dashboards the pickups carried broken bolts, dusty shotgun shells, and crushed cans of Hamm's; in the rear beds the trucks carried fifty-gallon fuel tanks, plastic canisters half full of hydraulic oil, broken chain-saw paddles and chains, flat iron plow lays, curved plow mold-boards, torn paper bags of bolts and nuts, hay chaff or sawdust.

The cars carried tattered infant seats, dented cans of Mountain Dew and Pepsi on the dashboard, torn "Masters of the Universe" comic books, empty Tootsie Roll wrappers. The cars' bumper stickers and drivers' doors read, "Mary Kay Cosmetics," "Aloe Vera," "Tupperware for Modern Living," "Herbalife for Longer Life," many with phone numbers in reflector letters. One dusty old Buick, jacked up in the rear and with furry dice hanging from the mirror, blue shag carpet in the back seat, and draw drapes all around, had painted on its side "If this buggy's rockin', don't bother knockin'."

"A man of taste and style," Guy murmured.

He joined the flow of people, some Indians, mostly whites, converging on the school. He felt like he was going to a basketball game. By the door two smiling Indians in tribal dress—long braids, leather vests, leather pants, plus enough drilled bone and turquoise to start a beadwork boutique in Berkeley—handed out fliers explaining the Anishinabe position on the White Earth land claims. The few whites who accepted the fliers glanced briefly at them, then crumpled them and threw them on the auditorium steps.

"Stanbrook—he'll put the sonsabitches in their place," someone said loudly.

The Indians did not stop smiling or stop handing out the leaflets.

Guy stepped through the doors into the foyer. He waited to hear the thud of basketballs and the blare of the school band, but there was only the drone of voices from inside the gym. He thought of a great gray mushroom hive of hornets that he and Tom once threw a stick into; how the humming inside suddenly rose in pitch like the sound of a motor pushed to high RPMs.

He stepped into the gym. Its air was a close, warm wall, barnlike and humid. The bleachers were two steep hillsides, one of brown faces, one of white faces already shiny from the heat. The basketball floor was a yellow valley between them. In the middle of the shiny floor stood a raised platform, two metal chairs, and a microphone.

Just inside the gym door was Bradley Wicks. His badge and pistol chain gleamed brass and silver; his brown pants and tan shirt were pressed with military-sharp creases. He stood holsterside to the crowd, his face fixed in a half smile, as if he were waiting for someone to take his photograph. Closer, Guy read the bullet-shaped tattoo on his right forearm: "'Nam, '69." Guy stared closer at Wick's lopsided face, the skin under his chin, around his neck and ears. Tiny, intersecting mouse trails of stitching covered the flesh.

"Pehrsson," Wicks said. "I was hoping I'd see you. We need to sit down and have a little talk."

Guy paused. Wicks's eyes returned to the passersby as he spoke. He watched them for weapons. "That day we met on the road—you remember, by the irrigator?"

Guy nodded.

"You dropped something," Wicks said. Still without looking at Guy, he reached into his shirt pocket and pulled out a clear plastic Baggie. Inside was the thimble-size brown-glass bottle of cocaine that Guy had thrown into

Hank Schroeder's field. Guy felt the gym contract. Felt the lights brighten. It was like he was in a basketball game where time had run out and the score was tied and his free throw was bouncing off the rim.

Wicks turned to stare at him, but Guy couldn't take his eyes from the tiny brown jar. "Took me a while to find it," Wicks said. "You see, I stopped down the road a ways and took a look back at you with my big glasses. It's a habit of mine. I saw you throw something. After you drove off I came back and looked for a long time. I was just about to give up when the sunlight caught the glass just right. My good luck, huh?" Wicks grinned.

"Your good luck, my bad," Guy said. He shrugged.

Wicks stared at him for a moment longer before looking back to the walkers. "I like you, Pehrsson," he said. "You got . . . style. That's it, style. You don't break for the door. You don't give me no bullshit about it not being yours." He turned again to Guy. "It took me a while to get the lab report back from Minneapolis. Those fuckers down there think the world of crime begins and ends on Hennepin Avenue. But we know better, huh, Pehrsson? I got a thumbprint of yours that's clear as bird shit on a windshield. Plus the lab report on the coke. Ninety-two-percent pure. The real shit." Wicks grinned again. "Like I said, Pehrsson, you're a man of style. You like the finer things in life. I like that."

Guy looked around, then back. "Get down to it, Brad," he said.

Wicks turned his gaze back to the stream of walkers. "No hurry," he said. "I'm on patrol tonight. Why don't I drive by the farm, pick you up. We'll take a little ride around the reservation. We can talk about what we oughta do. That is, if you're still in Minnesota tonight. Which I would recommend."

"Why would I want to leave?" Guy said. "Everybody here is so friendly."

Wicks's mouth curled in a grin. "Pehrsson, you're a real kick. I like you. I really do. See you tonight, right?"

Guy walked on.

From the crowd someone called his name. It was Madeline.

* * *

"Are you all right?" she asked immediately as Guy squeezed in beside her. "You look white."

"It's the light," Guy said, looking up briefly at the big fluorescent bulbs.

She stared at him for long moments, then turned to survey the crowd.

"Where's Tom?" Guy said.

"He'll come when Stanbrook comes," Madeline said. She looked to the far end of the gym, to the emergency fire door, then back to the podium.

Guy followed her eyes with his, then looked closer at the crowd. Below, close to the stage and centered in several rows of white faces and seed caps, was a large placard held by a fat woman. The sign read, "Township Defense League —Save Our Land for Our Children." Guy looked closer. The woman holding the sign was Mary Ann Hartmeir.

"Jesus," Guy said.

Madeline followed his gaze.

"Look closer," she said.

Guy stared. Seated near Mary Ann he saw Kurt Fenske. The regulars from Doc's, including two men with bandages across their noses. Doc himself. A collapsible wheelchair, then Jewell Hartmeir. And only one seat away from Jewell Hartmeir, Guy saw Martin.

"Shit," Guy murmured, but at that moment the crowd began to clap. From the right door white TV lights blinked on as Senator Howard Stanbrook trotted onto the gymnasium floor. Cassandra Silver and several short young men in blue and gray suits were visible in the foyer. Stanbrook was tanned and trim and light on his feet. He was over fifty but spent a lot of time in the congressional health spa, Guy guessed. His hair was walnut-brown and shiny. From thirty rows and a jump shot away, Guy could see the makeup, the blue eyeliner, the brown shadow that made his small eyes look larger.

As Stanbrook took the podium, from the left side of the gym the fire door swung open. Four huge, shirtless Indians wearing mirrored sunglasses, braids, leather pants, leather vests came through the door. They carried stubby, polished billy clubs under their arms. The clapping for Stanbrook petered out. The crowd turned to stare. Tom LittleWolf trailed the big Indians. Passing beneath the basketball net,

268

he looked up and for a moment altered his step, as if he might go up for a jump shot. Above him, on the gym wall in tall, faded letters, were the tomahawk logo and the words "Go! Fight! Win!—Flatwater Indians!"

Stanbrook stepped down from the podium and walked toward Tom with hand outstretched. Tom hesitated. Boos and hisses came from the crowd. Tom briefly shook Stanbrook's hand. Stanbrook smiled broadly and gestured for Tom to precede him onto the stage. Tom's escorts seated themselves cross-legged in a row in front of the podium. Then the local chairman of the Republican Party, the town barber, stammered through an introduction of Senator Stanbrook.

"Thank you so much, Bill, and what a pleasure it is . . ." Stanbrook began. His voice was resonant and smooth. Stanbrook began with an anecdote about President Reagan.

"Before I left Washington the President said to me, 'Howard, I hear you've got some Indian trouble out in Minnesota.'

"'Yessir,' I said. 'But I think we Minnesotans can work it out if we work together.'" A small ripple of applause came from the crowd.

"'Well, Howard,' the President said to me, 'if you have any trouble, just give me a call. After all, I've got a lot of experience when it comes to Indian trouble.'

"How's that, sir?" I said.

"'In the movies I played a cowboy, remember?'"

A wave of laughter swept the auditorium. Even some of the Indians grinned.

Stanbrook went on to talk of the spirit of compromise, the metaphor of the American melting pot. He quoted from Carl Sandburg. From Eisenhower. From Bruce Jenner. From Stevie Wonder. From Eldridge Cleaver. "That must be from Cleaver's later work," Madeline whispered.

Smoothly, Stanbrook moved from Cleaver and melting pots to the land on White Earth. "I bring to you today legislation that will clear disputed land titles on the White Earth Reservation, that will make restitution to heirs of Indians for whom the federal government failed as trustees nearly one hundred years ago.

"The families of current landowners bought and worked the land in good faith, assured that their purchase was

269

secure and legal under the prevailing laws. But a 1977 Minnesota Supreme Court decision, *The State of Minnesota* vs. *Zay Zah*, clouded their land titles. This prevented landowners from selling their land and from using it as collateral for farming or business loans," Stanbrook called to the crowd.

"You got that right," someone shouted from the crowd.

"Since the federal government failed the Indians by not clearing the sales so long ago, the federal government has a responsibility to make restitution."

Some of the Indians clapped, but then stopped when the rest of the crowd turned to stare at them.

"My bill, Senate Lands Bill 885, soon to be introduced, would clear land titles, make restitution, and prevent this issue from dragging through the courts for decades."

"How soon?" someone from the crowd shouted.

Stanbrook faltered momentarily. Then he loosened his tie and spoke louder still. "My bill, ladies and gentlemen, will offer twelve million dollars to the Indian heirs of White Earth—"

A sharp sucking in of breath came from the Indians in the crowd. Many turned to look at each other and grin.

"Twelve million dollars! That will mean thousands of dollars for every man, woman, and child—thousands of dollars to be reinvested by the proud natives of White Earth. Jobs! Industry! Self-determination!" The crowd, including some of the Indians, began to cheer and stamp its feet.

Tom LittleWolf quickly stepped forward. He took the microphone away from a surprised Stanbrook. "Money but no land!" Tom said. "You can't eat money! You can't walk on money! You can't hunt on money!" he called.

The whites jeered. A can of beer looped toward the podium; one of the big Indians leaped to his feet and deflected it. The other Indians stood with their billy clubs cocked.

"Easy—easy—steady, my friends," Stanbrook called. He quieted the crowd with his hands. "My Indian friend wishes to speak; let him speak. I've said my piece. I've made my offer."

The crowd cheered. Stanbrook waved.

Tom stood before the microphone and stared at the crowd.

"Pull the plug," some shouted. Others hissed.

Tom waited until the gym quieted to a general rustling. Then he pulled from inside his vest a thin, tattered, yellow book.

"This is a book, *Ten Little Injuns,* I remember reading as a child," Tom began. His voice was steady, resonant as he read:

> *"Ten little Injuns standing in a line,*
> *One went home and then there were nine.*
> *Nine little Injuns swinging on a gate,*
> *One tumbled off and then there were eight.*
> *Eight little Injuns never heard of heaven,*
> *One kicked the bucket and then there were seven.*
> *Seven little Injuns cutting up tricks,*
> *One went to bed and then there were six.*
> *Six little Injuns kicking all alive,*
> *One broke his neck and then there were five.*
> *Five little Injuns on a cellar door,*
> *One tumbled off and then there were four."*

Stanbrook's mouth slowly came open as he listened to Tom. Then he recovered himself and looked to the side for his aides. But even Cassandra Silver's eyes were fixed on Tom LittleWolf. As he read on, the gymnasium fell silent.

> *"Four little Injuns climbing up a tree,*
> *One fell down and then there were three.*
> *Three little Injuns out in a canoe,*
> *One fell overboard and then there were two.*
> *Two little Injuns fooling with a gun,*
> *One shot the other and then there was one.*
> *One little Injun living all alone,*
> *He got married and then there was none."*

Guy looked at Madeline. Her eyes glistened.

"We Indians," Tom began quietly, "are at the end of our lives as a people. For us the sun is setting, never to rise

271

again. We are nearly extinct. For a few minutes, then, I want to summarize how this came to be."

Tom began with the arrival of Columbus and moved rapidly forward in time as he spoke of Indians pushed west, always farther west. He told the story of the Chippewa/ Anishinabe in the Midwest, came quickly to the establishment of reservations in Minnesota. He worked his way toward the present without notes, with nothing in his hands except the small yellow children's book that he swung to punctuate the even flow of his words.

He told of the treaty of 1785 in which the Chippewa ceded all their land to what was now the state of Minnesota in return for smaller tracts of land for each band, the reservations.

In 1867 another treaty established 837,120 acres for the White Earth Reservation—tax-exempt, inalienable land.

In 1885 white settlers adopted a resolution demanding the opening of the reservation to white farmers and white timber companies.

1887, the Dawes Act, better known as the General Allotment Act. This congressional bill began the allotment of land to individual Indians with the intent that they could do with their land what they wished. The great timber companies began to set up operations in towns near the reservation such as Akeley and Park Rapids and Bemidji.

1889, the Dead and Down Timber Act. This permitted Indians to sell off timber that was dead or had fallen. Great timber fires became a regular occurrence on the reservation. Though the fires often were set by agents of the timber companies, many Indians burned their own forest allotments in order to sell their timber. For the next decade or more, the timber companies had a free hand on the reservation. The sawmill in the tiny town of Akeley became the biggest mill in the world.

1902, the Dead Allotment Act. Congress enacted a law allowing the sale of inherited interests by Indian heirs if approved by the Secretary of the Interior. This law marked the first inroad into the reservation for outsiders to acquire land as well as timber.

1904–1910. The Clapp Act. The Steenerson Act. The Clapp Amendment. The Burke Act. The Probate Act. Combined, all of these congressional bills gave whites the ability to buy Indian lands, which they usually did through liquor and fraud. The fraud became so blatant as to cause a congressional investigating committee to journey from Washington to Minneapolis, then on to Detroit Lakes.

Guy thought of the copy of the old congressional report he had seen in Cassandra Silver's briefcase. 1912. It had to be the same one.

". . . thousands of pages of printed testimony . . . land fraud, collusion . . . stripping of the White Earth lands . . ." Tom continued, his voice rising. People in the crowd were shifting in their seats and fanning themselves with handkerchiefs and feed caps.

"We don't want to hear that old shit," someone shouted. "That's all in the past—we want to hear about today!"

"Yeah—that's right—today!" several other voices called.

Tom paused briefly, then moved rapidly from 1912 forward. He paused at 1920 to describe fee patents, which were issued to all living adult mixed-blood Indians on White Earth. Fee patents removed their land from trust status, made it taxable. "What did we know about taxes?" he called to the crowd. "Nothing," he said in answer to himself. "Our lands went tax-forfeit and were bought up by whites—another way we lost our land!"

Guy looked at Madeline, then she at him. "Helmer," Guy whispered. "That's how he bought the farm. I remember him talking once about tax-forfeited land."

Madeline nodded. They stared at each other for long moments, then turned back to Tom.

"Today—yes, let us talk about today," he said, swinging his children's book at the crowd. "Today, of the original 837,120 acres of White Earth, only a few thousand acres—patches of land here and there—are owned by Indians. All the rest of the land is gone. Gone to farms. Gone to resorts. Gone to timber companies.

"So, too, are the Chippewa/Anishinabe people gone. They are gone to Indian ghettos in Minneapolis. They are gone to alcohol and drug rehabilitation centers. They are gone to prisons, where they grow their hair long, where they drum and chant, and sit in sweat lodges and dream of a better time. And they do not come back to White Earth. There is little left here for them. The Indian people are shrinking away, disappearing like smoke in the wind. But you can help us," Tom said suddenly to the crowd. "There are other lands to farm, other forests to cut trees on. Give us back—"

"You had your chance and you blew it!" someone shouted from the United Township Defense League section.

Tom stared.

"Yeah, what do Indians do with the land? Nothing—that's what. Farmland ought to be farmed, grown trees ought to be cut. That's what the land is for—to feed people and make houses for them."

"Without the land the Indian is nothing!" Tom called out to the crowd.

"Indians are nothing—you got that right!" someone shouted.

From somewhere near Guy's father a single egg arched toward the podium. It splattered across Tom's chest and face. More eggs came. Stanbrook leaped nimbly off the podium. Tom's Indian guards ran toward the egg throwers, who were seated in the Defense League. People shouted. The bleachers trembled and swayed as people coursed for the door. Stanbrook waved once to the crowd and was hustled to safety by his aides. Cassandra Silver was among them.

The fighting at floor level widened. Bradley Wicks shouted and waved his billy club. Finally he drew his .357 Magnum and fired it once into the ceiling of the auditorium. The bullet shattered an overhead light. Glass showered part of the crowd with fine, snowlike slivers. Dots of blood began to grow, then run on people's faces and arms. There were screams. People ran. Guy grabbed his mother and hustled her down the bleachers and across the floor toward the side door. Then he saw Tom, standing alone on the podium. He stood there staring at the fighting. Egg yolk dripped and ran down the black rivers of his braids.

"Turd—come on!" Guy hissed.

Tom looked around. His eyes were bright with tears.

"Come on, Tom," Madeline called.

Tom wiped his face and stepped down from the podium and walked slowly toward them.

"Keep him here, I'll bring the car," Guy said rapidly.

Outside, the sidewalks and street were filled with onlookers as two police cars wailed toward the gym with red lights flashing. Guy found the Mercedes. Beside it, two Indian boys in black T-shirts were lifting a battery from beneath the hood of a GMC pickup. They saw Guy. "You got some sort of crazy hood latch, man," one of them said to Guy.

"It's on the inside," Guy said, hurriedly unlocking the door. "People steal the battery otherwise."

The two boys grinned and trotted off with the pickup battery.

Back at the side door of the gym, Guy drove the Mercedes onto the sidewalk. Madeline came out pulling Tom along. Someone spotted Tom and shouted, "There he goes!"

The crowd surged around the Mercedes. In the swirl of people Guy saw the placard for the Township Defense League, and below it Mary Ann. Her big body blocked the path. For a long moment the crowd, unsure of what to do now that it had the Mercedes surrounded, fell silent. Mary Ann stared down at Guy, then Tom. She raised the heavy stick of her sign high above her head, raised it like a club above the hood of the Mercedes. The sign trembled. Suddenly Mary Ann's eyes gleamed with tears and she began to flail her sign from side to side. She cut a path for the Mercedes. "Let them pass, goddamnit!" she screamed. "Let them go!"

Chapter Thirty-One

Guy steered the Mercedes slowly down the dusty gravel of Chippewa Highway. Tom and Madeline sat in the rear. Nobody said anything. Outside, the sun was shining on the reservation fields. Green John Deere tractors pulled multi-row potato planters in wide black sweeps up and down the fields. Guy gave way to a big truck that approached rapidly from the rear; it went around them in a roar of dust. A pyramid of brown seed potatoes jiggled at its apex. Two potatoes tumbled over the side, then bounded, rubbery, down the road, where they thudded against the grille of the Mercedes. Following the truck were two others. A long tanker truck of herbicide. Another tanker of anhydrous ammonia fertilizer.

Tom stared straight ahead, did not seem to notice the trucks. "Twelve million dollars," he finally said, slowly. His face was as expressionless as the flat of a knife blade. "Twelve million dollars in return for the death of the Anishinabe." For the first time he looked out the side window. He stared at the fields for a long time. "Someone ought to cut Stanbrook's throat," he said softly.

"No," Madeline said quickly.

Tom turned to look at her. He narrowed his eyes. Then he looked at Guy the same way.

Tom wanted to work alone. Madeline and Guy left him at the Humphrey Center. Afterward, because they knew Martin was in town, they drove back to the farm together. There they took a long walk past the buildings, down the lane by the grove.

"Your Chevy," Madeline said. She stopped over the underground garage and scuffed the dirt with a shoe.

Guy smiled. "Soul on ice. I'll leave it there for now."

They walked on.

The sun was warm on their necks.

"So what's going to happen to Tom?" Guy said.

By the washout where Guy and Tom used to search for agates, Madeline paused to stare. She looked back toward the green timber of the reservation and said softly, "I don't know. He's got the right dreams but for the wrong times."

Back in the farmyard, Guy heard the phone ringing in the house. At first he did not want to answer it, but the bell continued to jingle. He trotted into the house. It was Cassandra Silver.

"Ricardo Losano is having a reception at his house this afternoon for the senator," she said. "Care to join us?"

Guy heard in the background a champagne cork pop and people laugh.

"Why would I want to?" he said.

She was silent for a moment. "Because most people never get close to a senator, that's why."

"Why would I want to get near Stanbrook?" Guy said.

"Look," Cassandra said, keeping her voice down, "I think you and I are on different sides of this whole Indian thing. I'm sorry about that, and there's not much I can do. But I can invite you to the party. If there's anything you'd like to say to Stanbrook, here's your chance."

"Why the sudden big heart?" Guy asked.

"Good question," she said, and the phone clicked dead.

Guy steered the Mercedes down the paved and winding treelined driveway that led to Ricardo Losano's house.

Madeline rode with him. She would try to talk to Stanbrook, tell him more about the Indians, about Tom Little Wolf, make him see.

Losano's house, made of red cedar and glass, sprawled across a hillside that overlooked the south bay of No Medicine Lake. Greening lawns, their sprinklers pulsing little rainbows in the late-afternoon sunlight, sloped down to the lake, to a screened gazebo and a two-story boathouse. Beyond, the lake water sparkled blue.

Guy parked. Madeline looked at Guy before they got out. Not wanting to put off Stanbrook with her battered Adidases and braids, she had pinned up her hair, wore a hint of pink lipstick, a dress, and low-heeled shoes. She looked trim and fresh. She swallowed, licked her tongue over her lips, tugged at her dress.

"You're gonna be the prettiest woman there," Guy said. He grinned and led her toward the wide oak doors and their brass potato knocker.

"My mother, Madeline LeCouerbrise Pehrsson," Guy said to Cassandra.

Cassandra's eyes flickered down Madeline's face to her dress, her shoes, then back up. "What a surprise," she said with a small smile, Cassandra, who did not like surprises. "Hello."

Then Cassandra turned to look at Guy. They stared at each other so long that Madeline looked away.

"Well, well—who have we here?" called a stout, swarthy man wearing a pink shirt and black bow tie. He was looking at Madeline. Ricardo Losano, after a brief wet handshake with Guy, steered Madeline away toward the center of the party. She looked back once to look round-eyed at Guy. He nodded slightly to her.

"Attractive woman, your mother," Cassandra said, leaning lightly against Guy. "Your father's a lucky man."

"They're separated," Guy said.

"I'm sorry," she said.

"You don't know my father," Guy replied.

He looked beyond into the long living room. Before the cathedral window with its lake view, steam rose from dried ice in a swan-shaped champagne bowl; the swan's beak exhaled steady, frosty breath toward the ceiling. Around the

278

swan, men in suits and ties, women in cocktail dresses stood with long-stemmed glasses and ate shrimp and crackers. They were all from somewhere other than Flatwater. In the center of the champagne drinkers was the tanned face and glinting white teeth of Howard Stanbrook.

"Victory party?" Guy asked.

"There are no victories in politics," Cassandra answered. "Only acceptable gains and losses."

"So which is this?"

She smiled. "We think today's town meeting went very well. We sensed wide support, a consensus."

"What about the egg throwing, the fighting, the police?"

"Ugly. Distasteful," Cassandra said.

"But not for the TV cameras or the newspapers," Guy said.

Cassandra shrugged. "The media make of things what they will. If the fighting makes the senator look like a peacemaker, we'll take the publicity as it comes."

"I'm sure you will," Guy said. He kept his voice even.

Cassandra took another glass of champagne and handed one to Guy. Ricardo Losano was talking earnestly with Madeline, who kept looking beyond to Stanbrook. Stanbrook was surrounded by women with short hair, red lipstick, and straight teeth. "It appears the senator is occupied," Cassandra said. "Let me show you around the house that potatoes built."

They passed down the wide hallway. A sauna. A deep conversation pit with fireplace. A grotto and indoor fountain. A swimming pool. A black-tile bar with "Happy Daze Are Here Again" stenciled in gold-leaf letters on the mirror behind. On the upper level were rows of bedrooms, all with balconies overlooking No Medicine Lake.

"Senate Command Post, Becker County," she said, opening a door to an office near the stairs. Inside, a secretary looked up from her paperback, *To Love and Honor.* She sat in front of a large, two-receiver phone with several rows of lighted buttons. On the desk were papers, some of which protruded carelessly from a brown leather briefcase that Guy recognized as Cassandra's. Guy saw the front page of the 1913 congressional report. He stared at it briefly, then followed Cassandra down the stairs to the champagne.

Madeline had edged closer to Stanbrook, to the outer ring

279

of women around him; Losano was regaling her with anecdotes about Ray Kroc and the American love affair with french fries. Two curly-haired men wearing wool suits and horn-rimmed glasses, lawyer types, angled in on Cassandra and pumped her hand. "Great fieldwork!" they said said in unison. Cassandra smiled modestly, introduced Guy.

"And what's your line?" one of the men said pleasantly to Guy.

"Cocaine," Guy answered.

Cassandra turned to stare.

"Which reminds me," Guy said to Cassandra, "I got busted today. Cocaine. I may need your help."

Cassandra laughed. "Great sense of humor for a Norwegian," she said to the lawyers. They laughed.

"Serious," Guy said to her. "But don't let me spoil the party. We can talk about it later." He excused himself and went for more champagne.

In a minute Cassandra was close behind him. "What the hell are you talking about?" she hissed.

Guy explained.

"Shit," she murmured. She began to blink rapidly, as if to clear her head of the champagne. She stared beyond Guy toward the sunlight from the big window. "Cocaine . . . Minnesota. I'll have to look up some things," she said. She turned back to him. "I'll have to know all the details, everything," she said quickly, looking about for something to write on.

"Later," Guy said. He stared at her for a moment. At the shiny fall of hair across her forehead, her perfect nose. He saw her as a kid. She was a long, straight-legged colt kicking up its heels, flashing in the sunlight. He wondered what she would be like if she'd been born in the Midwest; what he'd be like if he had been born in the East. What if he and Cassandra had met when they were twenty-one instead of thirty? His hand suddenly came up and touched her cheek. She met his gaze, and for an instant Guy saw his thoughts mirrored in her eyes. A backward mirror. If Guy was from the East. If they had met at Harvard or at the Hamptons. If . . . But then another of the tanned men tugged at Cassandra's sleeve.

"Bob," she said, "I thought you'd gone to Justice!"

"I thought I had too." Bob grinned and explained.

Finally Cassandra turned to introduce Guy. But Guy was gone.

Upstairs, Guy stepped into Stanbrook's temporary office. The secretary was out. Guy heard a toilet flush in an adjoining room. He went to the desk, to Cassandra's brief-case. He removed the 1913 congressional report, scanned it briefly, then slipped it inside his shirt and left.

Down the hallway he found a bedroom just off the main balcony. With the conversation murmuring and glasses tinkling below him, he sat in a deep-cushioned, white leather armchair and began to read.

62nd Congress, House of Representatives
INVESTIGATION OF THE WHITE EARTH
RESERVATION
Presented by James M. Graham, Illinois
Chairman, Expenditures in the
Interior Department
January 16, 1913

The 62nd Congress gave this committee general authority to investigate matters past and present concerning the White Earth Indians of Minnesota. Means were provided by the House to defray expenses of this work, including the journey to Minneapolis. Sessions were held from day to day in Minneapolis. For the convenience of the sub-committee, the Indians, and others, the subcommittee adjourned to the county courthouse in the city of Detroit Lakes, Minnesota, about 200 miles north of Minneapolis, where its sessions continued from February 5, 1912, through February 21, 1912.

At both Minneapolis and Detroit Lakes the attendance upon these sessions was large and betokened great interest. This was particularly true at Detroit Lakes, where a very capacious courtroom, with gallery, was packed to its utmost, a large portion of the audience being Indians.

During these sessions at Detroit Lakes your committee also visited the Indians in their homes (if such they might be called), saw their schools, hospitals, and other agency buildings, the trip occupying about three days, the party traveling the reservation in sleighs during the coldest period of the winter. . . .

The White Earth Indians are of the Ojibway or Chippewa Nation, a part of the grand division known as the Algonquins. They originally held sway from the west end of Lake Ontario through the Canadian province of Ontario, the northern portions of Wisconsin and Minnesota. They clung to the shores of the Great Lakes. They were a numerous people. When the French traders in their early period of their association with the white man began to furnish them [the Chippewa] with the white man's weapons, the [Chippewa] forced the Sioux, who inhabited western and southern Minnesota, farther and farther to the west and south until they practically came into possession of all the northern half of Minnesota.

The Chippewa . . . were participants in the third treaty made with the Indians within this country. This treaty was concluded at Fort McIntosh, Pennsylvania, 1785. This and subsequent treaties with them resulted in their removal to the north and west. By a treaty of 1867, there was set apart for their settlement and ownership the White Earth Indian Reservation in portions of what are now the counties of Becker, Mahnomen, and Clearwater, in northern Minnesota, embracing originally 36 townships.

The land on this reservation was an exceedingly desirable home for the Indians. It contained nearly every natural resource necessary to their subsistence and happiness. It embraced over 796,000 acres. It had very valuable forests of pine, probably 500,000,000 board feet in measure . . . several streams, a large number of beautiful lakes abound-

ing in fish, many of them bordered with wild rice marshes. The rice served as an inducement to game, and was used by the Indians as wheat is by white people. Large portions of this land were of great fertility, and being prairie were easy to break and cultivate. To the north stretched a great territory, sparsely settled and calculated to furnish good hunting for a long time in the future. It was a valuable heritage.

Downstairs several champagne corks popped like faraway deer rifles. A ripple of laughter swelled, then faded. Guy read on.

The first inroad upon the reservation was for the acquirement of four townships in the northeast corner, and was made by the lumber companies. There still remained 32 townships. But the four townships had not appeased the timber appetite of the sawmills. Until 1905 neither the pine nor the land it grew upon was allotted to individual Indians, whereby it could be sold by them. Congress soon enacted such legislation, the Clapp Amendment of June 21, 1906. This provided a means whereby not only the timber, but the lands, could be obtained from adult mixed-bloods, and from the full-bloods when declared competent, and if both of these provisions failed title might be obtained by the sale of the land for taxes.

As a consequence of this legislation the greatest harm resulted. Land sharks, anticipating passage of the Clapp Amendment, had, by means of twenty-five-dollar mortgages, tied up a large and valuable part of the reservation. The subsequent enactment of the Clapp Amendment was followed by a period of debauchery and shameless orgies. The white and mixed-blood land sharks, the hirelings of the lumber companies, and the alleged bankers in the villages along the Soo Line Railroad were engaged in taking deeds and mortgages indiscriminately from mixed- and full-bloods, adults and minors. The most persuasive arguments with the Indians were contained in bottles and jugs.

Guy looked up briefly. Below him the conversation still murmured, the glasses tinkled like wind chimes. He let his eyes travel across the room. Across the black-walnut dresser, its matching bed table, the marble lamp, the brown velour bedspread, the pale carpet. He ran his fingers over the leather on which he sat, traced its soft skin with his own.

On the day the Clapp Amendment went into effect the mortgages began to show up. The Indians wanted money quickly and they found no trouble in getting it. Thinking they were full-fledged businessmen because they were no longer under the eye of a guardian, they willingly listened to friendly offers of money. The land speculators were wise enough to allow the Indians to visit the saloons first and talk business later . . . for several days a sober half-breed was hard to find.

Below, at the party, voices strengthened, the beginning of argument, but they were not yet loud enough to break Guy's concentration.

Scenes more pitiful than these witnessed by your subcommittee during the trip over the reservation could hardly be imagined. In the district of Pine Point, in the southeast part of the reservation, where about 500 Indians live, nearly every man, woman, and child is afflicted with trachoma, and many are totally blind from its ravages. Twenty-five percent of these people suffer from tuberculosis and 40 percent from other dread diseases. Each hut visited was a chamber of horrors. Sometimes ten or more Indians were huddled together at night in a single room, trying vainly to keeping out the

*intense cold, but succeeding only in keeping out
the fresh air, with scanty bedclothes that reeked
with filth and vermin. In unbearable stench and
awful squalor little children, almost naked, aged
women, blind and helpless, men, once strong but
now broken by disease, live a life without hope.*

*Our party of the subcommittee consisted of 10 or
11 persons. Our entrance into their wretched huts
late in the night, after they had retired, and
without even the form of knocking, seemed to
provoke not the slightest sense of resentment; their
spirit seemed entirely broken, their hope entirely
gone. Their demeanor eloquently voiced the belief
that they had no rights left except the right to suffer
in silence.*

*Everywhere convincing evidence of poverty and
disease was plainly visible. But amid these condi-
tions, which would seemingly melt a heart of
stone, the land sharks continued to ply their nefari-
ous trade. Your subcommittee found in one deso-
late hut three women who, although blind, were
about to be ejected on a mortgage deal, and their
case was also typical of many others.*

*These White Earth Indians, the remnant of the
once powerful Chippewa Nation, are rapidly suc-
cumbing to the effects of the extreme poverty and
the white man's diseases, and, betrayed by their
lawful guardian and their mixed-blood relatives,
are now despoiled of their heritage.*

Suddenly Guy looked up and listened. Downstairs the
conversation had ceased, the tinkling glassware fallen silent.
A woman's voice rose and fell. It was Madeline.

Guy jammed the pages inside his shirt and ran to the
balcony. Below, Stanbrook was backed up against the smoking swan. Madeline was speaking rapidly. Stanbrook was
looking about for his aides, all of whom stared open-
mouthed at Madeline.

"You set aside land for whooping cranes—you save land
for bald eagles—you save land for grizzly bears—for moun-

285

tain sheep. You stop building dams and bridges because of some damn fish called a snail darter. And none of these are even people!"

"One of my staffers will help you," Stanbrook repeated. Several young men in suits stepped forward. Cassandra and two of the young lawyers conferred. Then the two lawyers came up behind Madeline.

"You don't know the Indians," Madeline said. She turned to include the rest of the room. "If you knew what it was like to be an Indian right now you couldn't stand here and drink champagne! But maybe you don't know about real people at all," she said, softer, as if she'd understood something for the first time. "Maybe people are just numbers to you. People are percentages on the voter polls, blocs on questionnaires. People to you are like . . . like blackbirds baked in a pie that every six years you cut up and eat."

The two men with artificial smiles each took Madeline by an elbow and began to ease her away from Stanbrook and toward the door. Guy came fast down the stairs. Cassandra called out to him but he didn't stop. The two men were carrying Madeline by her elbows through the door. Guy, pushing through the crowd, grabbed the shortest lawyer from behind. He locked his arm around the man's neck, then caught the second lawyer by his tie and jerked his face down under his other arm. Madeline stumbled free.

"Guy—no!" Cassandra shouted.

He looked back to the crowd. Everyone stared. He looked down to the lawyers, whose faces were turning red. He pushed them away, toward the party.

"Come on, Guy," Madeline said.

Guy went.

Just before the door slammed shut he heard Stanbrook say loudly, accusingly, "Who invited them, anyway?"

Out on the highway, Guy drove in silence. Madeline blinked back tears, then blew her nose and sat staring straight ahead.

"That's the second party today we've gotten chased from," Guy said after another minute. He turned to grin at Madeline, reached to touch her hair.

She did not smile. She shook her head. "Madwoman makes scene," she muttered.

286

Madwoman's son goes berserk, chokes lawyers in revenge attempt," Guy answered.

Madeline laughed once, and wiped at her eyes again. But then her smile faded. She shook her head from side to side and looked into her lap.

"Hey, you were great," Guy said.

"I blew it," she said.

"No you didn't."

"Yes I did. I should have kept calm, should have talked about unemployment on the reservation, about the alcoholism. I should have talked numbers, percentages. That's their language." Her eyes welled again with tears.

Guy was silent. "What's ours, I wonder," he murmured.

As they drove back to the reservation the sun's yellow deepened across the fields and trees. Short shadows grew from the bottom of fence posts and telephone poles. It was suppertime. However, neither of them was hungry after the crackers and shrimp and champagne. Neither did they have anywhere to be. So Guy drove.

He put in a tape, some Strauss waltzes. Along the highway sparrow hawks sat on the telephone cables, their little talons knuckled around the humming wire, their tails flexing for balance as they watched for mice twenty feet below in the grass of the ditch. When the car drew even the hawks always dropped away. The white undersides of their wings flashed in the sun as they dipped in low figure eights over the field, then planed back to their perch to stare down again.

Guy brought the car at sundown to the west side of No Medicine Lake. The lake was a waveless sheet of orange. He pulled over and stopped. "I want to check on something," he said. Madeline followed him. They walked through the orange light and the cooler shadows of the pines, downhill toward the water. Guy began to slip from tree to tree as he neared the shore. Madeline did the same without asking why.

Soon they stood behind a gnarled pine whose roots snaked like spider legs into the water. Among the roots, on the clear sand and rocky bottom, the water trembled. Fish. Hundreds of suckers spawning.

Madeline's eyes lit. Guy put his fingers to his lips, motioned for them to lie down. They lay on the bank and slowly eased their faces over the edge to watch the fish. The biggest suckers were the females, heavy-bellied, coarse-scaled. The females swam in the shallowest water, their dorsal fins exposed to air, sunlight glistening on their backs, their salmon-colored bellies dragging the rocks, feeling Braille-like the coarse grain of the sand and stone. They coursed back and forth. Suddenly they halted. They shuddered. A yellow tapioca of eggs spewed beneath them. At the same moment the darker, smaller male suckers arrowed in from deeper water. The males jostled each other and wildly sprayed pale jets of semen that disappeared in the sand-roiled water like milk in tea.

They watched the spawning fish until the sun pulled its light down into the west trees and the lake turned purple. Madeline shivered. Then they walked back up the hill and drove on to Tom's house.

Chapter Thirty-Two

It was dark by the time Guy drove back into the farmyard. Across by the machine shed, just beyond the yellow halo of the yard lamp, sat a car with a star on its side. Leaning against it, a pair of binoculars dangling from crossed arms, was Bradley Wicks.

"I was gettin' nervous," Wicks said. "I was thinking all sorts of funny things."

"Like I said," Guy said, slamming his door, "this is so much fun, why would I want to leave?"

Wicks grinned, his new teeth flashing in the yard light. "You're a kick, Pehrsson, really."

Guy glanced down at the binoculars. They were long-chambered and heavy, with several dials on them.

"You like these? Take a look," Wicks said. He held them out.

Guy fit the rubber cups to his eyes, moved them toward the yard light. Everything showed red.

"Your basic rose-colored glasses," Wicks said, grinning. "Here—you don't need no yard light with these." He pushed the glasses toward the dark grove. The trees leaped from a black wall to red, individual pines, their knobby cones, their sharp needles. "Brought them back from the last good war," Wicks said. "Dink glasses, I call them. Saved my life more than once."

Guy handed them back. He thought for a moment of pretending to drop them, but didn't.

"So let's round 'em up and ride," Wicks said, carefully fitting the glasses into a black leather case.

"One phone call," Guy said.

In the house Martin sat with a bottle of Jack Daniel's watching *Wild Kingdom*. Guy realized it was Saturday night. "What does Wicks want on a Saturday night?" Martin asked. "He wouldn't peep to me."

"Me," Guy said, dialing the Lumberjack Hotel. "I'm an honorary rider tonight."

"I'll be on patrol myself one of these nights," Martin said, pouring more whiskey into his coffee cup.

"How's that?" Guy said, turning and cradling the receiver as it rang the Lumberjack.

"The Defense League. We've had enough of gas stealing, cattle rustling, tire slashing, buildings burned. The sheriff's department says they don't have any money for more deputies, so we're gonna watch out for ourselves from now on. We've started our own patrol."

Guy stared at Martin. Cassandra answered her phone. Someone else spoke in her room. A man's voice. Impatient, resonant.

"Just a second," Cassandra said to Guy. Guy listened but the phone was silent. He could feel her palm over the receiver. "Okay, yes?" she said again to Guy.

"Maybe I'm interrupting something," Guy said.

"Maybe," she said. "Then again, maybe it needs it."

The man's voice spoke again.

"Interrupting?" Guy said.

"Yes."

They were both silent for a moment. "I'm leaving with Wicks now," Guy said.

"Don't talk about anything except the weather," she said immediately. "I'll meet you in . . . a half hour."

"All right."

"Where?"

Guy thought for a moment. "Call the dispatcher at the

290

sheriff's office. He can get through to Wicks's car. We'll meet somewhere east of No Medicine Lake."

The man's voice spoke again, closer to the phone this time. Guy recognized Stanbrook's voice.

"I'm sorry, I have to go," Cassandra said.

"Okay," Guy said. When she didn't reply he realized she was speaking to Stanbrook.

She returned to the phone. "Remember, only the weather," she said.

Before he left the house to join Wicks, Guy paused by Martin. Martin didn't look away from the TV.

"This Defense League patrol," Guy said. "Does the sheriff's department know about it?"

"I was telling Wicks, but he stopped me. He said he didn't want to know. He said what he didn't know couldn't hurt." Martin grinned conspiratorially.

"Somebody's going to get dead because of the Defense League," Guy answered. "You shouldn't hang around with those people."

Martin turned. "Who should I hang out with then—the goddamn Indians?"

"Hang out with me," Guy said softly.

"You're busy," Martin said. "Every night you're busy."

Guy paused. In the yard, Wicks honked the horn.

"After tonight I'm not busy anymore," Guy said. He stepped toward his father. But Martin turned away, poured more whiskey.

Wicks drove slowly north on the reservation. Yellow and red pinpoints of light blinked on his radio, which occasionally coughed with static.

"Some weather coming in," Wicks said, glancing down at the radio, then through the black windshield. "Can tell by the squawk box, plus my face. The wires," Wicks explained. "I got enough wires in my face to make a radio. Whenever the weather changes I can feel the wires tighten up. It's like my face is a banjo and every new weather front tunes it up a few notes. Wicks's Weather Radar." He grinned.

Wicks flashed the long, yellow arrow of his spotlight across the passing farmsteads. He let the light play in the darkest corners of the farms. Behind buildings. Underneath tractors. Along fuel barrels. Down the rows of trees in the black windbreaks that ran along the north sides of the buildings.

"I read once where some guy went to the dentist and afterwards he kept hearing voices," Wicks said. "Like radio announcers. Singers. It drove him crazy. Went to see a shrink, spent all sorts of money. Thought he was nuts. Turns out the metallic fillings in his teeth were picking up a local radio station. Truth," Wicks said, turning to Guy. "I read it in *Reader's Digest.*"

Guy nodded.

"The flyboys dropped us twenty miles inside Dinkland," Wicks said in the next breath. "Me and a spotter. I handled the rifle, he had the glasses. We'd find high ground and just lay there for three or four days. He'd watch the trails and I'd sleep or rub down the rifle. Sooner or later the Dinks would start to move on the trails. Then I'd set up my tripod, get the distance nailed down. We'd watch the Dinks through the glasses until we picked out who was in charge."

Wicks grinned. "Once we picked out a big fat northern Dink in full uniform. Even had some sort of lieutenant's cap with a brass star on it. He had a big, hairy mole on the right side of his neck too. We watched him set up a wide board and roll out a map on the board. He started to trace his finger along some trails on the map. The little Dinks were all sitting around him on the ground, watching. There was some breeze, five miles an hour, maybe less. The big Dink was out there sixteen hundred yards so I allowed eight inches. I waited. Finally the big Dink pulled his hand away from the map and turned to face the little Dinks. He put his hands on his hips. I could see his lips moving. I just knew what he was saying—'Any questions, class?' Just like old Mrs. Lincoln in history class, standing in front of those pull-down world maps. You remember her, right?" Wicks said to Guy.

"Right," Guy said evenly. He watched Wicks's hands on the steering wheel. His fingers were loose, slid easily back and forth as the road curved, as the wheel turned.

"Anyway, I let out my breath—you always shoot best with no air at all in your lungs," Wicks explained, "and squeezed off the round. From the recoil the shooter never gets to see what happens. But the spotter does. 'Bingo!' my spotter said, and started to crank up the radio real fast like to call the flyboys. I put the scope back on the Dinks. They were running around like bees with a rock thrown into their hive. The big Dink was down and the map behind looked like somebody'd thrown a bucket of bloody puke on it. 'Right in the kisser,' the spotter told me later.''

Wicks let the light play into a field. Two deer raised their heads; their eyes were four luminescent pearls.

"'Course I had my bad luck too," Wicks said. "My own fault, really. A sniper should never fire more than one round. Sniping is like poaching deer," Wicks said with a grin. "One shot sounds like it comes from everywhere and nowhere. The second shot gives away your location. One early morning I missed a Dink who was loaded down with mortar shells. I wanted to see him light up so I tried him once more, running. The chopper boys took a while to get to us. We took some fire. I remember my face going numb. Later the chopper pilot sent me a little plastic bag of my teeth they found on the chopper floor."

"But shit," Wicks said, his fingers tightening into fists around the steering wheel, "even that was better than this. Riding posse down the back roads. Scraping drunken Indians off the road. Filling out reports every goddamn minute of my life." He turned to Guy. "All these fuckin' Vietnam vets make such a big stink about their problems. Their head problems. Well, that's all bullshit. They're just pissed off and depressed because they can't ride around with loaded guns smoking the best fuckin' weed they'd ever get, only they didn't know it then."

Wicks looked back to the road. "Same with all this shit in the Middle East—the Arabs, the Jews, Lebanon. Shit, the magazines are full of it all the time, right? But you ever take a close look at the pictures, at the faces of those young boys with the AK-47s and grenade launchers and the automatic pistols? Hell—those boys are having the time of their lives. Going to school and gettin' married and raisin' kids is pretty thin soup compared to racin' around in the back of a truck with a bunch of your buddies and a fifty-caliber fire stick mounted on top. That fucking war over there goes on because what the hell would they do if it stopped? A lot of wars are like that. . . ."

Guy looked closely at Wicks for a moment. At that

moment Wicks's radio coughed and the dispatcher said Cassandra Silver's name.

Wicks gave his location. As he hung up the receiver he turned to Guy. "Your attorney, well, well," Wicks said. "I thought this was between you and me."

"Still could be," Guy said.

Wicks touched his shirt pocket, pulled out the cocaine bottle, glanced at it, then put it back. "I got a little deal for you. I need some information about some bad Indians," Wicks said. "They like to steal cattle, burn buildings when people are away, that sort of thing."

Guy waited.

"These bad Dinks—Indians, I mean—hang around the Humphrey Center, hang around your buddy Tom Little Wolf," Wicks said, turning to stare at Guy.

Guy met his gaze.

"I want to know what the fuck goes on in that Tribal Council Office. I want names. I want names 'cause I'm gonna sort out some bad apples, cart them off to graystone college in St. Cloud," Wicks said. "I figure there's about twenty Indians around here who need to be gone. And I want to be the one to tell them goodbye. You get me their names, anything else that will help, and I lose your little brown jug with your big thumbprint on it."

Ahead on the road Guy saw car lights, parked. It was Cassandra.

"Well?" Wicks said.

"Let me think about it," Guy said.

"No hurry," Wicks said. He glanced at his car clock. "It's eleven o'clock. I'll give you till midnight."

Cassandra joined them in Wicks's car. She carried a yellow legal pad, took the back seat. "I understand you're charging my client with possession of cocaine," she began.

Wicks turned off his radio.

"Once during a night drop the flyboys read their maps wrong and dropped us in a swamp," Wicks said softly, dreamily. "Time we got onto high ground, we looked like we were tarred and feathered. Only we were the feathers and the leeches were the tar. They were as long as a baby's arm. Each one we pulled off took a hunk of skin the size of a quarter."

Cassandra swallowed and looked at Guy. His hand out of sight behind the seat, Guy took away her pen.

They listened.

Wicks talked about *punji* stakes. About night watch. About the coral snake that his spotter leaned onto with his hand. The snake bit him in the soft flesh between his thumb and index finger. Wicks killed the snake, then took his knife and scooped away all the soft meat between the thumb and first finger like spooning seeds from a cantaloupe. But the snake had hit a vein. The spotter died in convulsions on the Medivac chopper.

Wicks talked in a low monotone. Once lightning flashed far away; Wicks flinched and jerked the steering wheel. The car slid half into the ditch, then back up. Cassandra's mouth hung open.

He talked on. Guy watched the clock. It was ten minutes to midnight.

In mid-sentence Wicks gunned the engine and hurtled the car forward. Ahead on the road Guy saw Indians running toward a truck. It was the truck with the high wooden rack in back. The rustlers. Some of the Indians, caught in Wicks's spotlight, scattered and ran across the road and into a field. The truck lurched from the ditch up onto the road. Wicks tried to block its path. But the truck, heavy-bumpered and tall, did not give way. Cassandra screamed. The Ford slammed into the front left wheel of the sheriff's car, spun it down into the opposite ditch. The car engine killed and would not start again. Wicks swore and jerked at the steering wheel.

"You fucking Dinks!" he screamed. He leaped out and emptied his pistol—crashing tongues of fire—at the Ford. Cassandra covered her ears and dropped from sight in the rear seat. The Indian truck raced away, unimpeded, into the night.

Then Wicks turned to stare across the road into the field where some of the Indians had run. He grinned. He uncased the heavy binoculars, strapped them on. Then he opened the trunk. The trunk was layered with weapons. Wicks thought a moment, then selected a short carbine that was like no deer rifle Guy had ever seen. He slammed a hand-long clip into the rifle. "Sent this back from the last good war, one piece at a time, U.S. mail," Wicks said. "You two stay in the car, keep the lights off. I'm goin' to round up some bad Dinks."

Faraway lightning, brief shudders of yellow on black, was the only color. When it struck Guy could see for an instant into the field. The field was unplowed grain stubble. Populating the field in dark humps, like elephants moving across savannah, were scores of great round straw bales. In one lightning strike, like a slide flashed onto a screen, Guy saw an Indian running from one big bale to another.

"Come out of the field with your hands up," Wicks shouted.

There was silence.

Wicks repeated the order.

"Come get us," a voice called from somewhere deeper in the field. A second Indian yipped fox-like from the left, a third barked from the right. For several minutes there was only silence. Cassandra held on to Guy.

Suddenly Wicks's rifle split the silence, one whiplike report that ended in a scream deeper in the field. "My leg—my leg!" someone began to scream. Then another burst of fire from Wicks's rifle.

"Stop him!" Cassandra cried. "He's killing them!"

Guy felt the round tube of a flashlight. He flashed it inside the car, on the dashboard, on the radio. He tried the switch labeled "Dispatch." A woman's voice answered.

"We need an ambulance," Guy said quickly and gave the location.

One of the switches said "Outside Microphone." Guy flipped the microphone switch. "Wicks," Guy said. His voice spilled metallic and hollow across the field. "Wicks, I called for an ambulance."

"Get off that radio!" Wicks screamed. "Get off or you'll end up in jail for interfering with a law officer!"

"I called for an ambulance, do you need help?" Guy repeated.

Wicks fired two rounds close over the roof of the car. Guy threw Cassandra to the floor and extinguished the flashlight.

"He's snapped—he's gone crazy—what are we going to do?" Cassandra breathed.

Guy thought for a moment. Then he reached out and felt Wicks's twelve-gauge standing upright in its holder. He fumbled briefly, then released the gun. Quietly he eased open the door away from the field and pushed Cassandra out. They crouched there, Guy with the twelve-gauge. Then Guy reached back inside for the radio transmitter. He took a deep breath.

"The law officer in the field has night-vision binoculars. He can see you when you can't see him," he called.

Glass rained on them. A rip of lightning on thunder. Cassandra flattened herself on the ground. But it was not lightning. Wicks had shot through his own car. Wires sputtered and sparked somewhere behind the dash. He screamed at them from somewhere in the field, "When I take care of these Dinks then I'm coming back for you, Pehrsson," Wicks shouted. "You and that bitch lawyer of yours. You interfered. You got in the way."

Guy leaned back against the side of the car.

"Now what?" Cassandra whispered. Her voice quavered once, then held.

Guy tried the radio. It was dead. Then he felt the twelve-gauge, jacked a shell into the chamber.

"I heard that, Pehrsson," Wicks called. He laughed. "That shell you just loaded? It's bird shot. Fifty yards and all it does is sting. What you need is a rifle, Pehrsson. 'Cept they're all locked in the trunk and I've got the key." He laughed again.

But the end of Wicks's laugh hooted. It was like someone had thumped him on the back in mid-laugh. Guy heard choking noises. Then a brief groaning.

"Wicks?" Guy called.

There was silence.

"Wicks . . ."

Suddenly the night was split by an Indian war cry—a high wailing scream that sounded all around them. Cassandra scrabbled toward Guy.

"Wicks?" Guy said again.

But there was only silence in the field.

They waited several minutes. Guy kept his finger on the trigger of the shotgun.

Nothing.

Carefully Guy eased back into the car. With the flashlight, he lit the dashboard, found the spotlight. Keeping his head down, he played the beam into the field. It brought no gunfire. No cursing from Wicks. He slowly raised his head

297

over the side of the car, then directed the beam among the round bales. Far out he saw someone lying on the stubble. Closer and to the right he saw two legs sticking out from behind a big straw bale.

"The shooting is over," he called into the field. "If you need medical help, stay where you are. The shooting is over." For long moments he looked at the shotgun in his hands, then laid it in the seat. He crossed the ditch. The barbed-wire fence squeaked as he swung over it; his heart raced at the noise. Then, parallel to the yellow path of light, he slowly walked into the field.

Guy approached the feet behind the bale. The feet were turned sideways. Behind him he heard the barbed wire squeak as Cassandra followed him into the field. He came around the bale and shone the flashlight down. Wicks. Wicks with a long steel arrow through his chest.

"Wicks!" Guy whispered. Wicks's eyes were open. A black thread of blood ran from his left nostril across his cheek. Guy knelt beside him. "Wicks—I'll get an ambulance." But in the bright glare of the flashlight, Wicks's eyes did not blink.

Guy started at a sudden gasp. Two steps behind him, Cassandra stared.

"Go back to the car, goddamnit," Guy said.

"No," she whispered, "Wicks . . . is he . . . ?"

"Dead." Guy turned the light to the other figure, then walked forward.

A young Indian lay staring up into the black sky. His eyes held the same empty stare as Wicks's. The Indian's left leg was exploded nearly in half just above the knee. The leg hung on mainly by the bloody fabric of his pants. Underneath his torn leg was a wide stain of blood. The blood was a dark red throw rug on the pale blond stubble of the field. Red earth, white earth.

"Not him, too," Cassandra whispered.

Guy put his hand on the side of the young Indian's neck. Nothing. Guy nodded and stood up.

Back at the car, Guy sat in silence with one arm around Cassandra, who breathed deeply, as if trying to catch her breath. Suddenly he pushed her away. "Wait here a minute," he said.

"Where . . ."

"Just one minute—I'll be right back."

She stared a moment, then nodded.

He walked back into the field and around the straw bale toward Wicks—then stumbled to a halt. Two Indians surrounded Wicks. One held the crossbow. One was kneeling on the ground beside Wicks. His knife was drawn and Wicks's cap was off.

The Indians stared up at Guy.

Guy stared at the Indian with the drawn knife. The Indian looked down at Wicks, then up to Guy.

"Don't," Guy said.

"Why not?" the Indian hissed. "Look at what he did to Sonny! Sonny's dead."

"So is Wicks," Guy said, looking to the Indian with the crossbow. He had seen him before at the Humphrey Center, had seen him arguing with Tom. "Wicks is dead. It's even."

"It's not even," the Indian said. "It's not close to being even."

They all were silent for a moment. The Indian with the crossbow suddenly stepped backward out of the light. "What do we do about him?" he said. Meaning Guy.

The Indian on the ground stood up. He still held the bare knife.

"Was that you on the loudspeaker?"

Guy nodded.

The Indian stared for a moment, then sheathed his knife. "Nothing," he said.

"He knows me," the crossbow Indian said.

"We know him," the other Indian said. "Come on." The Indians faded into the darkness.

Guy waited a few moments, then bent beside Wicks. Carefully he felt Wicks's pockets until he found it. He unsnapped Wicks's right shirt pocket and removed the little Baggie containing the tiny brown jar. He stood up, walked deeper into the field, and stuffed the Baggie far inside one of the big straw bales. In the distance sirens wailed.

He hurried back to Wicks's car. In the back seat he put his arm around Cassandra and she leaned close to him. At first she just curled against him. Then she put her other arm around him and slowly pulled him tighter. She hung on, and buried her face against his neck. Guy lowered his face and slowly kissed her hair, her ear, pulled her tighter against him. Her face turned up to his. Tears glinted on her cheeks. In the darkness their lips searched for each other. Their noses and chins collided as their lips found, then lost, then found each other again and again as they held each other.

But the sirens grew louder.

Finally they pulled away. They looked out the window. Across the black prairie, flashing red lights rose and fell like heat lightning before a storm.

Chapter Thirty-Three

Zhingwaak's story "The Crabs Who Went to War."

Once upon a time there was a village of crabs who lived by a stream. The young warrior crabs wanted adventure. One of them said, "Why don't we paint our shells, put feathers in our whiskers, fast, and learn something about war?"

"Yes, yes," all the other young crabs said.

One young crab went out from the village to find the most dangerous foe. Soon he found it, a raccoon. The raccoon lay there like a gray rock with fur. The raccoon was either dead or sleeping. So the young crab hopped back to the village and told the other crabs to come see what he had found.

The young warrior crabs in the village made ready to march on the raccoon. But an old lady crab, who long ago had had her hands bitten off by a raccoon, cried to them, "Don't go—don't go!"

But the young warrior crab who found the

raccoon, which was certainly dead, called out, "Don't listen to the Old Woman-Who-Knows-Nothing!"

So off the young crabs went.

Soon they found the raccoon. They formed a circle around him. They began to poke at him with their spears. They hopped back and forth with their spears. They sang, "Pick—jump! Pick—jump!" They kept picking at the raccoon and jumping back, picking and jumping, picking and jumping.

Suddenly the raccoon woke up from his nap. He whirled about and ate several of the warrior crabs in one bite. That day the raccoon had a feast of crabs without even having to hunt in the stream.

Back in the crab village the old woman crab worked alone to keep the campfire. She sang:

> Miskwaakone, miskwaakone.
> Fire blazes up, fire blazes up.
> Dibi misan, dibi misan.
> From where will the firewood come?

Chapter Thirty-Four

The day after the deaths of Bradley Wicks and James Allen "Sonny" Bowstring, Guy and Cassandra sat in the Flatwater courthouse with an FBI agent from Minneapolis, a small, immaculate man with thin brown hair combed forward, then looped across his forehead and secured with some sort of spray that smelled like strawberry jam.

Guy realized he was hungry. It was four in the afternoon; he had been in the courthouse since dawn. He drank more coffee. Cassandra sat slumped beside him. Their shoulders touched, but she drew away whenever someone walked by. The FBI man typed something. Guy paged through a tattered *House Beautiful* magazine. He looked at the pictures of people in their houses. He thought of his own living room in his own house in California. His couch. His books. His picture window. His plants. But the images of his own house were like photographs in the magazine. Photos of someone else's house.

"You walked into the field a second time," the agent said again.

Guy nodded yes. He waited.

"Why?"

"To make sure I had done everything necessary," Guy said carefully.

"Everything necessary," the agent said.

"To help anyone who needed help," Guy said.

The agent turned to Cassandra. "And that's when you heard voices for the second time?"

She nodded.

"Whose voices?"

"Voices. Just voices. I wasn't very close."

The agent squinted at her, then turned to Guy. "And it was then you saw the Indians."

Guy nodded.

"And how would you describe them?"

"Black hair, brown skin," Guy said.

The agent waited.

"We've been through this several times," Guy said. "You'll recall it was just after midnight, which means it was dark outside. Indians tend to look alike at night."

"But you grew up around Indians."

"I grew up with Indians in daylight. At night I slept."

The agent's lips turned down. He checked off something on his list, then turned to Cassandra. "What about the vehicle, the one that rammed the deputy's car?"

"Some sort of truck," Cassandra said. "We told you that." She lit another cigarette. It trembled briefly in her fingers.

"A blue truck," the agent said. "We have paint chips, blue ones." He stared at Guy.

"Blue, black." Guy shrugged. "It was dark. There was a storm. Check the weather report."

"We know about the weather that night," the agent said. He paused and looked at his notes again.

"There was a file in Wicks's car with your name on it," the agent said again to Guy. "An empty file."

Guy shrugged.

"Why were you riding with Wicks that night?"

"We went to the same high school," Guy said. "We were . . . acquaintances. I'm back here on vacation. He invited me along."

"And why were you along?" the agent said quickly to Cassandra.

She swallowed but did not look at Guy; they had talked about this. They had agreed on what to say. "I . . . wanted a closer look at reservation life," she said evenly.

"Which you got," the agent said.

Cassandra looked down to her cigarette ash.

The agent glanced over his papers once again, then checked his watch. For long moments he stared at Guy and Cassandra, then snapped shut his briefcase. The local police officers came into the room, stared as the agent stood up and slowly buttoned his overcoat. "Go for the truck," he said to them.

Guy took Cassandra back to the Lumberjack. She did not want him to come in. He returned in the morning and found her working, in bed, with the shades drawn. Opened books and yellow sheets of paper littered the bed and floor. Her ashtray overflowed.

"You slept?" Guy asked.

She shook her head no, and looked back to her papers.

"How about some breakfast then?"

"Not hungry."

Guy paused a moment. "You want to talk? About last night?"

"No—I just want to work—alone!" She stared at him with angry eyes.

"Suit yourself," Guy said, and left.

He hadn't been able to sleep either, so he did the next best thing.

Back on the farm, Guy drove Martin's big new John Deere tractor; Martin had gone to a Defense League meeting at Doc's. In the enclosed cab of the John Deere was a radio. There was air-conditioning. Tinted glass. A soft seat with a tiny, shock-absorber piston underneath, a seat that felt not unlike the one in his Mercedes. It was the first time Guy had driven a large tractor with a cab, and it took him several minutes to find the right switches and hydraulic levers. He did not turn on the radio or the air-conditioning.

He steered the tractor, the plow trailing, along the end of the field of oat stubble until he spotted the faint depression of the dead furrow, then lowered the plow. He brought up

305

the RPMs and headed downfield. He waited for the drag and pull, for the jolt in his spine of the plow irons scraping over stones. But the power of the big tractor drew the plow through the damp earth like a potter's knife through wet clay. In the new tractor he could not feel the plow, nor hear it scrape, nor smell the fresh-cut earth. It did not feel like he was plowing, but only driving a tractor down a field. He kept looking behind. Finally he stopped the tractor mid-field. He cranked open the windows of the cab as far as they would go. Left open the door.

He plowed in even rectangles about the field. Straight lines. Square corners. Turning left and left and left again. He reached the next dead furrow sometime toward midday. One land complete. Twenty acres. He stopped the tractor and got down. The pale green field was now a quarter black. The nearest overturned furrows glistened brightest, their moisture turned up to the light like the freshly cut dark meat of a peach. The sheen of each successive furrow dulled. At the dead furrow where he had begun, the overturned earth from sun and breeze had already dried on top and reflected no light.

He stooped and touched his hand to the damp soil. He felt the cool vertical edge that divided green earth from black. A gray and red-spotted salamander twisted its way down the square lane of the wheel furrow. The salamander was headed down a one-way path a half mile long. Guy hoped it would think to stop and wiggle up over the edge into softer dirt.

He stood up to look at the sky. It was high and blue and cloudless. The temperature had warmed to near seventy. Around him the plowed ground smelled like fresh coffee. He felt his heart start to beat faster. He looked back to the faraway farmyard, to the buildings. If he squinted his eyes, it all looked the same as it had when he was a boy.

Guy climbed back into the tractor and began a new land, a reverse path this time. As he drove, the sun played light and shadow across the field. The acres changed from green to black as easily as a painter drew his brush across a canvas. He forgot about the night out with Wicks.

About the FBI agent.

About Stanbrook.

About Cassandra.

About Tom and Mary Ann.

About Martin and Helmer and Madeline and Martin.

The rumble of the big diesel engine was like ocean surf. Repetitive. Hypnotic. Reassuring. Behind him the plow turned the earth in continuous waves, and soon, from the regularity of its rolling, he stopped watching the land turn. Forward and forward and forward he drove, the land beneath him bowing to the plow, bowing furrow by furrow by furrow, like a long line of black dominoes on a green table falling and falling. . . .

Suddenly a faraway thumping broke his trance. He jerked upright in the seat. He looked behind. The plow bucked and staggered like a cow with a broken back. The plow's rear axle had shattered, its rear wheel was nowhere to be seen. Guy cursed and grabbed for the throttle release.

He got out to inspect the damage. The plow was repairable, but barely so. Two acres of furrows lay twisted with high slabs of green and low clods of black earth. It was as if a truckload of tightly rolled sod had overturned on a freeway. He cursed again. The air was colder now, the sky partly cloudy. He looked from the broken plow beyond to the farm. He did not squint his eyes, and so saw it clearly this time. The farm looked the same as before. Only smaller.

Guy picked up Madeline at Tom's house. In the trunk of the Mercedes were the plow wheel and broken axle. Detroit Lakes had the nearest parts. He and Madeline would drive to Detroit Lakes, get the axle pulled and refitted, have lunch together, shop for a winter jacket for her.

A tall black column of smoke rose from behind No Medicine Town.

"Tire fire," Madeline explained. "For Sonny Bowstring. His funeral is this afternoon. Tonight there'll be dancing."

"You'll go?"

"Tonight, yes. But not today. Not to the funeral."

"You didn't know him?"

"I knew him pretty well, but Tom didn't want me to go. He said it would be a family affair." Briefly she looked away, across the reservation, then turned her eyes to the highway ahead.

* * *

In Detroit Lakes they dropped off the axle, then found a cafe on Main Street. They were talking about Howard Stanbrook when Guy turned to look at an old man limping by the window. The man was stooped, wore two winter jackets and a black wool cap jammed low over his forehead with the earflaps down. It was sixty degrees and sunny outside. The old man's lips twitched in some tight-lipped monologue. Something about the point of his chin, the length of his nose made Guy lean closer to the glass.

"It's old Henry Schroeder," Madeline said. "You remember him?"

Guy remembered him. He remembered Hank Schroeder had sold his farm to Ricardo Losano and, according to the late Brad Wicks, now lived on Easy Street.

Schroeder flailed his arms once and glanced through the window at Guy. He squinted briefly, rheumily, then looked away and walked on.

"Wait here," Guy said to Madeline.

"Mr. Schroeder, Henry Schroeder, Hank," Guy called, catching up with him.

Schroeder's blue eyes darted up from the sidewalk, then back down. He smelled strongly of piss in wool.

"I sent the check," Schroeder said quickly. "It's in the mail. I told you I'd send it. You got to have lots of insurance nowadays, I know that. You don't have insurance, they take everything from you. Leave you with nothing. I sent the check."

Guy stared for a moment. "I'm not your insurance man, I'm Guy Pehrsson."

Schroeder shook his head and kept walking.

"Helmer Pehrsson's my grandfather. You used to help us on the farm. Our farm was just south of yours."

For an instant Schroeder's eyelids ticked rapidly, but then he shook his head. "No. I never farmed. Never had a farm. Not me. I always lived in town. In town you've got to have lots of insurance. You don't have insurance, they take everything from you. I sent the check."

Guy glanced back to the cafe. Schroeder kept walking, rapidly, like some hard-shelled beetle trying to escape the sunlight. A block ahead was a four-story apartment build-

308

ing, plain brick without balconies. "Golden Age Apartments," the sign read. Nearing the door, Schroeder hunched his shoulders as though a sudden wind had risen. He paused and looked briefly side to side to make sure no one was watching, then ducked through the door.

Guy thought of Helmer. What for him in another year or two? What for Martin? For Madeline? What for himself?

He thought of Susan at Stanford. He saw her walking through a portico whose floor was slatted with sun and shadow; then she emerged into the full sunlight of the quadrangle, a flat yellow field of cobblestones below red-tiled roofs, but he was behind her and could not see her face. He called to her. She turned. It was Cassandra.

He shook his head to clear it, and turned back to the cafe where Madeline waited. At the door he paused and looked briefly down the street. Two cars waited at a red light, which did not change.

That evening, at the Lumberjack, the pink drapes glowed orange. Cassandra was out of bed and mostly dressed, though the curtains of her hotel room were still drawn. It was 7 P.M. Back from Detroit Lakes, Guy had driven to Flatwater to see Cassandra. He brought with him the congressional report.

Cassandra, dressed in jeans and a rumpled white nightshirt, sat barefoot at the pink writing table. Her briefcase and papers were spread across it. In front of her one white page was filled with black doodling.

"You've been out today?" he asked.

She was silent. A large ashtray full of cigarette butts sat by her right hand.

"You eat anything lately?"

"Not hungry," she murmured.

Guy swung her chair around, away from the desk, then swept all her papers into her briefcase. He pulled the drapery cord and opened the window. Yellow light spilled across the floor and pulled a wave of fresh air into the room. Cassandra shivered.

"Come on, let's go get something to eat," Guy said.

She didn't move from her chair. She squinted at the sunlight. "I've never seen a dead person before," she said.

"Well, now you have. Two of them."

She turned to stare at him.

"One with a four-point broadhead through his lungs, the other with his leg shot off."

Cassandra looked away.

"Both men bled to death—one filled up his own lungs, the other tried to fill up a field."

"Stop it!" she shouted.

"All right," Guy said. "I'll stop. I'll change the subject." He pulled the congressional report from his pocket and threw it onto the bed beside her. "You can't stop thinking about dead people. But you've never started thinking about living ones."

Cassandra looked sideways at the pages of the report. "What do you mean?" she said.

"This report."

"What about it? It's part of my research. That's what I do."

"Part of your research?" Guy repeated. He grabbed the report and held it close to her face. "This is your research?"

"Yes," she said cautiously.

"Look at what you've got underlined. Look!" He turned the pages for her.

"What do you mean?" she said angrily. "I don't know what you mean!"

"Jesus," Guy murmured. He leaned away from her, let the report drop beside her.

She was silent.

"You underlined dates. You underlined the names of treaties. You underlined the location of the hearings. You made notes about the acts of Congress and how they related to 1984," Guy said.

Cassandra stared, confused.

"But you never once underlined the name of a real person. Oh, maybe one or two old senators. But I'm talking about the Indians. Never once did you draw a line under tuberculosis. Under trachoma. Under firewood or lack of it. Under firewater and too much of it. Not once did you underline Indian shacks or cold weather." Guy stood up. "Maybe Madeline was right," he said. "People for you are just numbers to crunch, cards to play."

"What do you know about me? What do you know about politics?" she shouted.

"Just what I see," Guy said.

"Well, there's a lot you don't see. Politics is a rough game. It's bloody. But it's played for the benefit of the crowd, just like football or hockey or any other rough sport."

"And Stanbrook?" Guy said. "What about him? What's he to you?"

"I work for him. That's all."

"It didn't sound that way the other night on the phone."

"I was getting rid of him. I was glad you called. He tries stuff all the time. He's an asshole."

"Jesus Christ, then why do you work for him?" Guy said.

"Because Stanbrook for me is one rung on a ladder."

"Up," Guy said.

"Yes, up," Cassandra said. "Up—so that at some point I'll have some power. I'm a woman and so I'm second-team, can't you see that? The big boys have all the first-team spots and they aren't about to let go of them. I'm the water girl, just like all the rest of women in government. We stick to business. We do what's expected of us and twice that. We play all the little games. We become indispensable. We keep our eyes open. We wait."

"Which is all a way of saying you understand second-teamers—the little people—the ones who sit out the whole game." Guy said.

Cassandra stared. "You could put it that way," she said.

Guy was silent.

"Fuck you, if you don't believe me," she said.

"So prove it," Guy said softly. "Tonight."

Guy parked the Mercedes along the road at the end of a line of Indian cars. Cassandra rode with him. It was dark. The sound of a single drum came through the trees, where they could see a house-high pile of tires burning orange at the bottom, then red, then purple, then with black smoke that billowed darker even than the sky. A few Indians moved beside the fire behind a black lattice of oak trees. The tree trunks took quarter steps from the dancers, added a jerky rhythm to the dance.

"It's a tire fire for Sonny Bowstring," Guy explained. "His funeral was today."

311

Cassandra followed Guy past Indian cars, many filled with teenagers. From the cars came thudding music. REO Speedwagon. AC/DC. Twisted Sister. Prince. Guy recognized the songs because it was the same music that the young Chicanos at his company played loudly on their night shift. From some of the darkened Indian cars came the molasses smell of marijuana, the kiss of pop-top cans opening. A Becker County sheriff's car traveled by too fast to grab on to but slow enough to get a good look at the Indian cars. Three Indian kids scrambled from a car and pitched rocks after the sheriff's car. The stones fell short. The car did not stop.

"What if the Indians don't want us here?" Cassandra whispered, walking behind Guy, looking from the stone throwers to the fire ahead.

"Not to worry, of course they won't want us here."

Cassandra began to step on his heels.

Near the firelight they felt its heat on their faces. A tall Indian stepped forward to block their path. "Hey—this ain't Jellystone Park and we ain't bears."

Indian faces shone in the firelight as they turned to stare. A shorter Indian came from the side and said something to the tall Indian. Guy recognized the second Indian. He was the Indian who had knelt over Bradley Wicks with the knife.

The taller Indian looked back to Guy. "Him, maybe, but not her," the taller Indian said. "She's Stanbrook's spy."

"She's off duty," Guy said.

"So is Wicks—for good," the tall Indian said.

Cassandra's mouth came open.

"It's all right, Bobby," Tom LittleWolf said. Guy turned. Tom and Madeline stood behind them.

Madeline stared at Cassandra. "Well, here you are at our gathering," she said. "We don't have champagne."

"I'm sorry . . ." Cassandra began.

"About what?" Madeline said immediately. "About the champagne or about Indians?"

"Ladies, ladies," Tom said, his big teeth glinting white as he waved beyond for the drumming to begin anew, "let us be civilized."

* * *

Guy and Cassandra and Tom and Madeline stood in the steady glow of the fire. Cassandra's eyes moved from the dancers to the Indians who watched. Closest to the fire and to the dancers were the younger Indians, in their twenties, those with long hair and tribal dress. In the next ring were stockier Indians with shorter hair and department-store jackets; they stood in small groups, some with their backs to the firelight. They passed bottles. Beyond them, visible only when the tires shifted and threw the firelight farther back, were a few couples Guy's parents' age.

"This is a . . . powwow, right?" Cassandra asked Tom.

"More like a wake," Tom said. "Powwows are more formal dances. Powwows are like cotillions, only with Indians instead of debutantes."

Cassandra didn't answer. She stared at the Indians. "If this is a wake, where is the family?"

"Here and there," Tom said. "Some came, some didn't."

"Some went to the funeral but wouldn't come here?"

Tom nodded.

"Some went to both?" Cassandra asked.

"Yes. And some came only here, tonight." Tom let his eyes move among the Indians with the longest hair.

"There were a lot of teenagers out in the cars," Cassandra said. "Why aren't they here?"

"It's not important to them right now," Tom said. "Later it will be."

"Later . . . tonight?" Cassandra asked.

"No. Later. When they're older."

Cassandra looked among the crowd. "I don't see many older Indians."

"They're dead, remember?" Tom said.

At that moment an Indian came up behind Cassandra and tapped her on the shoulder. Cassandra turned. Her eyes widened. He was a fat Indian man and he held out to her a bottle in a paper sack. Cassandra stared at the bottle, then at the Indian. His face was sweaty in the firelight and pitted with smallpox craters deep enough to hold shadow. He smelled fruity with wine and smoke and sweat and piss. Cassandra's mouth came slowly open. She turned to Guy. Then she looked back at the fat Indian. Squinting,

313

she set her jaw, slowly raised the bottle, put her lips to its glass neck, and drank. An instant later she gagged and coughed and the wine spewed back out of her mouth. A moment after that she broke from the firelight and ran, stumbling among the trees, toward the road and the car.

Chapter Thirty-Five

The next morning in the Ford Guy and Kennedy started for Flatwater with a wagonload of oats and corn for grinding; Martin had let the bin run dry. Guy drove and thought about Cassandra, about what there was inside him that had stopped him from running after her. Suddenly ahead on the road he saw cars and people.

Indians. A line of Indians stood like fence posts driven into the road. Their corner post was the big green sign that marked the east boundary of White Earth. The Indians stood with their backs to Guy. Before them, like a chess player glaring across a table, was the tall, square face of a tanker truck with "Losano Potato Farms" painted on the door. The tanker was loaded with anhydrous ammonia fertilizer. The driver remained in his cab. He held a CB radio mike to his mouth and was counting Indians with a finger as he talked.

An Indian wearing mirrored sunglasses and a red head-band waved Guy to a stop, held out a flier.

"Customs check?" Guy said.

"You got it, man." The Indian grinned. Then his smile faded. "Read through this."

315

"White Earth Tribal Council Natural Resources Preservation Ordinance"—a long list of rules and regulations about land use.

The Indian jerked his head toward the tanker truck. "No chemical fertilizers, no herbicides, no pesticides are allowed on White Earth. It's all on the sheet," he said. He glanced briefly at Martin's truck and wagon before waving Guy on. "You farm on our land, you better read up."

Guy sat in the sunlight on the loading dock of the feed mill. Cassandra was not at the hotel or at the Caboose. He read the Indian flier. Faint oat dust drifted around him; below the floor grates the big grinder hummed its high, single note that was punctuated only by the crackle of ears of corn disintegrating to meal.

"Irrigation by farmers on the White Earth Reservation is theft of Anishinabe water *(nibi)*—theft of the greatest magnitude. One deep-water well for one irrigator can pump up to one thousand gallons per minute. One thousand gallons per minute times eight hours in a day is 480,000 gallons; 480,000 gallons per day times 15 or 20 days in a growing season equals nearly ten million gallons—from one well in one field. Ten million gallons times dozens of irrigators across the reservation equals billions of gallons of water stolen not only from the Anishinabe but from all people on the reservation, for all water to drink and cook with comes from the same underground table.

"The irrigator farmers pay only fifteen dollars a year to water a 160-acre field. In towns and cities the white and Indian families alike pay that much or more every month—and that only for water to cook and bathe with—why should this be so?"

Guy felt someone reading over his shoulder. Another farmer waiting for his feed. "What's that, that Indian bullshit?" the man said.

"Makes sense to me," Guy said, not looking up.

The man spit over the edge and turned away.

On the way back to the farm Guy had to stop a quarter mile from the green White Earth sign. Cars lined the shoulders. People walked rapidly forward, as if they were headed to an accident or an auction. Guy joined them but was stopped by a police cordon fifty yards from the tanker.

The big truck had not moved. Behind it were several other Losano Farms vehicles, including a pickup pulling a 500-gallon sausage tank of propane, two tall John Deere tractors with engines idling, and three trucks loaded with seed potatoes. In the crowd of Indians and farmers were TV men from Fargo and Alexandria and Duluth.

Centered in the crowd, Tom LittleWolf stood with arms folded across a sheaf of white papers. Tom was listening to Ricardo Losano. Losano's face was scarlet. The jerk of his jaw quivered his jowls; he shook a finger in Tom's face. Tom listened in silence. Tom the wooden Indian.

"Tell us again the Indian position," a reporter called.

"About the injunction," another said loudly.

Without expression, Tom read a statement: "The White Earth Anishinabe Council has filed a lawsuit of ten million dollars against Losano Brothers Farms. The suit is for use of and damage to Chippewa natural resources—namely our land and water. If the Indian people are to have a heritage that breaks the present cycle of poverty, it must be a heritage based on land—land that has belonged to the Indians from aboriginal times. Today the constant pumping of billions of gallons of water along with heavy use of dangerous chemical herbicides, pesticides, and fertilizers threatens the land and therefore the future of the Indian people on White Earth."

Tom paused and looked up. He held up another paper. "The Tribal Council has obtained a temporary court injunction that suspends all pumping of water and application of agricultural chemicals on reservation land."

"How did you get the injunction—on what basis?"

"Ownership of White Earth land is under litigation. The injunction is a common tool of law to prevent misuse of property or funds until conflicting legal claims are settled," Tom said.

"Suspends irrigation and use of chemicals—until when?" a reporter asked.

"Forever, we hope," Tom said, "or certainly until a court ruling."

"How soon before a court ruling?" someone asked.

"That's up to the courts."

"What about the potato crop? Right now, I mean," a Flatwater *Quill* reporter called out.

"Potatoes planted on the reservation must fend for themselves," Tom said. "Like the Indians who live here."

"Mr. Losano," a woman reporter called, "can you grow potatoes without irrigation or chemicals?"

"Sure," Losano said loudly, "if you want potatoes the size of rabbit shit." He turned to face the TV cameras. He struggled to keep his voice steady. "This country would go hungry if it weren't for irrigation and ag-chemicals. I don't know what the hell's the matter with these Indians. First, they're trying to sue me about land that's not even theirs—second, they're trying to ruin my potato crop. My french-fry plant employs two hundred and fifty people. If there aren't any potatoes to make into french fries, then two hundred and fifty people will be out of their jobs—it's that simple. If the public lets this happen, that's fine. I'll move my plant somewhere else."

"That's unlikely," Tom interjected. "If you're thinking of moving out, why are you buying up more and more reservation land?"

Losano stared.

Tom glanced at some figures on another sheet. "Our information shows that in the last four weeks Losano Farms has made purchase agreements for an additional two thousand-plus acres of land. Because of clouded title, the land is very cheap now. You buy the land at way below market price from worn-out old farmers, from scared young farmers. Then you plan, with Senator Stanbrook's help, to clear the title later—isn't that right?"

Losano's eyes bulged. His neck reddened. "Who the hell do you think you are? You . . . you goddamn parasite! That's what you Indians are, parasites on the land. You don't produce anything. You don't provide anything. You look for all the loopholes in the law and then take advantage of them. If this country had been left to the Indians, you wouldn't see farming, you wouldn't see towns and factories —all you'd see here would be . . . buffalo chips and tee-pees!"

At that instant a sharp hiss and then a rushing noise drowned out the reporters' voices.

"Run!" someone shouted.

Guy saw a white vapor cloud spew from behind the

propane tank. Two Indian boys dressed in black scrambled away from the gas tank and ran toward the woods. The battery boys—Guy thought instantly—the two boys he had seen stealing the pickup battery at the town meeting.

The crowd stampeded. Whites ran toward the police cordon. Indians fled down the road to their cars. Tom Little Wolf stood fast. He shouted and pointed toward the Indian boys who ran toward the woods, "Catch them!" Several Indians gave chase. The drivers whose tractors were parked closest to the propane tank gunned their engines to wheel away, but a radio station's van blocked their path. The propane cloud drifted over the trucks and tractors. The drivers leaped down from their cabs. Holding arms across their faces, coughing, they sprinted away. The white mist drifted over the green tractors like fog closing around trees. One tractor's engine still idled.

Tom still stood shouting directions to the other Indians. He was not looking at the gas cloud.

"Run—Turd—Run!" Guy shouted. Tom turned at Guy's voice. He saw the gas cloud among the tractors. He began to back away, then turned and walked quickly down the road, all the while looking over his shoulder. Tom was still only thirty yards from the trucks when light flashed around the green tractors. They bucked, once, against their weight like tied horses rearing from a flashbulb. The white sausage of the propane tank tore free from its trailer, slammed against the radio van, overturning it, bathing it in fire. Then the propane tank, like a tipped-over rocket, spun and slammed itself against the tanker truck. The ammonia tank ruptured and pressurized ammonia billowed into the air. Tom sprinted away.

The propane tank, on fire, tumbled down the road toward Tom. Guy saw Tom look behind once, then dive for the ditch flat-out, like he used to dive off the rocks into the shallow waters of No Medicine Lake. Coughing flame, the propane tank passed directly over Tom, skipped into the field, burning, hopping, a great white chicken with its head cut off and yellow fire for blood. A hundred yards into the field, the propane tank lurched ahead slower and slower, finally came to a stop, tried to heave itself forward one last time, then hissed and lay still.

In the foreground the tanker truck and the radio van burned. The two tractors and another truck also blazed. A TV man stood beside Guy, his camera whirring.

"Tom!" Guy called. "Tom!" Tom LittleWolf slowly pulled himself up from the ditch. His braids and the back of his shirt were burning. Guy pushed aside the policeman at the cordon, ran to Tom, and beat out the flames with his hands.

At Tom's house Tom sat shirtless and backward in a chair as Madeline clipped away his charred braids. Guy sat and watched. He wore mittens of white gauze. His palms ached; blisters had grown like toadstools, then popped. Tom shook his head again. "All ruined, all ruined . . ."

"Hair grows fast," Guy said.

Tom didn't look up.

That evening they watched themselves on TV. They watched the propane tank bounce. Smoke rise. Tom on fire in the ditch. Guy leaping on him, pounding his back. There were long closeups of Guy pulling Tom to his feet, supporting him until his head cleared, holding on to him.

Then the TV reporter stood framed against the backdrop of burning tractors and trucks: ". . . a violent clash of Indians and farmers . . . an apparently well-orchestrated attempt by the White Earth Indians to force their wishes upon reservation farmers, particularly upon the potato grower Ricardo Losano. While previously working within the boundaries of suits and countersuits and injunctions— in short, within the law—the incident today marks a new and lawless direction by the White Earth Tribal Council and its leader, Ma'iingaans."

Madeline turned off the TV.

The screen hissed and shrank gray to black. Tom and Madeline and Guy stared at one another.

Guy drove home to Martin's house after the 10 P.M. news. The yard was full of cars and trucks, twenty or thirty of them. Loud voices and the smell of cigarette smoke came through the open windows. The Defense League. Guy thought for a moment of sleeping up in the barn on his old cot in the hayloft. But he walked toward the house.

When he stepped through the door, conversation died.

Martin sat at the head of the table with his bottle of Jack Daniel's before him and a cigar in his mouth. Martin never smoked cigars.

Guy looked around the room. Looked at the men with caps on. At the staring faces. Jim Hanson. Kurt Fenske. The regulars from Doc's. Jewell Hartmeir. Mary Ann beside her father. Mary Ann's small blue eyes flickered to the floor, then back up, defiantly, to his.

"Maybe I'm at the wrong party," Guy said. "I'm looking to buy some Tupperware."

Mary Ann giggled. Several others laughed, but, when no one else laughed, fell silent. Martin looked down at Guy's bandaged hands. So did Kurt Fenske.

"The TV star," Fenske said.

"Coulda saved your hands and all the rest of us a lot of trouble today," someone else said.

Martin drew deeply on the cigar, then lurched forward to cough. He continued to cough until someone clapped him hard on the back. Recovering, wiping at his eyes, Martin slid the Jack Daniel's bottle across the table toward Guy. For his father's sake, Guy took a drink.

The loud talk resumed. In the haze of cigarette smoke Guy slipped through the crowd into his old bedroom and closed the door. He lay back on his bed looking up at the sloping walls, the low ceiling, the bulletin board. The brown and crumbly cork tiles were pinned with yellowed newspaper clippings of him and Tom playing basketball. A red FH school letter with tiny gold basketballs and bars and stars on it. A tail-feather fan from a partridge. A newspaper clipping of John Kennedy holding his coat at the throat, his hair tousled by wind as he spoke to a crowd. As he lay there staring, the door clicked. It was Mary Ann.

"Come in," Guy said.

For long moments they stared at each other. Then she looked about the room. "It's exactly the same," she said.

"Only smaller," Guy said.

She nodded and let herself smile. They stared another moment.

"How are your hands?" she said.

"Better."

"Let me see them," she said, in a mother's voice. She

321

came forward and took them and turned them over to inspect the bandages.

"Who did the doc-work, not you?"

"Madeline."

She nodded.

"Sit," Guy said to her, patting the bed.

She released his hands and sat on the end of the bed.

"How's Tom?" she said quietly without looking at Guy. She glanced at the door, then down at her hands.

"Lost a foot of his braids, but otherwise he's okay."

Mary Ann grinned briefly. Then her face fell again.

"They all want him off the reservation," Mary Ann whispered. "They think if it weren't for Tom, there'd be no trouble."

"What about you?" Guy asked.

Mary Ann's nose quivered. A tear grew like a pale pearl in the corner of her eye. She swallowed. "I don't know. In one way Tom's right. But I got my kids to think about. My job . . ." she said. She slapped away the tear before it could roll, shook her head as if to clear it. She turned to Guy. "Why couldn't things be like they used to be?" she said in a rising voice. "Every year we got older, the more mixed up things got," she said. "Look what's happened to us!" she said. Another tear grew, moved down the thick flesh of her cheek. But she shook her head again. The tear flew onto the pale bedspread and left no mark. "It's like a person goes through different lives all in the same life," Mary Ann said, softer now. "Tom used to be just a kid. Now he's an Indian. You used to be the reader, the thinker. Now you got rich and live in California. I wanted to be on TV. Now I got four kids and a job stripping rotten spots out of potatoes."

"Leave," Guy said. "Move to California if you like. I'll get you a job, find a better house for you."

Mary Ann's eyes gleamed for a moment, then she shook her head. "No. No moving. I moved around all my life, one damn moldy, piss-smelling crop house to the next, and I swore once I had kids they'd never have to move even once." She put her hand on his arm. "But thanks anyway." She stared down at her own hand. The fingers were chapped and starting to twist at the knuckles. Her fingernails were bitten down to red meat; flesh curled up like the round shell

322

of a snail into which the fingernail was retreating. She suddenly made fists.

"So you don't want to move, okay," Guy said. "But you need a better house. I can help you. I've got some money, plenty of it, I'll give you some. You need—"

"No," she said. "I ain't takin' money from nobody!"

"I'll lend it to you, then. You can pay it back whenever you can—next year, fifty years from now—it's just money, it doesn't matter to me."

"Well it matters like hell to me," she said, her cheeks coloring with anger. "We Hartmeirs don't need any help. We're doin' all right fer ourselves."

Guy was silent.

She looked back down to her lap, to her hands.

After a while she slowly shook her head. "But that ain't true. It ain't even my own words. That's what my daddy always says. Even the boys say it now. You hear something often enough, you believe it. And if you can't believe your own flesh and blood, who can you believe?"

Her eyes filled slowly with tears. "You ever wish you was somebody else?" she whispered, not looking at Guy.

Guy nodded.

"I do it a lot" she said. "It scares me sometimes. On the line at the potato plant sometimes I start to dream and I only snap out of it when the bell rings for break or quittin' time or my fingers hurt and there's blood on the potatoes 'cause I cut myself."

"Daydreaming is a way of getting through the day," Guy said. "Everybody does it."

"But I do it all the time," she said. "And it's not like I'm somebody else when I'm daydreaming. I'm not me and I'm not them. I'm not nobody." She turned to Guy.

Guy was silent.

"I mean when I'm home and the kids and Jewell are there all shouting and wanting something, then I'm me. But all day at work. That's when I think about being somebody else. That's when I'm nobody."

"Who do you think most about being?" Guy asked.

Mary Ann thought a moment.

"Princess Di, I think. Or if not her, then Marlene Evans on *Days of Our Lives.*"

323

Guy nodded.

Mary Ann looked down at her hands once again. "Sometimes I think TVs are like dollhouses but with real, little people inside," she said. "There's little houses and cars and people right inside the TV. Close your eyes sometime, and put your ear right on the side of the TV. It's like you're listening through a wall to the neighbors." She blinked and looked up suddenly to Guy. "You must think I'm nuts," she said, and lurched up from damn the bed.

"No," Guy said. He grabbed her before she could go through the door. "You're not nuts—you're just too damn bullheaded—like your father. You're too stubborn to let anybody help you. And you know what that means? It means the way things are is the way they're going to be—maybe not forever, but for a long time."

Mary Ann set her jaw.

"So let me help you. I can make things easier for you."

"No," she said. She pulled away from him. "That's not the way I was raised. And the way I was raised is the way I was raised—I can't change that."

"It doesn't have to be that way," Guy said.

But Mary Ann only stared at him with her lip pushed out until he swore and turned away.

"Now you're mad," she said.

Guy shook his head.

They stood in silence.

Mary Ann looked at her hand on the doorknob. She looked at both her hands, then up to Guy. She said, "If you want, there is one thing . . ."

The next morning Guy drove toward Ricardo Losano's frenchfry plant to meet Mary Ann. She wanted to show him around the factory. "That's all?" Guy had said.

"What d'ya mean 'that's all'? It's eight damn years of my life," Mary Ann answered.

He was supposed to arrive at exactly 11:35—no earlier, no later—on the west side of the building by the employees' entrance. Guy checked his watch, drove slower.

The potato factory squatted like an airport just beyond the north city limits of Flatwater. A tall, long terminal of gray concrete stretched parallel to the highway. The only color on its plain face was a giant yellow potato with beams of light streaming toward the name, painted in yellow cursive, of Ricardo Losano. The main building was silohigh, sixty or seventy feet, the equivalent of seven or eight stories.

Behind the main building, in a parallel row, were fourteen airplane hangar-size buildings made of galvanized steel. The steel buildings had doors that slid open full width; dump trucks and skid-steer loaders and a few tiny men came and went in and out of the dark mouths of the hangar-buildings.

Guy looked at his notes. "11:35. South side of main building, slot C, Visitors' Parking (in front of the cafeteria windows). Slot C only!" Mary Ann's exclamation point.

He drove slowly toward the main building, then circled behind as Mary Ann had said. He gave way to a long dump truck pyramided with potatoes. Some of the potatoes reflected sunlight off the wetness of their broken skins; others were shriveled and black. As the truck passed Guy squinted and pulled his face away from the smell. Brown juice dripped from the rear of the dump truck and led in a thin trail backward to the aluminum buildings.

Potato warehouses. Spring clean-out.

Guy remembered doing the same for his grandmother, carrying up from her basement a dripping bag of potatoes some of which had pushed long white sprout fingers through the weave of the burlap while others had melted to slime. Helmer's potato supply always came out even. He ate the last winter potato the day before new potatoes were ready.

Guy checked his watch: 11:34. He turned into slot C. On the concrete walls of the factory a narrow band of windows looked onto the parking lot. Behind the glass, people in white smocks and kerchiefs moved about carrying bag lunches and cans of Mountain Dew and Pepsi. Several women stared out the window as if they were waiting for someone. For an instant Guy remembered an old-age home near his factory in California: how the old people watched out their windows like pale watercolors framed and under glass.

Mary Ann, smockless and wearing a broad, flowered

dress and a blue kerchief tied up like rabbit ears, waved at Guy from the window closest to the door.

Guy stepped inside. The women at the tables and by the red Pepsi machine fell silent and turned to stare. Guy nodded. A woman even fatter than Mary Ann grinned at Guy with dark teeth.

"Come on," Mary Ann said, taking Guy by the arm and pulling him toward a large steel door. "If the fatties don't eat they'll be bitchy all afternoon."

Several women hooted at Mary Ann but nonetheless moved again to find chairs and dig into their lunch boxes and sacks with a clatter and rustle. From a wall of steel lockers beside the door Mary Ann hunched over her lock, spun the combination, then reached inside for a white hard hat and a set of earplugs for Guy.

"Put on the hat but save the plugs," she said to Guy. "We'll start across the road where the potatoes come in." She talked very loudly. So did all the women at the table, who fell silent again as Mary Ann guided Guy back out the door.

They crossed the parking lot. Mary Ann walked them past the Mercedes and paused to run her hand over the fender and roof. She put a finger into one of the shotgun-pellet dents. "Somebody shot your car!" she said, puzzled. "Indians, I suppose."

Guy didn't speak.

"Anyway," Mary Ann said, bringing Guy to the mouth of the nearest potato warehouse, "here's where the truckers bring in the spuds."

The building had strong breath, a warm exhalation of rotted potatoes and black dirt and stone dust and tractor exhaust.

"They're nearly empty now, 'cept for seed potatoes," Mary Ann said. She jerked her head back to the factory. "Line shifts get cut back in the spring when there ain't as many potatoes going through. People with least seniority gotta help in the warehouses and with planting. People been here a long time—like me—get to stay in the plant. Course there's two sides to that," she said. "In the spring it's cold and dirty in the warehouses and in the fields, but it's warm in the plant. But in the spring in the plant you get a lot more

326

rotten potatoes and so there's more strippin' to be done, more stink. Me? I done enough field work down in Georgia so I don't mind the stink long as I get to stay inside."

Guy nodded. He blinked as his eyes adjusted to the dim light. Deeper inside the warehouse two lines of women came into view. They wore coveralls and hard hats, worked with long rakes. They looked like coal miners. The women dislodged potatoes from the sides of the walls, then raked the potatoes in even lines toward a central grate. The women talked to each other without looking as they swung their rakes. To one side a male foreman worked on a broken rake handle.

The potatoes rolled ahead of the women's rakes and dropped through the grate. Guy heard faint splashing below.

"The spuds go in water through an underground pipe to the plant," Mary Ann explained, "a potato flume. The pumps are over here." She pulled him away from the women rakers and through wide swinging doors.

"Wear your plugs if you want," she called.

Inside was a great spaghetti of white pipes as large in diameter as Mary Ann. A squat turbine pump with a German name whined like an orchestra tuning at low C. The noise made Guy's ears pop. Below the floor a waterwheel full of potatoes turned and sloshed, turned and sloshed as the potatoes were sucked into the flume. Beneath the wheel, water coursed black and heavy with dirt. A small chain link conveyor turned through the black water, brought up stones. The glinting stones, some sharp-edged, most round like potatoes, traveled up to floor level, where they dropped with a clatter into a wheelbarrow. A woman with a wide face, wearing a black stocking cap pulled low across her forehead, stood between the handles of the barrow; she drew on a cigarette while she waited for the barrow to fill.

"Shitwork," Mary Ann called to Guy. "I know, I did it for a year."

Outside the warehouse a man sat leaned back in the cage of a skid-steer loader. Its engine idled. He was waiting for another wheelbarrow of stones to make a full bucket.

"Funny the stuff that comes in on the potatoes," Mary

327

Ann said. She pointed to the wall. Hung between nails on a piece of plywood were dozens of stone hammer heads and spear points and smaller, pale white arrowheads.

Mary Ann swung open the main factory door to a wave of noise and humid potato air. "Be careful, the floors are slippery," she shouted.

A faint sheen of cooking oil and humidity coated the gray-painted concrete floor. Mary Ann walked forward splay-footed, like she was on thin ice. Narrow stairs made of open grating crisscrossed up to several dump-truck-size bins. Guy carefully followed her upward.

At the top they looked down at the potatoes, now on a black, wet conveyor belt. The belt dumped the potatoes onto moving grates. Small potatoes fell away; big ones moved forward.

"The big ones turn into french fries, the little ones to hash browns, and those tiny ones go to hog farms," she called.

Beyond the sizing bins was a bank of gauges, a bird's nest of leg-thick piping that led to a large drum, similar in size to a ready-mix concrete truck. The mouth of the drum opened for a long swallow of potatoes, then closed. Black needles quivered and jumped in the white eyes of their gauges.

"Steam peeler," Mary Ann shouted. "It's just like a pressure cooker—three hundred and fifty degrees for a minute or so. The peelings get rolled off, then drop below. They end up cattle feed. The peeled potatoes get another washing."

"What's that?" Guy called, pointing to three bathtub-size, plastic-lined hoppers nearly full of a creamy white glue.

"Starch," she shouted. "It's trucked off somewhere and made into cornstarch to be used on babies' asses."

She waved for Guy to follow her back down the stairs. There she paused to wait for Guy, then pointed ahead to where a dozen women sat on tall stools along the conveyor belt. The women wore white hard hats, white smocks with the sleeves rolled up. Their arms were white. The black, wet conveyor belt came through plastic curtains carrying white, wet naked potatoes. The largest, roundest potatoes looked like slippery newborn babies.

"Strippers," Mary Ann called, nodding toward the

women. "That's what I do." They walked forward. Halfway to the women Mary Ann stopped. "It's slipperier here than anywhere—you better hang on to my arm."

Guy looped his arm through hers. If anything, the floor seemed drier.

Mary Ann brought him to the head of the stripping line.

"Hey!" Mary Ann called to the women, who looked up first at Mary Ann, then to Guy. They let their eyes run up and down Guy.

"This is Guy Pehrsson—from California," she called, still holding on to his arm.

The women grinned at Guy, their hands all the while snatching up potatoes from the conveyor. The women hardly looked down. Their fingernails were eyes on the end of their hands. With a small, hooked paring knife they struck at any color other than white. Brown and black fell away. White moved on.

"What are you, blind?" Mary Ann shouted, pointing to the belt.

"Saving some for you, honey," one of the stripper women shouted, flipping a rotten slice toward Mary Ann while still watching Guy.

Mary Ann tugged Guy away.

The women grinned. Their hands speared at the stream of white potatoes. As Guy walked away he felt their eyes moving on the dark back of his jacket.

Just ahead of the stripper tables, the potatoes funneled into a pipe that narrowed quickly to the diameter of a single potato. French fries spilled onto a conveyor belt.

"An air compressor accelerates 'em down the pipe through the blades," Mary Ann called. "It's like somebody come speeding around a corner on a motorcycle and suddenly running through a bunch of razor blades." She glanced at her watch, then pulled him along, quicker now.

They passed through a great room that shuddered. The floor shuddered. The walls shuddered. The ceiling shuddered as the french fries vibrated along shaking grates. Small fries fell away; larger fries continued. At the end of the shakers the fries accumulated in weigh-scale hoppers, then fell through pipes to the next floor below. Over the railing

Guy watched women bag the fries, sew them shut with power stitchers, then let the bags fall onto a conveyor belt.

Mary Ann hurried Guy along. It was 11:51.

Back in the employees' canteen, the women sat at tables eating their lunch and drinking from cans of pop. Most of the women still wore their white smocks and hard hats, some their earplugs. All turned to stare at Guy, then at Mary Ann, who still held his arm.

Guy nodded to the women. They grinned. Guy looked at the wall clock. "Aren't you going to eat?" he said to Mary Ann.

"Do I look like I need it?" she said. She took off her hard hat and fluffed up her blond hair. "Come on, we ain't gonna hang around here. Let's sit in your car until the whistle blows."

Outside, Guy opened the door of the Mercedes. Some of the women came to the window to stare.

Mary Ann sat silently, looking at the women through the windshield of the Mercedes. She touched the dashboard with her right hand. Behind the car two long refrigerated trucks rumbled toward the shipping doors.

"Where do the french fries go from here?" Guy asked.

Mary Ann shrugged. "McDonald's. Burger King. Hardee's. Denny's. All the chains, I guess."

"So in California I could eat a french fry that you made," Guy said.

Mary Ann grinned briefly. "S'pose so." She looked back at the women framed in the window. "The big shots from the burger companies fly in here to Flatwater in their little pissant jets and tell us how to make their fries," Mary Ann said, her mouth turning down. "They want every fry just so long, so thick, so crisp. They even taste them. It's funny to see, these tanned guys in their suits and ties sitting down to a package of fries and chewing on them like it was their last supper."

She stared for a moment.

"But the women," Mary Ann continued, "they're even funnier to watch. Whenever the strippers and packers hear there's taster-men coming they get all dolled up. They get permanents. They just happen to forget to have on their hard hats when the guys in ties walk by."

330

She looked back to the women in the windows. "They think someday one of those rich guys is going to notice them. They think he's going to say, 'Hey, what are you doin' in this goddamn oil pit? You're too pretty for this. I'm takin' you out of here.' And she doesn't even punch her time card that day because she knows she's never coming back and she don't need the money no more. She's gettin' on that little jet and she tells the pilot to fly low and fast over the plant and she gives everybody who's lookin' up the bird even though she knows they can't see her 'cause she's so small by then. She's on her way to New York or Denver or California." Her voice had softened to a near-whisper. "That's what all those dumb broads dream about," Mary Ann finished.

"And you?" Guy asked.

"I'm as dumb as they come around here," she said. She looked up at Guy. "I thought when you came back to Minnesota—that maybe you came back to see me."

Guy touched her hair. "I've got a girlfriend," he said softly.

"I figured that," she said.

They were both silent for long moments. She looked down at her hands.

"Besides, we're too different, anyway," she said.

Guy stroked her hair.

She glanced at her watch again. Suddenly she turned to him and blurted, "But I told the women that you was my boyfriend—that you'd come all the way from California to see me."

"I guessed that," Guy said.

"You did?" she said quickly.

Guy nodded. "But I didn't mind," he said.

"You didn't?"

"Why should I? You once were my girlfriend. Kind of."

Mary Ann grinned. Her cheeks colored slightly. "I gotta go, Guy," she said. "We got to be on the line when the whistle blows." She leaned over and kissed his cheek. "Thanks."

"For what?" Guy said.

"For not tellin' on me."

"They don't need to know," Guy said.

Mary Ann grinned. She got out of the car. So did Guy. He

331

came around and took her in his arms and kissed her. He kissed her a long time, kissed her as her big breasts pushed against him, kissed her until the whistle blew. Mary Ann's kiss was by far not the worst kiss he'd ever had. When he and Mary Ann looked up the cafeteria windows were filled with women who watched.

Chapter Thirty-Six

In the night the wind switched. Toward morning Guy awoke sweating in his blankets. Upstairs in Helmer's house he reached up to touch the ceiling that sloped behind his head. The boards were warm.

Hot, dry weather rolled up from South Dakota and hunkered over White Earth like a great brooder hen spreading her wings over a nest. The reservation greened. In the next two days Madeline's tulips shot blue-green spikes around the foundation of Martin's house and Tom's house too. Oats blushed chartreuse on the cheeks of some fields. Other new seeding, planted a day or two later, remained soberly brown. Yet even the brown fields, if Guy turned his head and looked from the corner of his eye, fuzzed pale yellow. And yellow was another huge of green because it could not become otherwise. Looking for color in new seedlings was like looking at faraway stars at night. Stare straight on and you saw nothing. But tilt your head . . . look to one side . . .

Guy planted oats for Martin, who was hard to find. He was always leaving. His Ford pickup jolted down the drive-way, then sped north or south. His contrail of dust drifted,

333

thinned across the fields. Another Defense League meeting. So Guy drilled oats for him, up and back, up and back the field, and left his own dusty trails.

He pulled the grain drill with Helmer's little tractor. The orange Allis was easier to turn, left no heavy tire tracks, and Guy could more easily stay wheel mark on wheel mark. He had only to look straight below him at the unwinding earth. Each pass of the grain drill left a sweep of tiny lines, as if he were pulling a wide comb straight down the field. As he planted he remembered the year Martin, drunk and angry, had seeded grain. The seedlings came through in wobbling green lanes. Some oats, double planted, grew brighter green. Other rows, paler, looped and curved back on themselves. Some parts of the field remained dark, had no oats at all. It was a field of paisley, green on brown.

Helmer said nothing to Martin about the planting. But daily he drove along the field and stared. Once, to Guy, Helmer said that the field was a lesson. That was all. A lesson. Late one night in June, Guy had awakened to tractor sounds in the dark. His father was disking under the oats. By then it was too late to replant, but the next day everyone seemed happier, and after that, nothing more was said.

As Guy planted, Helmer watched from his wheelchair by the gate. At noon the two of them ate sandwiches together at fieldside. The sandwiches were baloney and mayo or cold fried eggs with a swirl of catsup between white bread. They drank smoking black coffee from the thermos, then cooler water from the vinegar jug. The heat surrounded them like bathwater.

"Some stones out there," Helmer rumbled, staring far out in the field. "Have to get them stones off or you'll break a sickle come swathing time."

Come swathing time. Helmer assumed Guy would be here for swathing—and harvesttime too. Guy turned to Helmer. He must speak quickly, tell Helmer he would be leaving again. But his words, like divers turning upside down and backward in midair, transformed themselves even as they left his lips. He heard himself say, "We'll get the stones, Gramps. Don't worry."

"Should do it today," Helmer said, "before they settle. While they're sitting up."

"I can get them later with the big tractor and loader."

Helmer shook his head. "The John Deere's too heavy. Leaves ruts. Should use the Allis and the stone boat."

The stone boat. Guy had forgotten the stone boat. It was Helmer's invention, a long DeSoto car hood with a great, jutting nose. Helmer had turned it upside down, welded some curved steel cross-ribs to make it stronger, and added a hitch on the prow. Then, with the orange Allis and a chain, they pulled the car hood about the field. Guy or Martin had always ridden the stone boat, jumping on and off to load stones.

Guy looked back to the farm buildings. "Martin's gone," he said, "but I could get the bigger ones myself."

"Need two men," Helmer said.

They were silent. A bumblebee droned past.

"I'll ride the boat. You drive the Allis," Helmer said.

Guy turned to his grandfather.

"Won't hurt me," Helmer said. "I got one good arm. Bring around the boat and set me in it."

The stone boat lay rusty in the weeds by the fence. Guy dragged it free of the grass. Pale sprouts of grass grew underneath. A grass confetti ball of a mouse's nest tore open and spilled pink mice onto the dry dirt. The mice twisted in the sunlight like live shrimp. Guy stared for a moment, then kicked grass over them.

Behind the tractor, Guy lifted Helmer from his wheelchair and set him cross-legged in the stone boat.

"Okay?" Guy said.

Helmer nodded. "Let her go."

Guy climbed onto the Allis, looked back, and slowly let out the clutch. The chain tightened and the car hood scraped forward. Helmer sat straight upright, a Viking on the deck of his ship. As the stone boat rode the dry earth, Helmer's white hair flapped behind his cap, and he swiveled his head slowly side to side, squinting across the field for surface breaks, swells. Guy steered the tractor toward a squat melon of gray granite. He slowed the tractor, brought the stone alongside Helmer's right side. Helmer leaned over, rolled the stone on board. Guy drove on.

In this way they loaded stones. Helmer's boat left curving, looping trails across the field. Guy helped load the occasional big stones, basketball size or larger. The smaller ones Helmer pulled on board and stacked by himself. He arranged the stones in circles about him. He built layer on layer. As the stones rose in the boat, Helmer's legs were covered. Then he was sunk in stones up to his waist. Then to mid-chest.

"Dump?" Guy shouted, turning toward the fence.

"No," Helmer called back, and waved him on.

In one more half circle across the field, Helmer looked like a head poking out of a stone fireplace. Guy turned toward the washout without Helmer's wave. He stopped the tractor alongside the whitish mounds of old fieldstone and jumped down to check on his grandfather.

"Don't want to bury you," Guy said, grinning.

Helmer was silent for a moment. He looked down at the stones that covered him. "It don't feel that bad," he said.

Guy began to toss Helmer's rocks onto the larger pile beside them.

"Feels kind of cold. Heavy." Helmer fell silent. "Maybe that's what it's like."

Guy looked up. He halted a stone in mid-toss. Then he began to pitch away the stones as fast as he could clatter them onto the pile beside them.

Toward midafternoon, when they had dumped the last stones and drunk a jar of water, Helmer said, "Some farmers hate stones. Hate looking at them. Hate picking them. Martin. Martin hates stones," Helmer said. "But I never minded them." He spoke softer now, dreamier. "One thing, you can depend on stones. Pick them off the field in the spring, they come back the next spring. Stones move around underground. They come up just like seeds or roots. No difference really. Stones always come back." Helmer turned to Guy. "Like you, Guy-boy."

Guy swallowed and stared.

Helmer reached out his good arm.

Guy sank into it like he was five years old.

Late in the afternoon, Helmer dozed in his wheelchair. Guy finished the seeding, drawing closer to the north fence with each round. Across the road on Hank Schroeder's farm

336

the potato irrigator, under injunction, stood motionless. Its silver pipe bisected the 160-acre field like a table knife left in pie. The field itself, planted in machine-hilled rows, lay corrugated and flat and brown, a dull tongue-and-groove floor to the great blue room of the sky.

Twice that afternoon dusty white pickups with yellow potatoes painted on the doors stopped alongside the field. Men got out, walked into the field, knelt among the rows, did something with their hands, stood up to stare for a long time, then drove on. Later that afternoon, when Guy was on the last outside round of seeding, he stopped the tractor, ducked under the fence, and crossed the road to look at the potatoes.

Tiny potato leaves poked through the tops of the rows. The leaves were like green fingers, thousands of them reaching up from the ground into the light. The green leaves formed wobbly lines that straightened downfield. No other green—no quack grass, no wild oats, no volunteer corn—broke the surface of the soil.

Guy knelt beside one potato plant. The soil around the leaves was chalky dry. He dug with his fingers. Below, the soil was moist. But the wetness came from the rotting seed potato. The sharp hilling-up of the rows left more soil exposed to sunlight and heat, and therefore caused faster growth. But the hilling-up also left more soil exposed to the wind, to moisture loss. Two of five green leaves had curled under at their edges. Guy felt of one. Brittle, the leaf broke in half.

As he knelt a cool waft of air came up from the fresh dirt. He squinted. He scooped up another handful and held it closer to his nose. It smelled metallic. Smelled like the wood slats on the floor of the electroplating room of his company where acids were poured and rinsed, poured and rinsed. He stared closely at the dirt. It was as fine and black as potting soil. He clapped its dust from his hands and stood up.

Across the road he knelt and lifted a handful of Helmer's soil to his nose. Helmer's dirt smelled like rotted fence posts and leaves. Smelled like earthworms at the bottom of their can. He let the dirt sift through his fingers. When it was gone a whiskery skein of roots remained on his fingers. He raked them to the center of his hand, rubbed them with his thumb. The roots turned to slick, sweet mud. He looked across the dusty, reddening air of the field. Helmer waited in his wheelchair, a dark door in the wall of light.

That evening the sun went down scarlet. As tired from seeding oats as from a day at the beach, Guy fell asleep about the same time. Much later he woke to piss. In the darkness car lights flashed far out in Hank Schroeder's field, then went out. Guy watched at the window for a few moments, then returned to bed.

In the morning Guy was harrowing smooth the oats when he realized rain had fallen in the night—but only on the potatoes. Across the road the irrigator stood at a different angle, and the potato field was black with wetness. Over-spray had wet the road and left a crescent shadow across the dusty edge of Helmer's oats field. As Guy stared, a car came slowly along. It stopped where the road was wet. Two Indians got out. One took out a camera. The other held up the front page of a newspaper while the first Indian posi-tioned himself to get a picture of the newspaper, the wet road, and the irrigator in the background. Then the Indians drove north to the next field, the next irrigator.

That afternoon Guy called Cassandra. Her recorded voice spoke first and asked him to leave his name and number at the tone.

"Where are you? I want to see you," he said.

He called later but got the recording again. He left another message, the same as before.

That evening Guy drove to the Lumberjack Hotel, but Cassandra was not in her room. Mrs. Smythe, at the desk, said Cassandra came in late and left early. Always seemed to be in a hurry. "She's hardly ever here, why does she even pay for the room?" Mrs. Smythe grumbled.

He started driving back to the farm at sundown. A Losano Farms pickup passed him. A carload of Indians followed the pickup. When the pickup slowed, the Indians slowed. When the pickup turned, the Indian car turned the same way. The pickup slowed by the irrigator, then stopped. The Indians parked a few feet behind the pickup. For several minutes nothing happened. Suddenly the pickup lurched backward. Its heavy bumper slammed against the Indian car, which jerked from the impact. Guy heard the crunch and tinkle of glass. The Indian car backed up fast. It retreated a full quarter mile to the corner. There it stopped again.

Guy returned to the farm and parked the Mercedes. Then he walked in the blue twilight back toward Hank Schroeder's field. The Indian car still waited at the corner. The white pickup now sat in the center of the field beside the pump and generator. Darkness fell. The heat hung on. A few mosquitoes whined weakly in the dry grass. A tiny white eye of a satellite curved toward the big dipper. A yellow half-moon rose. But nothing else stirred.

Finally Guy turned back home. He had walked only a few yards when he heard a faint swish-swish, like bird wings, like an owl dropping from a tree into flight. He turned to look. Behind him, across the road, water began to sweep and swing above the irrigator pipe. The water slung itself forward and forward like surf at night. On its electric wheels, the irrigator began to crawl forward. The only sound was the hiss, chut-chut, hiss of the sweep of its night rain.

The Indian car's engine came on. Its wheels crunched on gravel, then receded toward No Medicine Town. The white pickup remained at the center of the field, a white smudge in the dark. Guy stood and watched for a few minutes more. Above the irrigator, sheets of water flapped like a line of swans flying single file low across the night field. The end nozzle gradually chut-chutted water onto the road, then onto Helmer's fence posts. Guy turned and went home to bed.

Much later in the night gunshots jerked him from sleep. He stumbled to the window. Car lights bounced and swung in Hank Schroeder's field. He pulled on his clothes and boots and ran outside to the pickup. There were faint shouts. A horn honked. Martin came running from his house with the shotgun. "Indian trouble—let's go," he called to Guy.

Guy paused. He looked down at the gun. "We don't need that," he said.

339

But Martin climbed inside with the gun.

Guy did not turn on the ignition.

"What the hell you waitin' for?" Martin said.

Guy stared at the gun. "We've got to talk."

"About what?"

"About that," Guy said, nodding at the gun.

"What about it?"

"This Defense League stuff. You're always carrying a gun. You're never home. Or if you are, you invite all the local thugs over to drink your whiskey and smoke cigars."

"Thugs, eh!" Martin said rapidly. "Maybe you forget. Those thugs are the people you grew up with. Those thugs are your neighbors."

"You act different when you're around them," Guy said quietly.

"Thugs, you call them," Martin said angrily, not listening. "Well, maybe I'm a thug, too, a thug trying to watch out for myself, like the other thugs. These are tough times. The goddamn Indians, the banks. Everybody's up against the wall."

"Not us," Guy said.

"What's that?" Martin said suspiciously.

"You and me is what I mean. We made some progress there for a few days. You know, after we had that fight. Things were pretty good between us. We had some jokes. I sprayed water on you. We even chased each other across the lawn." Guy's voice tightened. He stopped.

Martin did not come to his aid. He looked away out his window at the darkness.

Guy went on. He spoke softly. "When you hang out with those Defense League people, you're someone different. You're not yourself. That's not you, the point man on patrol with a cigar and twelve-gauge. You're not John Wayne."

"So you are maybe, is that it?"

"No," Guy said immediately. "That's not it. That's exactly not it. I'm only saying that we have to be who we are. That's the only important thing. The land, the Indians, none of that matters in the end. You and me, that's what matters."

They were both silent.

"Come on, goddamnit," Martin said, wrenching over the

340

ignition and starting the truck forward with a lurch. "Let's git after 'em."

But the Indians were gone. In Hank Schroeder's field the headlights of the Losano pickup shone on steel. Irrigator pipe lay on the ground. A geyser of water sprayed straight into the air like a single, tall plume of savannah grass. Two spans of the irrigator lay upside down, their wheels slowly grinding like a spent clock. Beyond the twisted pipe, toward the well, other spans remained upright, and their wheels strained to pull forward. But the irrigator's back was broken. It lay heaving slowly in place.

Two Losano men ran from the darkness into the headlights of the truck. One of them carried a rifle. "Sonsabitches—look what they did!" one of them shouted to Guy and Martin.

Guy squinted, then walked forward. In the track of the irrigator's big wheel was a grave-deep hole. The wheel had dropped into the hole. Downfield, beside the next span's wheel, was a crude wooden ramp. "The old high-low," Guy murmured. Like the Maxi-Burger, only bigger. As the irrigator had wound its way forward, one wheel had crawled up the ramp; just as it reached the top, the other wheel had dropped into the hole.

"Did you hit any of 'em?" Martin called, jacking a shell into the shotgun's chamber.

"I don't know," one of them said. "We thought we heard 'em. Took a few sound shots. What the hell can you do? They must have sneaked down the rows. Shit, we were right here!" The man's voice ended in a whine, as if he were explaining himself to Ricardo Losano.

"Let's go back," the other called, "we gotta turn it off, anyway."

"Then what?" the other man muttered, throwing the gun with a clatter into the pickup bed. The irrigator sprayed on in a growing lake of water.

"Then we got to radio in, that's what," the second man said.

Suddenly they turned their heads to listen. North, on the next field, car doors slammed. An engine accelerated. There was gunfire, then shouting.

341

"Shit," the two men said at once.

"Let's go!" Martin shouted to Guy.

Guy threw the truck keys to Martin and walked home alone.

The next morning, early, Guy met Tom at his house. Madeline was in her bathrobe. Tom's eyes were puffy and green-mooned.

"Seven irrigators," Guy said from the doorway. "They looked like crashed U-2s."

Tom shrugged. He drew deeply on his cigarette.

"You shouldn't have done it," Guy said.

"Why not? I'm tired of waiting," Tom said in rush of smoke. He scattered a sheaf of papers into the air. "Tired of the runaround. Yesterday I went into Flatwater to talk with the sheriff but he wouldn't even see me. I waited an hour. Too busy, his secretary said. Well, goddamnit, I'm tired of that shit. Now they got something to be real busy about."

Guy shook his head. "You're close, closer than you've ever been. But you blew it last night."

"No—they blew it!" Tom said angrily. "They were the ones using our water when they were under injunction. They were the ones breaking the law. All we did was enforce it."

"They won't see it that way."

Tom paused. He brought his dark eyes to bear squarely on Guy's blue ones. "What way do you see it?"

"Both ways," Guy said.

"That's not good enough," Tom said.

"What do you mean, 'not good enough'? It's the only way," Guy answered. "Especially for you. One way gets you somewhere. But one way doesn't get you back. You've got time, you've got the law—slow down, for Christ's sakes."

Tom stared. "I'd expect to hear that from Cassandra Silver, maybe, but not you, Tex."

"Don't get weird on me," Guy said. "Don't try to start some argument so you can write me off as just another paleface, because it ain't gonna work. So forget it," Guy said, his voice rising.

"Boys—boys," Madeline said.

Tom and Guy turned to stare.

342

"I meant . . ." Madeline said. She blushed crimson.

"Besides, I'll tell my mom," Guy said.

Tom's lips split into a grin that widened tooth by white tooth. Guy grinned. A moment later all three of them were laughing.

By midmorning of that same day, heat shimmered and bent the fields like the landscape was a reflection in an old mirror. Madeline pulled all the window shades in Tom's house, then made cold tea with lemon slices and plenty of ice cubes. Tom was at the Humphrey Center, working.

Toward noon Madeline wiped her brow and said, "I've got an idea. Let's pick up Tom, have a picnic lunch, and go for a swim. He needs a break," she said. "Plus nobody will know where he is for a couple of hours."

Guy helped make sandwiches.

The three of them spread their blanket on pine needles in dry sand. They were half shaded by a tall Norway pine. High above in the branches a red squirrel tsk-tsk-tsked at them. At the shoreline the water of No Medicine Lake pulsed slowly against the fine sand without break or splash. There were no boats. No gulls. No voices. A flat, shimmering heat.

They ate tuna-lettuce sandwiches and crunchy, cool wild rice with iced tea to wash it all down. Afterward Tom leaned back with his arms behind his head. In a minute his eyelids drifted together and his mouth went slack. Madeline stared down at Tom. She waved a fly away from his face. Guy chewed on a piece of grass. Madeline rubbed her eyes. She yawned, then smiled apologetically. "We didn't get much sleep last night."

"You were out in the potato fields with Tom?" Guy said, frowning.

"No. But I always wait up."

Guy was silent. He plucked up another spear of grass.

Madeline lay back with her head against Tom's arm. "Oh, Guy, what must you think of me?" she murmured sleepily.

Guy smiled. He shifted the shoot of grass to the other corner of his mouth, then looked far out across the lake. When he looked back Madeline's eyes were closed too.

While Tom and Madeline slept Guy walked down the shoreline. Coming around a bend, he drew up to watch a crane, a blue heron, flop up from the reeds into flight. He walked on. He found the broken stump of the old pine that had fallen onto the ice the winter of Zhingwaak's fish house. The smaller, round face of its sawn end was weathered and gray. The torn stump was like a chair. He sat and shaded his eyes as he watched the crane drifted back to its reeds. He looked farther down the shoreline for Tom and Madeline, but they were out of sight around the bend. He thought of Zhingwaak's story "The Rolling Head."

Once in an Indian village by a lake there was a teepee. In it lived a hunter and his wife and two little boys. Every evening when the hunter came back to his teepee he found the two boys crying.

"Why do you cry?" he asked them every time.

And the mother always said, "Oh, they just cry."

One evening the hunter returned to find the boys alone. He asked them, "My boys, why are you crying all the time?"

Then the oldest son told his father why. The son said that as soon as his father left the wigwam in the morning, the mother painted her face and put fresh bear grease in her hair to make it shiny. Then she braided her hair and tied it with a new strip of buckskin.

The father was very angry. The next day he hid himself and saw all that his son had told him. That night the father and mother argued. The father killed the wife with his knife.

Then he went to his boys and said, "My sons, I must leave you. When you see the sun setting red in the west, that means I will be dead too."

To the biggest boy he said, *"Ningos,* you must leave, too, and take little brother with you. But be careful. Your mother's head will follow you. Her head will keep calling to you. 'Wait—wait,' it will say, and other clever things too. But do not listen

344

to it," the hunter said, "or you will never escape."
Then he told them what to do each time the
rolling head drew too close.

The boys listened, then started out that same
afternoon.

Soon they heard the head rolling on the path
behind them. "Wait—wait," it called out in their
mother's voice. The boys did not listen. But soon
the head was very close behind.

The oldest son stopped and cut down some
thorn bushes as his father had told him. He threw
the thorn bushes over his shoulder onto the path
until he had built a mound of thorns that covered
the head.

Then they went on.

Only a little while later the boys heard the head
behind them again. "Wait, wait," the head called,
"I have food for you."

Little brother began to cry. "Let's turn back,"
he said to the big brother.

"No, we must not," the big brother said. He
remembered again what his father had told him.
This time he dug up flint rocks from the ground
and threw them over his shoulder. Bushes broke
into flames and made a burning wall. He pulled
his little brother along, away from the flames.

Soon they reached a lake. But the rolling head
was close behind them again. It called out in their
mother's voice, "Wait, wait—I must nurse little
brother."

Little brother cried again. "I want to go back, I
want to go back," he said to the big brother.

"No, we must escape," the big brother said.
"And there is how we'll do it."

On the shore of the lake was a great crane,
bigger than any crane in the world. And on the far
side of the lake stood another crane. The two
cranes then bent their heads toward each other.
Their long bills made a bridge. The two brothers
ran up the crane's legs and along the feathers of

his neck and then went across the bridge. The water was far below them. They ran onto the bill of the second crane, then slid down his neck and legs to the far shore.

Only then did they look behind. They saw the head rolling across the long bill of the first crane. But then the two cranes raised up their beaks. The mother's head fell into the lake below and did not come up again.

The littlest brother began to cry again. But the older brother pointed to the shore beside them. "Look, little brother," he said. The shore was thick with wild rice whose grains were as long and thick and brown as their fingers.

The little brother stopped crying. And they turned to explore this new land.

Guy stood up and turned back. As he came around the bend to the picnic spot, he heard laughter. Heard water splashing. He stopped to watch. Tom and Madeline were swimming and skating water at each other with their hands. Their clothes lay on the blanket. Once Tom chased Madeline and caught her and held her a long time. Guy looked away, behind him. He thought of turning back but suddenly Tom called out:

"Tex!"

Madeline turned and trod water. She watched.

Guy stared.

"Come on in," Tom called.

Guy waved.

Tom kicked back underwater like a brown otter.

Guy slowly came forward.

"Come on, Guy," Madeline called.

Guy smiled, shed his clothes.

Afterward the three of them lay wet and shiny and shivering on the woolen quilt, Tom in the middle. They clutched the blanket and waited for the sun to dry their skin. They lay like two slices of wheat bread with a peanut-butter center. Their teeth chattered and they laughed.

After a while, when they were warm, they sat up and

346

slipped into their clothes. Madeline did not turn away. Her small breasts hung flat and brown-nippled. Her stomach was wrinkled but tight. From her walking she had no fat.

In one moment, on the same blanket with his mother and Tom, Guy felt some anxious part of his childhood break up and fall away. An ice dam letting loose. A spring river flowing fully open for the first time. In one moment he saw his mother fully, saw her newly.

Tom helped Madeline up from the blanket and she held his hand to steady herself while she slipped on her shoes. Guy stared at their hands. The bridge of brown and white. He stared and felt nothing but sunlight striking all the way through him to his heart.

Chapter Thirty-Seven

The weather held hot. In the brilliant sky an occasional jet trail was the only cloud. It hung in place for hours, like a white cable stretched above the floor of the land. Nothing moved above. Little moved below, except Cassandra Silver.

"Hey—there's your girlfriend on TV," Martin said during the ten o'clock news." Guy walked quickly across the living room to watch.

". . . representing Senator Howard Stanbrook, aide Cassandra Silver has petitioned the district court judge to overturn an injunction that prohibits irrigation on the White Earth Reservation," a young woman newscaster said earnestly in her Midwestern nasal quack. She turned to Cassandra, who stood beside her on the courthouse steps.

"Miss Silver, what is the basis of your petition?"

"We feel the injunction puts undue hardship on the farmers of White Earth who use irrigation."

"Particularly the potato farmers?"

"Yes," Cassandra said.

"Do you expect to succeed in overturning the judge's decision?"

"Yes," Cassandra said.

"When will that decision come, do you think?"

"Soon," Cassandra answered.

"Tomorrow? This week?"

"It's up to the judge, of course," Cassandra said, smiling briefly, "but soon."

The newscaster turned back to the camera, which closed in on her round face and curly blond hair: ". . . decision could come too late to save this year's potato crop, which could mean massive layoffs at the Ricardo Losano French Fry Plant. . . . Jean Jacobsen, Channel 7 News."

Guy dialed the Lumberjack but got only Cassandra's recording. At the beep he said, "What the hell are you doing? I want to see you."

He saw Cassandra the next day in the Flatwater *Quill*. Her photo ran on page one, along with the lead article, "Violence on White Earth Threatens Federal Bill, Payoff." In the paragraphs that followed, Cassandra detailed the amount of federal money destined for the reservation and when it might be available—as soon as Christmas. But senators and congressmen from other states would be reluctant to vote for Stanbrook's bill until he could show them a violence-free, democratic consensus from the Indians of White Earth. And that could come only from the Indians themselves, Cassandra said.

On the page following the article about Cassandra was a large advertisement for a meeting, on White Earth, of "Indians for New Leadership." The meeting was scheduled for that evening at the Humphrey Center. Guy and Madeline went early.

Main Street of No Medicine Town and the Humphrey Center parking lot were filled with Indian cars, some battered and with windows missing, some shiny and newer. The lawn of the Humphrey Center was withered brown and looked dead, but the main hall was very much alive. It filled an hour before eight o'clock with short-haired Indians smelling of after-shave and deodorant, and with long-haired Indians smelling of patchouli, sage, and leather.

Cassandra Silver sat in the front row among some short-haired Indians in polyester suits. Guy and Madeline found seats at the far rear. Guy watched Cassandra. On either side of her the short-haired Indians periodically leaned close as she murmured something. They nodded each time. At exactly eight o'clock an Indian with a sweat-shiny face, a short-sleeved blue golf shirt that did not quite cover his belly, a white belt, and burgundy knit pants stepped forward to the microphone. He introduced Cassandra.

". . . fortunate to have with us . . ."

"Looks like the payoff pitch," Madeline whispered to Guy.

Cassandra took the podium. She was dressed in new blue jeans and a white cotton blouse with epaulets. She wore only a hint of lipstick, had parted her hair in the middle.

"I'm happy to be here and to be a part of a new direction for the residents of White Earth," she began.

"Go back to Washington," a long-haired Indian shouted from the rear, "nobody invited you here!"

"We invited her," the golf-shirted Indian called to the rear.

Cassandra waited for the shouting to die. Then she began to outline the main provisions of Stanbrook's bill.

"If Stanbrook cares so much, why the hell ain't he here?" another long-haired Indian interrupted. Other Indians in braids shouted at her.

Cassandra pressed on. Her jaw straightened with each interruption. The louder the audience became, the more resolutely she spoke. In speech-class fashion, her eyes moved back and forth among the front rows, then worked their way back. In mid-sentence her eyes fell upon Guy.

Her voice faltered, stopped. She stared. The hall slowly quieted. Indians in the front turned to look behind them. Cassandra pulled her eyes from Guy's and looked back to her papers on the podium.

"Excuse me," she murmured. She shuffled her papers, then began again.

When she finished to equal parts clapping and jeers, the heavy-set Indian in the golf shirt took the microphone. "Indians are here tonight because we're concerned just where the Tribal Council is taking this reservation. Indians never had any violence here on White Earth," he said.

"Except when the white man starved us and took our land," one of the leather-clad Indians shouted.

The Indian with the microphone ignored him. "There was no violence here—"

Another tribal Indian called, "Every day we don't have our land is violence against us!"

"Arrests, shootings," the fat Indian with the microphone called. "It's never been like this. Indians don't want it this way."

"That's the way it has to be," a braided Indian shouted.

"No—no," others shouted.

"The reservation is no better than its leadership, and right now White Earth is in bad shape. Tom LittleWolf came back here with a promise to use the law to help us—to protect us. But the chairman we've got now is not the chairman we elected. He doesn't even use the name we elected him by—that says it all!" the blue-shirted Indian called out.

Madeline looked sideways at Guy.

"Instead of the law all he's giving us is a lot of trouble and violence," the man called.

"That's right," people answered.

"That's why this meeting," the big Indian called with increasing confidence and volume. "We want new leadership—moderate leadership."

"That's right . . . hear!"

"Paint up and take it back!" an Indian in long braids shouted.

"It's too late—too complicated to get back the land. We Indians should support the Stanbrook bill. We can use the money for jobs and housing here on the reservation. We need a tribal chairman who understands that!"

There was shouting from the rear. The tribal Indians stood up, yelling. Short-haired Indians in the front rows also stood to shout. Guy and Madeline looked at each other briefly, then slipped down the row and through the side door.

Outside, Guy spotted Cassandra. She had opened the trunk of her Chevy for some well-dressed Indians who began to carry cardboard boxes from her car to theirs. Guy walked down the sidewalk toward her. She looked up, then straightened to watch him come.

"Hello," she said evenly to Guy and Madeline.

The sun beat in their faces. "Hot enough for you?" Guy said slowly.

"I do well in heat," she replied.

Guy looked into her trunk at the boxes. "What are these, air conditioners?"

"You might say that," Cassandra said.

Guy looked up from the boxes. "Goddammit, where have you been?" he said quickly. "I've been trying to find you."

"Working. And I didn't want to be found. By you."

Guy was silent.

"Excuse me," Madeline said, and walked away. They watched her go.

"She's never liked you, for some reason," Guy said.

"Being liked is not part of my job," Cassandra replied. "You made me forget that for a while."

"That's good," Guy said.

"No," Cassandra said quickly. "It only complicates things."

"What things?"

"My job. My life."

"Which are one and the same," Guy said.

"Yes—goddammit—at least for now," Cassandra said.

"So how do I complicate your life? I mean your job."

She looked at him angrily for a moment. "Whenever I'm with you things get . . . out of hand. Cars burn. Beds break. People get arrested, even killed, for God's sake. Suddenly everything is . . . off balance."

Guy waited.

"I come here with a job to do, a job I'm very good at, a job I've done before," she continued, faster now. "Then you come along and everything gets crazy and I start to forget just what it was I came here to do."

"And when I'm not around, you remember why you're here," Guy said.

"Yes," she said quickly, setting her jaw, "which is more, I'm starting to think, than you can say." She paused. "Just why are you here, anyway? Why did you come back? What are you trying to get done? I've never quite understood that." Her cheeks were flushed red.

Guy was silent.

352

"You come back to see your family," she continued before he could speak. "You argue with them. You get beat up, shot at regularly. You fight with your father. You spend lots of money on a farm that's going down the tubes. For a while I thought I had you figured out, but now I'm not so sure."

Guy paused. "Tell me what you had figured."

"I figured you were a loner. I saw that you didn't like to be backed into any corners where you might have to explain yourself. I found out you like books probably better than people. I know you made some money in California by being in the right place at the right time, and by not letting people get too close to you. You'd be a good boss in that respect. You can put everything behind you when you lock your company's door at night. Except that you don't work at night or even much during the day because you don't care a lot about money. This means you either don't understand how the world is run or you don't care—I haven't figured out which."

"Not bad so far," Guy said.

"But what I do know for sure," she said in a rush, as if to speak before the thought went away or changed, "is that my life seems much clearer to me when you're not in it."

Guy stared at Cassandra for long moments. In the last moment before one or both of them turned away, he spoke. "There's a big rock, as big as a car, down along the shore of No Medicine Lake," he said slowly. "I used to go there when I was a kid."

"Don't, Guy," she said, "please."

"You can dive from the rock into the water," Guy said. "All summer long the water stays cold but the rock stays warm."

They stared at each other. The red sun and the blazing asphalt shimmered around them, an envelope of heat.

Guy pulled himself up on the rock and stood in the sunlight above Cassandra. Behind him the sun shone orange on the water. He reached down to pull her up, but she stepped back. She looked back toward the car.

"All right," Guy said, "I'll show you how." While she watched, he shed his clothes. Then he dived backward into

353

the water. Its coldness grabbed at his nuts and made him whoop underwater. He emerged coughing. Cassandra laughed once. Then Guy turned, swam out a way. When he looked back Cassandra was on the rock pulling off her jeans and shirt. A moment later she soared off the rock in a long, white gleam of arms and back and legs. She surfaced gasping from the cold water.

"Come on—you have to swim to keep warm," Guy called.

They swam for a long time, then turned back to the big stone. They clambered up its smooth warm bulk, then lay belly-down, hugging the stone for warmth. They lay until the stone warmed their undersides and the late, red sun heated their backs. Then they dove in again.

This time they swam out a long way. When they slowed, the waves flowed past them and bent the sheet of the water into a washboard of orange. Far out, a pair of loons sat motionless, watching. Guy and Cassandra swam until their hearts pumped warm blood into the tips of their fingers and toes. Then they turned back to the shore. As they neared the big rock Cassandra suddenly drew up and began to tread water. On the big rock, like sparrows on a wire, stood a line of small Indian boys.

"Hello!" Guy called.

The Indian boys, seven or eight years old, stood silent.

"Aieeee!" the biggest Indian boy suddenly screamed as he sprang forward and curled into a cannonball. The rest of the kids leaped after him. Guy and Cassandra laughed at the rain of brown cannonballs and exploding water. For several minutes Guy and Cassandra watched the Indian boys dart and dive like tadpoles.

"Hey!" one of the Indian boys said. He looked up.

Atop the rock was a row, ascending in size, of white kids with curly blond hair. The kids were short-legged, strong, and wore homemade bathing suits.

"Jump in—y'all wanted to come—now what're ya waiting for?" a mother's voice called from behind. Mary Ann Hartmeir lumbered around the rock in a bright pink smock of a bathing suit.

Her eyes widened when she saw Guy and Cassandra. She started to step back.

"Mary Ann," Guy called, "come on in. But no wading—you have to jump from the rock!"

Mary Ann looked up at the big stone. "I can't get up there anymore," she said. "It's years since I been up there."

"She's too fat," called her biggest boy.

"No she's not!" her smallest girl said instantly.

Mary Ann looked up at her children, then out to Guy and Cassandra. She turned to the big boulder. She squatted. Like a great pink toad, she leaped onto its side and clung there.

"Come on, Mama," shrieked the youngest of her children.

"She ain't gonna make it," called the older boy.

The Indian kids swam closer to watch.

Mary Ann inched her way upward. Her toes spun against the stone, clawed for cracks. Catching one, she pushed off again, gained another few inches.

"Help her," Cassandra whispered, "she'll kill herself!"

Guy trod water and waited.

Slowly, like a bright caterpillar inching up the side of a basketball, Mary Ann pulled herself upward. Suddenly she scrabbled onto the summit. Then she threw over the side each of her children who had laughed. "You damn little farts, that'll teach you to laugh at your mama!"

The Indian boys below laughed and hooted.

Then Mary Ann leaped too. The Indian boys' mouths came open like full moons. They shrieked and churned the water to escape, but above them Mary Ann tucked under her legs, grabbed them tightly with her arms, and fell on them like an atomic bomb.

Later Guy and Cassandra and Mary Ann paddled and drifted farther out. Mary Ann floated on her back like a pink air mattress. Cassandra swam or trod water; she said she never could float, that she could actually walk across the bottom of a swimming pool.

"That's cuz your parents didn't feed you right," Mary Ann said. "You ain't got any preserves of body fat."

Onshore the Indian and the Hartmeir kids shouted and splashed and bombed each other from the big boulder. Their voices echoed across the water until sundown, when the loons started to call to each other.

The Hartmeirs left first.

A while later the Indian boys vanished all at once.

Guy and Cassandra finally emerged, shivering, beside the big boulder.

Cassandra leaned against the boulder, panting lightly, and tipped back her head and drew her hands tightly around her head to wring away the water from her hair. Water ran off the sharp ends of her breasts. Her teeth glinted white in the dusky light.

Guy stared.

She shook her head and flung away more water from her hair. When she opened her eyes she saw him watching her.

They stared at each other.

Guy came forward and put his arms in a hoop about her with his palms on the warm stone. He did not touch her. Her skin smelled of cold water and lake weed. Her breath warmed his neck. They stood that way for a long time staring at each other. The loons murmured.

At the same moment they reached to touch each other's faces. "Oh, Guy," she whispered. "Why?"

"Shhh," Guy said. He wiped water from her forehead and eyes. Her eyes still locked to his, they kissed for a long time. She trailed her hand down his chest and belly, then fit him inside her. Guy slowly pushed forward until her back was pressed against the face of the boulder. At first neither of them moved. Then, like small ripples on the water, they began to lap against each other. He let his hands drop to her shoulders, then to her breasts. Her cold hard nipples stood up straight and he warmed them with his fingers and then his tongue. She pulled him closer for warmth. For weight. For the touch of their skins that belonged no longer to separate flesh and bones, but, wherever they touched, to each other, to both at once, as did their breath and their lapping and lapping and lapping against the big stone. Cassandra spread her arms wide against the boulder and Guy moved harder and harder and harder against her. She moaned. A loon hooted quizzically. Cassandra called out; her knees buckled. Guy shouted, too, as they tipped backward into the shallow water. Its stones were rough and the water icy but they did not let go. They rolled and splashed and held and bit and held each other until they found themselves sprawled panting on sand.

Afterward they went, shivering, to find their clothes.
Which were gone.

Guy drove first to the farm. He turned the car heater on.
Cassandra rode on the far side of the front seat, naked.

"I don't believe this is happening," she said.

"At least it's dark."

"I should have known better," she said, ducking low in
the seat as they met a car.

Guy laughed. He drove faster.

"Don't speed for Christ's sakes—what if we get stopped?"

"We'll outrun them."

But no one stopped them, and Guy turned into the farm
driveway. A bunch of pickups sat by the front door of
Martin's house. Guy stopped the car and thought for a
moment. He slipped around the side of the house but his
bedroom screen would not come loose. So he walked
through the front door.

Talk died. Martin and several Defense League regulars
looked up to stare. Cigarettes dangled from lips; glasses of
beer hung in midair. Mary Ann grinned. She let her eyes
travel down his body, down the scratches on his chest and
legs.

"Wow," she whispered, looking at the scrapes on his
knees.

"Evening," Guy said to her. He nodded to the rest.

Martin nodded.

The rest stared.

Guy passed through to his room, dressed, and found
some jeans and a shirt for Cassandra.

On his way back through the living room Mary Ann and
the men turned to stare again. "Hot enough for you?" one of
the men asked Guy.

"Just right for me," Guy said, passing toward the screen
door.

Outside the house, Guy heard Martin say, "He's been
living in California."

Guy drove Cassandra to the Humphrey Center. As they
neared No Medicine Town Guy began to see posters tacked
on telephone poles and tied to stop signs: "Recall Tom Little
Wolf."

Guy braked the Mercedes hard and slid to a stop. He got out, tore down one of the posters, and brought it back to the car. Flatwater Printing Service. He turned to Cassandra.

She was silent.

He slammed the poster into a crumpled ball and threw it out the window. He drove on.

After a mile of silence, he said, slowly, "Tom could dive better off the big stone than anyone I ever saw. He had great spring." He stared straight ahead through the windshield. "Once we rigged up a big plank as a diving board. Tom would come running, dive onto the end of it with his hands, then go straight up in a triple backward somersault."

"I have to go," Cassandra said as he turned into the Humphrey Center. She looked for the door handle before the car had stopped moving.

Guy pressed the door-lock button with his elbow and all the doors clicked shut.

"He'd hang in the air longer than seemed natural. But that was only because he was so high above the water."

"I have to go. It's late. Unlock the doors, please."

"By the time he reached the water he was always head-first, arms straight out. Never much splash. Like a kingfisher," Guy said.

Cassandra pulled at her door handle, then tried the rear handle.

"Why are you doing this?" she said, her voice rising, choking.

"Tom and I spent a lot of time on that big stone. We talked about a lot of stuff there."

"I don't care!"

"Sometimes we wondered what would happen to us when we grew up. But Tom would never say much about that. I did most of the talking then."

"Let me out, I want to get out!"

"Once we'd been reading *Huck Finn* in school. Huck was always marking things in blood, right? So Tom and I did it too. We pricked our fingers with a jackknife and let some blood drip onto the rock. Then we mixed it around and swore we'd always save each other's lives when they needed saving. Dumb, huh? We were only nine or ten. Later we never said anything about it because we were old enough to know how dumb it was. It was more embarrassing than anything."

"I don't want to hear this. All I want to do is get out of this car—now!" Cassandra said.

"Sure," Guy said, releasing the locks.

She scrambled out and started to walk away. Then she came back.

"Why did you do that?" she shouted. "Why do you always have to ruin things?" At the end her voice caught.

Guy was silent.

"I understand you more and more," she said rapidly. "You're stuck in the past. You're back here from California wishing you could be nine years old again."

"Nine was a good year," Guy said.

"You can't deal with the present," Cassandra said. "But the present's here."

"No, the present comes and goes," Guy said quietly.

She stared at him.

"You couldn't make it where I come from," she said rapidly, her eyes flashing. "Out East you don't have time to be lonely and enigmatic—maybe in a Woody Allen movie but not in real life. You'd be lucky to hold down a job in your condition."

"My condition," Guy said.

"You're . . . damaged. From your past, I think," Cassandra said. "There's a lot of women out there who got damaged some way or another, but there's a lot of men too. Men just hide it better."

"I've nothing to hide," Guy said. Which was the point, he suddenly realized, he had been wanting to reach for a long time.

She stared down at him.

"What you see is everything."

"I need more than that," she said, her voice faltering.

"More than everything?" Guy said.

"Yes—more than everything!" Cassandra cried.

"Well, you can't have it," Guy shouted. "And I'm enough, goddamnit. I want you—with me—can't you see that?"

Cassandra's eyes widened and she clapped her hands to her ears. "Don't, don't," she said over and over to drown out his words. Suddenly she turned and ran.

Guy stopped himself from running after her. She stumbled into her car and threw it into gear. He watched her drive away.

When her car disappeared from sight she was still with him. He saw her at the Lumberjack, in her room, framed in the window, in sunlight, her clothes falling from her like leaves, like another skin.

Chapter Thirty-Eight

On his knees, Guy dug in the field with his jackknife. It was nine o'clock in the morning. The sun burned on his back like an iron left flat on its board and sweat bit at the corners of his eyes. He was checking his oats. Or rather, Martin's oats. Beneath the powdery dirt the kernels lay dry and flat. Some kernels had swelled and sprouted, then shriveled to black an inch beyond the belly of their husks like tiny, dried-up navel cords. Guy stood up and wiped his eyes.

Martin walked into the field, his legs vague in the dust that puffed forward from his boots at each step. He came over to Guy and looked down at his digging.

"How's it looking?"

"Not good," Guy said.

"Looks like one of them years," Martin said pleasantly enough.

Guy squinted at his father. Martin's tone of voice held the promise, the faint excitement of impending failure.

"Still time," Guy said, looking at the sky.

"No weather from here to Spokane," Martin said. "At least that's what the weatherman says," Martin added.

Guy snapped shut his jackknife.

His father walked away toward the machine shed. Guy remained in the field.

Why was he here, anyway? Just what was he hoping to do or say or feel? He shaded his eyes to look across the land, which shimmered with heat. There was only silence in the fields.

It was then he realized he had been waiting for something. A sign. A sign that something was ending. A door slamming. A final buzzer. A break beyond repair. A period at the end of a sentence. He had been waiting for the ending of something and then the beginning of something new.

But on the farm nothing ever ended. Or if it did, it ended so slowly that you mistook the ending for the middle of something else. A field of oats dried up from no rain. The same field drowned from too much rain. Neither the drying up nor the drowning came fast enough to be a real ending—like an accident or a death—for in the days and then weeks of heat or rain the oats faded in size and even in memory of their planting, as the burning up or the drowning became the real crop. So there were never any last rites. There was no taps. No rifle salutes. No flags lowered. No final bricks laid. There was no full harvest and there was no complete planting. There was only the endless middle of things.

One had, therefore, to choose his own endings.

One had to say, This broken axle is the end of this swather. I will not fix this machine again. I will not drive it anymore.

One said, This Angus cow is mean. It has always been mean. It deserves nothing more than to be shot and skinned and butchered and eaten by me and my family, against whom it has always directed its meanness.

This frost in August marks the last time I will try to grow corn this far north.

This south wind tells me I must sell my steers this week, for the market will only keep falling.

This field is not finished, but it is very late in the day and so this round of plowing or swathing or combining is the very last. No matter what. No matter how I feel or what I think when I'm nearly done with this, my last round, especially when I near the stone or the fence post or the gate where I declared this to be my last round, no matter what.

This hot wind tonight, by its steady, straight blowing, tells me everything I need to know about tomorrow.

Guy turned back to the house to pack.

In the yard he paused as Mary Ann's battered Galaxie turned into the driveway. She drove up to him. "So how you feelin' today, lover boy?" Mary Ann called.

Guy shrugged.

"You and that Silver woman would make a good couple if you could keep from killin' each other," Mary Ann said.

"I don't know," Guy said skeptically.

"You've been known to be wrong," Mary Ann said.

Guy smiled.

Mary Ann looked toward the house. "Where's your granddad?"

"In the barn." Guy answered. "Now with the stair ramp and the sidewalk he comes and goes as he pleases." Guy had seen him leave early, whirring his way toward the barn.

"In the barn. Figures," she said. "He knows today's bath day. Every ten days, on my day off, I come give him the twice-over. Get him in the tub and go after him with a scrub brush. He hates it," she said. "Usually pretends he's asleep when I come. Now with that sidewalk he figures he can hide in the barn. Well, he's got another think comin'," Mary Ann said, rocking herself up from the Galaxie seat.

"Need some help with him?" Guy said.

"Nope," Mary Ann said immediately. Then she blushed slightly and grinned. "Really, Guy, I don't," she said. "We got our routine. I took over from your father, who couldn't handle him right and didn't wash him good enough, anyway. So I do it. I don't mind."

Guy touched Mary Ann's cheek, then walked on toward the house.

Upstairs in the heat of the eaves bedroom, Guy packed. Once he heard Mary Ann laugh and he looked out the window into the yard. Martin leaned against Mary Ann's Galaxie. Mary Ann laughed again. Guy watched them. He suddenly realized that, what with the Defense League meetings and her helping with Helmer, Martin and Mary Ann spent a good deal of time together. He stood to the side of the window and watched them for long moments. Mary

363

Ann leaned against the car and folded her arms. She said something that made Martin grin. Then she laughed again. Soon he turned back to his suitcase. Their voices murmured on in the yard below.

Sometime later, Guy's hand was on the suitcase clasp when he heard Mary Ann shouting, crying out. He ran to the window. Martin stood across by the tractor, holding a can of oil, looking, frozen, across to Mary Ann. She stood by the open barn doors screaming for them to come.

The ambulance came up the road but left its red light and siren off. The sheriff's car followed. Both vehicles drove the speed limit. If there was a speed limit on gravel roads.

In the sunlight by the barn, Mary Ann and Guy stood on either side of Martin. Martin stared across the field. He watched the slow progress of the ambulance. His eyes were glazed. His breath came in shallow gulps, as if he had been hit hard in the gut.

"I shoulda checked on him. I shoulda been there . . ." he began.

"Stop that stuff right now," Mary Ann said, wiping her own eyes. "Don't even start."

Car doors slammed with a hollow sound. The ambulance driver and his assistant, along with the county coroner, who had ridden with the sheriff, all walked forward toward the barn. Guy met them halfway, spoke briefly with them. Mary Ann took Martin to the house. The other men went into the barn.

Guy waited outside. He leaned on the barn wall in the sunlight.

Voices came through the wooden wall. Soft voices. There was no argument. What had happened was clear at a glance. Helmer had reached, with his currycomb strapped on a broom handle, too far. The big white holstein had shied, of course, at the clatter of the wheelchair as it tipped across the gutter—had kicked at the sudden man come tumbling beneath her.

But the man just lay there. He was no trouble to her. Not this man. He never had been any trouble to her. Soon she chewed her cud again. She stood there chewing. Ruminating. Later her knees reminded her to lie down. And she had lain. When she settled onto the straw and concrete, the man was still there underneath her. But he was warm. And he was no trouble. She did not mind him there. Soon she did not think about him at all.

Guy realized he was staring but could not see. The sunlight on the white paint of the barn was burning his eyes. He squatted and stared down at the dirt between his boots. Bits of straw and hay floated across the red lake of his vision. Chaff on dirt. Then a daddy longlegs spider. The spider stepped carefully across a twig, a tiny hand striding on thinner fingers that left no sound, no track. Guy lowered his hand. The spider paused, then crawled onto his palm. He lifted the spider to his eyes. He wanted to see its mouth, its eyes, its face.

The ambulance driver came out and unloaded a gurney.

Guy stood and looked once more through the barn door. He wanted once more to see the tipped wheelchair. To see the long, blanketed form of his grandfather.

But his eyes failed him again. In their water he saw not Helmer but the great belly of the cow. He saw it as Helmer must have seen it. It was like lying on one's back and looking up at the sky, a sky curving not blue but white. A sky with a great sweep of fine white clouds all combed and swirling toward the center. A sky whose surface was painted pink with paths that wove their way across the whiteness, paths slowly throbbing with real blood.

But then the sky began to sway. To swell. To fill the whole horizon, the whole earth, as if the sky was falling or the earth was rising. It didn't matter which. For Helmer they were the same.

Martin began on the Jack Daniel's the afternoon of his father's death.

Guy unpacked his suitcase halfway.

At suppertime Guy milked the cows for Martin, who could not stand.

When Guy came in from chores broken dishes covered the floor in a sharp confetti. Beyond, lamps with crushed shades cowered in corners. To the right, the kitchen table lay on its back, two legs broken. The refrigerator lay on its side, its food pooling on the floor, its metal skin pockmarked by boot blows.

Walls were broken. The Sheetrock between the studs was

caved forward in large diamonds that repeated themselves all around the house.

"Martin?" Guy called.

No answer.

"Dad!"

Still nothing.

Guy rushed through the house jerking open doors, calling.

He found Martin underneath his bed, lying on his side, staring at the wall. He clutched a Jack Daniel's bottle.

Guy got down eye-level with his father. Martin squinted at Guy as if trying to recall his face.

Guy looked behind him at the mess. At floor level it looked like the house had tipped on its side, then fallen back. Not far away lay the kitchen clock, its hands still grinding. Six o'clock.

"You didn't make supper, then," Guy said.

His father stared.

"I'll see what I can find," Guy said. He glanced behind him again. "You must be hungry."

"The bastard," Martin murmured, still staring. "All my life, then he pulls the rug out."

"What's that?" Guy said, leaning down again.

"All my rug, then he pulls the life out—goddamn him."

"Come out of there!" Guy shouted, suddenly angry. He caught his father by the ankles and tried to pull him from underneath the bed. But Martin reached up and locked his fingers in the bedsprings. The whole bed skidded across the floor.

Guy kicked at the bed. Finally he called Mary Ann.

By eight o'clock Mary Ann had Martin cleaned up, in his pajamas, and part-way sober. Guy shoveled Sheetrock, splinters of wood, and broken dishes from the floor with a scoop shovel and pitched them out the door.

"Once I had a chance to work in Montana. On a big cattle ranch," Martin slurred.

Guy kept shoveling.

Martin stared down at his coffee. "I told the old man about it. He listened but he didn't say anything. Nothing. Not even 'Montana, huh?' Not a fucking word."

Martin paused. He looked around for the Jack Daniel's.

"Forget it," Mary Ann said, "you ain't drinkin' any more today."

Martin looked back to his coffee. He stared. "Talking to the old man was like talking to a barn wall—all you ever got back was an echo. Your own goddamn voice." He paused again. "I didn't go to Montana. I never brought it up again."

Guy stopped to look at Mary Ann.

"'Wait,' he always said," Martin muttered. "'Wait. Go slow. Slow and steady. There's no hurry.' Well, I waited, didn't I?" Martin said loudly, accusingly.

"Yes. You waited," Mary Ann said.

"You think it was easy, waiting? And waiting? And waiting!" Martin called, rising from his chair. He shouted at the door.

"Easy," Guy said.

"Not, not easy," Martin shouted. "What kind of life is waiting! That's what I want answered—what kind of life is that? Tell me, goddamnit—tell me!"

As Martin went at the walls with his fists, Guy caught him from behind.

"What kind of life is that!" Martin shrilled.

Guy had one of Cassandra's Valiums. Martin drank it down in a cup of coffee and Jack Daniel's. Then they got him to bed. Mary Ann sat on his legs—pinned him down. In three minutes he was asleep.

After Martin slept, Mary Ann talked.

"Maybe we ought to call somebody," she said, looking toward the bedroom where Martin snored.

"Like who?"

"I don't know," she said. "Somebody. Like a doctor. A doc could put him under for a week. He comes to, Helmer is buried, the farm's all his. Whole new ball game."

"Like Sleeping Beauty?" Guy said. "He wakes up a completely different person and everything is great? Well, he's no princess."

Mary Ann's cheeks reddened. "Sometimes you're no goddamned prince, either. When I got here you were swearing at your father and trying to pull him out from under the bed by his goddamn ankles. If you want to know, that wasn't the brightest thing I've ever seen!"

Guy looked away.

Mary Ann stood up. "Here's the deal," she said. "From now on—until after the funeral—I'll take care of your father. I'll cook for him. I'll look after him. I'll talk to him. I'll stay with him. I'll make sure he doesn't get too crazy. I'll be here first thing in the morning."

Guy began to speak.

"And don't tell me you don't need no help," she said immediately, "'cause it ain't true. You're no different than anybody. And neither is your daddy. He ain't that bad of a man," she said. "He just never had a chance."

"He had a chance—he just blew it by hanging around here all his life," Guy said.

"Nice, real nice," Mary Ann said, her face reddening again with anger. "Who does that sound like?"

Guy turned away.

"Fathers and sons," she muttered, heading through the door. "The things they do to each other. And don't do. I never did understand why."

368

Chapter Thirty-Nine

The next day Mary Ann stuck with Martin like gas on water.
In the morning she got him up, made him wash, shave,
dress. After that she fixed him breakfast. Martin waited at
the table. He stared out the window toward Helmer's house.
His face was fieldstone, a steady stare that told of cold bulk
below grade. He stared through the kitchen wall and chewed
his breakfast.

In the afternoon, while Mary Ann went home to check on
Jewell and a sick kid, Guy took his father to the machine
shed. He handed his father a broom. Martin swept. The
short jabs of his broom flung stray nuts and washers across
the concrete. Little wheels clinked and rolled until they
banged against the tin wall or bounded through the door
into bright sunlight. Guy sorted wrenches with one eye on
Martin. Once Martin's broom rhythm slowly scraped to a
stop; Guy turned to stare out the door with his father. A tiny
figure, far off, was walking up the road toward the farm.

The quick steps. The steady stride. It was Madeline.

Martin stiffened and brought the broom in front of him.
"What the hell does she want?" he said to himself.

Madeline came into the driveway. Guy stepped through

the doorway of the machine shop and called to her. She turned toward him and opened her mouth to speak, then saw Martin behind.

"I just heard. About Helmer. You should have told me," she said to Guy.

"I was coming this afternoon," Guy said.

She looked behind to Martin, who was still in shadow. Her brown eyes brimmed with tears.

"Martin—I'm so sorry. . . ."

"About what?" Martin said.

"About Helmer."

"That's all you're sorry about? Nothing else?"

Madeline set her jaw. "I'm sorry about your father," she said. "That's what I came to say."

"And now you've said it," Martin said, "so why don't you go back to your boyfriend. Or maybe I should just call him the boy. Or maybe just the friend—the family friend!"

"That's enough," Guy said. He realized he was standing exactly between his father and mother.

"Don't tell me what's enough," Martin shouted. He threw the broom behind him and lurched forward into the sunlight. Madeline stepped back. "From now on nobody's tellin' me nothing around here. This is my farm now. Anybody makes trouble, they pay the piper," Martin said, his eyes flaring wide in the bright light. "On this farm I'm the piper now!"

The rest of the day and all that evening the phone rang often for Martin. To some callers he said, "Nothing we could do . . . gone when we got there . . . 'preciate it . . . yup . . . yup."

But to many other callers Martin lowered his voice and turned so that Guy could not overhear. Defense League stuff, Guy guessed. After those calls Martin hummed a made-up toneless melody just beneath his breath. Hummed it over and over.

At milking time Martin swung the milkers udder to udder. Guy helped with the milking so he could stay near him. While the machines hissed and chucked, hissed and chucked, Martin stared out the barn door and hummed his little tune.

After chores they ate the supper that Mary Ann had cooked. Halfway through the roast beef Martin said loudly, "Somebody get me a drink."

Guy and Mary Ann glanced at each other.

"One," Mary Ann said. "And I'll pour."

Martin hummed his tune as Guy went to find a bottle of Jack Daniel's with the least whiskey in it.

Mary Ann poured.

Martin sipped the whiskey and smacked his lips.

Guy drew a breath and said, "Dad, we should talk about some things. Like the funeral. It's coming up fast."

"Talk away," Martin said, putting his boots on the table.

"Did Helmer have any instructions for his funeral that you know of? A will? Papers?"

"That little iron box in his writing desk," Martin said. "What's inside, I wouldn't know. It don't matter now anyway," he said, draining his drink and hoisting his empty glass to Helmer.

Guy swung open the door to his grandfather's house. He turned on the kitchen light. A mouse skittered away. Guy listened for the hum and click of Helmer's page-turning machine. For the whir of the wheelchair. But the doorway to the living room was dark and silent. He reached around the doorway for the light switch. When the light was on he went in.

He opened his grandfather's writing desk. He ran a finger over the smooth black cover of the Bible, around the rim of the pencil cup. The first drawer was filled with old implement manuals; one had on its cover a red combine faded to pink.

In the bottom drawer his wrist touched cold metal. The iron lockbox. But there was no key anywhere.

Back at Martin's house, Guy worked at the box hinges with a screwdriver. Mary Ann had gone home to put her kids to bed. Martin sat across the table and watched.

Guy finally levered open the lid. Carefully he turned over the box and emptied out the papers. Some were wrapped in oilskin—the farm abstract, the deed. There were no insurance policies. On the bottom of the pile, which meant it had been on top inside the iron box, was a faded, creamy sleeve of an envelope: "Last Will and Testament."

Guy pushed it toward his father's side of the table.

"Can we read this?" Martin said. He looked briefly at the door and then at the window that looked out on Helmer's house.

Guy was silent.

They stared at each other.

"I mean, why the hell can't we? Who's to stop us?" Martin said. He looked up once more to Guy, then jerked the pages from their sleeve. A single page of brighter, thinner paper fell away as Martin unfolded the will. Martin squinted first at the thicker, creamier paper. His lips moved as he read. Then he picked up the single page of new paper. He stared at it, then jerked his gaze back to the older pages. A croak of laughter came from his lips.

Martin kept laughing until he lost his breath. He started to choke and Guy came around the table and pulled his father up from his chair and clapped him on his back. Martin gasped for air. His eyes ran tears from his laughter.

"What the hell's so funny?" Guy said.

Wheezing, doubled over, Martin pushed the pages toward Guy.

Guy read the first page of the will, then the single-page codicil. The codicil, executed by a Flatwater lawyer and dated only a week before, began:

> Because of the state of mind of my son, Martin Pehrsson, namely his difficulties with matters of judgment and financial responsibility as they affect the farm and its operation and preservation; and considering that his son (my grandson), Guy Pehrsson, has recently come back to the farm, I hearby bequeath, with the understanding that my son, Martin will always have a place to live and work on the farm, my entire . . .

Guy's mouth fell open. He looked up to his father.

"Just tell me what to do, boss," Martin said, stooping and bowing. "Just put a shovel in my hand and I'm your man." Martin laughed in a high, whooping cackle.

372

Guy called Mary Ann. She sat on Martin until he fell asleep.

Later that night Guy jerked awake at the heavy crash of a shotgun.

"Dad!" he screamed.

But then the gun crashed again and again, outside. Guy ran through the door into the black heat. A yellow flash ripped the darkness near Helmer's house. Window glass crashed and tinkled. Guy's vision focused. In the moonlight he saw Martin outlined behind the gun. He was sitting on a kitchen chair in the dark on the lawn. Beside him was another chair stacked with boxes of shotgun shells. The shotgun blazed yellow again, slammed against wood this time. The report clapped back in echo from the face of the barn. Then the gun clicked empty and he started to reload.

"Dad," Guy called, stepping toward his father.

"Get back! I mean it!" Martin called, shoving shells into the gun. He swung and fired a round into the Mercedes. Glass sprayed in the moonlight and the car rocked. Guy cursed and dived for the grass. He crawled behind the big oak tree and waited, breathing hard.

But Martin turned the gun back to Helmer's house. The yellow spear leaped, the report crashed again and again. Guy lay there. He lost track of the times Martin fired. Forty. Fifty. In the thunder and echo, only the blaze of light from the gun barrel told which blast was real and which was echo.

Into his third box of shells, Martin grunted from pain and held the shotgun lower and lower on his shooting shoulder. Soon each report spun him halfway around in his chair. He began to load shells with his left hand.

"Dad," Guy called softly.

Martin whirled and shot through the Mercedes again. Guy flattened.

Car lights came fast down the road, slowed, and swung into the driveway. Martin stood up and followed the car with the gun barrel.

"It's Mary Ann," Guy called to Martin. The Galaxie skidded to a halt.

Martin's gun barrel wavered.

Still behind the tree, Guy shouted to Mary Ann, "Watch him—he's got a gun!"

373

"I'll watch him all right," Mary Ann said, striding forward. "I'll watch his ass under my stick if he don't put that gun away. How in hell are we supposed to sleep with somebody out shooting up the goddamn neighborhood! Give me that thing!"

Martin let her jerk away the gun. She threw it onto the grass, where it exploded again and they all jumped.

"Guy, get over here and help your daddy."

Guy came cautiously from behind the tree. Martin had fallen to his hands and knees. He began to cry, long heaving sobs. Mary Ann and Guy helped him up, then walked him back to bed. Mary Ann waited beside Martin's bed until he was asleep.

Afterward, on the front steps, Guy said, "Thanks."

Mary Ann shrugged.

They both grinned, then looked across the yard.

"Your poor damn Mercedes," Mary Ann said, "it's been goin' downhill ever since you came back."

In the moonlight the Mercedes sat with a vacant, punched-in stare. Shards of window glass lay on the hood and roof like snowflakes. Guy shrugged. "What the hell, it's only a car, right?"

Mary Ann grinned.

Guy walked her across the yard toward her car. He stopped by the two empty chairs on the lawn and the litter of spent shotgun shells. Beneath one of the chairs was a glass and a bottle of Jack Daniel's.

He turned to Mary Ann. "You in any hurry?"

"Not me," Mary Ann said. "I ain't goin' nowhere."

So they sat in the two chairs on the lawn between the two houses. They talked some, but after a while they fell silent. For a long time they sipped whiskey and watched the stars fall.

In the morning Guy milked the cows, then came in and made breakfast. Martin stumbled from his bedroom at nine o'clock. He squinted at Guy. Then he winced and held his right shoulder. Suddenly he looked up again; his eyes widened. He weaved across the living room to the window. He stared across at Helmer's house. At the Mercedes.

"Shit," Martin said.

374

"Come eat," Guy said. He poured two cups of coffee.

They ate the eggs and toast in silence.

"About the Mercedes . . ." Martin began.

"What Mercedes? You mean that shot-up junker in the yard?" Guy said immediately, when he had planned not to.

Martin was silent. He ate another bite of egg, then got up to look out the window again. He stared for a long time. "Bad part of it is," he said, "she looks kinda like an Indian car now."

Guy choked on his coffee. Then he began to laugh. He laughed until he had to go outside to catch his breath.

Chapter Forty

After Helmer's funeral there was lunch at Martin's house. Mary Ann had cleaned and cooked. Laid out on the kitchen table, which Guy had shored up with two-by-fours, was the food.

Hot dishes bubbled and popped in their glass dishes like steam pots in Yellowstone Park. Tuna-noodle casserole. Hamburger-tomato. Hamburger-pea-potato. Scalloped potatoes and ham. Wild rice-green bean-hamburger, and two other hot dishes not immediately identifiable.

Then the breads. White bread. Dark bread. Wheat bread. Rye bread. Yellow buns with sliced ham. White buns with sliced turkey.

Pickles. Dill pickles. Sweet pickles. Beet pickles. Carrot pickles. Chutney. Relishes.

Salads. Three-bean salad. Cold macaroni salad. Fruit salad, a mixture of chopped apples and walnuts and raisins, fruit cocktail and whipped cream.

Jell-Os. Strawberry-banana. Raspberry-banana. Black raspberry-pineapple. Lime with grated carrots. Lemon-lime with raisins. Orange Jell-O, cubed, in whipped cream. Cherry Jell-O with mandarin oranges.

At the far end of the table were the desserts, mostly bars

and pies. Raisin-coconut bars. Zucchini bars. Carrot bars. Brownies with walnuts. Plain brownies. And then the pies, mincemeat, apple, cherry, raisin, and a peach pie with a woven, crisscross crust.

Martin stood at the head of the table and shook hands. Guy had bought him a dark blue suit, white shirt, and striped tie. Martin's pale, thin hair was washed and fluffy and combed straight back. His teeth were brushed. His gums bled pink on his teeth. Guy remembered photographs he had once seen in a magazine, photos of New York City bums made over with fifty-dollar haircuts and five-hundred-dollar suits, "before" and "after" photos. But change the clothes, change the hair, the eyes remained the same. His father's eyes, small and blue and flecked with red, flickered about the room in pride and fear.

More car doors slammed in the yard. Feet thumped on the porch. People came inside without knocking. Farmers took off their caps. Their round faces were white above, brown below, cap lines their equator. Their eyes moved quickly to the food.

Mary Ann and Madeline served. Men with chapped cheeks and razor-burned necks passed down the line. Silverware was small in their brown fingers. Wives followed husbands. The farm women wore patterned dresses, long-sleeved sweaters, and bright brooches on the left side of their breast. At each hot dish the wives murmured, "Oh— that's a great plenty."

Conversations began with Helmer, turned to the weather, then fell silent. If someone else spoke, people turned to listen. But soon the house was crowded, and voices wove themselves into layers of talk and laughter. Voices swirled into the clink of silverware, the clack of serving forks on dishware, the sharp clatter of spoons swirling cream in coffee cups, then tap-tapping the rim of the cup. Soon there was noise enough that Guy no longer had to talk. Once he looked for Martin but could not spot him in the crowd.

The house warmed. The smells of food and coffee and people washed over Guy. Dime-store perfume. Baked beans. Mennen Skin Bracer. Tuna casserole. Cows. Dill pickles. Old manure on boots. Hydraulic oil. Cherry pie. Go-Jo hand cleaner. Soap. Aftershave. Perfume. Coffee.

Guy closed his eyes to draw in the smells. He turned his

head to take in fully the broad hum of voices and of people eating. He breathed in deeply. He listened for a long time. When he opened his eyes again, he was crying.

He went outside and sat on the steps. After several minutes in the fresh air he felt better. He felt hungry. He should eat. Eating would help. He took a deep breath and stood to go back inside. Then he saw his father.

Across the lawn, Martin stood braced against the side of Helmer's house. His face was pressed against the rough boards. His arms were outstretched. His fingers gripped the jagged holes of the shotgun blasts. He was trying to lift his father's house, or, if he could not lift it, take it all into his arms.

The last car had gone and Guy was walking to the barn when someone hissed at him from behind the granary. Guy whirled. "Tom—Jesus!"

"Red man sneak up on white farmer." Tom grinned.

Guy looked down at his coveralls. He shrugged. "Chores. A night off is the least I can do for Martin."

"That's why I came," Tom said seriously. "I'm sorry about *Naenimo*. Your grandfather."

"Naenimo," Guy repeated. He smiled. He had forgotten that word. Zhingwaak called all the old farmers *Naenimo*. He-Who-Saves-Something-for-Later.

"How's your father doing?"

"He's in the house," Guy said, "you could ask him."

Tom pretended to consider that for a moment, then grinned. "Indian not that brave."

Guy did the chores while Tom waited out of sight in the hayloft. When Guy was finished he climbed the loft ladder halfway. He called out Tom's name. In the dim light the loft was quiet but for a brief scuttle of pigeons overhead. He found Tom in their old hay house, stretched out asleep on the iron cot, a pen and some notes of paper on the floor where they had fallen from his hand.

Guy came alongside Tom and ran a fingernail across Tom's throat. Tom jumped awake. Guy stood grinning at him.

"White man sneak up on Indian," Tom said, blinking rapidly to wake up.

378

"White man sneak up on Indian who steals white man's mother," Guy added.

Tom touched his neck. "But white man not cut Indian's throat," he said.

Guy grinned and shook his head no.

At sundown Guy drove on the roads around No Medicine Town. Tom rode and talked.

"You see, Tex, I've got these plans for jobs on the reservation," Tom said. He was energized from his short nap, talked with moving hands and flashing eyes. "Wild rice," he said. "Paddy rice, but still wild. At the south end of the lake, where Doc's Tavern is, we divert water and create the paddies. Like they do in California," Tom said. "I've been reading all about it."

"What about Doc's?"

Tom grinned. "Doc always wanted to retire."

Guy shook his head at Tom.

"I'm serious, Tex. Wild rice paddies. Ten acres of paddies would create fifty jobs. Fifty!"

Guy let the car coast to a stop on the edge of No Medicine Town. Tom talked on. Through the open car window behind Tom, a van with a stepladder tied on top and an empty trailer behind sat by an Indian house. Two white men wearing yellow hard hats crouched at the base of a shiny white satellite TV antenna. An Indian woman and four small children watched the men work.

Guy's eyes fell back to Tom.

". . . then limited commercial fishing on No Medicine Lake," Tom continued, sorting through the notes of paper he had spread over the seat. "People don't eat as much meat anymore—chicken and fish, right? We'll raise the poultry, we'll raise the fish. Fresh walleyed pike—we could sell—"

"What about the white resorters, their fishermen?" Guy said.

"Once we get back the land the resorters can be relocated," Tom said quickly. "Not just thrown off, but a five-year plan. Give them enough time to find someplace else. There's plenty of lakes nearby—off the reservation."

Guy was silent. The men in hard hats stood up. One of them turned a crank at the base of the dish. The parabola turned. The second man said something to the Indians, then pointed into the sky. The Indian family looked up and turned their faces to follow the path of his arm.

"After the rice and fish operations, maybe a small wood manufacturing plant," Tom continued. "Small toys. Some furniture. Toothpicks. Chopsticks. You know how many people in the world use chopsticks?" Tom said, his eyes flashing. "Guess—"

Guy held up his hands.

"One billion!" Tom said. "Aspen and birch make the best chopsticks, and we've got both kinds of trees. We need more wood, we plant the fields to trees. Aspen has only a twenty-year growing cycle. Everything is here. Once we get the land, we've got everything we need, Tex."

"What about the farmers?" Guy said softly.

"Same as the resorters," Tom said, his eyes bright. "Instead of buying out the Indians, Stanbrook buys out the farmers. The farmers buy other farms—off the reservation. The land—"

"It's not gonna happen, goddamnit!" Guy said, slamming his fist on the dashboard. "Look, for chrissakes—open your damn eyes for once!" he said. He grabbed Tom by the shoulders and turned him to look out the window.

Tom stared at the Indian shack and the TV dish. The TV men slammed the doors to their van. The smallest and last Indian kid into the house let the screen door clack shut behind him. The van pulled away. Inside the house someone pulled a shade. Outside, the white eye of the TV dish stared blankly into the purple sky.

Tom turned away and looked through the windshield toward No Medicine Town.

"Turd, you've got to be realistic," Guy began.

"Why?" Tom said softly. "Why should I be realistic when this is reality?" He jerked his hand toward the Indian shack and its TV dish, toward the empty streets of No Medicine Town.

"Because dreamers have a longer way to fall than other people. They hit harder," Guy said.

Tom was silent.

"People worry about you is what I'm saying," Guy said. "Madeline. Me. We worry, goddamnit."

"Tex, oh Tex," Tom said. Suddenly he laughed. "You and

your mother. You know what? You hung around Indians too long and now you've got Indian hearts."

"So whose fault is that?" Guy said.

"Mine," Tom said. He reached out his brown hand to touch Guy's cheek. "All mine. And stop worrying, Tex. Nothing ever happens to me when you're around."

Tom slid out of the car.

Guy watched him walk away, moving quickly through the dusk toward the somber, staring totem at the Humphrey Center.

Chapter Forty-One

The next morning before the heat rose, Guy took Martin and the Mercedes to Flatwater. Martin drove the Ford pickup. The Mercedes followed at the end of a chain. One of Martin's shotgun blasts had blown away half the battery, its cables, and a good part of the ignition system. Guy steered the dead Mercedes. Once an Indian car passed them. The Indians slowed to look, and grinned.

In Flatwater, Guy left the Mercedes at the body shop. The owner took one look at the Mercedes and shook his head. His son, a wide-faced teenager in a black Bardahl cap, came out of the back room and ran his hand over the roof and down the trunk lid. "Engine good?" he asked.

"Yes," Guy said immediately.

The boy nodded and traced a greasy fingernail from the driver's door to the back. "She'd make a good pickup," he said.

"Don't do anything until my insurance man calls you," Guy said. "Nothing—no welding, no torches—nothing, okay?"

The owner and his son shrugged.

* * *

Afterward Guy brought Martin uptown.

"What's the deal here?" Martin said suspiciously as they walked into the lawyer's office.

"Something we've got to take care of," Guy said.

The lawyer, Ken Peterson, who had written the codicil to Helmer's will, was a small, pale man who sat in a tall-backed chair; his desk was an enormous, dark hulk of battered oak with a hand-high rail around its top that suggested the building tilted on occasion and the rail kept pencils and papers from sliding off the edge. Guy explained Helmer's will, the codicil, what he wanted to do.

"You mean you're giving the farm back to me!" Martin said immediately.

"What do I need with a farm here when I live in California?" Guy said.

"I'll be damned," Martin murmured. He scratched his head.

"I don't know," the lawyer said. He frowned as he looked over the codicil. "An estate, an inheritance is one thing, but an outright gift is another. There'll be a substantial gift tax. The Minnesota State Legislature—"

"I don't care about that," Guy said. "Just do it."

The lawyer shrugged, then paged through a file for the right form. As he typed Martin leaned back in his chair. He grinned. At length Martin said to the lawyer, "You see, my boy Guy here has got his own company out in California."

"I see," Peterson said, not looking up.

Afterward, as they climbed in the Ford, Martin said, "I suppose this means you'll be leaving soon."

Guy nodded.

Martin was silent for a while, then spit briefly out the window. He turned to Guy and said, "Shit, you just got here!"

Guy smiled as he turned the key. The starter clicked once and was silent. Dead battery.

"Goddamn this truck," Martin shouted, and kicked the dash.

They got out and tightened the cables, without success. Guy stepped back to survey the rusty Ford. He slowly looked up Mainstreet to the bodyshop. Then back to Martin. "Come on," he said suddenly to his father.

At the bodyshop the round-faced son and his father were sitting in the Mercedes. The son leaned forward through the vacant windshield and broke into a yellow-toothed grin. "It'd be a snap," he called to Guy. He pulled himself out through the windshield and crouched on the hood. He produced a grease pencil from somewhere inside his coveralls. Like a surgeon he rapidly began to draw black lines across the roof and the trunk lid and down the body of the car. "You cut the corner posts here and here. You fold down the roof and cut in a rear window—Plexiglas is plenty good," the boy said. "Then you cut off the trunk lid, you bolt down a couple of sheets of treated plywood for the rear bed, and there you have it!"

Guy covered his eyes.

When he opened them again, Martin and the bodyshop owner and his son all stared at him expectantly. Guy had a sudden vision of his father, air-conditioned to sixty degrees, blasted by fifty stereophonic watts of Tom T. Hall as he hummed toward Flatwater at 110 miles per hour, a thirty-thousand-dollar pickup hauling a hundred-dollar load of oats and corn for grinding. But what the hell. If Martin had a Mercedes pickup, at least the cows would not go hungry.

Guy grinned and tossed his father the keys.

That afternoon tractor tires spun in dry dirt. With the front loader Guy scooped away even lines of black dirt from a spot west of the grove and out of sight from the road. When the bucket scraped on wood, he parked the tractor. With a shovel he dug until he found the four corners of the underground garage that housed his old Chevy. Then with the tractor he began to dig again.

He passed through moist, reddish gravel to dry, white sand.

In two hours he had dug himself eye level to grade, then deeper still. Once he looked up and saw boots. Martin stood above him. "Was wondering when you'd dig up the old dinosaur," he called down to Guy.

A half hour later the tractor's scoop clunked on plank. Guy got down and dug with the shovel. He threw dirt into the tractor's bucket, and was about to climb on and dump it when Martin started up the tractor.

Guy straightened up to stare.

Martin backed the tractor out of the hole, dumped the sand, and then returned. Guy kept shoveling. When the tractor's bucket filled, Martin emptied it.

Once Martin called out to Guy, "Your Chevy's gonna be one big rust ball—you wait and see!"

Guy smiled. He wiped sweat from his eyes and watched Martin drive the tractor. He and his father had a machine between them. Each had something to hold on to—Martin the steering wheel, Guy the shovel. An engine was running. Hearing was difficult. When they did speak it was half sentences, brief commands, broken English, jerky hand signals. But it was a language of their own.

When Martin could no longer maneuver the tractor in the hole, he came down to help with a shovel and then with a crowbar. Guy and Martin pried at the plank face of the garage. The wood was soft and flaky, like the damp undersides of fallen logs. The rust-capped spikes pulled through the wood. The nails were shiny underneath.

Guy broke open a doorway wide enough to throw a beam of daylight into the garage. The Chevy sat square and silent. The headlights on its broad face were fogged and pupilless, the wide-set eyes of a strange Greek statue.

Martin pulled away more boards, made a doorway. Guy stepped inside. Chrome peeled and curled on the front bumper. The cheeks of the hubcaps were pitted through. A cluster of red cancers grew along the rocker panels and the bottoms of the doors. But the diesel fuel that Guy, twelve years ago, had poured over the car had drawn dust to form an oily shroud, a petroleum shrink-wrap around the Chevy.

"Be damned," Martin said. "She don't look that bad."

Guy opened the hood. The battery had leaked. Thin white tears of acid coursed down the fender well, and where they had frozen, had eaten through the metal. The radiator was dry. The fan belt lay slack. But the dipstick shone with cool, clean oil.

Martin went home for the pickup and some tools. Guy worked again with the shovel, smoothing a road up the hill. Two pickups turned into the yard, one with Losano Farms markings and another that Guy recognized from the Defense League. He kept swinging the shovel.

Finally Martin came with the pickup.

"What did the boys want today?" Guy said as he unloaded the air compressor.

"Nothin'," Martin said as he bent to lift the chain. Guy helped with the chain. It was Helmer's log chain from when he had cleared land. Guy had forgotten its weight. The chain links were as big as calves' hooves, the hook and clevis at either end bound by one-inch machine bolts. The chain was used for only the biggest jobs—logging, moving a granary to replace a foundation, pulling a combine from a soft spot in a field, hoisting up a truck bed to replace a broken axle. It was the chain they had used to lift the tractor off Jewel Hartmeir.

Martin hooked the clevis to the tractor. Guy secured the hook to the frame of the Chevy. He wiped the windshield enough to see, then got inside. The interior smelled of dust and incense and PineTree air freshener and old shotgun shells. Images of his past came like a cloudburst. But Martin started the tractor and the chain jerked tight.

Before they proceeded, Guy got out and Martin got down from the tractor. They checked once more, as they always had, as Martin had taught him, the chain and its fastening. Its iron links stretched between them as straight as a rod. Martin strummed the chain, then held it; for a moment Guy could feel his father through the iron.

"Okay," Martin said, stepping back, "let's roll."

The Chevy jerked and creaked forward.

Guy steered.

Martin gunned the tractor and the Chevy rolled from its garage into daylight. At the top of the earthen ramp the tractor spun in sand. The chain jerked and whipped, but the Chevy kept rising. Suddenly Guy could see tree trunks. Fields. Then buildings.

Martin gunned the tractor in the sand. As the Chevy crested at field level there was a sudden cracking noise—like a rifle report—and something slammed into the grille of the Chevy. The Chevy began to roll backward. Guy jammed on the brakes. The chain had broken.

Martin jumped down. He looked at the two new, bright ends, at the tiny eye of gray slag that had caused the break. He touched the new ends together as if by contact they

386

would weld themselves. "Shit," he muttered, "the old man's gonna be pissed."

Guy was silent.

Suddenly Martin looked up to Guy, then across to the house. "Goddamn," he said to Guy. He let the chain drop. He sat on the ground. His eyes welled with water. "Goddamn but it's hard."

That night rain spattered briefly on the roof, then quit. Come morning, the sun rose dusty red. By midday cows queued along the sides of the barn for the narrow shade of its eaves, or clustered beneath the scattered oak trees of the cow lot. Often the holsteins turned their noses north and huffed the air. Bumble-bees droned in the same direction. Both could smell water.

On Hank Schroeder's farm the potato irrigator turned clocklike around the field. Still under injunction, irrigators across the reservation spun shiny sheets of water onto the ground—thanks to Cassandra Silver. She had persuaded a judge to impose a small, daily fine on each irrigator. Until the matter was resolved, Ricardo Losano paid up and the irrigators circled the fields.

The next night, distant gunfire tattooed the dark. The yellow yard light by Martin's barn flickered and went out. The TV hissed and faded to black. Guy heard a faint thud, like a faraway thunderclap. They went outside onto the steps and looked north. Something burned in the sky.

"What the hell?" Martin said.

They drove fast in the pickup to investigate. A quarter mile from Schroeder's field a big electrical transformer burned on its pole, a tall sparkler stick jammed in the ground. Two Losano Farms pickups stood parked nearby, and men with guns clustered on the road in the headlights.

"Fuckin' Indians shot out the transformer," one of the men said to Guy.

Across the road the irrigator stood motionless, water dripping.

Then they all looked up. Across the prairie, farther north, gunfire crackled again, followed by another boom and thud, and a faint flare of light.

"This is fuckin' war," one of the Losano men muttered.

"Let's go after 'em," Martin said.

Pickup doors slammed and engines raced.

Guy walked home alone.

The next morning at 10 A.M. Guy looked up from beneath the hood of the Chevy. He listened. A faint, far-off rumble came from the east. A thunderstorm. But weather never came from the east. He stood up and shaded his eyes to see better. Beyond the cow lot, across the shimmering haze of the fields, a dust cloud grew on the road. A brown, lumbering tornado, lying on its side, of road dust. At the same moment he heard engine noise. Guy squinted and then began to make out the vague green shapes of tractors driving the dust before them. A half mile of tractors.

He turned quickly back to the farmyard. By the machine shed Martin stood running diesel fuel into the big John Deere. "What the hell's going on?" he called to Martin.

Martin only checked his watch, glanced at the dust cloud, and kept running fuel. Guy crossed the yard and came up to his father. "What is that?" he said, pointing to the long convoy of tractors.

Martin looked briefly at Guy, then away toward the dust. "You make trouble, you pay the piper," he said. "The potato boys and a lot of other farmers on the reservation have had enough of the Indian trouble."

"Where are they headed?" Guy asked.

Martin's eyes flickered, looked across to the inner reservation toward No Medicine Town, then back to Guy.

Guy was silent for long moments. Then he said to his father, "You don't have to join them."

Martin squinted up at Guy, then back to the caravan of green and brown.

"Stay here. With me," Guy said.

"No," Martin said suddenly. "I can't." He turned away, hung up the hose, and pulled himself up into the John Deere. He stared down at Guy. In the sunlight skeins of wrinkles showed around his father's eyes.

"Don't you see?" Martin said, looking back to the on-coming dust cloud. "This was my idea." He turned the key and his John Deere engine rumbled alive.

* * *

Guy drove the pickup fast toward Tom's house. He took the long way so he did not have to pass the slow-moving tractors. He pushed the Ford hard around the curves and through the trees until he skidded to a stop in Tom's yard. He rushed through the door without knocking. Madeline rose up, startled, from her writing desk.

"Where's Tom?" Guy called.

"At the Humphrey Center. Guy, what's . . . ?"

"Come on—and hurry," he said.

He explained as he drove.

"And Martin?" Madeline asked.

"He's with them."

Madeline was silent for a moment. "Last night—the power lines and the irrigators," Madeline said. "Tom had nothing to do with that. It was friends of Sonny Bowstring. They've been pushing Tom and pushing him—especially after Sonny was killed. They've got a lot of guns. So far he's held them back."

Guy stared at Madeline for a moment, then turned back to the road.

"Doesn't matter who did what," Guy said, "Tom's the one in trouble."

At the Humphrey Center, Guy and Madeline walked quickly to Bear Wing. Loud voices came from the Tribal Office. No music. Inside, Tom stood up against his desk with his arms folded as several long-haired Indians shouted at him. The shouting Indians were dressed darkly in jeans, black T-shirts, leather vests, and black slashes of charcoal across their cheekbones and foreheads. The night shift. Close behind them leaned several rifles and .30-30 Winchesters, and two Remington .30-06 automatics, one with a long scope.

"There's your problem right there," one of the Indians said as Guy and Madeline came through the door.

Tom turned to Madeline and Guy, then looked back to the other Indians. A vein in his neck began to pulse.

"Tom—come!" Madeline called.

"See what I mean?" the first Indian said.

Tom started to speak but Madeline cut him off. "The tractors—they're coming and you should get out," Madeline said. "Come with us."

389

Tom stared, confused. "Look," Madeline said, pulling him toward the window. The other Indians gathered behind Tom and Madeline. Over their heads and through the window Guy could see the dust cloud rising down the road, rolling toward No Medicine Town.

Tom and the other Indians stared.

"Shit, man, they're gonna terminate us for sure," one of the Indians said. He grabbed up a rifle.

Tom whirled and pulled away the rifle. "No—no guns!" he said.

The other Indians stared, first at Tom, then at each other, then back to Tom. "Fuck you, man," one of them finally said, "guns is all there's left."

"No, not yet—this is left," Tom said, sweeping his hand at the papers, the typewriters, the file cabinets.

"Nah," one of the other Indians said tiredly, "that's just papers, a fuckin' merry-go-round of papers that never stops."

One by one they picked up the rifles. Tom stared as they jacked shells into the chambers.

"All right—keep the guns but take them the hell out of here," Tom said rapidly. "You've got time. Go!"

The Indians looked back out the window. The lead tractor, tall and green, with four wide tires in front, was even with the junkyard on the edge of town. Most of the tractors pulled implements. Plows. Disks. Sprayers. Harrows. All were folded upright for highway travel.

"Forget it, man, we ain't gettin' our asses run over!" one of the Indians said.

"Besides," another said, turning back to Tom, "why the hell should we run? This is our place. Our land. That's the whole fuckin' point, right?"

Tom was silent.

"Tom, come with us," Madeline said. "You can leave!"

Tom stared at Madeline for a long moment. Then he grinned briefly and shook his head. "No, I'd better stay here. Somebody might shoot his toe off and need a Band-Aid or something."

Nobody said anything.

"Then I'll stay too," Madeline said.

"No," Tom said quickly. "Tex, take her home. I'll be there later."

Guy steered Madeline toward the door and down the hallway. Tom stood behind, outlined against the big mural, and watched them go. The other Indians started to flow out the door, but Tom pushed them back inside and closed the door behind him.

Guy and Madeline stepped through the front doors of the Humphrey Center just as the tractors rumbled into No Medicine Town. Two Indian boys who had been kicking a ball on the lawn now stood silent, holding the ball, watching. The ribs of the tractor tires whined on the asphalt and swirled up dust from the shoulders. The junkyard Labrador crouched flat in the back seat of his old Cadillac, only his head protruding, and barked frantically, soundlessly in the noise. Three Indian children scuttled across Main Street and into a store; like round loaves of pumpernickel bread, their heads slowly rose to peek out the window. Main Street was a narrow slot suddenly filled by tall tractors and dust and whirling bits of trash. At the grocery store a square of plate glass slipped and shattered like a sheet of ice falling from the face of a glacier. The tractors passed without slowing.

Guy looked for Martin, but in the haze and motion the tractors all looked alike. Behind the green-tinted windows of the tractor cabs the drivers were vague figures in feed caps and sunglasses.

The lead tractor, a tall, dual-tandem John Deere with a square rack of traction weights hung on its face like an extra jaw, headed toward the Humphrey Center. It pulled a field disk. The disk arms began to unfold.

"Jesus!" Guy said.

The two Indian boys on the lawn bolted for the door of the Humphrey Center.

The disk's multiple arms, each one a skewer of parabolas scoured shiny by the sandy soil, rose on hydraulic joints like a praying mantis arching its wings. Behind the second tractor toothed harrow arms spread, and farther back in the convoy sprayer booms dropped like arms of a railroad crossing.

Madeline stepped backward, behind Guy.

"Come, Guy," she said. She pulled his arm toward the Humphrey Center.

In the foyer one of the Indian boys said, "They're gonna crash the building over."

"No," Madeline said immediately. "It's only . . . a parade."

The Indian boys said nothing. As glass began to tremble they stepped farther back. The rolling bulk of the tractors vibrated the foyer like long, wobbly aftershocks of an earthquake. Among the tractors Guy saw a smaller, red Massey-Ferguson. The Hartmeir tractor. It carried a manure-bucket loader with the legless Jewell Hartmeir perched inside. Mary Ann drove. Just behind Mary Ann was Martin in his John Deere. Guy lost sight of them as the lead tractor veered from the road down into the ditch. Its wide disk settled onto the ground. Rolling blades sliced through the brown grass and rolled the sod belly-up, torn and dusty.

In the middle of the lawn stood the tall bear totem. The lead tractor swung its face straight at the trunk of the totem. Behind Guy down the hall someone swore—one of the night-shift Indians. Guy watched the tractor's nose close on the totem. Its square iron jaw slammed into the belly of the bear. In slow motion the bear broke in half. Like a tree toppling, the bear's gaze fell forward in a slow downward arc, gathering momentum as it fell. It crashed across the tractor cab, bounced down the green iron onto the spinning ribs of the tires, which pulled the broken bear beneath its wheels. There was a crackling noise of breaking wood. For a moment the bear jerked upright and free between the rear tractor wheels and disk. But then the disk blades pulled it down again. The rolling blades tore the totem into splinters and spread the bright chips of wood behind.

There was more shouting behind Guy. He looked back and saw Tom blocking his office door as Indians shouted and pointed. A sudden scrape and screeching noise jerked Guy's eyes back to the lawn. The lead tractor's disk caught the edge of the sidewalk, tore it loose from the ground, where it plowed along intact before the disk, then shattered into chunks of concrete that dispersed themselves, scraping and screeching, between the irons.

Other tractors crossed the ditch and surged onto the lawn. One pulled a chemical sprayer. Its thin pipe arms hissed a white mist that wet the ground and briefly settled the dust with a sour smell of herbicide. But the dust rose again behind a third tractor and its wide harrow.

Guy turned back to Tom just as the shouting Indians pushed their way past him into the hallway. Tom held on to three of them. All carried rifles. There was shouting and cursing, a stumbling fight and the clank of guns. Guy and Madeline ran to help.

"No—get back," Tom shouted, whether to the Indians or to Madeline, Guy was not sure. He hung on to two Indians with rifles but could not stop the roiling flow toward the door.

They crashed into the foyer, then outside into the path of a tractor, which veered suddenly at the sight of the guns. Tom and Madeline and Guy struggled for the rifles, but on the torn sod, among chunks of concrete, they fell.

A rifle went off with a dull clap. Someone cried out. They all froze, then got to their feet. Around them the tractors braked to a halt. Guy and Madeline and the other Indians all looked at each other.

Tom broke the silence. "Like spin the bottle," he said softly. "My unlucky day." He pushed aside his vest. High up on his white T-shirt grew a red rose.

Guy caught him as he fell.

"Tom!" Madeline screamed.

Tom's back bloomed bright red and Guy tried to cover the hole with his hand.

"Aw, Tex," Tom whispered, "I don't know if you can get me out of this one. . . ."

"Don't talk," Guy said.

Two nurses floated from the clinic like sea gulls and landed beside Tom. They pushed Guy and Madeline aside.

One by one the tractor engines shut off. The farmers opened the doors of the cabs and slowly climbed down. At first they lingered by their tractors. Then, slowly, they came forward, stepping carefully over the furrows. They paused in a ragged circle around Tom.

Tom's eyes squinted against the bright sun overhead. "Madeline," he said.

"I'm here," Madeline whispered. She held his head in her arms.

"Where's Tex?"

"Don't talk," Guy said, his voice breaking.

"Tex, you remember that time under the ice? When you saved me? I saw the big spring, Tex. I never realized it until now. But I saw it. It was just like the sun, darker, but like the sun . . . Tex?"

"Easy," Guy said.

Martin and Mary Ann came forward from the crowd and knelt beside Tom. They both spoke at once.

"Tom . . . we . . . didn't mean for anything like this to happen," Martin said hoarsely.

"No, Tom, never this—honest!" Mary Ann said, her voice a whisper.

"Honest Injun?" Tom said with a faint smile.

"Yes—honest Injun," Mary Ann said earnestly, her eyes starting to run tears.

"That's good enough for me," Tom said weakly. He turned his face away from the sun. "Maybe it was my fault," he whispered. "Maybe I overdreamed."

Chapter Forty-Two

Zhingwaak's story "The Boy Who Overdreamed."

One morning in a wigwam in an Indian village by a forest, a son awoke to find ashes in his dish. His father sat beside him.

The father said, *"Ningos,* your legs are getting long now. Soon you will need a *manido,* a dream spirit who looks out for you."

The son was very happy. At last he could go into the forest and have a dream. The father rubbed ashes on the boy's face and sent him off to the forest. After four days the boy had a dream. He returned happy and hungry to the wigwam.

But the boy's father told him to go back into the forest. To dream some more. The boy went back. He went on with his fasting and he had another dream. He came back to the wigwam even hungrier than before.

The father urged him to go back and fast one more day.

"*Noosag,* I have had my dreams, many dreams," the boy said to his father.

"One more day," the father said. "Go back."

The boy went and had another dream. He came back to the wigwam. But he was so hungry by now, he could not eat. The father was away hunting, so the boy fixed himself some paint and painted his face and combed his hair so he would look like *Opichi,* the robin. The boy sang:

Apegish izhi, idizoyaan ji-izhinaagoziyaan,
Dibishkoo go Opichi.
I want to change myself
Into a robin.

In a moment his nose grew sharp and his arms grew red feathers. He fluttered up onto the cross-beams of the wigwam. He perched there until his father returned.

The father recognized his son at once. *"Ningos, ningos*—come down," the father cried.

"I cannot," the boy answered. "I will fly away and return in spring. You will see my red breast on the day the snow deepest in the forest is gone."

Epilogue

For the first few days back in California Guy spent long
hours at his office and Madeline slept or worked some in his
yard. He found his company with three large accounts in
jeopardy, thanks to three bad batches of printed circuit
boards. His rose plants all needed pruning and repotting,
plus the lawn service, two brothers with a pickup full of
mowers, rakes, and shears, had split to Santa Rosa, where
presumably the grass was greener.

In the evenings Guy got home late. Madeline waited
supper. Neither talked much. After supper they usually had
a glass of wine, listened to part of an album, and were asleep
before nine. Guy gave Madeline the guest room that overlooked not the Bay City but the green hillside with its
eucalyptus trees. He hung a small bird feeder outside her
window. Kennedy slept in her room and, as he had in
Minnesota, stayed with her most of the day.

When they did talk it was never about Minnesota. About
Tom's death. About Martin or Mary Ann or Helmer or
Cassandra Silver. Rather, their conversation moved halt-
ingly within boundaries of the day just past. Guy told of
meetings with the three quality-control managers; how two

were warming up but the third looked impossible. Madeline told of finding a banana slug under the ivy, of someone's lost parrot that came to the bird feeder. She kept track of the birds in a little notebook. Some days Guy saw that she had done nothing at all in the yard or the house, but only made tiny notes that themselves looked like bird tracks. Madeline napped often, slept deeply, sometimes called out in her dreams, and awoke groggy. She did not want to go anywhere. She said little. She only worked some with the flowers, watched the birds, made notes, and slept. One night Guy awoke late and found Madeline standing in the dark living room. In the faint moonlight she stood before the Hundertwasser print, "Der Traum Des Toten Indianers," tracing her fingers over its lines. Its gray colors.

Later in the week, Susan called. She asked when he had returned and why he hadn't called. Guy did not recognize her voice; he had forgotten Susan. He recovered himself enough to lie and say he had gotten back just yesterday.

"Almost four weeks," Susan said. "I thought you said a two-week vacation." Her voice was surprisingly cheerful. People talked and laughed in the background. Guy guessed she and the other Stanford grad students had passed some sort of exam.

"I did," Guy said.

"You must have had a great time to stay so long!"

He started to speak but she said, "Anyway, you can tell me all about it. Friday afternoon there's an open house at the Stanford English Department. Wine and cheese. Can you come? We could have dinner later."

Guy was silent for a moment. "Sure," he said.

After he hung up he checked on Madeline. It was only eight o'clock in the evening but she was already asleep. He tucked the sheet tighter around her shoulders. Then sat on his deck with a glass of cold rosé. Below, in the flat, somber blocks of Palo Alto, streetlights faltered orange, then raced ahead like straight strikes of lightning far away. City lights.

Guy thought of Cassandra. She had come to Tom's funeral. Or at least he thought she had. He saw her once far back in the pews at the Catholic church, in sunglasses, a head taller than the Indians and the scattering of white farmers. Her head was bowed and she did not see him turn

398

to look. Later he tried to find her in the crowd but could not. That night, too, he thought he saw her at the wake. Beyond the tire fire, in the shadow of the trees, he saw her watching the dancers. Watching him. He pushed forward through the crowd, cut through the circle of dancers toward her. But she was not there. He walked the curving shore of the fire's glow, following its edge, where light lapped against shadow, searching, but did not find her. He asked. No one had seen a tall white woman. After a while he came to believe he had imagined her; that he had seen only firelight shining in the pale curves of birch trees. She never existed in the first place. All of this—Tom's death, Helmer's death, Mary Ann and her potato factory, Madeline and Tom, Cassandra, his trip back among them—all of it was a dream.

It was then he joined the dancers. He danced and remembered dancing with Tom in Flatwater that Fourth of July night long past. He danced until he was wet through with sweat, until his circles about the fire were stumbling lurches on the edges of the flame, until his voice had wailed itself to a hoarse whisper. He danced until he fell in the warm ashes, tasted their lye and soot, felt heat singe his hair and eyelids. Rough hands tumbled him away from the flames, and on his back he looked up to see Madeline and the darker moons of Indian faces. Above them the sky was pale blue, pale yellow, pale pink. They pulled him to his feet. He made his way to the Chevy. On the seat he found a dozen wilted red roses.

At the end of two weeks Madeline began to take short walks. Guy knew this because she mentioned houses she had seen in the neighborhood. He brought home a new pair of jogging shoes for her, blue ones with white stripes and Miracle Air-Piston heels that tilted the whole shoe forward. Madeline tried them on. She laced them tight and stood. She flexed up on tiptoe, then back. She smiled a half smile.

At night they talked more. They let the conversation touch down on the Midwest, on the reservation—but only lightly—like the birds that came and went from the feeder. Yet it was progress.

Two days later Guy returned from work to find both Madeline and Kennedy gone. She came back just before supper, breathing steadily, cheeks red, forehead shiny. She shrugged off a small backpack that held Kennedy, an empty water bottle, and her notepad. "Guy—guess what!" she said.

"What?" Guy said, grinning.

"I saw the ocean. I kept walking and walking up the hill, and suddenly I was on top. I wasn't even thinking about it, but when I looked up, there it was, this big sheet of light. I'd never seen the ocean before!"

Guy laughed. "Tomorrow," he said, "we'll take a picnic lunch. Tomorrow, the ocean!"

That afternoon Guy was to see Susan. He drove the '57 Chevy up Highway 280 and took the Palo Alto exit. He parked near the Stanford tennis courts and paused to watch two short-haired girls in their tennis whites hit the orange ball back and forth. One of the girls was tall, a trifle gangly, and wore a white headband over shiny brown hair. Her laugh tinkled like stream water. Guy found himself watching her through passing glance to steady stare to the far edge of good taste. A moment before he turned away, she smiled briefly at him as she jogged past. Guy smiled in return.

He passed Hoover Tower and headed toward the Quadrangle, but found himself walking slower and slower the closer he came to seeing Susan. He paused on the cobblestone walk outside the grad-student lounge. Inside he heard voices. Someone at the piano played a ragged imitation of Fats Domino's "Blueberry Hill." A wine cork popped. He stepped to one side and looked through the window. Clusters of grad students stood around a few men and women with graying hair. Susan stood with her back to the window. He could see only her dark hair and white blouse. Her shoulders seemed thin and bony, her hair too dark, her laugh too loud. He stepped away from the window before she saw him, before anyone saw him.

He walked back to the parking lot. As he neared the tennis courts he walked faster. He wanted to speak to the girl. But she was gone.

On the way home he stopped by his office. He was in a bad mood and did not want to go home to Madeline just yet. The receptionist said cheerily, "Present for you in your office."

"More bad boards?" he grumbled.

400

On his desk he found a bouquet of velvety red roses. Thirteen roses.

"Where'd these come from?" he asked. He touched their petals, smelled them.

"By messenger," she called back.

He bent to inspect the tag. There was nothing written on the tag except the variety, Scarlet Knight Rose, and the name of the greenhouse.

He called the greenhouse.

"Whoever sent them wouldn't give a name," a man with a heavy Chicano accent said, "but they knew where to call. Ain't many houses grow Scarlet Knights."

"Can you tell me where the order came from?" Guy asked.

"Hang on, my man," the Chicano said. Papers rustled. Then he spoke again. "Out East," he said. "Washington."

The next morning Guy hummed while he worked on the picnic lunch. Madeline helped.

"Six ham sandwiches?" Madeline said.

"Plus pickles, chips, blueberry muffins, apples, iced tea, and wine," Guy said.

"That's enough for an army," Madeline laughed.

"We'll eat it—you'll see," Guy said.

They drove at 10 A.M. up the narrow, winding road that led to Skyline Boulevard. On the sunlit hillsides, shaggy eucalyptus trees smelled like camphor. Nearing the summit, Madeline leaned forward to look.

"There!" she said excitedly as they topped the hill. Twenty miles away, the Pacific lay like a great blue field whose far end rose up into the sky.

Guy steered the Chevy down the long slope of land. Madeline watched the ocean and began to talk. She told him she was almost ready to go back. To Minnesota. To the reservation. She had her job at the Humphrey Center. She had Tom's house. Tom had told her what to do if this ever happened. He had planned. She talked more the closer they came to the ocean, more and faster, her words leaping forward like water flowing down a steepening hill.

Guy smiled and tried to speak on occasion, but couldn't get in a word. So he just grinned and listened as he maneuvered the Chevy around the curves, then down onto the flatter slopes and the fields planted with artichokes. The spiny artichokes grew on the last land before cliffs and salt water. Black sheets of plastic rippled in the sunlight. A line of Mexicans moved in another field that ran west to the cliffs. Land's end.

"Here we are," Guy said. He slowed the Chevy and parked behind a long line of cars.

"Hurry!" Madeline said, shading her eyes to look up at the water, then up toward the shriek of sea gulls. She headed down the rocky ravine toward the beach.

"Hey—wait," Guy laughed, lugging the blanket and the picnic basket.

But Madeline was already far ahead of him, leaping nimbly from stone to stone on her way down to the water.

When Guy reached the beach Madeline already stood barefoot on the glistening wet sand, holding her shoes, looking down at the foamy waves that ran uphill over her ankles, then rolled back. Guy stopped to watch her. She stood alone at the center on the long beach. To the left was a half mile of flat sand; far down were occasional dots of color, the umbrellas and blankets of people who wanted to be alone. To the right, where the shore curved white toward the brown cliffs, were the rest of the people. They clustered on blankets only a few feet apart like seals gathered on the same rock. Radios played. Around a volleyball net people leaped, with faint shouts, to thud the ball back and forth. Guy watched the players punch the white ball higher and higher in the blue air, trying to keep it from touching sand. Trying the impossible, for as long as they could leap and swing and shout, just for the fun of it.

Guy walked on to Madeline. She was staring out to sea and crying. He put his arm around her. They watched the waves for a long time. Finally she wiped her eyes and said, smiling, "I'm hungry."

"Me too," Guy said.

Then, at the same moment, in the same direction, they turned to walk up the beach toward the music and the cries of human voices.

Fine literature from Washington Square Press

MONKEYS Susan Minot
____ 63188/$5.95
A poignant first novel capturing the essence of family life
and all it embodies.

FAMILY AND FRIENDS Anita Brookner
____ 62575/$6.95
A moving and beautifully written story of widowed, artful
matriarch Sofka Dorn—and the binding net of affection
and obligation she weaves around her children, bringing
to the forefront a family coming apart as well as the
loyalties that make it endure.

AVAILABLE LIGHT Ellen Currie
____ 63205/$6.95
An extraordinary novel about love, marriage and family
told with wit, insight and bravado.

WALKING AFTER MIDNIGHT Maureen McCoy
____ 62301/$5.95
A high-spirited bittersweet account of Lottie Jay,
wisecracking and world-weary, coming to grips with
herself and her dreams in the modern world.

WHERE SHE WAS Anderson Ferrell
____ 62438/$6.95
A compelling tale of a woman confronting desire and
temptation in a small southern town.

IN THE PENNY ARCADE Steven Millhauser
____ 63090/$6.95
A masterful collection of short stories that takes place in
the never-never land of the romantic imagination.

PORTRAIT OF A ROMANTIC Steven Millhauser
____ 63089/$6.95
A portrait of romantic melancholy, of boyhood,
of school, and the agony of growing up.

WSP

Simon & Schuster Mail Order Dept. NTS
200 Old Tappan Rd., Old Tappan, N.J. 07675

Please send me the books I have checked above. I am enclosing $_____ (please add 75¢ to cover
postage and handling for each order. N.Y.S. and N.Y.C. residents please add appropriate sales tax). Send
check or money order—no cash or C.O.D.'s please. Allow up to six weeks for delivery. For purchases
over $10.00 you may use VISA: card number, expiration date and customer signature must be included.

Name_____

Address_____

City _____ State/Zip _____

VISA Card No. _____ Exp. Date_____

Signature _____